Debrianna Obara is an advertising professional, specializing in traditional and online media and marketing, with more than twenty years of agency experience. Through her work with the US Holocaust Memorial Museum, she came across a few brief references to Blok 42 or "The Puff" — the brothel of Auschwitz. An informed student of Polish language, history and literature, she had never heard of the brothel and soon discovered there is precious little information about the women who "worked" there. Only one account was published by a first-hand survivor, in German and anonymously, and it was never translated into other languages.

Debrianna earned a degree in journalism at the University of Florida, with a minor in Slavistics. She was an exchange student and later a language instructor at Adam Mickiewicz University. The middle daughter of Polish immigrants, she has always felt a deep connection with the plight of the Polish people and how World War II permanently altered every aspect of cultural and civic life.

Debrianna was raised in New York and currently lives in Southern California. *Blok 42* is her first novel.

Notes About the Polish Language

Many native English speakers are intimidated by the combinations of consonants that are common in the Polish language. It may be a surprise to you that Polish is a phonetic language, so once you learn how the combinations of letters sound, you can read Polish quite accurately. It is also worth noting, that the accent in Polish is almost always on the penultimate syllable. Female surnames usually end in 'A' and the corresponding male surname ends in "I" — so it is Pan Majewski (for a man) and Pani Majewska (for a woman). Pan is Polish for mister or sir, and is commonly used with both first and last names. Pani is Mrs. or Miss and also used with first and last names.

prz = psh like silencing a child, (przysięga = pshi-SHEN-ga)

rz = like the second g in garage

ci, cz = ch, like church (Wieliczka — Vyel-LEECH-ka)

sz, ś, si = sh, like shoot (Sikorski = She-KOR-ski)

w = like a V in English (Wanda = Vanda) unless at the end of the word, then like F (Kraków = KrakOOF)

j = like the y in English (Majewski — My-yef-ski)

ź, ż, zi = similar to rz, like the second g in garage

ł = like the W in English. (łapanka = Wa-PAHN-ka)

dz, dź = j like jeopardy (Łódź = WOOJ)

Ó = u as in uber

There are some vowels like ą and ę that are not found in English, but are more likely familiar to those who have studied French or Portuguese. Both are nasal vowels.

Polish Vocabulary / Key Places

Placki – a flat cake / pie

Kompot – compote, stewed fruit

Szarlotka — apple cake

Łapanka — round up

Mamo — Polish endearment for mother

Tata — Papa / Daddy

Krakowiak — folk dance from the Kraków region, Poland's most famous folk-dance style

Pozdrowenia — farewell / regards

Brewda – Surname for Henryk's aunt and uncle, pronounced Brev-da

Wieliczka — Henryk's hometown, also famous for its salt mines

Oświęcim — Polish town that housed military barracks, later converted by the Nazis into a concentration camp and called Auschwitz in German

Łódź — industrial city in Poland's north. After the war, it became a hub for the Polish Film Industry

Podgórze — neighborhood in Kraków where Polish Jews were forced to relocate to

Kazimierz – former Jewish neighborhood in Kraków; named after King Kazimierz, the Polish king who welcomed Jews to Poland in the 14th century when other nations were deporting Jews, effectively establishing the long-standing tradition of Poland being a safe haven for Jews in Europe

Kraków (Pol) / Krakau (Ger) — Crakow, city is Southern Poland, became the seat of the Nazi General Government in occupied Poland

German Vocabulary

Lebensraum – the concept that German people needed space to live, including taking over occupied lands for "living space"

Lebensborn – policy to increase the number of Aryan "racially pure" children in Nazi Germany

Nur für Deutsche – only for Germans / Germans only

Ordnungpolizei – Order Police

deutsches Mädchen – German young lady

für Polen – For Poles only

Vaterland – Fatherland

Sachertorte – a chocolate cake, of Austrian origin

Garderobe – wardrobe, furniture for storing clothes

Effektenlager – storage warehouse, used to store stolen items from transports at the camp

Volksdeutsche – People whose language, lineage and culture had German origins but who did not hold citizenship, favored as German subjects in occupied lands and who received special privileges

Frau – Miss/Mrs/woman

Herr – Mr

Krakau – German version of Cracow

Lager – Warehouse, stock room

BLOK 42

Debrianna Obara

BLOK 42

Vanguard Press

VANGUARD PAPERBACK

© Copyright 2024
Debrianna Obara

A CIP catalogue record for this title is
available from the British Library.

ISBN 978 1 80016 635 6

*Vanguard Press is an imprint of
Pegasus Elliot Mackenzie Publishers Ltd.*
www.pegasuspublishers.com

First Published in 2024

**Vanguard Press
Sheraton House Castle Park
Cambridge England**

Printed & Bound in Great Britain

To my parents

There are so many people to thank when one takes the first step towards the solitary yet deeply rewarding journey of writing a novel. I hope I haven't neglected the many people who showed me support over the years. Thank you.

I want to thank Peter Harris, the first person to read the very first draft of *Blok 42* — who said the words that gave me the confidence to pursue my dream: You are a true writer.

I also want to thank my parents, Christine and Julian Obara, who were not only tireless fans and supporters, but helped with the color and details that brought aspects of an old Poland to life. My dearest and beloved aunts, Sophie Freiman and Irena Pisarczyk: I not only thank you for reading my various drafts, but for joining me on my first research trip to Southern Poland. We will always have Kraków!

Other friends were key early readers — and I thank you all for your time, input, and candor. Thanks to Coleman Bigelow, Tammy Beauchamp, Graham Thomas, Danny Brophy, Marc Weiner, the late and much-loved Nancy Jenkins, the Włoch family, Christiane and Bernd Hohlen, and Susanne and Michael Detto. Aneta Mandarino was also crucial not only as a friend and reader, but as my Polish language instructor. Dziekuję wam wszystkym!

I want to thank Liliana Sikorska, author, educator, and friend, and Władysław Witalisz, dean of studies/faculty of philology at Jagiellonian University, for helping me with my on-site research. I also want to thank Dana Weinstein of the United States Holocaust Memorial Museum — it was when my path crossed with yours that I conceived of my novel.

Deepest gratitude to the women of Blok 42. Our society has chosen to bury your experiences and the place in history you should hold, and I truly hope this novel brings a spotlight of dignity and compassion to all those unknown victims.

And thank you to my readers. I hope you enjoy my novel. In certain ways, a first novel is based on a lifetime of experiences, conversations, and research. It is an honor to bring these to you.

Prologue

Auschwitz, Occupied Poland
October, 1944

"Just breathe in. Just breathe out," she whispered to herself.

She looked down at herself, naked under a sheer robe, on the edge of a well-used mattress. It was a single, but she would not be alone for long.

"*Nummer Eins*," the guard bellowed outside her room.

Number One walked in. He seemed quite old — maybe in his late forties or fifties — with gray skin stretched tightly over his skull. His eyes were dull and his skin had an odd yellow hue, reminding her of the hepatitis-diseased drunks that were once passed out on city park benches.

She struggled to get enough air into her lungs, and felt a wave of dizziness assail her. She was to have sex with this man. Perhaps if she just passed out, this nightmare would be over?

"*Fünfzehn Minuten*," the guard stated.

Fifteen minutes, she thought in panic.

Number One walked over to her, and she reflexively tightened the thin robe around her nakedness. He swallowed hard as he got closer and sat down on the lumpy bed next to her.

"What is your name?" he asked in Polish.

"No talking," yelled the guard. "You have fourteen minutes. Missionary position only."

She could smell him. He stank like the camp — the horrible stench of sweat, dirt and death. Her nose burned as she inhaled the chemical he had dipped himself in as he prepared for his visit with her.

He reached over to her, putting a rough and calloused hand against her smooth face. He leaned to kiss her and she recoiled.

"No kissing," stated the guard.

Number One paused awkwardly, then removed his hand from her face to open up her robe. He took in her full breasts, the smooth curve of her belly and her thighs pressed tightly together. He pushed her back onto the mattress, and her robe fell open further. He reached down with a strong hand to part her thighs.

She whimpered in resistance. She didn't want him to touch her. She didn't want to breathe in his sour smell. She didn't want *him*.

Feeling her resistance and clamped legs, his grip grew more forceful as he prised her knees apart and settled over her, pinning her with his weight. He awkwardly reached down to release his penis from his striped prisoner uniform.

She turned her head to the side, her eyes fixed on the window. She could not look at him, and she bit her lip hard to stifle another cry.

He entered her quickly and completely. She gasped with the shock of it, and felt bile in the back of her throat. She swallowed it down, squeezing her eyes together tightly as this stranger began his thrusts into her. Her breath came in short, shallow gasps as she breathed through her mouth to try to lessen her nausea.

Eventually, she opened her eyes. She let her pupils fix on an object in the distance through the panes of the window. Was that a top of a tree there? A willow tree? Yes, it was a willow tree. Solid and standing.

She focused on the glimpse of that tree until the man climaxed. She pushed him off of her, rolling to her side and belting her robe.

"Get out, *Nummer Eins*," the guard said after about thirty seconds.

The man stood up, stuffing himself back into his pants with shaking hands as he stumbled to the door. It opened, and the guard took him by his arm and pushed him out of the room.

She started to quietly cry, pulling herself into a fetal position. Her cries grew louder and more ragged as she struggled to gain control so she didn't hear it when the guard announced her next visitor.

"*Nummer Zwei*," the guard stated. "You have fifteen minutes."

Part One
1930 – 1936

Chapter One

S ixteen-year-old Aniela Majewska felt very grown-up taking the train to Wieliczka by herself. Smoothing down the skirt of her smart red sundress with capped white sleeves, she smiled to herself as the train left Kraków station.

She was off to see handsome Henryk Bartosz. Since the day Aniela met Henryk, when she was nine years old, she had been smitten. They met in the school library, when Henryk gallantly stepped in and stopped a classmate from bullying her. She had been tongue-tied then, wondering how a boy in her sister's grade would have bothered helping her; but he had smiled winningly, revealing a bright smile with one incisor overlapping slightly.

From that day on, Henryk walked Aniela and Irena home every day after school. Aniela, a little timid around him, let him do most of the talking. He talked about growing up on a small farm outside of Wieliczka. He spoke of his late father, who had been an engineer at the mines, and had managed hundreds of miners — Germans, Austrians, Transylvanians, Croats, and of course, Poles. He spoke of his father with great pride, but Aniela sensed that Henryk spoke of the man as if he were an icon or an image, with the distance and reverence of someone who only knows a person through the stories told about him.

One day after school, Henryk peeked inside Aniela's book bag.

"You always have a German book in your bag," he noted. "My dad loved languages, too."

"As does mine," Aniela agreed.

Aniela's own father, Professor Bogdan Majewski, taught Philosophy at Jagiellonian University, one of the country's most venerated institutions.

An admirer of German thinkers, opera and culture, he was fluent not only in German but in several other languages.

Aniela knew she took after her father in that she, too, had a good ear for languages and accents; so, trying to get over her shyness and impress Henryk, she often pretended to be a Russian diplomat, or a French maid, or a German opera singer. Her mimicry was good enough to get both Irena and Henryk guffawing, and so her confidence in front of this handsome older boy grew by the day.

Their daily journeys ended at the footsteps of their apartment building. The Majewskis lived on the second floor of an old, stately edifice with an inner courtyard and balcony looking over the street.

One day, her sister Irena suggested that she and Henryk study mathematics together once a week, and soon Henryk was invited past the threshold and into the Majewskis' home.

Bogdan Majewski and his wife, Kinga, immediately liked the young man that respectfully escorted their daughters home. Pan Majewski took a special interest in Henryk as he was a young "man of the house" and seemed mature beyond his years.

The reason the older man and young boy struck such a chord of simpatico was due to a mutual love of history and politics. The two would talk for hours about the sad days of partition, when Poland was split up between Russia, Prussia and Austria, each vying for their piece of Poland's flat, agrarian farmland. Pan Majewski would cite his favorite author, Henryk Sienkiewicz, the nation's sacred son, and remind young Henryk that their country had lost sovereignty before — but that as long as a nation's character remained alive in the language, in the arts, in music and expression, no identity could ever be erased.

Over time, Aniela began to feel excluded. She recognized that Irena and Henryk had much in common, studying the same subjects in school together. She felt like the silly, unwanted little sister, and while she recognized her resentfulness, she could not quash it. She sat in the corner of the living room, a book in her lap, and observed as the ties that drew young Henryk to her family strengthened.

Aniela tried to lose herself in more productive endeavors, as time in the Majewski household was to be spent in bettering oneself. She spent most of her time in one of three ways: with her head in a book; hanging around Irena and Henryk while they studied, pretending to be studying or reading; or practicing her dancing.

***

All that changed three weeks ago when a happy sixteenth birthday card arrived in the mail. Henryk had finally invited her to visit his family's farm in the town of Wieliczka. And he had invited Aniela *alone*.

Aniela turned her attention to her reflection, looking back at her through the smudged glass of the train. She kept her dark blonde hair long and often in braids, though a lot of other girls desired the permanent wave of movie stars these days. Her oval face, with pert nose and full lips, showcased light blue eyes that seemed ever brighter — surely excitement was a key factor, though the scarlet dress helped set them off. She didn't dwell on her beauty, and never felt comfortable attracting extra gazes. She detested the torment of boys who pulled her hair to try to get her attention or knocked books out of her hands in the library. Henryk was a different kind of boy. He truly looked at her, not staring or gaping like other idiots. He listened to her when she talked, and smiled often; his eyes — not green, not blue — were enigmatic to her, yet familiar all the same.

Irena declined to go to the train station, and instead had sulked around the house, barely uttering a word to Aniela. No matter. Nothing could dispel Aniela's anticipation and excitement. She just tried not to gloat, but Irena couldn't help but notice Aniela dancing around the house, spinning in circles, daydreaming away.

It wasn't long before the city ended and the rolling farmland and occasional patch of forest began. The trip took less than two hours, and the train pulled into the platform spouting clouds of dark smoke. Aniela peered out the window. Many well-dressed people were milling around, awaiting visitors, but she could not pick Henryk out.

Taking her suitcase, she made her way down the stairs and onto the platform, standing on her toes in hopes of spotting Henryk.

"Dancing girl!" Henryk exclaimed. He swept Aniela up in his arms in a big warm hug. "Welcome to Wieliczka!"

She was dazed by his burst of affection, and overcome by the contact against his strong frame. Too happy to find any words, she just stood there, beaming at him. After a moment, he reached for her suitcase.

"How was the ride? Did you enjoy the train? Are you hungry?" He seemed very excited, his words tripping over one another.

Aniela laughed, matching his excitement with her own. "It was great! I'm fine for now…"

"Here, follow me." He crooked her arm in his and started leading her to the street. "Mother is waiting with a wagon. We have a bit of a bumpy ride out to the farm."

A large draught horse was standing outside of the station, harnessed to a wagon with haystacks covered in woolen blankets.

Aniela waved to Henryk's mother.

"Welcome, Aniela!"

Aniela gave her cheeks three kisses and then Pani Bartosz motioned to get into the wagon. Henryk helped Aniela up and they sat on brittle hay bales, while Pani Bartosz took the reins and clucked to the horse, pulling forward with a jolt.

Wieliczka was a crowded, bustling town, with cobblestoned streets and a large town square, surrounded by well-kept store fronts and restaurants. Old tenement buildings created a low-profile. Before long, the road turned to dirt and the wagon and horse clopped along through rolling farmland.

"The salt mines are in the opposite direction," Henryk said, pointing. "We'll go. But first, I want to show you our farm!"

The road was rutted and Aniela lost her seat several times when the wagon hit a pothole, but Henryk was quick to put an arm around her. He smiled down at her, eyes twinkling. He pointed out the trees — apple, cherry, plum — and discussed the various farms and who lived in them, seeming to share every detail that flew into his head.

They arrived at the farm, where a quaint three-room house stood out against the fields with its bright robin's egg color. A couple waited outside the front door.

Stepping out of the wagon, Pani Bartosz introduced Aniela to Henryk's uncle and aunt, Sylwia and Walenty Brewda. The couple cared for and lived on the farm when Henryk and his mother lived in Kraków during the school year. Pani Brewda was about ten years younger than her sister and less severe, but she shared the same blonde hair, though with less gray. Her husband had a handlebar mustache and wavy dark brown hair, and his dark brown eyes twinkled with warmth. Pan Brewda darted a look of appreciation to Henryk.

"So now we finally get to meet the fine 'dancing girl' of Kraków that we have heard so much about!" he teased, winking at Aniela.

"I'm so happy to finally meet you," Aniela said a bit formally, and curtsied with a big grin.

"What city manners!" Pan Brewda teased. "No need for such airs out here, Miss Aniela. We are simple country folk."

Aniela blushed, and smiled back.

Henryk seemed impatient. "So, are you ready to see the rest of the place?"

Aniela glanced at the suitcase in the back of the wagon.

"At your service," Pan Brewda said, grabbing the suitcase from the wagon and putting it by the door. "It'll be in your room after the tour. Knowing Henryk, he'll start with the barn."

Henryk nodded and detached the horse from the wagon and led it to the barn. He walked with the horse to his right. The horse was a large, gray-dappled draught horse named Willow. Willow stood about sixteen hands high, and had a thick powerful neck, sloping shoulders, and a deep, powerful body. She was a gentle creature with warm brown eyes and uneven whiskers coming out of her chin.

"Do you want to groom her?" Henryk asked, and Aniela agreed.

Henryk clucked to Willow as he clipped her halter to two ropes on either side of an entryway outside of the barn. He brought out different brushes and showed Aniela how to lift the dirt from Willow's skin with a specific motion using a curry brush. Henryk seemed absorbed by the task, and Aniela could see the joy he took from caring for this horse and sharing this simple task with her. When they were done, Willow positively shone and Aniela could have sworn the horse puffed with pride, loving the attention and the sensation of being pampered. Aniela grinned, aware that she wasn't the only girl who liked Henryk's special attentions.

"Here," he said, digging into his pocket and handing Aniela a carrot. "Give her this. She'll love you forever."

He demonstrated by tucking her thumb so when Aniela offered the carrot, Willow wouldn't accidentally nibble on a digit. Willow found the carrot in Aniela's palm, and she giggled as the big, velvety nose grazed her palm and Willow took the carrot, leaving a wet trail in its wake.

Aniela looked up at Henryk's gentle face, and wiped her wet hand on his shirt with a playful grin.

"Well, do you want to ride her tomorrow?" he asked.

"I'd love to," she replied. "I have never been on a horse!"

"Well, we'll need to get you in more suitable riding clothes," he said, noting the sundress and sandals, all a bit dusty from the barn. "Did you pack anything more casual?"

"Let me think," Aniela said, reflecting on her suitcase filled with skirts, dresses and summer blouses. She really hadn't figured on the right attire for farm life.

"Don't worry, we'll figure something out."

Henryk unclipped Willow and led her back to the stall. He brought out a bale of hay, and asked Aniela to refresh the water and showed her how to measure out oats. The smells of the barn were fresh and pleasant. After feeding Willow, they tended the three dairy cows and a goat.

They returned to the farmhouse, which had flower boxes full of gardenias in the windows, which contrasted splendidly against the blue paint. It was a charming house, as if plucked right out of a fairytale and exactly as Henryk had described it. The main room, which functioned both as a living room and a kitchen, had a large stove in the middle of it. There were two rooms off the large kitchen, an outhouse around back, and a water pump in the yard. The conditions were quite simple compared to what Aniela was used to.

Henryk pulled a few straws of hay out of Aniela's braid, and tossed them outside with a grin. A large wooden table was set for five, and a vase filled with wild flowers was placed on a doily.

After they washed up by the water pump outside, Pani Bartosz urged everyone to sit down as she brought out a plate of pierogi — some filled with meat, others with mushrooms — a cabbage salad, sliced beets and a loaf of freshly baked bread.

Aniela spotted a picture of Henryk's parents on their wedding day on the wall. His father had a fashionable mustache, and wore a smart hat. But Pani Bartosz was almost unrecognizable to Aniela. Who was this buoyant teenager — perhaps eighteen or so — slight and very pretty? Her eyes seemed to sparkle despite the faded picture, with smooth skin and hair gleaming.

Aniela turned to Pani Bartosz and asked, "I can't help noticing the picture of your wedding day. How did you two meet?"

"Well, we grew up in Wieliczka," Pani Bartosz said, pointing to her sister. "On a farm, along with our five brothers. When Henryk's father arrived as the new engineer at the salt mine, all the young girls vied for his attention. They all wanted to nab a husband."

"You can imagine," Pani Brewda interjected. "A handsome, college-educated man from Warsaw. The country girls couldn't contain themselves."

"That is true," Pani Bartosz said. "But I wasn't going to make a fool out of myself like all the other girls did, throwing themselves at him!"

"You didn't need to," Pani Brewda said. "My sister was the town beauty. It didn't take long before he noticed her."

"Anyway," Pani Bartosz said, "Witold, Henryk's father, *did* notice me and asked to court me. The other girls were jealous. He was so cosmopolitan, you see. He spoke German and some Hungarian to the workers at the mine — he was good with languages…"

"Like Aniela," Henryk interjected.

"Yes, like Aniela. And he got along with everyone. He was well-liked and popular. And he was a fierce patriot. He detested the partition, and wanted nothing more than to see our people and lands restored. That was before the Great War, of course."

She was referring to the third partition of Poland, which had wiped Poland off the map for a hundred and twenty-three years.

"How old were you?" Aniela asked.

"I was eighteen and he was twenty-six. We were married within a year, and he bought this large house in town near the mines. But I insisted on having farmland. I was always happiest on a farm. I had no chance to have my own, with the boys inheriting the family farm. I only knew how to work with my hands — what use was I in a big house by the salt mines? He thought it was crazy, but he wanted to make me happy so he bought some land."

"And it's a good thing you insisted," Pan Brewda said.

"Yes, that big old house was destroyed in 1915 by retreating Russians. When most townspeople had nothing, we had this little farm, and so we were better off than so many."

"Better off?" Henryk said, noticeably angry. "How so? The war *broke* him. He was betrayed and disillusioned…"

Pani Bartosz shot her son a dark look, silencing him. She looked deeply into her brandy glass.

"Well, what's done is done. Let's not burden Aniela with such talk, especially on her first night with us."

There was an awkward silence and Henryk stood up moodily, running his fingers angrily through his hair.

"Fine, mother," he said in a clipped voice.

"Well, Aniela," Pani Bartosz said, focusing her attention on their guest. "You'll be sleeping in Henryk's room — we have the bed all set up for you when you're ready."

"Where are you sleeping?" Aniela asked Henryk.

"I'll sleep in the barn. Willow could use some company," he quipped.

"Oh, but I couldn't…"

"It's already settled, my dear," Pani Bartosz interrupted. "We don't have a guest room, and you are Henryk's guest, so please do not mention it. We absolutely insist."

"Okay, then," Aniela said, not wanting to add to the tension that she felt had sprung between mother and son.

"Let's take a walk," Henryk said to Aniela.

"Of course," Aniela said, then looked at the dirty dishes on the table. "But let me help clean up first…"

"Nonsense!" Pani Bartosz said quickly. "You are our honored guest. Your father's kindness and support for Henryk's studies have meant the world to this family. You are not to lift a finger while you are here!"

Aniela smiled, pleased that Henryk and her father had always gotten along so well. As Henryk's own father had died when he was a child, Henryk soon came to Pan Majewski for advice about his studies. And as a professor at the prestigious Jagiellonian University in Kraków, Pan Majewski steered Henryk down the path to education with a glowing letter of recommendation.

Henryk led Aniela outside. It was already late and she noticed that the night sky was much darker out in the country, where few homes had electricity. The moon cast its pale glow over the fields as she tried to keep pace with his longer strides. He was deep in thought, so Aniela kept quiet.

"You know, my mother is right," he said at last. "I am deeply and forever indebted to your father for helping me with my university application. Without his letter of recommendation, I'm sure a country boy like me would've been easily overlooked."

"Country boy?" Aniela queried. "Seems to me that you are both country boy and city boy. You fit wherever you are. It's one of the many qualities I admire about you."

Henryk stopped short, looking down at Aniela's shining eyes, and she grew embarrassed. She feared she had revealed too much. Maybe she had been singled out for this visit as his way to thank her for her father's support? Perhaps Irena would be getting an invitation, too. Pani Bartosz had mentioned there was no guest room, so maybe the invitation had to be issued one at a time?

"You think I fit in the city as well as the country?" he pressed.

"Yes, Henryk," Aniela continued. "I believe you do. It sounds like you take after your father in that way."

That made him smile, and they continued their walk. Aniela meant what she had said. Henryk was easy-going and well-liked wherever he went. She knew he and his mother had moved to Kraków years ago, leaving farm life behind in order to give Henryk a better chance of a future and to provide a steady income for his mother. His mother was a gifted and competent seamstress, and the elite of Kraków appreciated the quality of work she produced. Mother and son had built a life where summers were spent working their old farm and the school year was spent in the city.

Aniela felt she stuck out, never really blending in, and she preferred to be invisible, often hiding in plain sight in her dance troupe, or sequestering herself in the library with her best friend, Ewa.

After their walk, they returned to the farmhouse and Henryk left her at the doorway to his bedroom.

"Sleep well, dancing girl," he said softly.

"Good night, Henryk," Aniela said. "Thank you for a great first day."

He touched the tip of her nose with his finger softly, teasingly.

"It'll just get better," he promised, and returned to the barn. With a sigh, Aniela closed the door to the bedroom and got ready for bed. It was a small, simple room with a single bed, a table and bureau. Aniela's suitcase stood in the corner, and she took out her nightgown and changed quickly, slipping into Henryk's bed, feeling like she was doing something terribly intimate. She could smell him in the room — that earthy, male scent that was somehow piney but with what she knew now was a hint of the barn aromas. Hay? Wood shavings? Aniela lay in the bed in which Henryk lay down every night, and she breathed in the smell of Henryk all around her.

Chapter 2

Lipstick and Leads

S unlight streamed through Henryk's bedroom window while Aniela selected a blouse from her suitcase. With dismay, Aniela noticed that there was bright red lipstick smeared prominently on the collar.

"How on earth...?" Aniela muttered.

Aniela pulled out another dress from the case. It, too, had red lipstick prominently smeared on it, this time on the bodice.

A wave of dread washed over Aniela, as she examined all of her packed clothes. All had been sullied with a smear of lipstick.

"Irena..." Aniela breathed, shocked by the sabotage.

Well, her older sister had certainly been determined to make her mark on Aniela's trip.

Aniela's brain fumbled with a response. What to do? All her clothes were stained and unwearable! She heard noises through the door and peeked her head around to see who was in the kitchen. Henryk's aunt was already trimming pole beans. She looked up as Aniela peeked through the doorway.

"Oh, good morning," Pani Brewda said with a smile.

"Good morning," Aniela said, a look of indecisiveness on her face.

Pani Brewda paused. "Is something wrong, dear?"

"Not exactly," Aniela said quietly. "I seem to have a bit of trouble with what to wear."

Pani Brewda lay down the paring knife on the table and stood up. "Do you need some help?"

Aniela quickly nodded and ushered Henryk's aunt into the bedroom.

Aniela picked up a few marred articles of clothing and displayed them to Pani Brewda.

"You see," Aniela said stiltedly, "It... appears... that red lipstick melted on my clothes in my suitcase."

Pani Brewda took an item, eyeing it carefully. The lipstick formed a clear, marked line on the lapel of a pink shirt. She took the next article, a sundress, which also sported a clear, marked line of brazen red.

She looked up at Aniela. "Perhaps, dear, this was no accident?"

Aniela sighed unhappily. "Yes, I'm sure it was my sister Irena. She was jealous that Henryk invited me out for a visit, and this is her shade of red lipstick."

Pani Brewda nodded knowingly. "Jealousy, especially between siblings, can be nasty. Fear not, Aniela. We'll fix this. In the meantime, I can lend you something to wear."

Aniela exhaled and reached out to hug Pani Brewda.

"Thank you!" she exclaimed. "It's so embarrassing to have such… antics ruin my visit."

"Nonsense," Pani Brewda said. "Nothing will be ruined. I'm sure my sister knows how to remove wax from clothes…"

"It would be so embarrassing to have her know Irena's act of spite," Aniela whispered.

"It'll remain between us," Pani Brewda promised. "Wait here and I will fetch you some clothes. I dare say what you packed is far too nice for the back of a horse anyway. I know Henryk is eager to take you out today…"

Dressed in borrowed long pants and a button-down shirt, Aniela met Henryk and Willow by a tree stump. He helped her up, then raised himself onto Willow's bare back, so Aniela was seated in front of him, and he held the lead reins.

Willow was a workhorse, and her broad back swayed as Henryk clucked to her and signaled forward. With dangling legs, Aniela clutched Willow's braided mane to find her balance.

"Just lean back if you need to," Henryk advised. Aniela complied and enjoyed the hard comfort of his chest and arms. With a leisurely pace, they ambled through fields of hay and barley, and eventually approached a stream that bordered the farm to the east.

"So, what happened last night at dinner?" Aniela asked.

"Well," Henryk said, "it's a bit of a touchy subject. My father was friends with a lot of German co-workers from the mine. During the war, he expected support from them regarding Poland's bid for sovereignty. This put him at odds with a lot of the people around here, many of whom thought the Russians would deliver us from Prussian dominance.

"My father was assured by his friends, many of them connected to Max von Baden and other influentials, that Germany would stand by Poland. Our house was attacked by Russians, who scorched everything in their retreat. My father was injured while trying to protect us — stabbed in the leg by a bayonet. The wound never healed. Soon after, my father asked his German friends to help, but instead the Germans started arresting Poles in their plan to 'Germanize' Central Europe. Many of his friends and employees were sent to labor camps. He tried to intercede, and through his connections, was able to keep us from being removed. But he could do nothing for entire families that were packed up and sent to camps.

"We were betrayed by the Russians *and* the Germans, and my father never recovered from that blow. He was convinced that the Germans could be trusted. In the end, it was Woodrow Wilson and the Americans who insisted on Poland's right to statehood."

Willow nickered as Henryk paused, lost in thought.

"Within two years, my dad's leg had gotten so infected that he contracted gangrene. Like everyone, those years were tough on us. My mother gave birth to my brother, who died before he was six months old. His name was Tadek. And then my older brother Szymon died of tuberculosis. And shortly after that, my dad died. At the end of his life, he was very bitter — distrustful of the Germans, the Russians, pro-American and fiercely patriotic. I think if he had lived, he may have wanted us to immigrate to New York. I have a distant uncle who lives there."

Aniela wished she could see his face, and tried to peer over her shoulder, but Henryk's head was lowered.

"You never told me that, Henryk," she said. "I'm sorry."

Hours later, the pair returned to the farm. They were both parched from a day outside in the fresh air and felt their skin growing tighter from the strong summer sun. Pani Brewda motioned to Aniela to enter the house.

"Take a look," Pani Brewda said conspiratorially, leading Aniela into Henryk's bedroom.

All of Aniela's clothes were pinned to a makeshift clothesline across the room. Every item was fresh and clean, with no evidence of lipstick stains.

"How did you...?" Aniela breathed.

Pani Brewda laughed. "Of course my sister, as a seamstress, knew the very trick. Don't worry, I didn't let on that my question about removing lipstick was due to this act of retaliation. Turns out that all I needed to do was use brown paper and an iron to melt the lipstick off the clothes, and soak up the wax onto the paper. It took a bit of elbow grease, but everything is as good as new!"

"You did this for me while Henryk and I were out riding?" Aniela said, moved and brimming with gratitude.

"Of course, my dear!" Pani Brewda said. "I am no stranger to a little sisterly jealousy myself, and I regret some outbursts during my own younger days. It was good to right this wrong, and it's a reminder to take the higher road and ignore the sin of jealousy."

Aniela hugged Pani Brewda again. "How can I ever thank you?"

"No need," Pani Brewda said with a smile. "I can't have your visit, which meant so very much to Henryk, marred in any way!"

Aniela and Pani Brewda giggled at her pun. The two walked outside, where Henryk took Aniela by the hand and led her to the rabbit hutch. Aniela smiled over her shoulder to Pani Brewda as she was led inside.

Chapter 3

Salt Mines

The following day, Henryk took Aniela to the famous salt mines of Wieliczka. They entered Danilowicz Hall, where they met with an engineer who had worked with Henryk's father. Pan Szymański broke into a large grin upon seeing Henryk walk in, displaying glints of gold teeth.

"Henryk," Pan Szymański exclaimed, "you look just like your father."

He grabbed Henryk and gave him a warm hug. Pan Szymański's eyes welled up a bit as he took a good look at Henryk.

"It's been a while, son. You've grown," Pan Szymański remarked, wiping his eyes, and turned to Aniela.

"This is Aniela Majewska. My... uh, friend from school."

"So nice to meet you, Aniela," Pan Szymański said sincerely. His eyes twinkled. "I see you have good taste in friends."

Henryk blushed a bit. Without missing a beat, Pan Szymański reached for a carafe and poured cups of tea as he began talking about the history of the mine. "Henryk, you may know some of these old stories since your father worked here... but since this is your friend's first visit, perhaps she would like to know more about it? Yes? This mine is famous throughout Poland and beyond. It sits on a salt deposit that is about thirteen and a half million years old, and that took twenty thousand years to form."

"That is incredible," Aniela said, sipping the tea.

"The mine is our country's oldest commercial enterprise. Salt has been historically an important part of civilization's advancements. We have used salt to cure meats, to bring taste to food, and as you'll soon see, the air down there is so fresh and pure, many people have come to Wieliczka to heal respiratory illnesses." Henryk gulped down his tea impatiently and placed the glass cup down on the table.

"Shall we get started, then?" he said, as Aniela took a final sip of the tea.

"Let's," she said happily.

Pan Szymański gave them each a hard hat, before leading them to the mineshaft, a rickety, wooden box that was cut straight down through the earth a hundred and thirty-five meters below.

"As we go down, you'll see that it gets colder, so I'm glad you brought a sweater," Pan Szymański said as the mineshaft door closed. There was just one dim light above in the shaft, casting eerie shadows on their faces as the three of them jerkily started their descent. "Year round, it's a steady fifteen degrees Celsius. This mine has been operating since the thirteenth century, and many famous people have come from all over to tour our chambers. Copernicus, Goethe and Chopin, to name a few…"

Aniela leaned into Henryk, squeezing his arm. The elevator went down and still farther down, and the light cut out several times, plunging them into a complete darkness. But then it flickered back on and Aniela's eyes sought Pan Szymański's calm and amiable face, his gold teeth sparkling in the muted light.

After a while they came to a stop, and Pan Szymański pushed open the doors.

A whoosh of cool, crisp air hit them. The air had a humid quality and Aniela took a deep breath, enjoying the freshness in her lungs. Rivulets of water streamed across the cut paths as they stepped onto the first footpath. It took a minute for her eyes to adjust. They were in an underground cavern, dug out by the hands of laborers who had chipped away the rock salt with pickaxes. The salt was below them, in the walls and in the ceiling. Crisscrossed cedar beams supported the hallways, keeping the corridors from falling in on themselves. The salt wasn't white, like table salt, but was a light gray color and almost looked like a combination of ice and rock.

Pan Szymański turned on his flashlight as they stepped out. He reached into his sack and pulled out two more flashlights, passing one to Henryk and one to Aniela.

"You probably won't need these as we have lights to all the major chambers, but this may help you watch your step."

Pan Szymański pulled out a small chisel from his pocket, and deftly cut off a piece of salt from the wall and handed it Aniela. "Here you are,

Aniela, a little token."

She looked at the small jagged piece of rock salt, which fit easily in her hand.

"You can eat this?" she asked.

"Well, everything is a process," Pan Szymański said. "First, the rock salt has to be taken out. It's then sent to the surface, where we use a brining solution to break down the salt, steam it, condensate it, refine it, and eventually it is turned into table salt. For years, we were famous for our salt. The finest salt was mined from these chambers and sent to the best families on Wawel Hill. The barrels had the national bird on it, and it became known as Eagle Salt."

Pan Szymański led them slowly through a walkway that opened up into a room with salt stalagmites in the midst of statues of dwarves and gnomes merrily frozen in their work of excavating the mine.

"The miners were artisans," he said. "Over the years they would take out the salt and leave an empty chamber in the process. They used their pickaxes and chisels to carve creatures, statues, and saints in their wake. Each chamber is a little different. Over time, I believe there must have been quite a competition to see what could be carved or who could do it the best."

The statues were whimsical and beautifully carved. Each dwarf had a different expression and gleamed smoothly under the dim light. Aniela found it hard to believe that these statues were made from the rough, dull salt that she held in her palm.

Pan Szymański guided them deeper into the mine and into a huge chamber with a staircase down to an amazing sight. "This is our most famous chamber: St. Kinga's Chapel."

Aniela's eyes grew large as she took in St. Kinga's Chapel, a church deeply underground made out of salt. The staircase they descended was carved out of salt, as was the floor, which looked like marble tiles but was etched and carved from the same salt. There was even an altar entirely carved out of salt. It was truly spectacular.

"St. Kinga's Chapel was completed in 1896 and commemorates the engagement of King Bolesław of Poland to Princess Kinga of Hungary. As legend has it, Kinga was a noblewoman from Hungary who was to marry the King of Kraków, Bolesław. So prized was this salt that she asked for a lump of salt for her dowry. She supposedly threw her engagement ring in a mineshaft in Hungary and then was taken here to Wieliczka. She asked the miners to dig through the salt until they hit rock, and legend has it that they split open a rock and found her engagement ring."

Henryk snorted, "Preposterous legend. They evidently had no understanding of geology."

"Well, while I doubt that there is a word of truth to the story," Pan Szymański conceded, "it could be possible because of the underground water that flows through the mine. Water is the most destructive and dangerous part of the mine, as salt is soluble, and can cause unstable conditions. But imagine Kinga had thrown the ring in Maramaros, which is at the outer edge of this salt formation, and imagine that it fell into a subterranean stream that flowed all the way through the formation to Wieliczka and got trapped between a rock and a hard place…" He chuckled at his play on words. "It is just possible, though very unlikely."

"The part of the story that doesn't make sense to me is why she'd throw the ring into the mine in the first place," Aniela observed.

"Ah, the mysteries of women," Pan Szymański said.

"As written by men," Aniela quipped, earning a snort from Henryk.

They spent several hours exploring the various caverns. There were saints, animals, mythical creatures — every chamber held another sculpture, another marvel. They saw old equipment, cordoned off behind ropes, which showed just how difficult the work must have been for the men who worked down in the mines centuries ago. Aniela marveled at the giant winches and barrows, and felt pity for the beasts that had lived and died there, pulling harnesses in monotonous circles, never to see the sun again.

Pan Szymański was especially fond of a lovely statue of Saint Barbara, the patron saint of miners. He genuflected before it, and Henryk and Aniela respectfully followed suit. They walked chamber to chamber through intricate tunnels and hand-carved staircases. When they got to the sculpture of King Kazimierz the Great, Pan Szymański excused himself, giving Henryk a little nod, and disappeared up a flight of stairs.

Aniela leaned toward the statue of the King, examining the intricate carved details that made up his flowing beard and coronated head. Henryk approached her and took her hands in his, looking at Aniela intently in the dim light. He had such a serious expression on his face that Aniela instinctively held her breath.

"Aniela," he said a bit shakily, and cleared his throat. "I have known you since you were just a girl. Now that you are sixteen, I was hoping… I wanted to ask you…"

He swallowed hard. Aniela blushed deeply, but she kept her eyes locked on his face; his eyes were so earnest, they seemed to be pleading.

"What I'm trying to ask, after all this time, are you ready to be my girl?"

"Your girl?" she repeated.

"Yes, my girl," he continued. "I want to… court you; I guess that's the old-fashioned way of saying it. I want you to be not only my dancing girl, but… *my* girl."

In the shadowy light, she could not see the deep richness of his eyes — it was as if he was washed in sepia tones — but she could feel the energy pulsing through his sweating hands that grasped her own. After all the years of having a crush on Henryk, fearing that he may be more interested in Irena, daring herself to impress him, he was asking her to be *his* girl.

"Yes," she breathed happily.

Henryk threw his head back and whooped, his voice echoing through the caverns. He bent down and gently kissed her.

His lips were surprisingly soft and she could feel the slight roughness of his stubble on her cheeks. It was her first kiss, so often imagined, and she melted into him. The feel of his taut body pressed so close as his hands tangled in her hair and then circled her waist, overwhelmed her. It was an unaccustomed feeling to taste him and have him taste her. She felt an odd unfurling of desire deep in her belly, and was engulfed by the nearness of him. He slowly drew away, looking at her with blazing eyes. Breathless, Aniela leant into him.

"Oh my," Aniela whispered, head spinning.

Henryk hugged her to him, his head resting on hers. "Oh my indeed, dancing girl. Oh my indeed."

Chapter 4

Supernatural Strength

They bade farewell to Pan Szymański in a cloud of euphoria. They walked to the nearest tram station, but Aniela's focus was completely on Henryk's hand holding hers. Though she had touched Henryk a million times over the years they had known one another, somehow the feel of his hand clasping hers felt profoundly different and new.

She noted how small her hand felt in his, and it briefly made her think of her father's hand, and how she used to hold it during Sunday mass. She could feel the warmth of Henryk's body next to hers, and she thrilled when he lifted her hand to his lips and kissed it, as if to assure himself that she was still there.

Henryk was an average size man, but he suddenly seemed taller and larger. He was standing so straight, his chest puffed out a bit. *He is proud*, she realized.

When the tram arrived, Aniela stepped in as Henryk paid the fares, punching a paper ticket.

"Henryk!" a voice exclaimed from the rear of the tram.

Two young men, about Henryk's age, waved them over.

"There he is," said the taller one, a lanky blond man with a thin mustache and overalls. "Our savior, Lord Henryk Christ himself."

The other man laughed and slapped Henryk on the back, eyeing Aniela with obvious interest.

"How's the leg, Marian?" Henryk asked the shorter man, who was leaning heavily onto the tram bench.

"It's good, it's good," Marian responded, flexing his left leg. "Healing every day."

"Excellent," Henryk said. "Fellows, I'd like to introduce you to my… girlfriend, Aniela."

Henryk smiled smugly down at Aniela.

"I knew it!" Marian said. "From the moment I saw her with you, I knew this was the fancy city girl you told us about. And man, you were not exaggerating."

Marian looked Aniela over from head to toe, and she felt that familiar sense of discomfort, the feeling she got when certain men looked at her and through her at the same time.

"Nice to meet you," Aniela said, trying to break his gaze.

"And I'm Józef," said the taller man, bowing while taking her hand and kissing it. "I can see why Henryk had his sights on you."

Henryk turned a slight shade of pink and Aniela felt relieved that she wasn't the only one blushing like a fool.

"I owe you, my friend," Marian said. "Let's stop off at the city square and have drinks at my brother's pub. My treat, of course. The least I can do."

Henryk looked at Aniela, a question in his eyes. "Would you mind a little detour?"

"Of course not," she said, and Marian and Józef hooted.

A couple of stops later, they all got off and walked to a pub. It was a cozy place with a large wooden bar with rural hunting pictures and flags adorning the rough stucco walls. They sat down at a table closest to the open door and summer air.

Marian's brother, Wiktor, brightened when the group walked in. He was at least ten years older than Marian, but had the same dark eyes and prominent nose.

"There he is, our hero, our life-saver," Wiktor said, placing a bottle of vodka and glasses on the table. He pulled a chair up from another table and sat down.

Aniela glanced at Henryk, but he looked embarrassed and said nothing.

"Where are my manners?" Wiktor said, as he kissed her hand and passed her a glass.

"So," Aniela said, "will someone tell me what Henryk did?"

"He didn't tell you?" Józef exclaimed. He punched Henryk in the ribs.

"Idiot. How could you not tell her about saving Marian's leg? And maybe his life?"

Marian took a swig and leaned forward, clearly relishing the story he was about to tell. "I was taking my father's wagon to town with Józef. The wheel got stuck in a huge pothole and I was pushing against it to try to get the wagon loose. Well, it was pretty muddy and I fell in front of the wheel just as the horse pulled the wagon forward, crushing me. My leg was completely pinned."

"You wouldn't believe the sound he made," Józef interrupted. "I thought he had been cut in half. I couldn't get the horse to move, and Marian was stuck under that wheel. Henryk must've heard the screams, because he came sprinting across the field. He took one look at poor Marian, pinned under the entire weight of the wagon, writhing in pain…"

"It was excruciating," Marian agreed.

"And Henryk…" Józef continued, "Henryk grabbed the wheel, and I don't know how he did this, he picked up the side of the wagon enough for Marian to free his leg."

Henryk looked down at his hands, surprisingly bashful.

"You picked up the wagon?" Aniela asked, trying to meet his eyes.

"Can you believe it?" Wiktor chimed in. "The wagon was loaded with bags of barley. It must've weighed over two hundred kilos. It's hard to believe…"

"But it's true," Józef said. "I saw it with my own eyes. He picked up the wagon by the spoke of the wheel. The veins on his neck and his arms were popping out. Marian was able to move enough to free his leg. It was the most amazing thing I'd ever seen."

Marian rubbed his hands up and down his left leg. "Luckily, due to the mud, I had a huge bruise and a deep cut, but I didn't break my leg.

"It was amazing, Henryk," Marian said, his eyes shining in awe and gratitude. "You are Hercules, my friend."

The guys teased and ribbed each other, trading stories and downing vodka after vodka, and Aniela tried to join in. But it was hard — they were older, and friends for years, and kept talking about people from the town whose names she didn't know, and stories of adventures from years gone by. She smiled politely and laughed when everyone else did, and as they grew louder and more raucous, Aniela sat sipping her drink till her head swam.

The men seemed to want to impress her with their tales and bravado, and they started arm-wrestling each other, pushing Aniela even more to the outside. She felt she was tacitly being asked to *ooh* and *aah* like a puppet observing their manly competition.

Henryk's speech grew slurred and sloppy, and the guys were increasingly physical with one another — slapping one another in play, hiding Marian's hat, and re-living past conquests. Józef and Marian teased Henryk about his fancy life and high-class friends from the city.

"Some life you have in Kraków where the 'girls are so much prettier and the people more cultured'," Marian intoned in a singsong voice.

"But as you can see," Henryk said, pulling Aniela roughly to his side so that she almost fell out of the chair and onto him, "I was right about the Kraków girls, wasn't I?" he said, holding her face in his hands. Aniela tried to pull away, but his grip was too strong.

Wiktor, Józef and Marian stared at her drunkenly and lewdly, as Aniela tried to wiggle free from Henryk's grip. He had pulled her practically onto his lap, and had her face in his hands, as if showing off a sow at the market.

Henryk kissed Aniela hard and drunkenly, before slapping her backside. "Dancing girl, why don't you do a little twirl for us?"

Aniela took a step back from the table, swaying a little from the abrupt shove. Her blood surged in her veins with anger and indignation.

"Do your own damn twirl," Aniela said, and ran to the door and out of the bar, feeling the evening air on her heated face.

She was furious and had to get away from those drunken, crowing men. She felt belittled and hurt, and shocked that Henryk could treat her like that. Aniela stormed ahead with tears streaming down her face, when Henryk caught up to her.

"Aniela, stop!" he shouted, breathing hard as he grabbed her by the arm and turned her to face him. "Please."

She glared at him, noticing his dilated pupils and red cheeks. His hands on her arms were firm. "Please stop," he said again.

"You are the one who should stop," she said angrily. "What happened to you in there? Is that who you really are?"

"No, Aniela, please listen," Henryk implored. "I'm sorry. I drank too much. I was so happy that you'd said yes to be my girl. I got carried away…"

"Carried away?" she snapped. "I fail to see how celebrating a happy day together should result in you parading me in front of your friends like a... a floozy. It was demeaning."

"I'm sorry," he said helplessly.

She pulled away from his grip, and started marching furiously away. Henryk ran in front of her and tried to block the way with this body.

"You shouldn't go..." he said.

"Why not?" she snapped.

"Well," Henryk said, a smile teasing the corners of his mouth. "That's the way back to the salt mines and away from the farm."

"Oh," she said, and reversed direction.

"Aniela, please," Henryk implored, sobering up a bit. "Let's walk home. Don't go off on your own, even if you never want to speak to me again."

He led her to the main street and started their journey back to the farm. It was a couple of kilometers and they walked in silence for a long way.

"You are right, I know," Henryk said quietly. "I acted like an ass."

"You did," she agreed, tone clipped.

"I'm really sorry."

Aniela stopped and looked at him squarely. "I thought you were different from the other boys. I thought you saw me for who I am. I thought I was more than just a pretty face from Kraków," she said bitterly.

"I do, you are," Henryk said, taking her hands. "I have no excuse. I wanted to impress the guys. I felt so powerful, so special being seen with you. I have wanted this for so long. So long."

Aniela looked up at his face, searching it, trying to see the man from the salt mines and not the one from the bar. Just a few hours ago, his mouth had found hers and they had melted into one another in the dim light of the mines.

"You promise me, right here and now, that you'll never treat me like a plaything or trophy ever again."

"I promise," Henryk said quickly and sincerely. "Please, kiss me and forgive your foolish man."

And so she did.

And then she recalled something her father had said when she had come home in tears after a boy in school pulled her braids and pushed her books off her desk.

"Very few are immune to beauty," he had said. "There are those who want to honor it, and those who want to admire it. Others want to protect it, or control it. But beware that, for some, they seek only to destroy it. Beauty inspires imitation, extreme jealousy and an unmitigated desire to possess. Great beauty brings out both the best and worst in all of us. But precious few are truly indifferent."

Chapter 5

The Sweetness of Summer

The final days spent in Wieliczka were a whirlwind. Henryk's uncle and aunt were delighted to hear that Henryk and Aniela were officially a couple, and Pani Brewda doted on Aniela with affection, while Pan Brewda teased Henryk about "picking the most beautiful peach" from the orchard.

Henryk and Aniela seemed to take turns blushing from the jokes and the knowing looks. Pani Bartosz asked Aniela if she wanted to go currant-picking, just the girls, and she gladly accepted. The farm was surrounded by a large border of currant bushes, and they gently picked the ripened fruit growing in clusters, glistening like red pearls.

"The problem with sweet fruit, like berries, is that everyone wants to partake in the summer harvest," said Pani Bartosz. "We lose a fair amount of berries to the birds, but you'll also find insects and small animals feasting on the currants."

"And who can blame them?" Pani Brewda said.

Pani Bartosz continued, "Growing up on a farm, we were taught that everything had to serve a purpose. The currant bushes not only provide us with delicious fruit, they also serve to break the wind coming off the fields during the winter."

"So what are we going to make with all these currants?" Aniela inquired.

"We'll make most of it into jam," Pani Bartosz said. "I will show you later how we do that. And Sylwia will use some to make brandy."

"And we'll put aside a small amount for dessert tonight," Pani Brewda said.

They returned and dropped off their baskets onto the table, and washed hands at the pump outside, scrubbing until their skin tingled in an effort to remove the stains.

Henryk came out of the stable. He smiled broadly. "Well?" he gestured.

"Look in the kitchen," Aniela boasted.

He peeked his head in, seeing the table overrun with baskets of currants, and whistled appreciatively. He took Aniela's hand in his, still slightly pink from the currants, and kissed her palm sweetly.

"Not bad for a city girl," he teased. She stood up on her tiptoes and quickly kissed him on his mouth, while his mother and aunt busied themselves in the kitchen.

"Why does everyone take every opportunity to remind me that I'm a city girl?" Aniela asked, eyes beseeching.

Henryk paused, considering his words. "Well, around here, people don't really trust city people. My father was considered an outsider and didn't find his place until he married a local girl. Even then, some people thought him high and mighty with his foreign friends, educated speech and manners."

"So, are you saying that people are suspicious of me?"

"Perhaps a little bit. They may think I'm reaching a bit too high in courting a girl whose father is a respected university professor."

"Who thinks that?" Aniela pressed.

"Not since they've met you," Henryk assured. "But certainly my aunt and uncle were worried when they heard me speak of you, and your family, and my devotion to the Majewskis. They didn't want me to get my hopes dashed - if you were too fine a lady to see a guy like me."

Aniela pointed her toe idly. She looked up, her voice very soft. "A guy like you? I always thought that we were the same."

Henryk laughed. "Which is one of the many qualities I... like so much about you. But most people in the city look at country folk as the great unwashed, the uneducated and backward. At the same time, country people see city people as the bourgeoisie that exploits the working class with no regard of how hard people toil and how difficult their lives really are. Neither side looks at the other as 'the same'."

Aniela nodded. "I must admit that this week on the farm has shown me a world I hadn't known. But this life has its beauty and I can see the charm and honor in living a country life. Surely there is merit in both ways."

"Not everyone is that open-minded," Henryk said, matter-of-factly. He leaned over and kissed Aniela on the forehead. "You really need to read *With Fire and Sword*, Aniela. You know I love that book. It sums up centuries of bitterness between the aristocracy and the peasantry. That bitterness is as old as time and as part of our Polish identity as vodka."

Pani Bartosz emerged from the house, holding empty baskets.

"Come, you two," she said. "Let's go to the garden."

The garden seemed like Eden. Aniela reflected on the recent discussion of city versus country living, and was reminded of how disconnected she was from all that went into making life sustainable. In their bright Kraków apartment, Aniela's family spent their days listening to music, reading books, studying, or playing cards. They enjoyed family outings to the theater, and appreciated symphonies and the arts. Had she ever stopped to consider what it took to grow a tomato or keep their pantry full?

The Majewskis' housekeeper, Pani Geba, did much of the shopping on market days, and she was the one who chopped and peeled and prepared most family meals. Aniela had been sheltered from this reality. She felt in awe of Pani Bartosz, who was clearly at home in this environment. Henryk's mother seemed to know everything — how to grow and harvest beautiful fruits and vegetables, how to kill and then prepare a meal, how to make soap and chop firewood — and all on top of her tremendous talent as a seamstress. Compared to her, Aniela felt one-dimensional and useless.

"Please teach me how to cook," Aniela implored Pani Bartosz, who was stooped over, snipping herbs.

The older woman straightened, eyes twinkling warmly. "Of course, it would be my pleasure."

Aniela spent the whole of the afternoon shadowing Pani Bartosz as she confidently turned raw ingredients into delicious dishes. She was covered in sweat from the heat of the large Russian stove, coupled by the closed kitchen, which only let in the occasional summer breeze.

Aniela stepped outside to get some fresh air, seeing Henryk pumping water.

"Not such a city girl now?" Aniela called, twirling in the sunshine as she patted her apron, filling the courtyard with a fine mist of flour.

"It appears to be so," he said, passing her a cup of water, their hands brushing. Aniela sipped the cool well water and passed it back to him. He closed his eyes as he sipped the water. She liked the way the sunbeams caught the hair on his arms, giving them an almost golden back-glow. He caught her staring at him and lowered the ladle.

"Everything okay, dancing girl?" he inquired.

Too shy to admit she had been drinking him in, not unlike the way he was drinking in the water, she just nodded, feeling her rosy cheeks grow even hotter.

Chapter 6

Unwanted Advance

December, 1930

It was the time of year that Aniela's dance troupe performed their Christmas recital at the town hall. All their practice paid off, and the dancers performed their routines flawlessly.

Pulsing with jubilation, the troupe wanted to celebrate. They chose trendy Café Gwiazda, which had an exciting atmosphere with a live band and a dance floor. A cloud of cigarette smoke hung in the air.

"Wow," Ewa said, admiring the women with their finger waves and loose-fitting dresses.

"Very elegant," Aniela agreed with her friend, noting the men in high-waisted trousers with suspenders or belts, and crisp shirts.

Upon entering the café, Aniela's gaze was drawn to the couples on the dance floor who were displaying the latest dance craze with the foxtrot, or something called "swing". The troupe downed several drinks, but before long they, too, were all on the dance floor, trying out the new moves, watching more experienced couples and giving it a go with their partners.

As usual, Aniela danced with Leon. Compared to folk dancing, swing dance was entirely different. It was not an easy rhythm to grasp, as the timing was unsyncopated. They bumped into one another and stepped on each other's toes, laughing as they tried to figure out the steps. Before long, they, too, were inventing moves and flying around the dance floor as the band filled the room with their relentless energy.

Aniela loved the wild abandon of this new dance form and found the modern music exhilarating. Leon, however, was dripping in sweat, and had a serious look of concentration on his face as he led her through each dance.

In swing dancing, every decision was in Leon's hands. He cued Aniela with his hands or a change in direction, and her job was to follow his lead. It was fun to just live in the moment, and often the anticipation of wondering what move he'd do next had her giggling when she had predicted correctly.

She and Leon had danced together since they were both nine. Aniela's mother, Kinga Majewska, had enrolled her in traditional folk dancing lessons, called *krakowiak*. She learned to dance high-energy polkas, waltz to the polonaise or glide to a lively *oberek*, a twirling dance in triple time, similar to a mazurka but usually faster. They practiced weekly, and there were older girls and boys among the younger ones. Aniela loved it.

It was through folk dancing that Aniela could take center stage, lose herself in the music and movements, yet blend in as part of the ensemble.

Their dance instructor, Pani Ostrowska, was an elegant woman who still wore her dark hair in a low bun, heavily streaked with gray. When Pani Ostrowska demonstrated a move, she would spring to life, like a gazelle. She danced through her fingertips, every motion a demonstration of control and elegance.

Aniela couldn't help remembering their first dance recital, seven years prior. Pani Ostrowska gave instructions to the mothers on proper attire for their upcoming recital.

"Are you excited about your first dance recital, your first *krakowiak*?" asked Pani Majewska.

Both the dance and the dress were called *krakowiak*. The dress was a traditional costume that drew on the country folk traditions of the region. The girls wore blue skirts with a floral apron tied over them, white peasant tops with puffy sleeves, and a corset-like vest made of dark blue wool. The boots were laced up above the ankles and were a soft, dyed red leather. Ribbons and flowers were woven into their hair, and all the girls were required to have braids.

Aniela looked up from her German verb drills. "Yes, mama, so very much."

"We'll have to get you fitted," Pani Majewska said.

Henryk, who was studying with Irena, had looked up and said quietly, "Pani Majewska, I'm not sure if you are aware, but my mother is a seamstress. She is very talented…"

A slightly embarrassed look crossed Pani Majewska's face. "I hadn't realized your mother was a seamstress. Of course we will come to her to get the dress made…"

Henryk smiled quickly. "She would greatly appreciate the opportunity, I'm sure. She will not disappoint."

Aniela took in the slight flush on Henryk's face. She bit her lip in commiseration, sensing his discomfort from across the room. While the Majewski family lived comfortably as faculty and intellectuals amongst the educated elite, Henryk's small family evidently did not. Henryk's father had been an educated man, too, an engineer, but died when Henryk was very young. She hadn't really thought about how Henryk and his mother made a living in the city, and felt ashamed that she had never considered his family might not live in the same lifestyle as her own. She shot Henryk a look of encouragement, but his head was lowered and focused on the book in his lap.

The next day, Kinga Majewska brought Aniela to Henryk's mother, Pani Bartosz, for a fitting. Aniela had seen Henryk's mother at school a couple of times over the last months, and had the impression that she was forever mulling over some deep problem in her mind, furrowing her brow and biting her lip.

Pani Bartosz offered swatches of fabrics so she could choose the small embellishments that were to be sewn onto the apron, vest or corset. Aniela picked small flowers to be appliquéd to the dress.

Pani Majewska reached for her purse. "Here is half the payment," she said, laying the zlotys on the table.

"It's too much, Pani!" protested Pani Bartosz. "Really, ten percent is enough!"

"Nonsense!" Pani Majewska said firmly. After a moment, Pani Bartosz nodded her head, and thanked Pani Majewska profusely.

A couple of days later, while walking home with Irena and Henryk, Aniela practiced her steps, sashaying around and zigzagging to and fro.

"You sure are excited about your recital, dancing girl," Henryk remarked.

Aniela smiled and curtsied in front of him, as the girls did to their partners when starting a dance in class. "Shall we begin?"

She took Henryk's hand and tried to engage him in a simple three-beat polka, but he immediately turned red, dropping her hand.

"I'm no dancer, Aniela," he declined, walking ahead.

Aniela moved on to Irena. "Shall we?" she encouraged.

"I don't know the boy's part," Irena stated, and continued on her way.

"No bother," Aniela stated, unperturbed. "I'll dance on my own."

But tonight, Aniela was not alone; rather, she swing danced with Leon for hours, only stopping to grab a drink. Aniela was so wrapped up in the spirit of fun, she had not noticed that their crowd had thinned and that there were only a few dancers left.

"Leon," Aniela panted, "it's getting late. I really must be going home."

"All right," he said, wiping his brow on his sleeve.

Aniela spotted Ewa, and kissed her goodbye, and began bundling up. Leon waved to Ewa, took Aniela by her elbow and led her out of the café.

"I live on Pijarska Street," she offered.

Leon kept his hand on Aniela as they walked, their hot cheeks tingling in the cool December air. Leon seemed edgy, so Aniela tried to break the ice with conversation. "Tonight was so much fun…"

"It was amazing," he said seriously.

Aniela nodded, carefully planting steps on the slick cobblestone street.

"So," Leon said, "would you like to go dancing with me again some time?"

Aniela's instinct was to quickly agree, as it had been such a fun evening, and the two made such good and natural dance partners. But when she glanced at Leon's face, she saw something written in his features that she had not seen before. It was an intense look, one that revealed a lot more rode on her answer than dancing. She paused, considering her response.

"I did have a lovely time, Leon," Aniela answered carefully. "But I think it only fair to tell you that I'm seeing someone. Henryk Bartosz. He's not much of a dancer, so if you are looking for a dance partner, I would love to go again…" She trailed off awkwardly.

Leon's face grew red. "You think I want someone just to *dance* with? You could have mentioned your boyfriend before I spent the whole night dancing with you…" he spat.

He took his hand off her elbow and shoved his hands angrily into his pockets.

How had I missed the signs? Aniela wondered, biting her lip. She had never thought to mention her relationship to Leon. While they had been dance partners for years, and chatted easily at weekly lessons, she had never seen Leon as anything but a boy in her class. He was red-faced and breathing heavily, and she felt ashamed she had unwittingly hurt him. She regretted letting loose on the dance floor with him and thinking that was all there was to it.

He walked the final blocks to her apartment in silence, his eyes never meeting hers.

"I'm sorry, Leon," Aniela ventured, as she turned to the door of her building. "I didn't mean to hurt your feelings."

"Fine," Leon said gruffly. "I guess I was dreaming that a girl that looks like you would go with me anyway."

And with that, he turned and left her on the icy doorstep. She watched his sullen figure walk away. She knew that her relationship with Leon would likely never be the same again. After Christmas break, Leon quit the dance troupe and Aniela felt melancholic at having somehow spoiled what once had been a fine partnership.

Chapter 7

Class Concerns

A niela turned eighteen and was a proud freshman at Jagiellonian University. Among the seven thousand six hundred or so students enrolled, about twenty-nine percent were women, a great advancement from the nineteenth century when, as legend had it, a girl by the name of Nawojka entered the university in male disguise. But since 1897, the university had made the formal decision to admit female students.

Aniela was excited about her decision to pursue a degree in German Studies. Many of the fellow female students were enrolled in the romance languages, history, pedagogy, or art. Ewa also enrolled and was accepted, to Aniela's great comfort and delight. Ewa decided to pursue a degree in Russian, so the two old friends had no classes together at first. They agreed to minor in English so that they could attend the same classes and have a study partner. As English is a Germanic language, Aniela had a bit of an advantage, as so many of the words were similar or related.

With Ewa's smiling face greeting Aniela during class, she soon found this to be her favorite course at the university. And Henryk, who asked to see her class schedule, made sure to meet her after class and walk her home, as he had always done.

***

The Majewskis' home life was full of contradictions, like many educated households of their day. Aniela's mother, Kinga, was a true believer. She sat in awe of the clergy and their power, and saw them as a direct extension of the Pope and God himself.

Bogdan Majewkski's views on religion were less straightforward. He went to church mainly as a gesture to his wife's faith and as homage to Poland's long-standing Catholic traditions. But he was a philosopher, a man of the world, and in private moments at home, he expressed grave doubts about the validity of any organized religion.

But since Poland had been restored to statehood in 1918, there was much debate about what kind of country Poland should be. Was it a Catholic country? What role did minorities have? Who were its allies? After one hundred and twenty-three years of partition by the Russians, Austrians and Prussians, finally Poles had a voice in their own identity. Heated discussions erupted about the meaning of Polish statehood.

One Friday evening after dinner, Henryk and Bogdan Majewski started debating which road Poland should take, while Aniela readied herself for their usual Friday evening out.

Bogdan cited how the *de facto* President, Piłsudski, gained national respect and prestige during the Great War when his negotiations helped Poland regain statehood.

"Piłsudski did something that many of us thought would never happen," Bogdan said, sipping his ale. "He ensured we regained statehood. But his main goal was to create a stable nation in Central Europe that was inclusive of Poland's minorities spread out throughout greater Poland, Lithuania and the Ukraine: Jews, Russian and Greek Orthodox, Protestants, Muslims."

"For that," Henryk said, "we can be eternally grateful. One needs such a leader in uncertain times."

"I respect Piłsudski's desire to create distance between the two powers that flank us and build consensus with Romania and Hungary to oppose any future foreign aggression," Bogdan said. "I respect German culture, language and philosophy, and I do believe we can build a new bridge of understanding between a suspicious Poland toward the Vaterland to the west."

"What do you think of the argument that Poland should be made up of Catholic, ethnic Poles — and that the minorities, including Germans and Jews, should be relocated out of Poland's borders?" Henryk probed.

Henryk was referring to the leading politician espousing this nationalistic and exclusionary view, Roman Dmówski. Dmówski, like the

National Socialist Party gaining traction in Germany, blamed the Treaty of Versailles and a Judeo-Masonic conspiracy in the West that was unfriendly towards Poland and his party beliefs. His party wanted the borders limited to greater Poland, and not stretching to the Lithuanian and Ukrainian states.

"I think it's hogwash. We must come together as one country, as Piłsudski envisions, and not get caught up in petty differences," Bogdan said with conviction. His eyes fell on Henryk, his voice growing gentler. "My son, we all lost so much during the Great War. I know that war resulted in the loss of your father. The horrors of that war, the carnage, the simple and inexhaustible loss of life, all so senseless... that has left a mark on Europe's collective memory."

"You may be right," Henryk said. "But I'm not so certain. There's so much anger, it seems to me it has to be placed somewhere. We will need stronger allies than Hungary and Romania if we are to be in charge of our destiny. France and Britain must be our allies, and maybe America."

"Maybe so," Bogdan said, idly stroking his mustache. "It is always wise to have allies. But ultimately, it is diplomacy and compromise, and fear of another war, that will keep us safe."

"In any case," Henryk said, "when I graduate from university, it'll be my time to do my compulsory service. Like the great winged *husaria*, I hope to be a cavalry man, though those days may be soon behind us..."

Bogdan grinned. "I see you have been swept up by the battle stories as told by Sienkiewicz. During the days of partition, simply having a copy of *Fire and Sword* on a bookshelf was a quiet form of resistance."

Henryk smiled. "Yes, our tradition of being on horseback is something that gets my blood pumping." His face grew rueful. "But the truth is, my experience with horses is limited to the plough and idle walks on the backside of Willow. I doubt I'll be good enough."

Bogdan patted his hand. "You are young, bright and talented, my boy. You'll do fine."

***

Before long, Henryk graduated with a degree in political theory and a desire to make a mark on the world. But this also meant it was time for Henryk to perform his mandatory two-year military service.

The Polish military was based on the American military model, with four divisions such as land forces, navy, air forces and special forces. All men of age had to report to a service center, and take both a written and a physical test to determine where their talents would lead them.

As a college graduate with a firmly middle-class background, Henryk was bound for the "Middle Army" — a division of the military that was designed for men with an education who were not from top aristocratic families. Therefore, those in the Middle Army were not bound to be officers or infantry, but to do technical and skilled jobs in the middle of the ranks. In order to qualify, he had to endure hours of testing on Polish history, current events, mathematics, physics, and foreign languages. There was an extensive psychological test, and questions that aimed at determining the morality and ethical make-up of each man.

The physical test consisted of strength and endurance trials, from long runs carrying heavy equipment to performing squat thrusts, push-ups and sit-ups with a barking man and his stopwatch, to crawling and scrambling over obstacles. Upon completion, each cadet's file was given a letter to denote his physical fitness.

Some weeks after the tests, Henryk received a letter on official military stationery citing that he was to be stationed in Inowrocław. It gave him some comfort, as it was where his father had done his service, back when Poland was part of Prussia.

Henryk and Aniela cherished their summer together. Henryk returned home to Wieliczka, as he did every year to help with the family farm, but the young lovers saw each other almost every weekend.

On some weekends, he returned to Kraków, and the pair strolled through Planty Park, a former moat and now was a ring of green grass around Wawel Castle. They strolled the public gardens, dined at cafés, saw a movie, or just picnicked. Aniela loved those lazy summer days, lying on a blanket, as comfortable in each other's company and silences as an old married couple. And of course, there were the times the two passionately kissed and groped each other, behaving like teenagers and not resembling an old married couple at all. Those times, they prayed for privacy, and their passionate encounters were left unfulfilled, each dreaming of the day they could express feelings openly and without hiding.

When Aniela visited Henryk and his family in Wieliczka, they spent their time similarly there — they often took Willow out and rode through the rolling countryside together, something that Aniela truly loved. From time to time, they'd see Henryk's old friends and stop to get a beer and pay a visit. Henryk was always on his best behavior, drinking just a beer or two, making sure to include Aniela in all conversations and activities, and Aniela began to relax around his friends and grew to like and tease them, as they did her.

Back and forth, between Wieliczka and Kraków, they traveled until the crisp chill in the air of late summer let them know that their time was coming to an end.

It was on an August summer evening that Henryk escorted Aniela for a walk. The sun had not yet set, and Henryk took Aniela's hand and led her to the babbling stream that bordered the farm. There was a great willow tree by the stream. Henryk held Aniela's hand a little too hard; he grew quiet and serious and led her under it. He had set up a picnic, and had laid down a blanket.

"Please," he gestured, somewhat formally. "Please sit down."

Aniela tucked her legs under her and sat down on the soft blanket. Henryk sat down next to her. His eyes were searching hers intensely, and Aniela grew quiet.

He seemed lost in thought and then jerkily reached back for the basket. "Oh, I brought brandy. Would you like some?"

"Yes," Aniela said, watching as he reached for the homemade brandy and filled up two glasses. His hands were unsteady, and he spilled some on the blanket. He cursed under his breath.

"It's okay, Henryk," Aniela said, trying to calm his agitated mood.

He was nervous and unsettled. She reached over and took his hand in hers. He was so warm, his hand sweating.

"Henryk?" she said, softly.

He let out a long, tortured breath. "Aniela," he said. "My dearest, my beautiful dancing girl…"

Aniela's eyes encouraged him to continue.

"I have loved you, I think, from the first time I saw you… in that library, with that fool trying to impress you…"

"Julian," she said, though he didn't appear to hear.

"And since then, I've seen you grow into this… golden-haired goddess… You are not some cold, untouchable icon to be worshiped from afar… you are clever, and honest, and kind, and you are warm and your lips taste like peaches and when your body molds to mine, I am so…"

He stopped, shaking his head. "I had this all planned out. I'm sorry. I can't offer you subscriptions to opera houses and philharmonics. But I have something to offer. What I'm trying to say is, I have loved you for so long. And I have waited for you. And now, I think it's time, I'm ready to ask you… to ask you what I have always wanted to ask you. Aniela, my beautiful dancing girl, will you marry me?"

Aniela examined the eyes locked on her face. His jaw was tense, a vein throbbed in his temple and she felt a wave of love and devotion sweep over her. Aniela's face softened and turned to his, eyes luminescent with unspilled tears of joy. She saw his own expression ease a bit, a flash of relief brightening his eyes even more.

"I will marry you, Henryk," she said, taking that face in her hands and kissing his lips. "I love you. It's what I have always wanted, too."

Henryk groaned with happiness, and he kissed her with such fervor and force, Aniela was forced down onto her back on the blanket. Henryk covered her with his body, kissing her gratefully and frantically.

"Yes, yes, yes," he murmured between kisses. "These are the best words a man can hear!" Aniela started giggling, as he kissed her like a man slightly mad.

She kissed him back, matching his wild energy, kissing his nose, his cheek, his mouth… wherever she could. At last, he stopped and looked deeply into her eyes.

"I did ask your parents' permission," Henryk said softly. "And they accepted, of course, but they are worried that we are so young. I promised them that we would wait until I'm back from my service, and after you graduate from college. I'll get a good job and take care of you. Will you wait for me, my sweet?"

"I'll wait, my love. Forever, if I need to."

Henryk laughed and pulled them up, reaching into the basket.

"I almost forgot!" He pulled out a small sachet, tied with a ribbon. He untied the ribbon and emptied the sachet into his hand. A small, delicate ring landed in his large, rough palm. He picked the ring up, took her hand, and slid the ring onto her finger.

It was made from white gold, decorated with eight small gems encrusted in the thick face and three individual larger diamonds, each separated and set off by two smaller diamonds laid out vertically. It glittered in the fading light, and the ring's weight felt natural on her slim finger. It fit perfectly.

"It's the most beautiful thing I've even seen."

Henryk squeezed her hand, his eyes never leaving Aniela's face. "Yes, my darling. I agree."

Chapter 8

To Inowrocław

Aniela cried the whole way to the train station. Henryk, dressed in his dark green uniform, a smart cap, and with a duffel bag in his hand, tried to soothe Aniela by hugging her to him and kissing her hair. Pani Bartosz wore a stern expression, and kept her emotions in check. As the black train pulled into the platform, Pani Bartosz stepped aside to give the young lovers a moment of privacy.

"You'll write to me," Henryk stated, squeezing Aniela's shoulders urgently. "And wait for me."

"Of course," she promised.

He took her hand and looked at the ring. He swallowed a lump in his throat and urgently sought her eyes.

"You won't fall for some fool who flatters you with compliments, fine dinners, and candy while I'm sweating like a grunt?" He was trying to sound as if he was joking, but she heard a worried undercurrent in his tight voice.

"Never," she said.

"I'm sorry that I won't be here to protect you," he whispered.

"I'm fine, Henryk," she reassured him. "I can take care of myself."

He grunted. "I know you can. It's others that seem to lose themselves around you. Just be careful, Aniela. You don't know the weapon you wield."

"I'll be fine," Aniela sniffled, trying to avoid breaking down altogether on the platform.

"Well, then…" He grabbed her face in his hands and kissed Aniela tenderly, before he moved to say farewell to his mother. Pani Bartosz stood very still, but the corner of her eye twitched, betraying her inner emotions. Her only son was about to leave her, and she was both proud and devastated.

"Wear clean socks," she said abruptly. "And eat regularly, my son."

"I will, mamo." Henryk hugged his mother to him, the two stiff and awkward but full of emotion.

And with that, Henryk ascended the stairs up to the train and stepped inside. He turned back, taking a final look at the women he was leaving behind, and waved quickly — trying to reassure them with a tight smile.

The doors closed and Henryk was gone.

Chapter 9

Concerning Danzig

March, 1935

Kinga Majewska wore her thick blonde hair down to her shoulders, which complemented her sparkling light blue eyes. She had been raised in a well-off family with two brothers, and watched from the sidelines as the boys were given opportunities that she wasn't. Their mother had died when she was only ten, and Kinga grew up taken care of materially, but overlooked and rudderless in a masculine home. Her father never wanted to talk about the death of his wife, and threw himself into his work. So Kinga devoted herself to the study of the piano, an appropriate pastime for a girl. Kinga adored her gentle piano teacher, and saw the old woman as a surrogate mother. But when her teacher died of a heart attack when Kinga was just fifteen, she felt like she had lost a mother anew.

At eighteen, Kinga met her brother's professor at a graduation ceremony. She was immediately drawn to the older professor, and felt truly seen when he asked why she was not enrolled at the university, too.

"Nobody ever asked me whether I wanted to study," Kinga said simply. "In fact, I am rarely asked what I want at all."

Bogdan looked at the beautiful woman in front of him, and vowed that he would spend the rest of his life asking her what she wanted and finding ways to fulfil her every wish. So, with the clarity of an old bachelor man overtaken by love at first sight, he courted Kinga.

Six months later, Bogdan asked Kinga's father for permission to marry. Kinga worried that her father might think her too young, too rash to know her heart. But he accepted Bogdan's offer quickly. There was an odd gleam of relief in her father's eyes. Years later, when looking in the mirror, Kinga was struck by how similar she looked to her late mother and she belatedly wondered if it had caused her father unbearable grief to see her face every day.

In the security of her new home, Kinga embraced life with her husband, pushing away thoughts of her sad childhood. And slowly, the ties that bound her to the past withered away.

Professor Majewski displayed an elegance that comes naturally to those accustomed to soft music and the smell of leather-bound books in well-heated rooms. The professor walked with a cane, not so much because he needed it, but for the gravitas and security of it. While his well-stamped passport and his knowledge of foreign books could be a bit intimidating, Henryk was nevertheless drawn to him.

"Herr Ausfelder writes that the chancellor of Germany is increasing his rhetoric regarding the illegality of the Treaty of Versailles, and is threatening to leave the League of Nations," Bogdan Majewski said idly, looking down at a letter in his lap.

Herr Ausfelder was Aniela's father's old university friend, and Aniela recalled many summer vacations spent in Dresden at Herr Ausfelder's stately home, listening to the two men talk philosophy and theory into the wee hours of the night.

Aniela looked up, taking a break from reading a German book. Never as keen on politics as her father, and sensing he missed Henryk to discuss these matters with, she tried to contribute.

"What will that mean, Papa?"

"Well, Danzig is a free city — protected by the League of Nations. If Hitler leaves the League of Nations, I fear that his next move may be to take over the city. The Germans have long believed it was their port, and they resented losing it in the war."

Danzig, a city on the Baltic Sea, had long been an important port city. Habituated by many ethnic Germans, Germany had long claimed it as part of their territory. However, Danzig lay in the north of Poland. Poles called the city Gdańsk; it was a strategic city as it allowed access to the Baltic and maritime trade.

"Wilson's 14 Points restored our sovereignty. The thirteenth point declared an independent Polish state would be erected, including territories indisputably inhabited by Polish populations, and critically, we would be assured free and secure access to the sea. In order to not hand over Gdańsk directly to Poles or Germans — as populations on both sides made claims to the city — the League of Nations declared it an international, free city."

Her father looked down at the letter in his lap. "I hope that Herr Ausfelder is exaggerating, but he has concerns that the Chancellor is preparing for war. He worries that if Hitler leaves the League of Nations, he will eventually annex parts of Poland, starting with Gdańsk. The last thing we friends want to see is our countries at war again."

She took his hand in hers, noted it was growing thin and wrinkled with age. Her heart went out to him, this aging patriot who had lived most of his life without a country to truly call his own. The skin on his face had deep lines, and his blue eyes — once so bright and cheerful — were losing their luster. His teeth had yellowed with time, and he had his share of gold teeth now. Aniela suddenly saw him as he really was — an old man.

"You, of all people," Aniela said, stroking his hand. "You know the Germans are a proud people, which have brought out some of the best qualities of our shared European culture. You love their philosophers, their music, their language. Let us hope that there are more voices like yours and Herr Ausfelder's in Germany. The wise ones, the reflective ones will prevail. A new Chancellor is high on campaign promises, but you know how politicians are. He'll likely get nothing done and these promises — which alarm us now — will come to naught."

"Yes," he said, smiling weakly. "You are probably right. That is quite true that politicians make great speeches and promises, and oftentimes, it is nothing but hot air. But dear Herr Ausfelder is no alarmist… It would break my heart to imagine my two girls, and all the young people who are the future of Poland, having to experience war like we once did."

Chapter 10

A Hero Dies

Kraków
May, 1935

Aniela returned home to find her parents and Irena huddled around the wireless. She was shushed as she walked through the door.

"What's going on?" she whispered.

Pan Majewski put his finger to his lips to quiet Aniela, as he listened carefully to the voice of Benjamin Noga.

"…*Marshal Józef Klemens Piłsudski is dead,*" said the voice. "*He died today at Belweder Palace in Warsaw, after fighting a secret but ultimately deadly battle with liver cancer. Within a half hour of the announcement of his death, people flooded the streets of Warsaw to pay respect to one of our greatest citizens. While many have criticized Piłsudski's authoritarian regime and his increasing focus on military and foreign affairs over democratic ones, let us never forget the important role Piłsudski played in securing Poland's independence as a free state and his heroic victory in the Battle of Warsaw against the invading Soviets in 1920, defending our beloved Motherland as she was rebuilding after partition. Marshal Piłsudski is credited with being a leading orchestrator of the miracle on the Vistula…*"

The phone rang, and everyone jumped. Aniela ran to get it.

"Hello?" she said into the black receiver.

"Aniela? It's Henryk." Her heart constricted as she heard Henryk's deep voice through the crackling connection. Phone calls were very expensive, and there was but one phone for the entire barracks.

"You heard the news?"

"Yes," she said. "We're all crowded around the wireless."

"They say there is to be a funeral procession by train around the country. And his wife and daughters want him buried in Kraków."

"Yes?"

"My unit will likely be coming to Kraków to attend the funeral. We should be there in five days or so."

Aniela was flooded with a rush of excitement at the mere thought of seeing Henryk again, then felt a rush of guilt as Marshal Piłsudski's death was the reason for bringing Henryk home.

"I'll be home, dancing girl. That's why I'm calling."

"I cannot wait to see you," she breathed.

"I am not on leave, of course," Henryk explained, "but I will see you. After the ceremonies. I promise."

"How strange to be celebrating over a funeral."

Henryk grunted. "He is a great man who will be dearly missed, but right now, all I want is to kiss your gorgeous lips and feel you in my arms."

She heard male laughter and hoots in the background, for no cadet was ever truly alone.

"Sorry that we are not alone," she offered, imagining his cheeks growing red with embarrassment.

The phone went dead and Aniela held the receiver, just basking in the memory of that brief connection, and unwilling to step back into reality.

But reality soon seeped in. As Henryk had said, Madame Piłsudska and her two daughters traveled the nation by rail, with her husband's body in a coffin and millions of Poles lining the route to pay their respects.

A week later, the convoy made its way to Kraków, where a very large funeral procession was to be held. The city was awhirl since the news of the funeral. The streets were cleaned and scrubbed, awaiting the foreign and local dignitaries. Garbage was removed from every corner. Shopkeepers scrubbed windows and stoops. Big banners were unfurled and hung from windows. Dance instructor, Pani Ostrowska, called on her troupe to march in the procession in folk costumes, along with other dancers from all over the region.

On Saturday, May 17th, the city was ready. Despite the banners, streamers and flags, the mood was festive and celebratory. Never had Aniela seen so many people in one place. The city was bursting. There were onlookers on the parapets of buildings, dressed in their colorful best.

Peasant women wore red kerchiefs around their heads. The peasant men wore oddly shaped hats, sporting falcon feathers.

The city's Jews were also decked out in their finest, and they, too, mourned the loss of Piłsudski — a defender of minorities. The men dressed in long dark caftans, wearing hats made of beaver pelts, with their long curls peering from both sides of their bearded faces.

There were uniformed soldiers, many on horseback, their steeds gleaming in the May sunshine and the riders sitting stiffly and proudly.

Aniela marched along the route through the old city with Ewa, Pani Ostrowska, and hundreds of other dancers in costume. The noise was deafening. The police eventually pulled the dancers to the side behind barricades as the official procession began.

Through old city gates and under brick arches emblazoned with tapestries, the long funeral procession marched. Piłsudski was laid in a coffin on a gun carriage covered in wreaths, with his faithful charger preceding his coffin. On either side of him, military men wearing beautiful uniforms adorned with medals, ribbons, and gleaming brass buttons somberly accompanied the cavalcade.

The retinue slowly made their way through the streets, steadily heading to Wawel Castle, the former seat of Polish nobility, which was situated up a hill paved with cobblestones. As the coffin went by, everyone grew silent and bowed heads in respect.

Behind the gun carriage and the beautifully decorated coffin, President Mościcki walked stoically, holding the arm of the widowed Madame Piłsudska. She was dressed completely in black, and no feature could be seen through the veil that covered her countenance. Her daughters and other foreign dignitaries followed.

Aniela overheard a man behind her, "See how beloved and respected dear Piłsudski is! France has sent Minister Pierre Laval and Marshal Henri Petain… and look, there's Field Marshal Lord Cavan of Great Britain."

Aniela stood on her tiptoes to glimpse these important people. Polish security forces kept the crowds at bay, as other dignitaries continued their march to Wawel Castle. She saw a rather portly man in a brand-new uniform. He was adorned with a sash and a large star pinned to his right lapel. From the medals and his position in the parade, she knew he was very important. The official looked furtively around, as if uncomfortable, at the masses of Poles dressed in traditional costume, and she noted three security forces protecting him alone.

"Who is that?" she asked.

The same man commented, "That's Minister Hermann Goering of Germany. He's head of their air force."

The procession rolled on, while the dancers jostled for position in the crushing crowds. They heard the throbbing pulse of the drums beating from blocks away.

Piłsudski's coffin was carried to St. Leonard's Crypt in Wawel Castle. The hill to the castle was lined with flags from ninety regiments of infantry and other branches of military, and soldiers and officers lined the hill as the procession made its way up to the castle.

There was no chance for the dancers to get into the church to attend the funeral service, but they heard the salute of a hundred and one guns and the band and drums from many blocks away. With the mixture of peasants in traditional garb, Kraków's intelligentsia dressed in their very best, polished soldiers displaying their shining uniforms with precision and pride, and Christians, Jews and Russian Orthodox all mingling together, Aniela felt an overwhelming sense of national pride and unity.

She felt so lucky to be Polish, to be Krakovian, and to have witnessed such an amazing event in homage to a most revered citizen. The city of Kraków had shown the world what was truly at the heart of Poland, and it gleamed like a precious jewel.

Chapter 11

Stolen Moments

It took Aniela hours to make it back home as the festivities wound down, and she was but half a block away from the apartment when a pair of strong hands encircled her from behind and lifted her into the air. She squealed indignantly, then felt Henryk's face against her own, as he hugged her from behind.

"I've found you, my dancing girl," he laughed.

"You always sneak up on me!" she squealed in return.

He put Aniela down and spun her around, and kissed her so long and hard, she felt dizzy. And when his lips finally broke from hers, she was able to gaze up at him. There he stood, wearing his dark green, wool uniform, and smelling of tobacco. A leather strap crossed his wide chest and he sported a wide leather belt.

"Henryk." She was at a loss for words. He always had this effect on her.

"Boy, have I missed you. These last five days dragged by so slowly…"

She giggled, hugging him back. They stood wrapped in one another's arms until the world crept back in.

Finally, she said, "I have missed you so much, too! Come on, let's go to my home; my parents will be thrilled to see you."

Entering her apartment, Aniela called out, "Look who I found…"

Her parents rushed to Henryk and hugged him warmly, everyone laughing and talking at once. Henryk took off his hat and sat down in the sitting room, and everyone was preoccupied with the events of the day.

"They'll keep Marshal Piłsudski's body on display at St. Leonard's Crypt for two years," Henryk stated. "So there will be plenty of time for people from near and far to pay their respects."

"His heart will be taken to Wilno and buried with his mother," Pani

Majewska said. "Is it true that they are moving royalty from the crypt to make room for Piłsudski's body?"

"That is what I heard," Pan Majewski agreed. "He is displacing King Władisław IV and Queen Cecelia Renata."

"Hmmm," Pani Majewska murmured. "When were they alive?"

"In the 1600s, I believe," Pan Majewski answered. "I'm not sure where they will be moved, but it is said that Marshal Piłsudski will be laid next to Sobieski and Kościuszko."

They nodded appreciatively at this news, as Sobieski was revered for having saved Christendom from Turkish invaders in the 1600s, and Kościuszko was well-known in Poland, Belorussia and in the US as a military hero from revolutionary times.

"So what now, I wonder?" Pan Majewski mused. "Now that Piłsudski is gone?"

"It is hard to say," Henryk commiserated. "Piłsudski appointed Rydz-Śmigły in charge of the army, but already there is a feeling that conditions will deteriorate. The question is, will Hitler honor the non-aggression pact that he signed with Piłsudski?"

Pan Majewski squirmed in his seat, and Aniela knew he was thinking of Herr Ausfelder's recent letters and the rumblings that Germany was gearing up for war and had its eye on Poland again.

Aniela squeezed her father's hand under the table, trying to give him reassurance, and then reached to hold Henryk's strong hand. Even on such a momentous day, it was hard not to realize that they might be drifting toward a storm.

***

Henryk and Aniela talked well into the night, and at long last, he had to go and visit his mother before being due back to his unit. Aniela felt the dread of being separated again. With a warm, lingering kiss, he was gone.

Irena came in at almost midnight, and as Aniela lay awake in her bed, she overheard her mother scold her for coming back so late.

The major excitement, in the Majewski household at least, was that Irena had a suitor, a fellow musician, whom she had met at the large funeral procession. His name was Adam Perelmuter. He was a tall, lanky man, with thick dark hair, deep eyes and a warm, open expression. Irena blossomed around Adam, and while Aniela was so pleased to see her sister so happy and content in her new-found love, their easy and growing intimacy made her miss Henryk all the more. Adam was about five years older than Irena, and played the cello beautifully at the old opera house.

Before long, Irena had introduced Adam to Pan and Pani Majewski, and he was dropping by once a week to have supper, just as Henryk had once done. Many an evening, Irena and Adam pulled out their instruments and regaled the family with classical duets. Pani Majewska's eyes shone with pride and she seemed transported by their melodies. When Aniela saw that look on her mother's face, she felt a pang of envy — as her mother had a deep and profound love of music, and while Aniela had the gifts of dance and languages, music was a bond Pani Majewska shared with Irena alone.

Aniela surmised that it was Adam's deep and abiding love of music that won her mother over. At first, she was a bit wary of him — with his dark looks and prominent bone structure, Pani Majewska had quietly asked Irena, upon hearing his name, "Is he Jewish?"

Irena shrugged. "What of it?"

Pani Majewska furrowed her brow. "Nothing, I suppose. I see how fond you are of him, so I'm sure he is a lovely person. It's just that… there are so many challenges in life; it is good to choose a partner who is similar to you. Having a similar upbringing, similar views, similar religions… it is one less thing to have conflict over…"

Irena bristled at this statement. "His mother said the exact same thing! Why can't people see what we *do* have in common? We're both musicians, we both play stringed instruments, we both imagine a country free of those old-fashioned distinctions of class and religion. All your reasons, to us, seem like petty, antiquated excuses!"

Pani Majewska quickly reached out to take Irena's hand. "I'm sorry to have upset you. I only want what is best for you; but of course, you must follow your heart."

Irena calmed a bit at this. Pani Majewska was never one to invite conflict, and she quickly defused the situation whenever disagreement arose at home.

Pan Majewski, who was listening from his study, called out, "Does that mean you are communists, then?"

Irena paused at this. "We are both very intrigued by the promise of a fair and more equitable society... So, yes, I suppose you can say we are *interested* in communist teachings."

Pan Majewski harrumphed under his breath and turned back to his book.

Chapter 12

Working Man

1936

With Henryk's departure, along with thousands of other visitors from near and far, life soon settled back into its old routine. The banners were folded up, the flags removed, dust settled again on the streets and pavements. Although a steady stream of curious visitors still made their way to Piłsudski's glass-covered coffin, Kraków returned to its old self.

By the time that Henryk's two years of mandatory service was over, Adam and Irena were engaged. And of course, Henryk and Aniela had an understanding that once she graduated, they, too, were to be married. Their parents faced the prospect of losing two daughters to marriage within a year.

Pani Majewska, as usual, looked on the bright side. "I'm not losing my daughters," she stated firmly. "A mother never loses a daughter in marriage. Daughters are for life. We are gaining two sons."

Henryk returned from service during Aniela's senior year. Eager to find a job, he found one at the *Kraków Times*. His beat was writing lifestyle articles and stories for the local government section. His days at the paper were long and erratic, and he was expected to log at least two stories daily, even when there was not much news to report. As such, he spent innumerable hours perusing documents at city hall and other government buildings, looking for a scoop. He got to know the clerks, the judges, the local politicians.

Henryk and Aniela picked up old habits and frequented the movies, to cafés to listen to live music, or sometimes they just strolled the city arm in arm, finding a park bench to snuggle into, making wedding plans.

They agreed that they would marry at the end of June in St. Adalbert's

Church, and then take the ultra-modern Luxtorpeda train to Zakopane for a week-long honeymoon. A honeymoon was a rather cosmopolitan idea, newly brought in from the West. It would be just the two of them: something very precious after years of stolen moments and park bench kisses.

Aniela took her winter exams, and scored well. Henryk began looking for apartments that he could afford, and eventually found a small but cozy one through a contact he made at the newspaper. It was on the border of the Old Town and had a small balcony with a nice view of a rear courtyard. He brought Aniela to see it, and he nervously showed her around the tidy and modest apartment, his eyes eager for approval.

He couldn't have picked a nicer day. The street was lined with trees beginning to bud, bulbs were pushing through the soil in the tree wells, and the smell was fresh. The building had an old carved wooden door with wrought-iron windows and a vestibule lined with worn but clean marble. Few buildings had modern elevators, so they walked up three flights to the empty, rear apartment. The agent was already in the apartment and let them in.

The living room and kitchen were nicely appointed and cheery. They walked into the bedroom. It was a modest-sized room, big enough for a bed and a wardrobe. There was a deep bay window in this room, and Aniela imagined curling up with a book in that sill on a summer morning, looking over to see Henryk sleeping peacefully in their bed.

It was warm and charming. "I can see us being very happy here," she said to Henryk, grabbing his hand and squeezing it.

The agent led them to the bathroom, which had a claw-foot bathtub, pedestal sink and a toilet that flushed by pull chain on the wall. There was also a second room; it had perhaps been a maid's quarters once upon a time, as it was in the rear with a small window and facing a small alleyway between buildings.

"This could be used as a small study," the agent said. "Or a nursery."

Aniela caught Henryk's gleaming eyes and blushed deeply. Just two more months and this would all be theirs and their lives together would begin in earnest.

"I can't wait," Henryk whispered in her ear. From the look on his face, she knew what he was thinking, and her blush deepened.

***

Henryk burst through the door to his and his mother's apartment, a bound in his step. He removed his hat and casually tossed it onto a hook.

"Mamo," he called. "We found it!"

Pani Bartosz came out of the kitchen, an apron tied around her waist. "What did you find?"

"Paradise," Henryk said, dropping himself onto the couch, his whole lithe body emanating relief. He stroked the growing stubble on his chin, a lopsided grin splitting his face. He looked at his mother proudly.

"I took Aniela to an apartment on Józef Sarego Street," he said. "I was tipped off from a guy at the paper that one of the apartments was available. I had scoped it out first, of course. I needed to make sure it was fitting for the daughter of Professor Majewski. It was charming and bright. I hoped it wouldn't be too small or too modest for her, but she loved it. We are to begin our lives together there, as man and wife. I'm so happy, I can hardly believe it!"

Pani Bartosz smiled tightly and sat down across from Henryk. He had leaned back, his face turned to the ceiling, a smile on his face.

"I'll spare you the need to offer me to move in with you," Pani Bartosz said, voice level and controlled. "I won't have you feeling the burden of taking care of your old mother when you have a fancy wife to keep."

Henryk snapped up straight, his eyes trained on his mother's restrained face. "What are you saying?"

"I'm saying that it is time for me to face some facts," Pani Bartosz said. "The economy is slowing down; my custom tailoring work is drying up. And the truth is: you are marrying into a very fine family; one that has helped us out since the fortunate day you met Aniela. I want my only son to have every chance at a successful life and happy marriage. You don't need me living with you as you begin your life with Aniela, and I know I couldn't afford to live in Kraków on my own…"

"I'd never let you," Henryk interrupted.

"And I know that, too," Pani Bartosz said, her eyes softening. "Which is why I'm telling you now that I'm moving back to Wieliczka. It is my farm. I am not homeless, and I'll be of greater use there with Sylwia and

75

Walenty than I am hanging around a pair of newlyweds."

"But mamo…" Henryk said.

"It's decided, Henryk," Pani Bartosz said, getting up and wiping her hands on her apron. "I have some *placki* to finish…" She exited into the kitchen, leaving Henryk staring after her with surprised eyes.

Henryk hated to admit it to himself, but he felt relieved. Upon seeing Aniela's joyful and beaming face, he had immediately asked the agency to draw up a rental contract and returned home to share the jovial news.

With a sense of shame, he realized that he hadn't even thought of his mother taking the room, the one he joked could be a nursery. The two of them had lived their strange, co-dependent existence from the time he was nine and became the man of the house, her substitute husband as well as only surviving child. But as much as he loved his stern and competent mother, he had to acknowledge that they often grated on each other's nerves and that he was itching to be free of the chains that bound her to him. He wanted to be with Aniela, and Aniela alone. All Henryk could think was that at long last, he would have Aniela Majewska — soon to be Aniela Bartosz — to himself, and he didn't want to share her. With anyone.

Chapter 13

Union

On Saturday morning, June 26th, 1937, Aniela walked the few blocks to St. Adalbert's Church, holding her father's arm tightly. He was growing thinner with age, but his presence next to her gave her the same sense of safety and comfort as it always had. It was growing warmer and she could feel a bead of sweat trickle down her back. Irena and her mother trailed behind, holding up the end of Aniela's dress to ensure it wouldn't collect any street dust or debris.

This was the same walk they had always done as a family. Dressed in her beautiful cream Art Deco-inspired dress, Aniela tried to see herself as others might — as an elegant young woman, dressed in a striking and modern wedding dress, strolling down Grodzka Street with her family, about to start a new and exciting chapter of her life and create a family of her own. Couples stopped short upon seeing her, and smiled warmly, calling, "Best of luck, Miss!"; and men tipped their hats, calling, "Congratulations, beautiful bride!"

And then they entered the ornate and beautiful church of her childhood, where a church volunteer — an older woman in her sixties — greeted them warmly and told them where to wait while she cued the organist to begin the wedding march.

And from there, it all seemed to go by in a blur. Aniela's father's eyes watered as he took her face in his hands and said, "Daughter, I am so proud to deliver you to a young man I have long regarded as a son. Today marks a very happy day for our family."

He kissed her hand and handed it to Henryk, who was waiting, his eyes locked on hers. Her parents and his mother proceeded down the aisle and took their seats. Henryk took Aniela's elbow, and together, they, too, walked down the aisle. She was moved by the beaming faces nestled in the pews. There were the smiling faces of Ewa, Henryk's friends from Wieliczka — Józef and Marian — and Aniela's beloved teacher and mentor, Pani Ostrowska. Aniela felt so moved and overwhelmed by the show of love and support that it was difficult for her to keep her composure.

She glanced at the man beside her. Henryk was grinning with such a look of pure joy that it settled her stomach and she found herself grinning right back at him. In that instance, butterflies subsided and she felt a sense of calm and security.

They approached the altar. The priest began the ceremony, welcoming the parishioners, reminding them of the importance of marriage in the eyes of the church and the blessed nature of the sacrament. Aniela tried to follow along, but she was lost in her keen awareness of Henryk standing next to her, shoulders touching. She could hear him breathing deeply, and see a slight sheen of sweat on his forehead. The knowledge that he was as excited and nervous as she was reminded her that they were in this together, in every way.

Aniela Bianka and Henryk August vowed to love and cherish one another, affirming fidelity in sickness and in health. They exchanged rings, and she looked up at him, eyes shining with unshed tears of joy. He could see adoration in her gaze, and he swallowed with emotion.

Aniela heard the priest pronounce, "By the power vested in me, by the laws of God — our Holy Father, the son and the Holy Spirit, I pronounce you man and wife."

Aniela turned her face up to Henryk and his warm lips found hers, and they kissed deeply and she forgot everything. It was just him and her. She had found her home, her true place.

Chapter 14

Wedding Night

T he Tatra Mountains displayed their green peaks in the distance. They were in Zakopane, having arrived at the glorious Grand Stamary Hotel. They had dinner plans to eat *al fresco* in the restaurant below, followed by a musical performance in the great ballroom of the hotel.

The pair had little taste for food due to the anticipation of their wedding night. Neighboring couples couldn't help turning their eyes to the young, beautiful couple lost in each other. Though she was exhilarated by the beautiful evening with the big band, the well-heeled people, and the pride over having the most handsome, ardent man on her arm, she wanted to be alone with him. Henryk's eyes displayed his hunger for her, and after toying with his food, he stated, "Let's go to our room, dancing girl."

Her mouth dry, she took his hand and he led her up the curving staircase to their suite on the third floor. Henryk took the key out of his pocket and gave Aniela a look that told her to stay put as he unlocked the door, swung it open, and switched on a light.

He then picked Aniela up, easily carrying her in his arms as he walked through the doorway. He laid her down on the bed, and seeing his face change from playful to dark and serious, the smile left Aniela's face and she stared back at him, lips parted and leaning back on her elbows. Henryk's eyes drank her in, from her shapely lips, to her collarbones, down to breasts jutted towards him.

His voice was deep and husky. "I have waited so long to make love to you, Aniela. And at long last, our wedding night is here. Finally, you will be mine in every possible way."

She reached up to him, beckoning him towards her. He obeyed and she kissed him deeply and without reservation. He tasted a little of vodka, and she found the flavor of him intoxicating. She took his strong jaw in her hands and kissed his beautiful full lips, his cheek — which was a bit roughened by the nascent stubble — and moved to his cheekbone, so high and perfectly sculpted, and to his ear. She took the lobe and put it into her mouth, and peeked over to see his reaction.

His face exhibited a mixture of pleasure and agony, something she had never seen before, and she was emboldened by her effect on him. Henryk reached behind and found the zipper of her dress. Aniela got off the bed to wiggle out of the dress, and he stared at her intensely as she was reduced to a thin slip. Her breasts displayed her excitement, and she saw his eyes resting on her erect nipples, then traveled lower to her waistline, and legs in their hosiery.

"Do you want me to change into my trousseau?" she asked nervously, taking in his intense gaze.

"Hell no," Henryk growled. "The last thing I want is to see you in more clothes. Please let me undress you…"

Henryk leapt off the bed, and slowly pulled down the straps of her slip, until it fell to the floor in a heap. Aniela's breasts sprang to attention at this action, and he leaned over to kiss her neck and sternum, and finally put his mouth on her breast. The feeling of his warm mouth on her erect nipple sent a jolt of sensation through her, and she lost her balance momentarily and grabbed his shoulders for support. His tongue flicked the nipple and one hand cupped her heavy breast, while another hand explored her lower back and came to rest on her panties.

"God, you're beautiful," Henryk said, and slowly started pulling her panties down. For a moment, she felt embarrassed — nobody had ever seen her like this, and she felt vulnerable by her body's reaction to his every touch. She was losing control, and swayed again.

He caught her and flung the panties on the floor, then started rolling down her hosiery until she was completely naked and back on the bed. She wanted to undress him, too, but he quickly shed himself of his shirt and trousers, pausing to gauge Aniela's reaction before removing his underpants.

The lamp behind him gave him an almost ethereal glow, and Aniela forgot her embarrassment and inhaled in appreciation at his male beauty. She knew from touching him that he was trim and hard, but she had no idea that he was rippling with muscles. His shoulders were broad and sculpted, his chest well defined and covered in dark brown hair. Muscles rippled along his ribs, down his chiseled stomach to the waistband of his underpants.

"Are you ready, my love?" he whispered.

"Yes, Henryk. You are magnificent..."

Henryk grunted, removed the last of his clothes, and lay next to her on the bed. He took her face in his hands and kissed her mouth very gently.

"No, it's you that is a vision to behold..." His kiss grew deeper and more intense, and Aniela arched in passion. He kissed her throbbing breasts again, and his hand danced across her skin, cupping her breasts, caressing her belly, grazing her hip, before traveling to her inner thighs and gently parting her legs.

"Is this okay?" Henryk whispered between kisses, and Aniela groaned in response. She felt like a dam had broken somewhere inside of her. Every fiber was pulsing with blood, every nerve ending was at attention, and she felt a throbbing wetness between her thighs.

Henryk's fingers gently moved from soft inner thigh to her labia, and he grazed her flesh with the tips of his fingers. Aniela almost jumped from the sensation, and her hips automatically lifted to his waiting, tentative fingers. Seeing her reaction, Henryk's eyes grew even darker, and he slowly began touching her. Her lips parted for him, so swollen with blood and desire, and he felt her wetness on his fingers.

"Oh, God, Aniela," he moaned, kissing her passionately while his fingers explored. Her legs parted for him, and her body took over as she started moving up and down, coveting those fingers toying with her most forbidden and tender area. He found her clitoris, and stroked her in tender up and down motions, and she felt such a force of passion and energy throbbing through her, she thought she may die from this new sensation. She muffled cries by kissing him even more deeply, back arched to him, breasts flattened against his chest, while his hand stroked her until she felt she would burst. And then she did burst, losing all control as spasms took over her body. She heard a high-pitched squeal between panting breaths and realized it was she who made those sounds.

Her eyes were pressed closed and her head thrown back, and she felt Henryk's weight move over her shaking body. Aniela opened her eyes to see him guiding himself into her. She forgot to be scared, and there was a part of her that wondered at the size of him, but again her body took over. She arched towards him, feeling the tip of his manhood. His eyes grew wide, his jaw clenched, and Aniela could tell that the feeling was ambrosia to him. She bucked up again, taking him inside of her a little more.

"This may hurt, my love," Henryk whispered. "But I don't think I can wait any longer."

And with that, he sank down completely into her. Aniela gasped as she felt him enter her for the first time and she experienced a sharp pain. He was completely still for a few moments, buried in her, and breathing heavily into her neck. He pulled his weight onto his forearms.

"Are you okay?" he asked, his eyes taking on a pleading look amidst his desire.

The pain subsided, leaving a dull feeling of being stretched as her body slowly grew accustomed to him. Finally, she answered by swiveling her hips, grinding him into her, as some primitive age-old dance took over. She couldn't find her voice and nodded, as she grabbed hold of his hair.

Henryk groaned deeply in her hair. "My God. You're dancing even when you make love...!"

She forgot all coherent thought, as his arm encircled her from behind, and he held her up to him as he met each of her motions with a thrust of his own. They found a rhythm, and she matched his eagerly.

At last, Henryk whispered coarsely, "I'm coming..." — and he convulsed on top of her, his motions less rhythmic and more frenzied as his climax took over. His face took on an almost savage look and she stared up at him in awe until he collapsed, panting on top of her.

She was breathing heavily, too, and it took her a moment to realize that his full weight was constricting her a bit, so she wiggled out from under him.

"Must breathe," she panted.

"So sorry," Henryk said, moving over and lying next to her. He grabbed her and pulled her on top of him. "That's better..."

After several moments, he whispered, "Was that okay for you?"

With head pressed against his chest, where the sweat from their lovemaking glistened on damp cheeks, she felt his thundering heart slow its pace.

"Hmmm," she murmured, feeling as if in a trance.

"What was that?" Henryk asked again.

"I am finding it hard to form words, Henryk," she murmured. "It was a bit painful at first, but... so much better than I could have ever imagined."

Henryk laughed, and she felt pride surging through his body. "You are amazing, my dancing girl. I know I will never, ever get tired of exploring that delicious body of yours..."

"And that was just our first time," she said dreamily. "Doesn't everything improve with a little practice?"

Henryk laughed, kissing the top of her head. "I'll make it my life's mission to find every way imaginable to pleasure you, even if I have to practice myself to death!"

Part Two
1937 – 1944

Chapter 15

Łódź and Sienkiewicz

Back home, the newlyweds began their life together. Though they had each known the other for years, the newness of their daily intimacies was a treasure. Aniela experienced the pride of turning their sweet apartment into a cozy and warm home, making sure to buy fresh flowers each week, and spending hours at the farmers' market picking out the evening's menu. She kept an eye on her budget, knowing how hard Henryk worked, and was determined to be the ideal, frugal housewife. Aniela appreciated when Henryk's mother visited, as she was a great source of advice on how to pick the best vegetables, fruit and cuts of meat and who often had good ideas on how to bring the ingredients together.

Aniela loved greeting Henryk after a long day at the newsroom, with dinner warming in the oven and the table set with an eyelet tablecloth and matching napkins. Henryk's eyes lit up when he saw his waiting wife, and he grabbed her around her trim waist and picked her up while kissing warm lips. He loved the comfort of seeing her first thing in the morning and the moment he came home, and they soon fell into a relaxed pattern together. Henryk praised Aniela for her efforts making dinner, and regaled her with the latest buzz from the newsroom. Though disappointed that she had not found a job since graduating, it helped that Pani Ostrowska asked Aniela to assist teaching folk dance classes several times a week.

Months later, Henryk came home with news he would write a series of articles on the Polish Film Industry as well as the economic boom in Łódź. It was a great honor, and a sign of the editor's confidence in his skills. He was excited about the trip, and had twelve-hour days of interviews set up along with Tomek, the photojournalist from the paper, at a conference in Łódź.

Aniela was a whirlwind of activity, making sure everything was ready for his first business trip. She had all his suits pressed and folded carefully in the leather suitcase. She made sure his shoes were shined, that he had enough business cards in his briefcase, and she went to the bank to get cash for the trip.

Aniela rose early to make Henryk breakfast before he left for the train. He kissed her deeply, bemoaning the week's absence, adjusted his hat, and was off.

Aniela went to her parents' apartment for a visit.

"Everybody seems to have gone mad with classifications," her father lamented. "Years ago, we accepted all kinds of students — but now the administration is limiting the number of Jews, or making it uncomfortable for those Jews who are enrolled. It's unconscionable!"

"You know what I saw while shopping last week?" her mother said. "The shop on Floriańska Street, you know, the one I go to for sundries? There was a sign on the window saying, 'Polish shop'."

Aniela shook her head sadly. "Adam had mentioned those were sprouting up."

Pan Majewski shook his head. "Things are getting worse. That is exactly what Herr Ausfelder wrote had started happening in Germany! First, they segregate who is 'German' versus 'Jewish', and they punish the Jews by declaring those shops alien. I never thought I'd see such a thing here in Kraków."

"Polish shop indeed," Pani Majewska scoffed. "Is the shop run by Jews any *less* Polish, I wonder?"

"There is just too much nationalism since Piłsudski died," her father said. "Everyone wants their own state, to divide themselves up even further. The Ukrainians, the Zionists… nobody is happy co-existing any more."

"Maybe it's time to move to America?" Aniela said, an eyebrow raised.

Her father chuckled. "And leave Poland? Never! I waited the better part of my life to see my homeland restored; I am not going anywhere. Even Poland, with our tradition of great romantic poets and Sienkiewicz, is not immune to the baser politics happening inside and outside of our borders…"

He tapped his cane idly on the parquet floor. "Anyway," her father continued, "we need all the different factions here. I firmly believe that is what makes us different, and with time, we may follow in American footsteps by showing the world that diverse societies are the strongest.

Imagine Poland as Europe's beacon of multiculturalism and inclusion. We'd be the pearl of the continent."

Aniela left her parents and walked back to her apartment in a pensive mood. She felt aimless. With Henryk gone, she didn't feel motivated by the usual chores and obligations. She did not need to cook something just for herself; she was happy with cold sausage and bread. She didn't need to clean and tidy the apartment; it was already organized, and why bother dusting until Henryk was due back?

She had scanned the paper for jobs while visiting her parents, and there was nothing to apply for. She considered dropping by and visiting Pani Ostrowska, or perhaps seeing if Ewa wanted to meet after work, but her feet took her back to her apartment.

The apartment was filled with late-afternoon warmth. She grabbed a pillow from her bed and hugged it to herself while idly perusing the bookshelf. Her eyes stopped at the title *With Fire and Sword*, Henryk's favorite book by his namesake, Henryk Sienkiewicz, whom her father had just mentioned. The book he was always telling her to read, the book that she had promised to read when she had time.

Aniela smiled, pulling the book from the shelf. She had time. She could read this book all day — and all night — should she wish. Aniela moved to the large sun-drenched windowsill and propped the pillow up and opened up Henryk's favorite book. What better way to welcome him back home than by sharing his favorite author?

Aniela sat in the windowsill until the light faded. She spent days lost in the book, leaving the apartment only to run an errand or teach a dance class, but largely cloistering herself in the world of Poland in the seventeenth century.

It was a hefty, daunting book, more than a thousand pages that transported Aniela to the days when Poland and Lithuania formed the great Polish-Lithuanian Commonwealth, an empire that was vast in territory, controlling the whole of Eastern Europe. The story began in 1647, when this empire was one of the strongest and largest in Europe, and the territory provided a natural border between the warring religions of the Tartars, Cossacks and pagans.

The book followed the paths of two men, Bogdan Hmyelnitzki, who helped spark a Cossack peasant rebellion that destabilized the area and brought battles and bloodshed throughout the land, and Jan Skrzetuski, a dashing Polish lieutenant, who loyally served his Prince and defended the commonwealth.

A running theme throughout the book was the love triangle for the heart of Helena, with whom Jan fell madly in love. He was astounded by her dark beauty, her purity and elegant, feminine manners. Of course, Bogdan also fell in love with Helena, and this rivalry fortified the book as Helena was absconded, feared for dead, hidden in a monastery, dressed as a boy, and eventually reunited with a victorious Jan.

As Aniela read chapter after chapter, she found that, for all its courtly love and medieval politics, it mostly chronicled the bloody devastation of battle after battle, as villages were pillaged and bodies left on stakes in retribution. Women were raped at every turn, children slaughtered in their beds, and entire towns of Jews reduced to ashes as the region boiled over in violent chaos.

After some time, she had to put the book down. In her whole life, she had either been with her family, or in church, or dance class, or school. And if she had found herself alone for a scant handful of minutes, she was never without some obligation. She missed Henryk.

Aniela stretched and pointed her toes as she contemplated this indulgent freedom. Phone calls from Łódź were expensive, so she knew that Henryk would not call. What she wanted now was to take an evening stroll after her meal, to read into the wee hours of the morning, sleeping in and waking without an alarm. She thought of Henryk, bustling around an unfamiliar city — meeting with contacts and laboring to find a story, an angle that would please his editors — while she slept in, meandered to the market to see if anything caught her fancy, and read his favorite book.

She doubted that she could have endless weeks like this, but in its own way, she felt like she had truly settled into her own home. She enjoyed the flowers from the market on the kitchen table, the unmade bed. She felt like the luckiest bride in Kraków as she turned another page.

Chapter 16

Harmony

Aniela took special care with her appearance the day Henryk was due home, wearing the red polka-dot dress with cinched waist that Henryk liked. Dabbing her wrists with perfume, she brushed her hair until it shone, and accented her high cheekbones with rouge.

She had arisen early, made fresh bread in order to still have that lovely aroma when Henryk arrived. The house was immaculate, as she had washed all the curtains and bed linens as well as the usual dusting, polishing and scrubbing.

Aniela walked to the station, arriving early. Henryk stepped onto the platform to find the smiling face of his wife. He could hardly contain his excitement upon seeing her in his favorite dress, and rushed down the steps to swoop her into his arms. He kissed her hard on the mouth, not caring if anyone was witnessing this public spectacle.

"I missed you," Henryk growled into her ear.

"Me, too." Aniela kissed him back.

And with that, the beaming pair made their way back to their apartment. Henryk burst forth with stories about Łódź and his interviews. The city was bustling with an intoxicating and sometimes chaotic energy, it being the most modern and industrial of Polish cities. It was not exactly beautiful, but pulsing with life.

He drew on a cigarette and spoke about the great brick factories producing buttons, shoes, textiles, woolens, machine parts. Then there were the film makers at the conference, each representing the studios — all the many people who made a living in the world of sound film.

Aniela listened attentively, as Henryk spoke of the stores which boasted both locally made products as well as the fanciest imports from around the globe. Scottish whisky, Russian caviar, French champagne, all could be found on Wschodnia Street. Also impressive was the new wealth of the industrialists that were helping to build and shape Łódź, a city very different from Kraków, which had for centuries been the seat of the Polish monarchy. In Łódź, one could walk by and see the stunning mansion of Izreal Poznański taking up a whole building corner and half a block. The castles there belonged to self-made men.

Henryk also spoke of seeing the well-kept Jewish cemetery in which Poznański had been buried in a mausoleum, a beautiful edifice with mosaic tiles and details.

"You wouldn't believe this mausoleum," Henryk said. "It was bigger than many *homes* I've seen, and it makes the crypts of St. Mary's look tiny in comparison. People in Łódź leave the mark on the city by their industry, and leave themselves a castle in death."

Henryk continued, "You could hardly tell that there is a Depression by the bustling shopping district. People there seem to be doing quite well, though the studio executives I interviewed had lots of concerns. And everyone complains about union issues, the trade embargoes with Russia — and how this may affect the export of Łódźian textiles."

Henryk looked down and kissed his listening wife. "You would have liked it, I think. Plus, there are a lot of German speakers, so you'd have had a chance to use your degree."

Aniela grimaced slightly at the reminder that she still had not found work using her German language skills. "Of course, there's plenty of Polish being spoken, but so many people speak Yiddish — it really is such a melting pot. You hear French and Russian, too. But I suppose they all speak the same language: pursuit of money."

Aniela chuckled at this. "So were you pleased with the interviews? Did you manage to get good articles?"

Henryk adjusted the hat on his head. "Well, I'm happy with the interviews. I met so many fascinating people. Socialists. Bundists. Capitalists. But it seemed to me that every interview led back to public policy and national politics. My editor, well, he admonished me not to be too focused on the political aspect of our film industry. He wanted me to take a lighter, more featurish approach to the stories."

Aniela sensed his frustration and disappointment.

"I've made it no secret that I'd love to cover politics and not just be a junior feature writer, but even at the paper, there are politics! I suppose I need to put in my dues before being moved to the political beat, but I will need to rework some of my articles to be 'lighter'."

"I'm sorry, Henryk," Aniela offered. "But remember, you haven't been at the paper long, and this was your first assignment outside of Kraków. Certainly that shows that they believe enough in you, in your future?"

"I guess," Henryk mumbled grumpily. "But I can't help it if I see the political side to even so-called lighter subject-matter. I wish I could just say: Look around, politics is influencing every moment of our lives."

Aniela quietly thought whether politics, with its rising anti-German and overall nationalistic fervor, was also responsible for her poor working prospects.

Moments later, Aniela unlocked the door to their apartment and proudly welcomed Henryk home. The apartment was warm, tranquil and filled with sunshine. Henryk was immediately assailed by the smell of freshly baked bread.

"Come, come," Aniela said, taking his jacket and hat. "I have lunch all ready for you. You must be hungry." She tied an apron around her waist and busily grabbed the carafe with freshly percolated coffee, a plate with sliced ham and kielbasa, and a cabbage and carrot salad with vinegar and caraway seeds. She took out the bread, still warming in the oven, and started to slice it into thick, hearty slices.

Henryk quickly shook off his mood and sat down at the table, enjoying being fussed over. He pulled Aniela onto his lap, kissing her deeply.

"This is where everything is just perfect," he said, nibbling her full lower lip. "Here with my beautiful bride, in our cozy apartment, a delicious meal on the table and bedroom sheets just begging to be tousled…"

Aniela whispered, "I wanted your homecoming to be very special. It's your first business trip."

"You've succeeded," Henryk said contentedly.

Aniela got up and finished preparing the table, and they happily dug into their meal. Henryk noticed *With Fire and Sword* on the side table by the sofa.

His eyes widened with delight. "I see my favorite book there. Does that mean that you've read it?"

Aniela nodded proudly. Henryk whooped with glee. "Wow, I have been pushing that on you for years! So… what did you think? Did you enjoy it?"

Aniela paused, picking her words very carefully. "It is a grand sweeping story and I can see why so many people love it."

Henryk paused, sensing that she was hedging, and cocked his head inquisitively. "But did *you*?"

Aniela took a deep breath. "Me? Well, I can see why you did. And that is really the lens through which I read the book…"

Henryk interrupted, "Just tell me what *you* thought of it."

Aniela equivocated again. "I don't think the book was really intended for someone like me, so…"

"Someone like you?"

"As a woman," Aniela said, a tad testily.

"What does that mean?" Henryk asked, perplexed. "You don't think that the book was meant for women as well as men?"

Aniela inhaled, putting aside her concerns for discretion of her husband's obvious devotion to the book. "What I mean is: the book was a thousand pages and spanned decades of Polish history, and I think that there were exactly two female characters. One was a conniving shrew of a woman and the other was a vapid, beautiful princess. Aside from the princess's beauty and purity, she had very little to contribute to the story. It is basically one bloody battle after another, where entire villagers are brutally wiped out. Women are raped without a second thought, children slayed, and fields burned in a frenzy of revenge."

Henryk was momentarily speechless.

"So, no, Henryk," she continued. "I think the book was not meant for someone like me. It fans the patriotic flames where men imagine that battle and war are virtuous things, and sweeps aside the moral questions of whether any of the destruction, the murder and mayhem was worth the cause that each side was fighting for."

"Was it worth the cause?" Henryk practically sputtered. "It was about the great Polish-Lithuanian empire and how they put down the sordid Cossack rebellion…"

"But who were these Polish and Lithuanian noblemen but the gentry, the landowners, the aristocracy and the elite? Why is their cause so righteous that simple farmers and peasants should pay with their lives and livelihood, to be slaughtered without a second thought?"

Henryk was truly speechless now. "But surely you must have loved the brave warrior, Jan, and his romantic love for the beautiful Helena."

Aniela's cheeks grew warm as she turned to Henryk fully, her eyes flashing with feeling. "I appreciate that this knight had feelings for the princess Helena. Truly I do. But from what I could read, he really fell in love with her because she was exquisitely beautiful and a shy, sheltered girl with little knowledge of the world."

"Yes," Henryk interrupted. "Her purity was a model for all womanhood…"

"See, that," Aniela countered, "is what I simply did not like. Yes, Helena is beautiful and pure, and those are values that are held most high by men. Never once do we hear about Helena's other qualities; it was as if she were reduced to her looks and her virginity."

"But surely in those times, these were the qualities more revered in women," Henryk offered.

"Ah, that may be true of noblewomen. In fact, so important is purity to a noblewoman that the threat of being dishonored by rape is enough for Helena to consider suicide." Aniela stood up and started pacing the kitchen. "In the meantime, scores of peasant women were raped by soldiers of both armies as they vied for battle positions. Should all of these women also commit suicide for their unpardonable crime of being in the path of these… barbarous men?"

Henryk tapped his fingers angrily on the table. "I think you are missing the point. The point is that the cause of the Polish army was noble, and the love of its lead knight was noble, too. Surely that moved your heart."

"I fail to see what is so noble about a cause in which thousands of people are killed senselessly and carelessly; mere pawns, while the lives of a knight and his lady love are held in such high regard," Aniela said shrilly.

Henryk's voice started to rise. "Helena considering suicide is surely an example of… such devotion, such love for Jan that she'd rather die than be… despoiled for him."

"And you think that just?" Aniela refuted, her voice rising to meet his. "Purity in a beautiful woman is so important that her life can be discarded because she is a victim — yes, a victim — of rape and therefore worthless? Should I ever be raped by a marauding soldier, would you expect me to just end my own life there and then?"

Henryk slammed his hands on the table. "That is not the point, Aniela! You are baiting me now. Of course not! You are being deliberately obtuse and contrary."

"I think you'll find that I simply don't agree with you, Henryk. That is allowed after all, is it not?" Aniela said, her voice low and seething with indignation.

Henryk, at a loss for words, sat at the table and stared at his angry wife. Her face was cold and her arms folded tightly across her chest. He reached into his breast pocket for a cigarette and found an empty pack.

"Some homecoming!" he exclaimed, grabbing his hat and jacket.

"Where are you going?"

"For a damned smoke, woman," Henryk said, slamming the door behind him.

Aniela stood there for several moments. She didn't see eye to eye with Henryk about his favorite book, but why was he so mad? Did he really expect her to agree with him on every matter? And why was he so bent on not listening to her interpretation of the book? Was it truly more sacred to him than having an honest discourse with his own wife?

Aniela sat down angrily, her face flushed. A profound feeling of hurt assailed her. After a few moments, her eyes focused on the half-eaten meal left on Henryk's plate, the untouched coffee emitting a swirl of steam. The flowers she had arranged so prettily in the vase now seemed to mock her with their optimism.

Now what have I done? Aniela thought with rising regret. She had striven to make his return perfect, so why had he stormed off angrily — looking for comfort in one of his detestable cigarettes, instead of making love to her in that bed as he had alluded to just minutes earlier? How had the mood shifted so quickly and completely?

Aniela felt the ire drain from her like water through a sieve. She grabbed her coat and key, and ran out of the apartment and down the stairs. She needed to find him and to patch things up. As she burst through the front door of the apartment, she hesitated. Would he have gone to the tobacconist?

Aniela turned right and started running down the street. She spotted Henryk the next block over, his head down in his coat.

"Henryk!" Aniela called. "Please wait!"

Henryk paused, turning to see Aniela sprinting toward him, her face flushed and eyes sparkling with tears. He quickly dropped the cigarette he had been puffing, stamping it under foot. Henryk looked at her sternly, his jaw clenched. "What?"

Aniela pulled up short and looked at her glowering man. "I just wanted to say… I'm sorry we fought. I don't want to fight with you, Henryk."

Henryk exhaled deeply, and gruffly said, "Me either… It's just that…"

He stopped abruptly. Henryk cocked his head to the side, eyes focused on some faraway point. "Did you hear that?"

Aniela stopped, listening intently. "No, what did you hear?"

"It sounded like a baby mewing," Henryk said, his voice returning to its normal deep timbre, and no longer laced with anger.

Then they both heard it. A pitiful, weak cry, not from a human baby, but from some despondent animal.

"I think it's coming from here," she said softly, as they walked to the sewer grate on the side of the street. They heard the high-pitched wail again.

"Look there, Henryk," Aniela said, bending over and looking into the sewer. "It's a kitten! It fell through the grates and is trapped!"

Henryk peered over to see where Aniela was pointing. Sure enough, a small ball of seemingly black fur was curled up on a jagged stone from the wall down to the city's sewer system. The tiny animal had fallen through the grates, which were far too narrow for a human hand or arm to reach through.

"Oh, the poor little thing," Aniela said. "Who knows how long it's been trapped there?"

Henryk thought quickly. There was no way to get an arm through the openings of the grates, and if the kitten were jostled in any way, it could easily fall off its stone perch and down into the stinking sewers below. He took off his jacket and laid it down on the street in front of the grate. He knelt on the jacket and placed his hands on both sides of the grate, grabbing the metal with his fingers as tightly as he could. It wasn't a great hold, but he had his fingers wrapped around each side as he pulled up with all his might.

The grate was solidly placed, and at first, it didn't budge at all.

Henryk's forehead registered his effort, as beads of sweat popped up on his brow and the veins of his temples throbbed.

"We may need to find some kind of tool," Aniela offered. "Maybe I can see if our neighbor has a crowbar…?"

Henryk grunted as he bore down on the grate again, and this time there was the sound of metal rasping and groaning as he moved the heaving piece of metal first one centimeter, and then several centimeters up.

"Hurry, Aniela," Henryk panted. "There is probably just enough room for you to get your hand in and grab it. Grab it by the scruff of its neck!"

Aniela quickly got on her knees next to Henryk and leaned into him — practically in his lap, as she angled her arm through the narrow opening he had created. She felt the kitten with her fingers and it tensed up in fear, and she worried that she'd frighten it enough to lose its grip on the stone. She had to move quickly. She grabbed the extra skin on the neck and pulled it roughly out through the opening.

Once her arm was free, Henryk dropped the grate, and it clattered with a loud bang. The kitten, petrified and dirty, clasped onto Aniela's chest, and she felt its tiny claws prick her skin through her coat.

Now, in the bright of day, she could see the kitten better. It wasn't actually black, though it was very dirty, but tortoiseshell — the beautiful marbled color of female cats both black and orange. She held it to her chest and stroked it, trying to calm that skipping heart she could feel clinging to her chest.

Henryk dusted off his coat and looked down at Aniela, his eyes filled with concern.

Aniela pulled the kitten off of her a bit so Henryk could see, and the kitten's little paws stretched out with infant claws to stay pressed to her.

"Female, about four or five weeks old," Henryk offered.

Aniela raised shining eyes to Henryk. "Let's get this little thing home, clean it up and get it some food. Who knows how long it's been since she's eaten?"

Once there, they were once again a team. Aniela put a small saucer of warm milk out, and to their delight, the kitten began lapping it up, splattering milk everywhere and even stepping into the bowl in its exuberance to be eating.

"That is a good sign," Henryk said, pleased with the little kitten's display.

Henryk laid out a pan with old newspaper as a makeshift litter box, saying, "I'll go out later for some wood chips or sand, but this will have to do."

After its meal, Aniela took a warm rag and began to bathe the kitten both to remove the splattered milk as well as the grime from the sewer. The kitten mewed pitifully at first, but then seemed to like the warm feeling of being bathed and emitted a small purr of comfort.

"She's purring!" Aniela exclaimed.

Henryk put out a finger and scratched the kitten under her wet but clean chin, and the purr grew louder and more pronounced.

"We have to keep her," Aniela stated.

"Of course," Henryk agreed. "We do. This little creature knows how to take the air out of an argument, so we owe her now."

Aniela chortled. "Yes, she sure did. What shall we name her, then?"

Henryk thought for a moment and his face lit up as an idea came to him. "Harmony!" he exclaimed. "Let's call her Harmony and let her be a reminder to us to end all arguments with her."

Aniela beamed in agreement. "I love it. Harmony it is."

Harmony purred even louder, her belly full of warm milk, her orange and black fur clean, and closed her eyes. She was quickly asleep on Aniela's lap.

Henryk gazed at the two, a grin on his face.

"And Henryk, I thank you for your amazing strength. As you pulled up that grate, I couldn't help remembering the wagon you lifted when Marian's leg was trapped. This is not the first life you have saved."

Henryk kissed Aniela gently on the forehead. "Now this is truly the best homecoming," he murmured. "I have my beautiful dancing girl *and* a beautiful purring girl."

Aniela smiled back and kissed him warmly. She then placed Harmony in a basket with a soft blanket on the floor. She stood up and took Henryk's hand and led him to the bedroom.

Chapter 17

Nesting

It was like they had their own baby. Aniela thrilled in restoring the skinny, malnourished animal into a thriving kitten. With a visit to the vet, good food, brushing and gentle direction on manners, Harmony became a source of much joy for Aniela and Henryk.

Harmony gazed at Aniela adoringly, slow blinked as a greeting, and chirped with an odd high-pitched noise that was more bird than cat.

Aniela and Henryk were, in short, in love with the kitten.

Henryk grumbled playfully when Harmony joined them in bed, walking all over them and settling on Aniela's pillow above her head. Sometimes, Harmony would gently play with Aniela's lashes, softly batting her paw against Aniela's smooth cheek.

On a late, uncharacteristically mild Spring evening, Henryk suggested a walk around Planty Park. Aniela clasped Henryk's arm in hers as they strolled leisurely. It had been several months now since finding Harmony, and since that night, Aniela and Henryk often looked back and laughed at their first fight. How stupid they were to fight over a book! And how easily their anger was dismissed when there was a chance to save a life.

They sat hand in hand on the park bench, nestled into one another like turtle doves.

"Henryk?" Aniela said. "Do you think you could do something for me? Something that would please me tremendously?"

Henryk played with the soft tendrils of hair escaping her chignon. "Anything," he stated.

"Well," Aniela said, casting her eyes down, "I don't want you to take this the wrong way... but I would love kissing you even more without the taste of cigarettes. Would you mind cutting back on smoking, just a bit?"

Henryk looked surprised, but quickly recovered. "Consider it done."

Chapter 18

Anschluss in Austria

September, 1938

They couldn't believe it. Hitler had waltzed into Austria and took over the country with only the *threat* of force. No armies met the German soldiers at the border, and no sizeable resistance was mounted.

It was a cold March day, and Aniela, her parents and Henryk sat in the living room of her family's apartment. They sipped tea as they kept returning to the news that had shaken them.

What did it all mean?

"Mark my words," Henryk said. "They will unify Austria and Germany. Then they'll go after Hungary. They'll claim that Poland belongs to them, too; they've done it before."

Pan Majewski took a less alarmist view. "Well, given that Austria and Germany share a common language, history and customs, this is not surprising that they desire to unite. It is perhaps how we Poles think of places like Lwów and Vilnius — they are Polish cities; they represent the diaspora. But we are well aware that Lithuanians and Ukrainians claim those areas as their own."

"Well, if those Krauts lay one boot on Polish soil," Henryk warned, "the French will come to our aid. The world's strongest army will honor their pact, and won't tolerate Germany imposing itself on us. Not after the Treaty of Versailles."

Pani Majewska quietly said, "I believe the Treaty of Versailles expressly forbade Austria and Germany from attempting reunion."

"There will be no German boots on our soil, my son," Pan Majewski said calmly. "Remember, Hitler signed a non-aggression pact with our dearly departed Piłsudski back in '34. We are shielded by our agreements."

"Agreements, huh?" Henryk pressed. "I'm working on a story about how Germans feel about their so-called agreements. Were you aware that we have large quantities of frozen credits in Germany due to exchange restrictions and transport dues? We have sent our butter, our produce, our pigs to Germany, yet they refuse to pay the bill due to what they call 'Corridor' issues. They take what they want, then change the rules, invent tariffs and other difficulties. They have forced many of our farmers into dire financial circumstances."

Pan Majewski thoughtfully tapped his cane on the floor. "No, I was not aware. But certainly, this sounds like the type of problem that can be solved by diplomacy."

And then, in September, the Polish population watched with disbelieving eyes as Hitler claimed the Reich's right to take over a large piece of Czechoslovakia, called by the Germans "the Sudetenland".

This maneuver was closer to home, and did not bode well, given the similarities. Like Poland, Czechoslovakia had been formed in 1918 by the Treaty of Versailles and was a young country. Like Poland, it was made up of various nationalities. A quarter of the people living in the mountainous regions of Bohemia, Moravia and Czech Silesia were of German descent, but had Czechs, Poles, Ruthenians, Slovaks and Hungarians co-existing. Poland, too, had large populations who spoke various languages such as Yiddish, German, Russian, Lithuanian and Ukrainian.

Most of the German speakers in the mountainous regions were feeling the effects of the Depression and protective trade agreements. The area was heavily dependent on exports, which were not faring well as the whole world was pinching pennies and nervously counting its change. Their factories that produced textiles, costume jewelry and glass were suffering, and unemployment was high.

Some locals were nervous and saw joining the National Socialist Party of Germany as a path out of economic misery. Hitler exploited the rising populist movement, and claimed that it was justified to unify German populations and that Sudetenland belonged with Germany. The Czech government reached out to its British, French and American allies to help withstand the onslaught.

Months of tense negotiations began. Hitler threatened to unleash a war on all of Europe if the Sudetenland was not "returned". The Czechs had most of its army's defensive positions in the region, and flatly rejected the idea that the area belonged to Germany and should be "returned".

And yet, to the shock of both Czech and Polish citizens, British Prime Minister Neville Chamberlain met with Adolf Hitler on September 15th, 1938, and agreed to his demands. No representative from the Czech government was at the meeting. Hitler was able to take hold of a region rich with manufacturing assets, including the Skoda automobile company as well as the North Bohemian basin rich in brown coal. Without firing a shot.

A few weeks later, the leaders of Britain, France, Italy, and Germany held a conference. They dubbed it the Munich Pact, and officially, all agreed to the German annexation of the Sudetenland in exchange for a pledge of peace from Hitler. Franklin Roosevelt agreed to the solution in absentia. The Czech people were offered up like a lamb on a plate to a wolf who promised to never dine again.

Henryk was among the many Poles that cried in anguish, "Appeasement! Chamberlain and Daladier showed no spine!"

One by one, the democratically elected officials of Czechoslovakia resigned rather than tolerate the insult. Aniela's father, as usual, tried to put forth a positive spin. "Henryk, my son. It does seem like a tremendous offering to give to the Germans, especially without consulting a single of our Slavic brethren in the future of their own country. I agree — it's not a solution that anyone can stomach without indigestion. But can't you see? Such a huge sacrifice in the name of peace?"

Henryk shook his head, slowly and emphatically. "You say that now. But how would you feel if it were Poland — not Czechoslovakia — that is to be carved up and offered to the Germans?"

"That would never happen," Pan Majewski said firmly. "Our non-aggression pact, our strong and unfaltering alliance with France… We are protected."

Henryk said nothing, a muscle skipping in his clenched jaw. He wished with every fiber of his being that his father-in-law was right, that his position as a man who had seen the Great War, who was well-educated and traveled, and who had seen Poland reemerge like a phoenix from the ashes, gave him a perspective that was somehow more nuanced than his own.

But he doubted it.

Chapter 19

Work, Finally

1938

"**A** man I interviewed in Łódź called today. He has two cousins — brothers — who own a glass and crystal factory in Kraków, and unfortunately one of the brothers had a stroke. The older brother, Antoni Urban, is in desperate need of someone local who can help him with foreign correspondence. He asked me if I knew anyone local who was proficient in German, so, of course, I suggested you!"

"Really?" Aniela said, excited and nervous.

"Yes," Henryk continued. "It's a chance for you to really use your language skills, and you'd be helping a family that is going through a very rough time. Would you be up for it?"

Aniela agreed. She learned that one brother, Roman, was paralyzed on the left side of his body, and he struggled to talk and communicate. Antoni was left running the company by himself and had grown more and more overwhelmed by the task.

Within a week, Aniela arrived at Antoni's office and was greeted by a disheveled middle-aged man with thinning hair and a worried expression. He smiled with relief as he introduced himself, looking lost amidst the chaos of his office. There was a large wooden desk, nearly completely covered by stacks of folders and papers. Filing cabinets lined one side of the office, doors left open and files trapped and preventing closure. The room smelled of dust, perhaps of old sweat.

She was excited and nervous about helping Antoni, never having done any work with contracts or business matters. But upon seeing the disorganized state of his office, she took comfort in the fact that she could help him in more ways than one. She could start by airing out the place, and then help organize the folders and contracts.

Antoni didn't appear to know where to start. He pointed absently at a pile on the left side of the desk.

"Can you translate those?" he asked. "They all have come from Vienna, and from the letterhead and signature, there appear to be new people in charge. Since the Nazis have taken over Austria, we have not been paid. I need to know what my options are, and may need help with drafting correspondence. Can you help with that?"

Aniela nodded, picking up the first folder, noticing a coffee ring staining the outside. She flipped it open and observed the letterhead: it was her first close-up look at the stern, serious-looking stamp of an eagle, its wings spread, head turned to left, its talons grasping a wreath with a crisp swastika centered inside.

***

Three months later, Antoni and Aniela left the Kraków Main Train station for Vienna. She had a job to do, and she was nervous. Antoni's largest foreign client, department store Wiederman's, had refused to pay a large bill. Antoni desperately needed the cash, and had never even met the client, as this was his brother's milieu.

From the correspondence that Aniela had translated, they learned that Wiederman's had been newly taken over. Antoni, in a somewhat desperate gamble, had decided to meet the new businessman in charge, Herr Müchter, in hopes of not only securing the overdue payment, but to negotiate new business terms in order to continue the contracts. Aniela had taken a night course in shorthand and stenography and felt up to the task ahead of her.

Upon entering into Austria, Antoni and Aniela immediately felt a change. The border control men, wearing stiff and starched dark green uniforms, brusquely took each passport and examined each passenger with cold eyes. They wore the iron cross on their lapels, as symbols of the Nazi government.

One of the border control men inspected Aniela's passport with such intensity that she felt a trickle of dread creep up her spine.

"*Polnische?*" the man barked. He was a man of average height, maybe only a few years older than Aniela, with pale eyes and lashes so pale they framed his eyes like specs of sand. His mouth was set in a firm, grim line.

"*Ja*," Aniela responded, trying to keep her voice calm.

"What is your business in Austria?" he asked, casting those eerie eyes on Antoni.

Aniela answered, "We are traveling to Vienna to meet clients."

His eyes raked over her, but eventually he stamped her passport and moved on. Aniela breathed a sigh of relief and looked at Antoni. Something was different here. This was not just some humorless, punctilious border control man taking his job a bit too seriously. The feeling of threat was in the air; hostility palpable.

By mid-afternoon, they arrived in Vienna's main train station, Südbahnhof. The beautiful, glass-infused building with bow windows and iron beams was breathtaking. There were flags adorning this building everywhere. Huge red, white and black flags with crisp swastikas streamed from the beams.

They made their way off the platform and onto the main street. They reviewed the map and decided to walk to their meeting, both eager to stretch their legs and see some of the city. Aniela's father had studied at the University of Vienna, and it was here that he met his lifetime friend, Herr Ausfelder of Dresden, with whom the family spent many summer vacations. She wished they had time to visit the university so she could imagine her father as a young man, chatting about the Secessionist movement and eating *sachertorte*.

But this was no holiday. They approached the Vienna State Opera House, and heard the din of hundreds of people crowded around some spectacle. Curious, Aniela and Antoni wove through the throngs of people. The atmosphere was festive. People were excitedly straining to view whatever show was being put on, and cheered and laughed with excitement. Women were dressed smartly, their lips and nails gaily painted bright reddish orange. Their teeth gleamed against the bright lipstick, and Aniela watched the feminine necks thrown back in glee as they laughed and giggled, straining to see over taller shoulders. The men all had lapel pins, each showing a variation of a soon-to-be familiar sight: black swastikas in a white circle, surrounded by a red border.

Aniela jostled through the crowd, her eye level scanning the lapel pins.

Gott mit uns. God is with us.

Frie und Deutsch. Wollen wir sein. Free and German. We want to be.

National-Sozialstische D.A.P.

Her eyes met Antoni's hazel eyes as they drew closer to the inner circle.

"Dirty Jews!" she heard a man yell to her right. "Now you see what it means to do real work!"

"Not so high and mighty now?" a woman taunted to her left.

Aniela pushed through a gap, finally able to view what drew the crowds. She gasped in horror, and instinctively grasped Antoni's sleeve.

In the center of this large crowd, she saw Jewish men on their hands and knees scrubbing the cobblestones with toothbrushes. The men were ashen, their faces frozen in fear as they frantically scrubbed the ground with numb and bruised hands. There were about ten men from age twenty to fifty. Some of the men were dressed in traditional dark robes, with yarmulkes askew, bearded with tight curls around their faces. Others wore fine suits and oxfords; they could have easily blended into any crowd. She saw blood dripping down the side of several of the men's faces.

Nazi soldiers with guns flanked the men.

"Faster, you filthy swine!"

"There! Dirty Jew! You missed a spot!"

Aniela felt Antoni cover her hand as they stared aghast.

"This is horrible," she whispered.

She saw an older, dark-haired woman leaning on her husband. The woman pointed to one of the men in suits, who was keeping his eyes down as he scrubbed frantically.

"Look, dear," she said over the crowd. "Isn't that the high-and-mighty surgeon, Herr Hirschl?"

"Yes, my treasure," the man responded. "It certainly is!"

The woman managed between her laughter, "Not so high and mighty now..."

"Let's get away from here," Antoni said, leading Aniela away. She had never seen such blatant, unadulterated joy at inflicting pain on someone else. She shook her head in shock, trying to process the outright cruelty.

Gott mit uns? Her brain seized on the lapel slogan. God is with us? How could these people invoke God when humiliating both strangers and neighbors alike? How could they exhibit such glee in watching other people reduced and degraded?

They made their way through the crowd, and stopped at a street corner. Aniela leaned against a streetlight, breathing heavily. Antoni was at a loss for words, pale and drawn. Quite a long time passed, and eventually, Antoni gathered himself together and said, glancing worriedly at his watch, "We should go."

They made their way to the address where a secretary greeted them. She was in her forties, with a grim look around her mouth.

Aniela spoke in German, "Good afternoon. We have an appointment with the new director, Herr Müchter."

The woman looked down at her book, shuffling piles of papers from one side to another, as if trying to buy herself some time. After a few moments, she looked up, not meeting Aniela's or Antoni's eyes. "I'll see if Herr Müchter is available."

She quietly entered an office through a closed door. Moments later, she came back and asked Aniela and Antoni to sit.

"Herr Müchter is a very busy man," she stated. "He will see you when he is ready."

Aniela and Antoni exchanged nervous looks. From the horror outside, to the cold welcome, things were off to a rocky start. Aniela looked around the office. The furniture was wood and large, giving the room a cold, stoic look. On the wall to her left, a framed picture of Adolf Hitler looked down to his right, as if looking down on them.

Half an hour passed. The secretary sat stiffly at her desk, busily arranging papers in folders.

Aniela stood up and walked over to her, smiling warmly. "Did you work with the old director, Herr Klein, by chance?"

The woman started, looking over her shoulder. Her eyes softened.

"Yes, I did," she whispered. "For almost twenty years. The new director kept me on as I know the filing system, and have connections with all the suppliers... Things are a bit... different... now that Herr Klein is no longer in charge."

Aniela nodded, sensing the woman's nervousness, and tried to encourage her with a smile. "What happened to Herr Klein, if I may ask?"

The secretary lowered her eyes. When she raised them, they were full of fear. "He's been... removed from this job. Herr Müchter is now in charge."

"Removed from his job?" Aniela repeated. "You mean fired?"

"No," the secretary whispered conspiratorially. "Removed. This business was seized by the Nazi party. You know, Herr Klein is a Jew."

Aniela paused, at a loss for words. "So the business was just... taken from him? Just like that?"

"Just like that," the secretary responded. "Müchter is the director now."

Before Aniela could ask what became of Herr Klein, the secretary's phone rang and she quickly picked it up.

"*Ja, stimmt*," she said brusquely on the phone. She placed the phone in the receiver and motioned to Aniela and Antoni. "He is ready to see you now."

The two were led into a large office, complete with an enormous desk in front of a window and a regal-looking leather chair. A portly man in a dark suit, sporting the Nazi pin in his lapel, sat head-down, reading a file. He did not look up as they entered. Aniela and Antoni stood, shoulder to shoulder, awkwardly waiting to be invited to take the seats in front of the desk. Aniela looked at Antoni, a question in her eyes, unsure how to proceed.

Eventually, Herr Müchter looked up and waved a hand for them to sit. He was a man in his late forties or early fifties, with a face that showed the ravages of fatty food, stiff pours and decades of cigars.

Aniela squinted a bit to adjust to the light, and began in careful German, "Herr Müchter, we thank you for agreeing to meet us. I'm Aniela Bartosz, the personal secretary and translator for Mister Antoni Urban, who is President of Urban Brothers Glassware and Crystal, whom your company has contracted."

"I do not recall accepting any such meeting," Herr Müchter barked.

Aniela felt color rising in her cheeks, as she herself had set up and confirmed the meeting with the secretary outside.

"In any case," she continued, trying to sound confident, "we are here, and Mister Urban was hoping to come to terms regarding the contract with your firm."

Herr Müchter looked over at her, eyes scouring, and then shifted to Antoni.

"I am the director of this firm," the man said tersely. "I'm not obliged to fulfill any contracts or obligations put in place by a Jew. I'd rather not waste any more time discussing trivial details with a Polack any more than I would with a Jew."

Aniela's eyes widened and her cheeks grew warmer, as she turned to Antoni to translate Herr Müchter's insults.

Antoni looked at Herr Müchter. "Tell him," he said to Aniela, never breaking his gaze, "that this firm owes me money for services rendered. It is of no concern how he came to his position, but rather to insist on his honoring the contract which we have right here. Not only is it right, it is also legal."

Aniela translated Antoni's statement to Herr Müchter, who slammed his hands down on the table in disgust.

"You think that trotting out a beautiful young woman to translate your mongrel language will make any difference to me?" he shouted. "I owe you nothing, you will get nothing!"

He picked up the phone and angrily pushed several buttons.

"This meeting is over," Herr Müchter shouted. "Show them out immediately."

The secretary walked in, her eyes downcast, and she quietly showed Antoni and Aniela out.

Her face registered a deep embarrassment and she whispered, "My apologies. I had hoped the meeting would have gone… better."

Herr Müchter yelled through the door, "*Schmittchen*, get in here!"

The secretary scuttled into the office, closing the door behind her. Aniela and Antoni took their coats from the wardrobe and made their way to the exit as the sounds of Herr Müchter dressing down his secretary followed them.

When their train pulled out of the station, Aniela caught sight of a poster. It was an anti-Semitic poster that read '*Die Juden sind unser Unglück!*' The Jews are our misfortune!

She failed to see how the abused people on the street had caused anyone misfortune, and in despair, she clenched her jaw so hard that she gave herself a headache. It was a somber train ride back to Kraków. Aniela apologized, feeling that due to her lack of diplomacy or language skills, or both, she had not been up to the task that Antoni had set in front of her.

Antoni was quiet, staring absently out the window.

"We desperately needed that payment," he mused sadly. "But seeing what the Nazis have turned Vienna into… I'd rather never set foot in this God-forsaken city again, money be damned."

They were enveloped by a cloud of shock and powerlessness. Neither could have done a thing to help the Jewish men humiliated in the street. Neither could they have negotiated Herr Müchter into seeing reason.

Chapter 20

Refugees and Expectations

Jews from Czechoslovakia and Austria flooded Poland, many being blocked at the border. Poland was not eager to take them in. Their economy was faltering. Very little foreign investment was to be had; the banks were not lending money. In fear of pending war, the Polish government put in orders for armaments, ordering fighter planes, submarines and tanks on credit. The instability in the region virtually froze international trade, and the mood across Europe was dark. And it was not only Poland that shut down its borders to the desperate and fleeing refugees. France, Holland, England, the United States — almost each and every country stated that they could not absorb the refugees, claiming economic hardship.

To make it worse, there were declarations by nationalistic parties that denied the Jews (or any refugees) the right to enter Poland. These groups maintained that these people were not Poles and would only drain the country of its resources. They viewed the Jewish people as disloyal to the Polish state, as during Poland's rebirth in 1918, many Jews in Western Poland had voted in plebiscites to be incorporated into Germany. And many Jews spoke German or Yiddish at home, which also drove a linguistical wedge.

***

Aniela reviewed a stack of unpaid invoices. She sat at her desk, ignoring the wintry air seeping through the factory windows.

Antoni was on the phone in his office, the door closed. She heard his voice rise with tension, and sighed deeply. He was under a tremendous amount of strain, and it could be seen in his face — new lines appeared around his hazel eyes, and his thinning hair was perpetually disheveled. He was gaining weight, yet hardly eating, surely a sign of a body that was suffering against all the stresses.

His brother, Roman, was out of the hospital, yet half his face was frozen and his left hand was curled like a claw. Antoni not only felt the extra burden of running the family business without his brother's much-needed help, but now felt the additional financial responsibility. Contracts had been cancelled, or cut in half. Others, like many of the contracts that had been drafted in former Austria or Czechoslovakia, were now worthless, as the regime had had little interest in making good on pre-existing contracts and littler interest in payments.

Aniela heard the bang of the receiver. Antoni stalked out of his office, sweat stains visible. He paced back and forth a few moments, then sat down angrily in the chair. His gaze fell on the stack of unpaid invoices.

"I don't know how much longer I can go on like this," he said, voice flat. "You see what is going on here. No cash flow. Products sitting in warehouses. Getting an invoice paid is like moving a glacier."

Aniela nodded, her eyes intent.

"I can't pay you any more, Aniela," Antoni said, his voice growing rough with emotion. "I cannot see a way out of this, either. If a lender could just advance me the money, we could keep weathering the storm, but with no capital or cash to pay anybody…"

Aniela reached across the desk, and Antoni took her hand and kissed it with great respect.

"I never wanted it to end this way, my dear," he continued. "I can pay you to the end of the month, but I'm afraid that this business is going to be shuttered."

Aniela worked through the month, and had a tearful farewell with Antoni. She knew he was wracked by feelings of powerlessness and guilt. She had caught him staring at a photo of himself and Roman in happier and younger days, where they had their arms thrown over each other's backs, smiles on their faces.

Antoni, though in his fifties, had become an old man. His shoulders were stooped, his stubble — which appeared more and more as he grew weary of daily shaving — was completely gray. Even his skin tone had become a pallid gray color, with dark, almost garnet circles under his eyes.

On her last day, Aniela wandered home through Planty Park, noting that there were other men like Antoni peppering the city. She spotted an old man feeding pigeons as he sat on a park bench, wearing a wool coat that now seemed oversized. Was he about Antoni's age? His mouth was downturned, and he emanated a sense of melancholy as he sprinkled breadcrumbs. The pigeons fluttered in a frenzy, and she wondered if these were his only friends, his only purpose. How sad this man appeared, living out pointless days, slowly marching towards an end. Was he once a man of vigor, of energy, of purpose?

Young men take for granted their strength and fortitude, she mused. They throw it around carelessly, chasing women, bragging and boasting about victories and conquests, real or imagined. They puff up their chests, grab a cigarette and drink with no concern, not even an inkling, that one day that strength will fade. Their arms will lose their sinew, their lower backs will start to ache, and each morning they will get out of bed with a groan. Women seem aware that their beauty is an ephemeral offering, and exploit it or cling to it in their own fashion. But for most men, aging is a brutal shock.

Aniela found her eyes welling up again. Since Antoni told her he was closing the factory, she had been very sensitive. She became acutely aware of all the listless men, many loitering around the milk bars, slowly drinking themselves into a stupor. But even among this gaggle of overlooked masculinity, there was always one man sitting quietly on the bench, his hands wrapped around his bottle of beer like it was mother's milk. He would not look up, engage with the world or the other men, simply staring down into the bottle as if expecting salvation.

What will become of Antoni? Aniela worried. She was not aware of him having any true hobbies, and with all this time on his hands, she wondered if he would descend into depression.

She suspected her tender feelings and weepiness ran deeper than usual and after a visit to Dr Rozenberg, she knew why.

"I'm pregnant," Aniela said to Henryk, as they sat, legs entwined, reading on the sofa.

Her eyes sought his. His eyes were bright, and he blinked quickly.

"That is wonderful news," he said, moving to take her in his arms.

"Are you happy?"

"Deliriously."

But unspoken between them was the uncertainty amidst all the talk of war.

Chapter 21

A Stroll Through the Park

June, 1939

It was a beautiful summer day, perfect for an anniversary, and Aniela suggested a picnic by the river. Children scampered about, squealing in delight, begging parents for money for cotton candy.

They settled by the banks, sipping homemade kompot. Quietly, Henryk reached over to place a package onto Aniela's lap, gently stroking her four-month pregnant belly. She smiled at him, and pulled the paper open to unveil a beautiful box. It was rectangular in shape and had an intricate pattern of inlaid wood that featured a folk dancer in the center, surrounded by musical notes. There were many different, tiny pieces so carefully woven together, it was truly a work of tremendous craftsmanship. Her hand smoothed the top of the box, marveling at the sleek finish and exquisite details.

"Henryk," Aniela said, eyes bright with emotion. "It is so beautiful…"

"See? The dancing girl?" he asked, his eyes searching.

"Yes, it is lovely," Aniela said, again smoothing the finish with her finger.

"It's you, of course. My uncle helped me make this. We have been secretly working on this together for quite a while."

"You made this?" Aniela said, a lump in her throat.

"I did. We did," Henryk said, his voice raspy. "Open it."

Aniela slowly lifted the lid, and nestled on the plush red velvet lining a pair of amber and silver earrings caught the light.

"It's a start," Henryk promised, squeezing Aniela's hands. "One day, this box will be filled up with jewels that will pale against your beauty."

"Oh, Henryk," Aniela said, putting the box aside to give him a hug.

"This is so beautiful. Happy anniversary."

Aniela pulled a wrapped gift out of her purse and handed it to him.

Henryk obliged and unwrapped the elongated box. Inside was a fine leather case, with the gold script 'Audemar, Piguet & Co.' on top. Henryk lifted his eyes to meet Aniela's. Audemar, Piquet & Co. was a well-known jeweler and watchmaker from Switzerland, and the leather box itself spoke of centuries of craftsmanship and care. With an intake of air, Henryk flipped open the case. A very fine men's watch shone brilliantly against blue silk lining. It was rectangular in shape, with an eighteen-carat gold watch face set against a shiny ostrich leather wristband with a gold clasp.

"This is a very fine watch," Henryk said, his eyes fixed.

"Do you like it?" Aniela pressed. "My father and I thought it would suit you well. It belonged to my grandfather."

Henryk swallowed with emotion, took the wristwatch out and put it around his wrist.

"One day," he said quietly, "I hope to buy you something as fine as this…"

"You deserve lovely things in your life," she said.

"I already have lovely things in my life," he said quietly. "I know of no richer man."

Chapter 22

Called Up

In early August, Aniela went to see Dr Rozenberg for a routine checkup. He was pleased with Aniela's progress, and charted her weight and blood pressure with distracted eyes and a worried look on his face.

Confused by the worried countenance despite his comments that all appeared to be going well, Aniela pressed, "Is everything okay, doctor? You seem upset."

Dr Rozenberg's brown eyes stared into Aniela's large, worried ones. He exhaled deeply.

"I'm a bit rattled by the news. The Germans just revoked all medical licenses for its Jewish citizens. The right to work, to use one's education, is illegal now in Germany. It's total madness."

Aniela kept her counsel, finding no reason to share her experience in Vienna, where that awful couple twittered with glee upon degrading a surgeon in public. She left the office with a heavy heart, with no words or thoughts to comfort him or herself.

Despite it being summer, there was a distinct chill in the air. The talk of war and the escalating demands of Nazi Germany could not be ignored, and while normal life limped along, everyone was consumed with fear and worry.

There was a dizzying number of pacts that summer, but the most chilling was the neutrality pact between Nazi Germany and the Soviet Union. It was signed on August 23rd, 1939, by foreign ministers Joachim von Ribbentrop and Wyacheslav Molotov, and was called the Molotov-Ribbentrop Pact. Two days later, Poland and Britain signed yet another treaty in which they promised mutual assistance.

Then Henryk received a letter on a Polish Army letterhead, calling him up to service.

Aniela stood in their living room, her hand on her growing belly, reading the letter with dread. Her face drained of color as she looked at her husband in disbelief. Henryk ran his hands through his thick hair.

"It is happening," he said.

"What is happening?" she said, her voice a whisper, not able to formulate the words in her mind.

"We are going to war."

***

Aniela watched her husband don his uniform. Adam had also been called up, Tomek from the newspaper, boys — now men — that she had grown up with now wore the dark green wool uniforms and set off to an unknown future.

Henryk stood in the bedroom, looking down at his expecting wife, and tried to imprint the image of her in his mind. He breathed deeply, taking in her wavy golden hair and observing with tenderness the tendrils curling against her flushed cheeks. Her face was reddened and pink, and tears streamed down her face as she breathed shallowly.

"It's okay, dancing girl," Henryk said tenderly, brushing a damp curl away from her forehead. He knew he was speaking in platitudes. Nobody could foretell their future; the only thing that was assured was uncertainty.

Her heart was beating erratically, and her voice cracked as a strangulated cry escaped. Henryk hugged her to him one last time, noting the hard, growing belly of his child pressing against him through the uniform. Would he be back to see his own child born? Would he even be alive?

On one hand, he was as furious and dedicated to fighting back the Nazis as any other red-blooded Pole. He had long been suspicious of Germany and looked forward to beating those Krauts back and giving them the defeat they truly deserved.

But when he looked at his sweet, beautiful wife, he was assailed by a desire to just *stay*. Could there be some world in which he could do his duty, yet remain here, watching over her? His brow knitted with fear as he imagined her unprotected, and in need of him.

They had already decided that she would return to her parents' home, under their watchful protection. But he felt the hard stone of terror deep in his belly that he could not shift. It lay there, unrelenting and unmoving, and felt such a sense of powerlessness, he could weep.

He pulled himself away from Aniela, and stiffly moved to the dresser. He opened up the top drawer and pulled out the leather case of his beloved watch. Aniela's eyes widened as he flipped it open, seeing the watch back in the box, and not on his wrist.

"I cannot take this, my love," Henryk said quietly. "I vowed never to take this off, as it is one of my most prized possessions."

"I'll save it for your return," Aniela said softly, her eyes glistening. Henryk nodded, his throat tight, and he kissed her forehead one final time.

Chapter 23

War Begins

September, 1939

T he city seemed to be drained of its young men overnight. Troops were mobilized throughout the land, with a focus on the Polish Corridor in the north that was being threatened by Nazis, as well as troops on the Slovakian border. Deployment was so fast and decisive; nobody knew where their men were going or how long they'd be there.

On September 1st, Germany attacked. The war began with swift and brutal attacks across three fronts. The *Blitzkrieg* included tactical airfare and armored vehicle units that strafed anyone in their path, including fleeing civilians. The order was to attack everyone and anyone, not just military targets. Poland's one and a half million soldiers fought valiantly, but were overwhelmed across all fronts by the might of the German war operation. The Germans attacked from the north, from East Prussia, where the Polish military had amassed most of the troops. But Poland was also attacked from the southwest, in Silesia, as troops stormed into Katowice and towards Kraków. More troops came from the north, towards Bydgoszcz and en route to the capital, Warsaw.

The Majewskis were glued to the wireless, which announced the outbreak of war and concluded with the playing of the national anthem and Chopin's *Polonaise in A Major*. War was no surprise to anyone after such a buildup, and many hooted with jubilation, expecting a swift and easy victory… for people had been conditioned by propaganda that highlighted German weakness and promoted the strength of the Polish-French-British alliance.

But the Germans did not advance along broad fronts, as in previous wars, but concentrated their forces in highly mobile armored columns that tore into Poland, and then broke off into smaller, nimble units.

The Polish military fought with outdated equipment, including tanks that were a third the size of the German Panzers. It was quickly clear that the Poles were at a severe disadvantage.

The orders placed by the Polish government for increased weaponry stood in warehouses abroad, undelivered. Their calls for loans to finance a war were unheeded. Pleas for military assistance from Britain and France, allies that had sworn to protect Poland's sovereignty, went unanswered. On September 3rd, Britain and France declared war on Germany, but no military assistance came Poland's way. Despite this, the Polish government and high command misled the people into believing that the British and French were engaging the Germans in the west.

Nobody could conceive that these two powerful allies would simply do nothing to help Poland.

The British blamed the French for not using their mighty army and air force to aid their ally, while the French emphasized Britain's general lack of war preparation. By September 8th, their bickering ceased; they finally agreed on something: neither would send any support.

The Polish military leaders were in disarray. The expected help did not come. Significant tactical errors were made and radio and communication lines were severed or failed to work. Many underestimated the strength of the German forces and took matters into their own hands, without coordinating with other units or battalions. Entire platoons were stranded, with no orders or context.

Within days, Kraków was overrun by refugees fleeing the west. It was a pitiful sight to see families putting their entire possessions in carts and wheelbarrows. And Krakovians began to panic upon hearing the stories. Should they evacuate, too?

Aniela sat with Irena and her parents in her living room, worrying over this decision. Should she evacuate the city, as Irena urged, along with her parents, and head east? Or should they hunker down in Kraków, and hope for the best? Given the hordes of people flooding into Kraków from the parts of Poland already overrun, it was hard to imagine that there was a safe place to go.

"I'm staying," Aniela said, her voice firm. "I don't know if that's the right decision, but I cannot see myself fleeing in my condition. My first priority is this baby, and we have the best chance in Kraków."

Pani Majewska reached over to take her daughter's hands. "We will stay, too. It is a horrible decision to make, whether to flee or to stay, but we will remain here with our children. In our home."

Irena sighed, a look of disappointment on her face. "We could always try to bribe our way to the Romanian border. We have resources, we may be successful."

Aniela looked at her sister, fear and resignation on her stiff face. "You may be right, but I cannot do that. Furthermore, I'm not sure our father can manage that any better than I can."

"I understand," Irena whispered, sadly. She looked at her aging father, his hands on his cane even while sitting. "I will stay. We're family."

And five days later, Kraków was overrun by German troops that flooded the city in columns of tanks, infantry, and armored vehicles. The city reverberated with the low, grumbling sounds of machinery. The frightened citizens hid inside their homes and basements, their hearts in their mouths.

Kraków had fallen.

Chapter 24

Henryk's Service

Henryk was part of the Polish reserve, which had barely been called up and mobilized when the Germans attacked. The unit was under General Stefan Dąb-Biernacki, a medaled general who had fought in various campaigns in the Great War.

Along with tens of thousands of other men, Henryk was transported to the Northern Front, about forty kilometers north of Zamość. His role as a specialist was to operate and fire the heavy 20mm gun that had been retrofitted onto a tank. The job required the strength of a very powerful man, and was not suited for a particularly big man given the size of the tankette or the target a larger man represented. It also required the skills of a marksman, and Henryk offered both. He was part of the first tank battalion, within a small tankette squadron comprised of thirteen tankettes.

By the time they arrived, war was already under way. The Nazis had attacked viciously, and the Polish high command was in disarray. There were modest victories by Polish troops, but each victory was isolated and lacked coordination with other units, or the support of aircraft. Within a week, units were being pushed back and the troops struggled with lack of food, petrol or even maps of the area.

On September 17th, the Russians attacked, without even a declaration of war. The Red Army rolled in from the East and the Polish army was overwhelmed anew. Many Poles, who had more in common culturally and historically with fellow Russian Slavs than Germans, were shocked by the aggression.

A major advantage for the Germans was the Panzer tank. Until the Germans rolled across the flat Polish countryside in these modern, new tanks, most of the Polish tanks of the time were not armored, and were the size of a car, called tankettes. (It was a tracked armored fighting vehicle that resembled a small tank, intended for light infantry support and scouting.)

The tankettes formed the bulk of the Polish forces, and were the only armored fighting vehicles available to the troops. Tankettes were a Polish design based on the chassis designed by Englishman John Carden Loyd. About five hundred and seventy-five had been produced in Poland since 1931, and they included an improved and powerful engine and armor up to 8mm thick, but few had machine guns. Some had light armaments of a single machine gun, and only twenty-four of the total were completed and equipped with 20mm machine guns. Luckily, Henryk manned one of four tankettes out of his brigade of thirteen with a machine gun.

It was September 18th, and Henryk and the other men were given orders to head southwards from Chelm to the town of Krasnystaw. Their orders were to take back the city which had fallen to the Germans.

In two columns, the men made their way south. For forty kilometers, the soldiers comprised of cavalry, scores of infantry on foot, and tankettes and armored vehicles kicked up dust in a steady plume. Dąb-Biernacki ordered an attack at night, and the men fanned out to take back the city. Henryk heard the deep boom of enemy cannon as his tank battalion slowly made its way towards the city. Moments later, one of the tankettes was struck, thrown upwards and flung onto its side, as if it weighed nothing. Henryk watched in amazement, stunned to see how easily the vehicle could be made useless. The men inside struggled to escape the burning tank, and threw themselves out the hatch in a frantic frenzy.

Overhead, low-flying Luftwaffe opened fire, and the fleeing soldiers were cut down in seconds, as the planes swept by, mowing down rows of Polish infantry like blades of grass.

Flares, streaks of cannon and machine gun fire swept by the unit, and created a somewhat stunning display. Henryk noted idly that there was a perverse sense of beauty in watching flares light up the skies, like childhood fireworks, only to land with a tremendous thud, splaying the dry earth, twisting metal, and obliterating uniformed men in an arc of chaotic energy.

If the icy grip of fear had not been at their throats, it would be tempting to just watch for a second — so other-worldly and violent, it was hard to look away. But the men had a grim job to do, and continued advancing, using outdated tankettes while trying to avoid cannon fire, the superior weaponry of the German tanks, and the overhead threat of the Luftwaffe.

The men were initially successful, and despite heavy losses, the battalion advanced slowly. Inch by inch, they crawled their way to the city, pushing their enemy back. Each inch was fought with the lives of men. Each inch brought heartbreak to someone back home.

But this early fall day turned slowly into one of dust and blood, as men were slayed, vehicles ripped up and reduced to nothing, and the Poles struggled to advance.

The tanks represented the frontline, and as Henryk manned the heavy machine gun, he maintained a focus that made everything else besides his target disappear. The gun was huge, and Henryk's muscles were coiled from the stress and sizable strength needed to maneuver the carriage. His whole body ached from the pressure of his task, adrenaline driving away fatigue.

It became clear that actually destroying or disabling the German tanks with their cannon was unlikely. Yet the men pressed on. The night progressed and casualties mounted. Morale began to flag.

Then, the Germans ordered an attack on their rear. Now the men could neither advance nor retreat, and were slaughtered at every turn, and by the end of that long, bloody night, the Polish army had to admit that they could not capture Krasnystaw, and must retreat. Those who were lucky enough to avoid the bullets and cannon, managed to regroup at the base camp. They had fought all night and had little to show for the effort.

The next day, a messenger brought news that a battle in Tomaszów-Lubelski was taking place, and that the unit's help was needed. The men mobilized and headed towards Tomaszów, seventy kilometers away. The men marched their way further south, where huge numbers of soldiers and equipment were already engaged.

On September 20th, Henryk's platoon joined the battle. The soldiers were exhausted on both sides, and the Germans were astounded by the strength of the Polish resistance. Field Marshal Wilhelm List called in for support, and added to the German advantage.

Over two grueling days, the fighting kept on, and the number of men and machinery was staggering. Without aerial support and firm communication lines, Henryk had no way of knowing that over a hundred thousand soldiers were amassing on the region — German, Polish and Russian.

The Polish losses were heavy, and the men became more and more despondent as their compatriots morphed into corpses. The machinery slowly failed, as gnarled tankettes littered the battlefield and vehicles were ditched. Bodies were scattered everywhere — hanging out of broken-down vehicles, bits of men were strewn in trees, dead soldiers with morose and surprised faces staring blankly up at the darkening skies. And most of the dead men wore the green wool uniforms of the Polish army, soaked with blood, blackening with time.

Henryk's tankette limped on, and he kept firing on the German forces with muscles twisted and tense. He was soaked to the skin, and viewed his targets with glassy eyes. There had been little provisions and the effects of hunger, sleep deprivation and thirst were adding to the heightened state of continual stress and fear.

And finally, their ammunition ran out. Henryk turned to the tank operator, Arek, and said grimly, "We are sitting ducks. We must evacuate."

Arek nodded and the two men hugged briefly, before preparing to exit the tank. They had seen what chances the men had in trying to evacuate a disabled tank. They knew that a mad sprint to the adjacent tree-line was better than being burned alive in a metal tankette. The tankette had somehow transformed from protective womb to coffin. Henryk lobbed a smoke bomb out of the tank, waited a few moments, hoping the diversion would provide enough cover to get to the forest. The tree-line seemed very far away, perhaps the length of four soccer fields, and he prayed he had enough strength in his legs to get him there.

Henryk genuflected, thinking of Aniela and their unborn baby, of his mother and the people who were depending on him at home, and set off, running like the wind.

Chapter 25

Henryk's Fate

He could not feel his legs. His brain felt scrambled, his eyes gritty. He was lying, face down, on the battlefield. He blinked, trying to gather his wits, and tasted dirt.

Okay, he said to himself, drawing a deep breath in an effort to stay calm. *I am alive.*

He was lying on the cold earth — he realized that the chill was pressing against him, and he blessed the awareness. At least he had some feeling.

He turned his head and focused upward. Yes, he noted, the skies were darkening — so what time would it be? Maybe five p.m.?

He shifted his attention to his legs. Why could he not feel them?

Henryk pushed himself up and over to assess the condition of his legs, afraid of what he may find. With a stifled groan, he realized that it was Arek's torso that pinned his legs under its dead weight, and his comrade's blood had soaked his legs and cooled. Grunting, he pushed Arek's torso off of him and saw his stricken face as Arek rolled off of Henryk and to the side. Henryk gagged at seeing an eyeball dangling by a single tendon hanging out of Arek's skull.

Henryk started to shiver, realizing he was numb and cold from the dried sweat and blood soaking him. His senses were coming back to him — his ears were buzzing, but could make out the faint sounds of distant gun and cannon fire. It sounded quite an expanse away, and Henryk hoped that he was not lying in the midst of an active battlefield.

His hands and arms appeared to be in working order. He began experiencing the pins and needles of blood returning to his legs. He wiggled his toes and flexed his ankles, and rolled onto his side. His gun lay just a few feet from him, the leather strap that had crisscrossed his chest shredded by the blast.

Henryk tried to remember exactly what had happened. He recalled exiting the tank and running. The ground was uneven and full of divots, and he struggled to sprint through the terrain. Arek was behind him and the two men had zigzagged their way in a death run to safety.

Henryk didn't recall hearing cannon fire, or the sounds of bullets whizzing by his helmet, but he knew they were targeted. But it was poor, unlucky Arek Bukowski who'd been hit full force by cannon, his body ripped apart and thrown into the air, landing on Henryk and knocking him out cold.

Henryk shivered again. At least Arek's death was quick; there was no way Arek could have felt any pain or the grim recognition that his time was up. It was over for him in less than a second.

Vision clearing, Henryk noted figures in the distance. He squinted: it was a troop of German infantry, five men, with bayonets. They were checking each prone Polish soldier for signs of life. With a jab from a bayonet to the heart, the Germans ensured they were truly dead.

Henryk exhaled deeply. He needed to move — and fast. He rolled onto his belly and began crawling towards the trees, making sure to keep his head low and his movements small. He tucked his gun into his pants on his back, held by his belt. He needed to get to the forest before the men made their way towards him, and there was no time to waste.

Henryk slowly crawled toward the trees. His elbows dug into the hard earth, and his legs dragged behind him. It was arduous work, and torturously slow. He pressed forward, not willing to look back. His goal was ahead, not behind, and he kept his eyes focused on the blades of grass in front of him as he crawled. And crawled. Every muscle in his body began screaming in agony.

At long last, Henryk saw he was only about a hundred meters away. He hesitated, weighing his options. Should he spring to his feet and run — or would that simply draw attention to him? Or should he continue the painstaking journey on his belly?

Thinking of Arek's lifeless and mutilated body, he continued on his belly. Finally, he reached his goal. Henryk flipped over, panting, and looked back over the pitch. The Germans were still methodically bayonetting each body, making their way across the field in organized rows of death. They each had their heads pointed down as they performed their macabre task, and were at least three hundred meters away from Henryk.

He sprang up and sprinted into the forest, his legs feeling awkward, wooden, as if they belonged to someone else. No shots were fired his way and he stumbled into the forest, pine needles snapping under his feet.

He continued running, not sure where he was going, intent on finding safety among the tall trees and gathering darkness.

Chapter 26

Poland is Lost

October, 1939

Poland had not surrendered, but she was lost.

Her citizens wept in bitterness as news filtered in that the Polish government had escaped through the Romanian border. No official surrender was made, but with their flight, it was clear that the Poland that once existed was no more. Warsaw had been encircled by the German armies and bombed mercilessly, and finally the capital city surrendered on September 27th, 1939.

With no capital, and no government, the remaining citizens waited in dread. The enemies had proven victorious, and citizens swallowed the hard lump of their familiar reality: they had yet again lost independence.

The Russians and Germans quickly agreed on how to carve up the vast conquered territory. The German Reich annexed territories along Germany's eastern border: West Prussia, Poznań, Upper Silesia, and the former Free City of Danzig. The remainder of German-occupied Poland (including the cities of Kraków, Radom, Lublin and Warsaw) was organized as the so-called *Generalgouvernement* or General Government under a civilian governor-general, the Nazi party lawyer Hans Frank.

Hans Frank and the General Government decided to make the capital of their newly occupied territory in Kraków, which had not suffered the bombs and destruction of Warsaw, and which seemed pleasant enough (to many Nazis' surprise, given their views on Slavic inferiority), with its medieval architecture, tree-lined streets, and gracious homes and boulevards. They took a look at the Wawel Castle, with its high walls and views over the lower-lying areas, and decided that this would be a perfect place for their headquarters. The seat of centuries of Polish monarchies, where patriots like Józef Piłsudski and King Kazimierz the Great were buried, became the new home of the Nazi ruling elite.

The Nazis entered the castle and surrounding museums, plucking art off the walls and sending the paintings back to their homes, where a Da Vinci or Rembrandt, anyone would agree, would look perfectly at home.

The demarcation line agreed to in August, 1939, in secret by the Molotov-Ribbentrop Pact, divided Eastern Europe, with Germany occupying most of the Polish land west of the Bug River. This new and arbitrary line threw people into chaos, as the Russians and Germans patrolled the line and set up border checks, dividing families, employees and neighbors. Families that fled east now faced difficulties returning home in the west. There was a tremendous confusion as scores of Poles were being thrown out of their homes as the occupying Nazis attempted to "Germanize" the area, offering stolen homes to Germans willing to move east and experience *Lebensraum*. The former residents were herded onto unheated cattle cars and "shifted" to the south.

Poland became a land of refugees. Millions were uprooted, and families turned to one another in need, only to learn that their loved ones were in another zone, now as difficult to reach as Mars. Borders were closed, and desperate people tried to bribe their way out. A few managed through the Romanian border, as Romania was sympathetic to the plight of the Polish people, but eventually yielded to pressures from the Reich to seal the border. Poles were trapped in their own country, but it was their country no more. Europe also closed its door to Poles desperate to flee, as had America and other countries around the world. Political asylum or immigration: this avenue, too, was closing.

A proclamation was signed by the newly appointed Governor-General, Hans Frank, accompanied by a note of a compulsory call-up for work. The proclamation was posted all over the city and read:

Inhabitants of the General Government! Victorious German arms have, once and for all, put an end to the Polish State. Behind you lies an episode in history which you should forget forthwith; it belongs to the past and will never return.

The Fuehrer has decided to form a German Government of part of the territory of the Polish State to place me at its head. The General

Government can become the refuge of the Polish people if they will submit loyally and completely to the orders of the German authorities and accomplish the tasks set them in the German war effort. Every attempt to oppose the new German order will be ruthlessly suppressed.

Poles were expected to carry an identity card, and only Poles that worked would get a ration card. The best restaurants and shops soon displayed signs — *"Nur für Deutsche"* — and Poles were relegated to specific stores, neighborhoods, and tramlines. Kraków began morphing in other ways, each a cut against its citizenry's soul. Street signs, often extolling Polish patriots, poets and artists, were ripped away and replaced with German street signs. A city-wide curfew was set.

People like the Majewskis, who lived their entire lives in Kraków, were now second-class citizens. The city flooded with Germans — some were high-ranking Nazis like Hans Frank and his ilk, donning black uniforms, tall leather boots, and driving around in Mercedes and BMW cars and motorcycles. Others wore the green uniforms of the occupying stormtroopers, and their job was to police and harass the citizenry. People were stopped countless times a day, as the Germans made their demands for work or identification cards. People began whispering about *"łapankas"* or roundups, where groups of citizens, often young men and women, were rounded up and shipped off to concentration camps or conscripted for labor. Polish teenagers were sent to farms and stone quarries in Germany or elsewhere in occupied Poland, and forced to work for German families or businessmen who wanted the free labor in easy exchange for party support.

Loudspeakers were installed on every street corner and regularly blared messages in Polish and German reinforcing German superiority and the futility of resistance. Everyone was forced to hand over their wireless. All local newspapers ceased publishing, but a German-produced propaganda newspaper in Polish immediately hit the streets. Cars were confiscated, and Poles were relegated to using bicycles or traveling on foot.

People disappeared at an alarming rate, as mass arrests took place, and the Germans routed streets, seeking out military and government people in hiding. The young began putting gray streaks in their hair. Young men grew mustaches and women changed hairstyles and fashions to appear older and more dignified. Small talk disappeared, as people set about their business, and didn't look up or linger.

There was news that in the Russian-occupied part of Poland, food was in short supply as the Russians had looted all the farms while forcing the population to use the ruble; but here in the General Government, Polish zlotys were still accepted and in circulation, which prevented any immediate economic disaster.

Being in her childhood bedroom, around the familiar smells and objects, made Aniela miss Henryk even more. He should be here with her in Kraków, wrapping his arms around her large belly. She missed their bright yellow bedroom, and the magic that they made there. Again, she cursed the Nazis and their heartless intrusion into everyone's life, but especially her more private one.

Since Henryk had been called up to battle, she had not heard from him. Aniela willed herself to stay calm and collected for the sake of the baby, but her brain kept returning to Henryk. In fact, nobody had news from any of the men in Henryk's battalion. Mail service was still suspended, and the phone lines had been severed during the six weeks of fighting. Most people had no idea the fate of loved ones, whether on the battlefield, in other cities, captured as PoWs or stranded in different sectors of occupied Poland.

Chapter 27

A Simple Lecture

"The Poles do not need universities or secondary schools; the Polish lands
are to be converted into an intellectual desert."
- Hans Frank, Governor-General of the General Government

It was the first week of November, and Pan Majewski was already dressed for a meeting at the university. His wife fussed over him, adjusting his tie.

"So what did the rector say?" Pani Majewska asked, her voice tight.

"He ordered us professors to attend a lecture about the German plans for Polish education," Pan Majewski said, fiddling with the corners of his mustache. "It's entitled *The Attitude of the National Socialist Movement Toward Science and Learning.*"

"Do you think they'll shut down the university?" Aniela said.

"Why should they?" Pan Majewski countered. "Let us not forget I lived most of my life under German rule. I know how these people operate. They will carry on as they always have. We Poles can expect them to set harsh but civilized rules, and we will bend them to our own advantage, as we have always done. We will ensure that our children are educated and that our Polishness will endure... for however long it takes until France pushes them out."

Aniela nodded, comforted by her father's sage words.

Pan Majewski kissed Aniela on the forehead. "It would please me, dear daughter, if you can withstand having my first grandchild until I return from the Collegium Novum. Can you manage that?"

Aniela smiled, chuckling as she stroked her belly. "You know it is not up to me, but I will do my very best."

Pan Majewski smiled. "Well, that is the best anyone can ask for." He turned to his wife and kissed her on the cheek. "I'll see you both after the lecture."

Pan Majewski exited the apartment, looking dapper in his best three-piece tweed suit, hat, and light wool coat. His cane tapped the steps in a familiar cadence as he descended the hall stairway.

But Pan Majewski was wrong. He sat with a hundred and eighty-three other professors, doctors and lecturers from three universities at the gathering of educators. All the men were dressed in their best, and greeted each other warmly, amongst the towering ceilings inlaid with carved wood and oil paintings of great Polish kings and battles.

The men stood when SS-Obersturmbannführer Bruno Müller strode into the room, wearing a black uniform emblazoned with an iron cross on his lapel. He addressed them in German, and his voice cut through them like shards of glass.

"Gentlemen, we have been informed that at the university you start classes, seminars and exams without our consent," he stated. "You don't seem to realize the plight you're in. This kind of conduct is a hostile act against Germany."

Pan Majewski shifted in his seat, glancing at his colleagues with concern. A hostile act?

"As a matter of fact," Herr Müller continued, "the university was always a major hotbed for the scientific struggle against Germany and at the center of anti-German propaganda."

Several men tried to protest, but were silenced by Müller's harsh words, "The University is closed."

The rector, Professor Tadeusz Lehr-Spławiński, stood up to argue, but Herr Müller rolled over him with the shocking news, "You'll all go to a labor camp, where you'll have enough time to think about your behavior."

Dozens of stormtroopers burst through the doors into the hall and grabbed the men at gunpoint. The professors stumbled as they were pushed roughly down the marble staircases of the stately building to the street, where transport trucks were waiting. Men in their fifties and sixties feebly tried to protest, but were easily subdued and overwhelmed. The elite and educated — representing Poland's best and brightest — were forced into the trucks and hauled away.

Aniela was sitting on the divan, reading with Harmony pressed against her lap, when the phone rang. She glanced at the clock — it was two p.m. Maybe her father had news from the lecture?

"Hello," Pani Majewska said. "Oh, hello, Pani Beata... how is every...? What? When? They did what? Oh, my God. Yes, yes, I understand."

She hung up the phone and walked into the living room, a dazed look on her very pale face.

"Mama?" Aniela queried.

"That was Beata, the department's secretary," she said, her voice thin and distant. "She just rang to tell us that your father — and all the other professors — were rounded up."

Aniela dropped her book, her eyes wide. "Rounded up?"

"She said that the Germans forced all the professors into trucks and drove them away. They took them to a work camp."

Aniela stared at her mother, not comprehending. "A work camp? For professors? What does this mean?"

"I have no idea," Pani Majewska said, turning eyes brimming with tears to her daughter.

She sat down and put a cold hand on Aniela's. "I have no earthly idea," she repeated in a raw whisper.

Chapter 28

Montelupich

Irena burst into the apartment, bringing in a gust of cool air with her. It was a bitterly cold November day, and it perfectly matched the feeling of dread that was hanging over all of them.

"I've information they were transported to a prison on Montelupich Street," Irena said breathlessly. "I spoke to an eyewitness, a graduate student. He witnessed the professors being pushed into trucks. He said the soldiers hit some of the men with rifle butts. Several employees and students tried to resist, and they were rounded up, too!"

"We must go to this prison," Pani Majewska stated. "We will reason with these Germans; we have to convince them they made a mistake."

Irena opened up a desk drawer and pulled out a map of Kraków, muttering to herself. "Where on earth is Montelupich Street? Aha!" Irena exclaimed, grabbing a pen and circling a spot on the map. "Put on your coat. Let's go."

Aniela rose to her feet awkwardly, leading with her belly.

"My German is very strong," she said. "Let me come, too."

Irena and Pani Majewska stared at her, as they took in her lumbering form. Pani Majewska shook her head.

"I'm sorry, Aniela. You cannot go in your condition. We made a promise to Henryk, and your father would never forgive us if we let you come with us."

"But I can manage," Aniela protested.

"Who knows if the trams will be working today?" Irena interrupted brusquely. "We may have to walk for ages... Aniela, you will only slow us down, and every second may count."

Aniela nodded, her throat dry.

Irena and Pani Majewska encircled her and hugged her, sandwiching her and her swelling belly between them.

"Good luck," Aniela said hoarsely, watching them go. She sat down heavily on the couch as Harmony weaved around her ankles.

She looked at the tortoiseshell cat. "We have nothing now to do but wait."

***

At long last, Irena and Pani Majewska approached the prison. It was a beautiful old building from the 1500s, a glorious edifice now perverted by the presence of German soldiers carrying handheld machine guns and the plaque to the right of the entrance that read: *Sicherheits-Polizei-Gefängnis Montelupich.*

A small crowd of twenty well-dressed women gathered, beseeching the Germans for information. The German guards stood stoically, and ordered the women to step back when one got too close to the entrance.

"Tell us where they are," a woman implored in German accented with the rolling *r* of Polish.

"They are professors and scholars," another woman said. "Not criminals."

Irena and Pani Majewska joined the crowd, and they, too, pressed the guards for information. They stood shoulder to shoulder, keeping warm as best they could. Many of the women recognized or knew one another from faculty parties and events, and they drew strength from their kinship.

They appealed for hours, using a variety of tactics. Some tried to engage the guards in conversation, even offering warm tea from Thermoses. Others admonished the guards, chiding, "How can you detain university professors and doctors with no charge? Where is your sense of decency?"

But their entreaties fell on deaf ears. Finally, just as the sun was beginning to set and the day grew even colder, a uniformed officer stepped through the double-entry doors and addressed the crowd.

"Ladies. The men you are asking about have been transported to barracks at Mazowiecka. They are not here. You are ordered to disperse, or we shall arrest you." With that, he nodded at the guards, who rushed toward the women.

The women, fearful of the men with machine guns, had no choice but to make their sad way back home.

Chapter 29

Wanda

For more than two tense weeks, they waited for news. A week into the interminable wait, they learned that the men had been transferred to a detention center in Wrocław. They had heard that the men were seen crammed into cattle cars.

"Cattle cars?" Aniela said, her hand on her throat. "Surely the men would freeze. Father only had a light wool coat…"

Aniela closed her eyes, trying to imagine her father as she last saw him, dapper in his fine suit and preparing for a lecture. She grimaced as she recalled him allaying her fears, reminding her how Germans behaved in the past, and telling her not to fret or have his grandchild without him.

What was he doing now? Was he in some squalid prison without heat or blankets? He was a man in his late sixties, with a cane — how would he survive such conditions? Would they treat the men with even a modicum of respect and dignity?

Aniela gasped as she felt a pop, then a trickle of hot moisture between her legs.

"Irena," she whispered. "Get mama. My water just broke."

Aniela stood up and gingerly made her way to the bathroom to grab a towel.

"Oh, papa," she whispered. "You and Henryk are going to miss an eventful day… I'm going to have a baby."

Pani Majewska burst into the bathroom.

"Not to worry, my darling," she soothed. "I called Dr Rozenberg. He asked if you had any contractions."

She bent over with a sharp intake of air as her first contraction assailed her.

For hours, Aniela paced as the contractions came — each time stronger than the last one and with less time in between. She was soon panting from exhaustion and shining with sweat. Irena and Pani Majewska took turns walking with Aniela, their bodies pressed against her side as Aniela paused to catch her breath or shuffled around the room in small circles of anxiety.

"Do lie down," Pani Majewska coaxed. "Dr Rozenberg will be here any moment. You know it's not easy to get around the city, so just hold on a bit longer and try to breathe."

Aniela obeyed and lay down, pale and clammy. Her mother handed her a cup of tea. "Please try to drink this if you can, dear."

Aniela took the cup with unsteady hands and sipped the tea, only to hand it back when another strong contraction wracked her body. Irena jumped up when they heard a light knock on the door.

"Finally!" her sister exclaimed.

Dr Rozenberg entered, quickly taking off his coat and hat as he made his way to Aniela.

"How many hours have you been experiencing contractions?" he asked.

Aniela turned glazed eyes to her mother.

"Five hours," Pani Majewska said.

"Hmmmn," Dr Rozenberg said. "I apologize for how long it took me to get here. The streets were swarming with soldiers and checkpoints today. I did my best."

"Of course, of course," Pani Majewska said. "What can we get you, doctor?"

"Take me to your kitchen," he said. "Let me wash up and get some water boiling. I fear we may be in for a long night."

Aniela was indeed in for a long, tiring night. As women had done since the dawn of time, she grunted and pushed, holding the hands of her mother and sister as the baby inside slowly inched its way toward the world. Tears streaked her face, and her bottom lip was red and swollen from where she clenched it between her teeth. With the doctor's calm encouragement, she labored on as seconds bled into minutes and then hours.

Between bursts of pain so deep and primal, Aniela sought flashes of Henryk's handsome face in her mind's eye. She conjured his eyes the color of the Vistula, his lopsided smile, and tried to imagine him beside her.

And then, with one final thrust, her baby slipped into the doctor's palms. The infant squeaked in protest, and Aniela sobbed with emotion, hearing her baby for the first time.

"It's a girl," Dr Rozenberg said, and cut the umbilical cord. "A healthy girl, Aniela."

Moments later, the baby was wiped down and swaddled and placed into Aniela's exhausted arms.

This tiny girl was a wartime baby, born in an occupied city, to a nation that had been torn asunder. Her grandfather was locked in a prison, her father was lost on some battlefield, but she still had a mother who would protect her at all costs.

Chapter 30

Postcard

Aniela stared at her baby, memorizing every detail. She noted the round head, a bit oblong from its journey through the birth canal, which sported a tuft of dark hair. She examined the round face with full cheeks and the cupid's bow mouth. She marveled at the tiny fists and perfectly formed nails, the smooth, hairless skin that was warm to the touch, and the legs that curled up naturally. There was a little heart-shaped birthmark behind the baby's left knee. She wished for Henryk, and for the millionth time, wondered where he was and what he was doing. She refused to entertain the thought that he might not be alive at all.

She lifted the baby to her right breast and tried to get accustomed to the strange new experience. The baby's mouth was surprisingly strong as she sought out the nipple, and Aniela adjusted herself in the bed.

Dr Rozenberg peeked in, and with Aniela's nod, stepped into the room. He watched as the infant suckled.

"She looks robust," he said, adjusting his glasses. "How are you feeling?"

Her lip was swollen and there were circles under her bright eyes, but there was also a glow about Aniela, something Dr Rozenberg had seen many times with new mothers.

"I'm tired, and I'm sore," Aniela offered. "But I am well."

"Glad to hear it," he said. "We've got a healthy girl on our hands. She may lose a little weight at first. Let me know if you have any trouble breastfeeding her or if she isn't gaining weight."

Aniela nodded.

"I'll be back in a few days to check on you both," he said, reaching for his coat that was resting on the back of a chair. "It's not easy getting around the city these days, as you know. But I'll return."

"Thank you," Aniela smiled with gratitude. She looked down at her nursing daughter, and amended, "*We* thank you."

Smiling, he shrugged on his coat. Aniela's eyes were drawn to the yellow star emblazoned on an armband that was sewn onto his left coat sleeve. She had seen those in Vienna, and she drew her breath in sharply upon recognition.

"Oh, this?" Dr Rozenberg said, sadly looking down at the Star of David. "The governor-general laid out an edict that all Jews must wear it. It's only been a few days; I'm not sure I'll ever get used to it."

***

Later that day, Pani Bartosz visited. She entered the bedroom, where mother and baby lay newly washed and resting. Aniela lay on her side, her eyes only half open, her baby right next to her.

Pani Bartosz rushed over, and her face blossomed into an unguarded smile of pure joy as she looked down at the baby.

"Amazing," she whispered. "She looks just like Henryk did as a baby."

Aniela scooted herself up and picked up the baby carefully. She motioned for her mother-in-law to sit on the bed.

"Would you like to hold her?" Aniela offered.

Pani Bartosz sat down and gratefully took the baby in her arms. She held the baby naturally, as a woman who had borne children does without a second thought.

"I had forgotten how small and delicate babies are," she murmured.

"She is perfect," Aniela said, a trace of pride in her voice. "All ten fingers and toes. Perfect little ears, and look at the fingernails... the same shape as Henryk's!"

Pani Bartosz gently touched the little hands, which immediately clenched around her finger. After several moments, Pani Bartosz looked up, her throat bobbing with emotion.

"Henryk would be so happy. And so proud," she said, eyes misting. "What a happy day it is to meet this new member of our family... but every mother has a heavy heart when her son is away at war."

Aniela's eyes welled up. "I know. I wish he were here. We had discussed naming her Wanda, the name of the legendary daughter of King

Krak, the founder of Kraków..."

"He is here with us," Pani Bartosz said, voice tight with emotion. "The proof is right here."

For weeks, Aniela stayed in her nest. She bonded with her baby, and convalesced as her mother worried over her. Irena stopped by every day, too, but she said she was busy trying to procure work with one of the few remaining orchestras or symphonies. Since the Nazis had invaded, the arts in Kraków dried up and work for musicians was scarce. The ironic part was that there were more edicts that every Polish citizen now required a work card, and everyone was scrambling. The mood was one of great uncertainty.

There was still no word from Henryk. Pani Majewska received a call from the old university secretary (now unemployed) that the professors had been transported to Sachsenhausen, wherever that was. The family hoped that perhaps a postcard would be delivered with news of Pan Majewski by Christmas. They could not conceive of the Germans being so heartless as to not allow the men to write home to their families. But no such postcard was delivered.

Irena, however, was delighted to receive a weathered postcard from Adam. The note had taken over two months to make its way to Kraków, but revealed the news that Adam was being held as a Prisoner of War in Russia. Irena stared at the card with stunned eyes, reading the two simple lines over and over. They were all relieved to hear that he was alive, but it was not clear from the brief note if he was well.

This note brought hope to Irena, but underscored to Pani Majewska and Aniela the absence of any news from Pan Majewski or Henryk. Neither could ignore the cloud hanging over the apartment — in reality the city, and the whole country, too — as women tried to carry on with their daily lives, constantly aware of what was absent. A missing husband, a lost father, a vanished brother — every woman felt the fear of the unknown clutching her heart.

Chapter 31

Blending In

The neighborhood was changing. Entire streets that lined the castle had become Germanized. More and more, restaurants and shops sported signs "For Germans only". It became routine to see policemen and military men checking identification cards on street corners, or turning people away as they tried to get on a tram or walk down a once-familiar street.

Despite this, Aniela donned her coat and bundled Wanda up to take a walk to visit her dance instructor, Pani Ostrowska.

It seemed to Aniela that less people were on the street, though it was already twelve thirty. Just a short time ago, people would have been busy buying groceries on their lunch break, or leaving office jobs to eat a lunch. Now, she noticed, she and Wanda strolled down a side street virtually alone. Being cooped up in the apartment, nursing Wanda, had cut Aniela off from the changes that were happening, and she sadly realized that Kraków was becoming less familiar and recognizable.

As she approached a street corner, two young German soldiers stepped out of a café. They wore brown woolen uniforms, each donning an armband with the familiar swastika.

Aniela darted her eyes away, hoping not to make eye contact with the men.

"Hey, you," one of the men called in German. "Not so fast."

Aniela stopped, reluctantly turning her face to the man who called her. The soldier was in his mid-twenties, probably her age, with reddish blond hair and ruddy skin. He was tall and skinny, and his Adam's apple protruded in his neck.

"Look, Vogel," he called to his friend. "Who knew that such a beautiful girl could be found right here in Kraków?" He turned to Aniela, standing straighter to reach his full height.

"Please show your identification card," he said, his voice deepening with authority.

Aniela fumbled with her purse, looking for the ID cards that every Pole under the General Government was now forced to carry.

The other man turned to Aniela and took her by the arm, looking down at her with blazing eyes.

"You really are a looker, huh?" he said. "Do you speak German?"

Aniela responded, "Yes, I speak German."

He looked down at the pram. "Your baby?"

"Yes, of course," Aniela responded, passing her ID to the man.

"Aniela Bartosz," the man read. "And where is your husband these days, Aniela Bartosz?"

Aniela paused, her throat working. "I'm not sure. He was called up to fight."

"A soldier, huh?" Vogel said. "Well, we slaughtered the Polish fighters, didn't we, Bürger? They put up a good fight, but they had no chance against our superiority."

What did they want? Just to lord it over her that her husband was missing in action? Why not let her pass?

"So, no word from Mr Bartosz?" Vogel continued.

Aniela shook her head. "Not as of yet."

"Well, you may need to start looking for another man. He's probably in his grave," he said, handing her ID back to her. "Perhaps you'd be up for taking a coffee with me some time?"

Stunned, Aniela spluttered her response, "I'm a married woman."

Vogel and Bürger turned to each other and laughed.

"At least for now," Vogel said, grinning and displaying crooked teeth. "Maybe you'll change your mind when you're officially a widow."

"On your way," Bürger said, and the two men stepped aside to let her pass.

Aniela hurried away, rattled by the coarse exchange. Tears flooded her eyes as she considered that those uncouth soldiers might have been speaking the truth. Was Henryk dead and decaying in some forgotten battlefield, never to return home to her? Never to meet his daughter?

She tried to calm herself by talking to Wanda, her voice tight with emotion. "Don't listen to those bad men, Wanda. It's pure intimidation — they have no idea about the strength of your father. They haven't seen what I have seen. Did I tell you about how he saved Marian's leg by lifting an entire wagon himself? Or when he lifted a sewer grate to free Harmony? They are spewing that… drivel just to rattle us, that's all."

Aniela continued on her way, and was stopped again by another pair of soldiers.

By the time Aniela arrived, she was over an hour late and brimming with emotion. She felt violated and demeaned, and missed Henryk more than ever.

Pani Ostrowska took one look at her face. "What happened?"

Aniela told her the stories of being hassled by the soldiers, and their taunts about Henryk likely being dead.

"I wish Henryk were here," Aniela said simply.

Pani Ostrowska took her hand and squeezed it. "Many of our soldiers are PoWs in Russia and Germany. The fact that you have heard nothing is likely good news, not bad, Aniela."

Aniela wiped her eyes. "I hope you're right."

"Me, too," she said. "But be careful going out. The Germans keep sending more and more soldiers, not to mention their citizens, to claim what is ours. They all have such a blasted sense of entitlement; it is not safe for anyone — especially not a beautiful young woman on her own."

"I will try," Aniela said. "It's just hard to be cooped up in the apartment with my mother and baby all day long. But now I see that going outside is not what it used to be."

"I fear nothing will ever be what it used to be ever again."

Chapter 32

A Little Humanity

Several months had elapsed since Aniela had moved out of her apartment and in with her mother. Wanda's fuzzy dark hair had fallen out and was growing back very pale blonde. Her eyes had also lightened, and were turning more like the color of turquoise, like Aniela's and her grandmother's eyes.

She was a good baby, gaining weight and sleeping soundly. She spent hours staring at her surroundings with curious eyes, and fussed and cried only when she had gas, was soiled or hungry.

Aniela recovered her pre-baby figure, and aside from her larger breasts, looked very much like the woman she had been before giving birth. The faint circles under her eyes were barely visible, she was sleeping more as she and her mother split duties and adjusted to the schedule of caring for a newborn.

It was a warm late April day. Aniela and her mother strolled along, pushing the pram with Wanda bundled up. Pani Majewska paused at a store window.

"Oh, look," she said, peering through the shop glass. "There is hardly any line. Do you mind if I pop in and pick up a few things for dinner with the rations card?"

"Not at all," Aniela said. "I'll stay out here, as the fresh air will do us good."

Pani Majewska nodded, and scurried into the store. Aniela adjusted Wanda's blanket and turned her face to the sun, enjoying the warming rays. It felt like winter was finally loosening its grip, and Aniela smiled inwardly. Maybe with the better weather, Henryk could more easily make his way back home? The roads and bridges destroyed during the six-week campaign were one by one being repaired. Mail, phone service and trains were slowly returning to normal schedules. Though the border between the Russian zone and the German zone was tightening, it was getting a bit easier to live daily life as the ravages of battle were gradually swept away. Aniela thought about Ewa, whose family had fled east during the Nazi assault. She wondered if she was trapped now in the Russian zone.

If only, Aniela mused, her father and husband could be returned to her.

Her reverie was broken by two young boys shouting cuss words. A bit surprised to hear such coarse language from children, Aniela turned her attention on their outburst.

To her chagrin, she saw the boys were following a stooped-over, elderly Jewish man. The man was dressed in a kaftan marked with a yellow star, a yarmulke with ear locks, and was trying to get away from the boys who were following him, imitating his shuffling gait.

"Can't move any faster, you dirty Jew?" one of the boys laughed.

The other boy picked up a handful of pebbles and began tossing them at the man's back, sticking his tongue out at the man.

Aniela gasped. Of course, she knew children could be cruel — she had been teased enough in her childhood to know that firsthand — but she was stunned by the venomous cruelty of these two boys.

Her mother exited the store carrying her parcel. She took one look at Aniela's shocked expression and the boys harassing the old man. They had grown even bolder and were poking the man with a stick, laughing and smirking with glee.

"Hold this," Pani Majewska said, thrusting the bag into Aniela's hands. She strode up to the boys and grabbed one by the ear.

"Mind your manners, young man," she scolded, twisting his ear. "How dare you act like the Nazis do, teasing this man? Your mother would be so ashamed of you."

She turned to the other boy, who was staring at her like a deer caught in the crosshairs.

"And you," she said. "You run along before I box your ears as well."

She released the boy's ear, and the boys — red-faced with shame — quickly turned and ran down the street, ducking into an alley. Pani Majewska turned to the man, who was watching with wide eyes, rheumy with age.

"Are you okay, sir?" Pani Majewska said, taking his arm. "Did those boys hurt you?"

"No, no," the man said, speaking in a thin voice. "Just my pride, dear lady. There is no dignity in being tormented by schoolchildren…"

"Do you need help getting to your destination?" Pani Majewska inquired, eyes filled with concern.

"No, thank you," the man said, embarrassed. "I am fine. Please, continue on your way and thank you for coming to my rescue."

"Of course," Pani Majewska said, lowering her voice. "We Poles must stick together."

Mother and daughter took their leave, and walked in silence the rest of the way home. Aniela was in awe of her mother's decisive action. She had come to the man's defense and scolded those rude children without a second's hesitation. She was proud of her mother's action, but chided herself for doing nothing. The children were Polish children, not the Blue Police or stormtroopers. Why had she not acted?

Aniela felt humbled and shamed. If they were to survive this harsh Nazi occupation, there would need to be solidarity between its citizens, and acts like the one performed by her mother would need to be commonplace to keep the dignity and pride of her people intact.

Aniela turned to her mother and reached over to squeeze her hand. "I'm so proud of you, Mama."

***

A week later, Pani Ostrowska stopped by for a visit, and sat in the living room across from mother and daughter. She was dressed primly in a long wool skirt, cardigan and elegant scarf, her long gray hair in a bun.

"She really is such a lovely baby," Pani Ostrowska said, holding a sleeping Wanda in her arms. "What a lovely disposition she has… takes after her mother."

Aniela smiled brightly and said, "I've been keeping a diary of all the little daily changes. It seems every day we witness some 'first'. I am recording it all so that I can catch my father and Henryk up on every detail when they return home."

"Yes, it really is amazing to witness the developments," Pani

Majewska interjected. "Just this week, Wanda was trying to speak. I swear she was saying ba… ba… ba… for *babcia* [grandma]."

Aniela turned conspiratorially to Pani Ostrowska. "We are in a tight competition to see if Wanda will say *mama* or *babcia* first."

"So," Pani Majewska said, "what have you been up to?"

Pani Ostrowska looked up with sad eyes. "You are well aware that the Nazis shut down all schools of higher learning."

Mother and daughter nodded sadly in agreement.

"Well, it's not just secondary schools and universities that have been shut down," Pani Ostrowska continued. "They have banned all cultural education. Aniela, I'm afraid that teaching Polish folk dance is now considered a crime.

"I have been approached by some of the parents and older students about continuing their dance education. With the Germans moving in, taking over the best apartments, closing schools and shops, people are looking for ways to mark their resistance."

Aniela nodded, her brow furrowed. "So are you considering taking the lessons underground, then?"

Pani Ostrowska lowered her voice conspiratorially. "In truth, I am. Payment will not be what it used to be, but I have dedicated my life to preserving and passing on our folk traditions. Who knows how long the Nazis will rule over us? We must preserve our way of life and our traditions, just as we did under partition."

Pani Majewska chimed in, "I'm sure my husband would be doing the same, if he were here." Her voice cracked a bit, but she quickly recovered. "There is talk, of course, that France is finally arming up and will join our fight. We may be free by year's end, God willing."

"I pray for that," Pani Ostrowska said. "Aniela, I wanted to ask you whether you'd join me in teaching classes underground. You don't need to answer now, as I'm still trying to find a location that would accommodate dancers that is safe and free from prying eyes. But my hope is that you will help me keep the school running."

Aniela paused, looking at her sleeping daughter in Pani Ostrowska's arms. With a slow nod, she promised to think it over.

After her old dance teacher left, Aniela pondered what Henryk and her father would advise. Her mother believed that Pan Majewski would have taught university students underground, if he were here. Aniela agreed with her. Her father was a patriot and he would not forgo his lifelong passion and goal of educating Polish youth due to a mere detail like occupation.

And Henryk? Aniela's knee-jerk reaction was that he would support a decision to teach folk dance. He was a lot more cynical about Germany than her father, and she imagined his hatred for the Nazis had intensified after the bitter defeat of the Polish army and the exile of their government, now situated in Paris.

But she had Wanda to think of. Until Henryk returned — *not if* — she chanted inwardly, she was Wanda's sole parent and needed to protect her baby during uncertain times. Would she be putting not only herself but Wanda at risk?

Since October, 1939, General-Governor Hans Frank had ordered the mobilization of the pre-war police in service to the Germans, on pain of death. In addition to the policemen who were ordered to serve the *Ordnungspolizei*, the *Ordnungspolizei* had also been actively recruiting young Polish men sympathetic to the German cause or simply wanting power and security with the Blue Police. The pay was impossible to find elsewhere — two hundred and fifty to three hundred and fifty zlotys — and the Nazis cleverly allowed the men to earn bonuses, including keeping up to ten percent of confiscated goods. Aniela had heard that many young Polish men were being lured into the "Blue Police" — a subordinate arm of the German *Ordnungspolizei*, whose role was to enforce Nazi rule and laws onto the occupied population.

They sought candidates who qualified as *"Volksdeutsch"* — Poles with direct German lineage, surnames or proof that they had German blood coursing through their veins. The concept of *Volksdeutsch* derived from the Nazi ideology that Germans were their own race, and that over the many years of German occupation on Slavic lands, there were true Germans nestled among the so-called sub-humans.

The Nazis even took Jagiellonian University, the most respected university in Poland, and converted it into a research facility dedicated to studying archives in pursuit of proving German racial purity among the occupied population. They encouraged Poles with German ethnicity to step forward, and awarded those who did with plum jobs within the Blue Police or within the administration. Poles of German ethnicity were persuaded by better social status and food if they registered as *Volksdeutsch*, and the Nazis actively encouraged such registration, often deploying terror assaults if one refused.

Before long, the Blue Police became a much-feared organization, as people saw the boys and men that they grew up with — who once protected and served the local population — now coopted into doing the bidding of the Nazis. The Blue Police were all Poles; they spoke the language, they knew their communities, and they were a fearsome adversary for anyone that wanted to resist. Many a Pole spat behind their backs, seeing their conscription into the Blue Police as collaboration, and nobody trusted the sight of the navy-blue uniform, stripped of national insignia.

Aniela wondered if joining Pani Ostrowska underground would put her on a collision course with the Blue Police, or worse: the *Ordnungspolizei*. Justice was not a familiar sight any more around the city, as "enemies" of the Third Reich were quickly dispatched to a work camp or hanged from the gallows in the main square, as an example to other Polish freedom fighters and citizens.

But Aniela's heart pulsed with the love of dance. Teaching was not an active resistance, such as those men fighting from safe havens in the forest, who set off bombs at Nazi strongholds or circulated clandestine information through the underground press. No, her act of resistance was smaller and less significant, but still a way of asserting and preserving her Polish identity. She thought of Wanda, too little to don a *krakowiak* and dance, but she wanted her daughter to have the same opportunities that she did, no matter what the cost.

Chapter 33

France Falls

May 10th, 1940

Germany had invaded France as well as the lowland countries of the Netherlands, Belgium and Luxembourg. Expectations were high that France, with the world's best military, would stop the invading Nazis in their tracks.

Everyone was confident the French would be victorious. In quiet voices, people speculated that by the end of the year, Poland would be free of its German occupiers. Older folks reminisced fondly about France — they never forgot that when Poland regained statehood in 1918, France was the only Western power that offered Poland unqualified support. Nor would they forget the heroism of France in the Great War.

Luxembourg surrendered after just one day of fighting. Three days later, German newspapers and citywide wirelesses proudly announced that Holland had also surrendered. Krakovians heard the news with disbelief. Just four days? Ah, yes, people rationalized, Holland had not mobilized or militarized appropriately.

But France — she will surely prevail.

Belgium surrendered next. Again, propaganda freely celebrated the Nazi victory. The Germans flouted their superior air power, they cited the force and vigor of their troops, the might of the Panzer tanks, and the shock and awe of the blitzkrieg. On June 14th, the Nazis took Paris, the capital of France, and its beating heart.

Eight days later, on June 22nd, France surrendered. The Germans celebrated their victory by ringing every church bell throughout Kraków. They flooded into the streets, drunk and wild with joy, while Poles fled to their homes and closed their windows. It was a blisteringly hot day, but still windows remained shut, and the Majewskis, in their sweltering apartment, fanned themselves and wished that there was enough cotton to block their ears.

They were in shock. Brutal, unforgiving, relentless shock. France had fallen in less time than Poland had endured. Poland, a country reborn just twenty-two years ago, fighting a war with the Nazis to the West and the Russians on the East, had fought and outlasted the great armies of France. It was inconceivable.

Since Poland's disastrous defeat, many Poles blamed their government in exile for not reading the signs of war, for not being prepared, for not calling up the men soon enough, and certainly for not waging a winning defense strategy. But now that France had fallen — so quickly and decisively — people found room in their hearts to forgive their failed governmental and military leaders. Maybe they had not been betrayed by incompetence, if even France — mighty France — could not prevail.

Like Poland, France was split — yet France had a government in the south friendly to the Nazis in power called the Vichy. The Polish government, in exile and operating in Paris, was forced to flee again. They fled to London.

With France fallen, who was left to resist? Just Great Britain — a country a lot less known and familiar to Poland than France.

Despite the heat inside and the carousing outside, Wanda was quiet, hanging onto the bar of her crib in the living room. Aniela stared at her daughter, now seven months old, amazed at how implacable she seemed to be. She bitterly noted that the crib resembled a jail cell, and bleakly admitted to herself that each and every one of them was in some kind of prison or another.

"I don't know how she manages to be so quiet in this heat and with all the commotion outside," Aniela said, mopping her brow.

Irena looked at her niece, and back at her sister. "Well, it's simple really. She is a war baby. Babies born in times of war have the good sense not to cry."

Chapter 34

A Package

With all the celebrations outside, and the altering of life in the streets, life turned inwards. It was summer, yet Poles could no longer linger at the parks, or idle time away at cafés and milk bars. Life became something to be lived in the shadows, hidden from public scrutiny.

The Polish Resistance made its presence known by acts of sabotage, often with smuggled-in information on what was happening outside of Poland. The Home Army, as it was called, also helped with forging documents, intelligence-gathering, assassinations, installing spies within the General Government and maintaining contact between ordinary Poles and their government in exile. The Polish nation had never surrendered, and the German occupiers increased the severity of punishments when a partisan was captured.

Bodies dangling from a rope became a common sight outside Cloth Hall. People whispered warnings that any partisan caught would not only be executed, but their relatives would also be targeted, rounded up, and sent off to some unknown destiny. For every German that was killed by the Home Army, ten random Poles were killed. Life was boiled down to one of getting by, and trusting no one.

It seemed that every discussion led to Britain, as interest had intensified in Poland's last standing ally. Who were the British exactly, famous for their practicality and vast empire? Would they be able to do what the Poles and the French could not do — push back the mighty German army and bring peace and freedom back to Poland and Europe?

People began sharing books about Britain, and taking clandestine private English language lessons in the hopes of being able to speak a few sentences in English when the day of liberation came. It all depended on the new Prime Minister, Winston Churchill, who had supplanted Neville Chamberlain. Churchill was reportedly known for his military ability, and Poles clung to the idea that this capable and powerful man could rise up, alone, and square off against Hitler and the Third Reich.

Days later, Irena arrived carrying a tiny wad of paper. Over the kitchen table, she carefully unfolded it until it turned into a leaflet. It contained an appeal by British airmen to the Polish population not to weaken, and it promised an early beginning to a big air offensive against the Germans.

"Where did you get this?" Pani Majewska asked in awe.

"I have my ways," Irena said.

Aniela looked at her sister with appraising eyes, wondering what she was up to. Was she, perhaps, involved with the underground movement in some way?

"God bless the British," Pani Majewska said, clenching her hands in front of her chest passionately. "With France on her knees, we desperately need this reminder to keep fighting on and to not give up faith."

Aniela narrowed her eyes. "But where did it come from?"

"Where do you think? The British were over Kraków last night," Irena said. "They dropped leaflets."

"The British were over Kraków last night?" Aniela probed skeptically. "How do we even know if these are real? Perhaps it was done by our own people to cheer us up, like it has mother."

Irena's mouth opened, and she turned to her mother, at a loss for words.

"But but…" she spluttered. "It has to be real. It's in English."

"Precisely," Aniela said. "Don't you think the British — the practical British — would have had the time, talent and resources to have this translated before sending a covert mission into enemy territory?"

"But it's in English," Irena repeated quietly, looking down at the leaflet with new eyes.

"Well, yes," Aniela said. "It's in English. Let us assume that it came from the British then, shall we? The note wants us to be hopeful, so let's be optimistic. God knows, we need something to feel good about."

Yet, two days later, the postman delivered a large wooden box to the Majewski family. The postman, a man in his late forties and dressed in his postal uniform, passed the box to Aniela and beat a hasty retreat. Aniela grimaced at his quick departure; in the old days, they would have chatted idly and he may have lingered, expecting a tip. But these days, even the postman spared no time for pleasantries.

Aniela placed the box on the kitchen table, as her mother stepped into the room.

"It's postmarked from Germany," Aniela said, noting the stamps that read *Deutsches Reich* in that familiar typeface and black swastika.

"Will you read the note?" Pani Majewska said, sitting down, her face pale.

"Of course," Aniela said, reading in German. "The Sachsenhausen commandant regrets to inform that on May 18th, 1940, Professor Bogdan Majewski died in jail of an untreated cardiac defect."

Aniela dropped the note in horror.

Her mother carefully unwrapped the package and took out a small wooden box. Inside were ashes, gray and coarse. She stared at them incredulously.

"This can't be," Aniela whispered, staring with disbelief at the ashes. "May 18th? That was over a month and a half ago..."

Pani Majewska took the box, hugging it to her chest, and wept. "My dear Bogdan. Can this be all that is really left of you?"

Aniela sat down, her body stiff and numb with shock. Her dear father, proud patriot, educator of Polish youth, scholar and polyglot — was he really dead? The father who always tried to see the best in everyone, who taught her the joy of language and literature, about the honor of cherishing one's birthright, and the responsibility to one's fellow man — was he really and truly gone?

Her brain couldn't quite wrap itself around the fact. She sat bleakly across from her mother, the wooden box between them, until the tears came and swept them both away.

Chapter 35

Mourning

The women Bogdan Majewski left behind held a private ceremony at St. Adalbert's Church to honor a life cut short. The Nazis discouraged funerals and public acts of mourning, so only a dozen mourners returned to their apartment. Pani Bartosz squeezed Aniela's hand as she entered, her face pale with grief.

"My boy loved him like a father," she said, as Aniela's eyes filled again. "It was a great injustice for that boy to lose his father so young, but I bless the day you came into his life, and with it, your father. I didn't know it at the time, but Henryk so dearly needed a father-figure."

Aniela wiped her eyes as Pani Bartosz continued, "Your father was an intellectual, just like Henryk's father; but he was also a philosopher, a historian, a cultured man of the world. I am certain that it was his influence, not mine, that led Henryk to being a newspaperman. His influence was tremendous."

Aniela hugged her mother-in-law to her, and they sat down on the sofa, facing one another.

"I appreciate your words," Aniela said, her voice hoarse. "It makes me miss the two most important men in my life all the more."

"I understand," Pani Bartosz said. "Now that you have Wanda, you know how deep and intense a mother's love is. I mourn Henryk's absence every day."

"He will be despondent when he hears the news," Aniela continued, fiddling with her hands in her lap.

"Yes," Pani Bartosz said. "But let's remember to honor the wonderful life your father did live. These days, so many people's lives are cut short before they'd had the chance to fulfill their destinies. Your father accomplished much to be proud of. And his blood still runs in your and Wanda's veins."

Aniela looked at her daughter, now seven months old. "That is a comforting reminder that he lives on in Wanda."

Aniela found her mother, who was standing in the corner, conversing with Pani Ostrowska. Her face was tight, there were circles under her blue eyes, and she had an ashen look. Aniela grimaced as she saw the stress of the last two weeks etched onto her mother, from the slope of her shoulders to the dullness of her eyes.

Again, Aniela cursed the Nazis who had thrust themselves into everyone's lives, bringing misery, loss and death.

Chapter 36

Proper Work ID

Weeks later, Aniela said to her mother, "I heard that the old glass factory has a new director. I'm thinking I will go and see if there's need of a secretary or office worker."

Pani Majewska nodded.

"I don't see another way. We need the income," Aniela said. "I'll go tomorrow morning and try to be back by noon in order to breastfeed Wanda."

"Yes, of course," Pani Majewska said, reaching down to scratch Harmony.

Pani Majewska continued, "It's in times like these that I really appreciate the company of animals."

The next day, Aniela made it to the factory by nine. She didn't have an appointment, and had no idea how long it would take. She entered the building and made it to her old office.

A man was sitting at the desk, wearing a dark gray suit, his hair disheveled. He was in his late fifties, and was of average height and had a belly pressing against the buttons of his shirt. There was a coffee stain on his lapel, and he rifled through papers with one hand and sipped a mug of coffee with the other.

She knocked on the door, and he jumped.

"Sorry!" he said in German. "You surprised me. What can I do for you?"

"Good morning," Aniela said, very formally. The window was closed and the room was stuffy and smelled of old coffee, cigarettes and male perspiration. "My name is Aniela Bartosz and I used to be the secretary and office manager for this factory when Antoni Urban ran it. I stopped by to see if you, sir, by chance, had any need for secretarial services, since I have experience and know the business?"

The man looked at Aniela as if she was from Mars. "Are you a Pole?"

"Yes," Aniela said, hoping that he was asking because of her lack of accent. "But as you can see, I am fluent in German."

"And you used to work here?" he pressed, his eyes skeptical. "A beautiful young woman?"

"Why, yes. I majored in German language and literature at university. Pan Urban had a lot of business contracts in Hungary and Austria, so my language skills were of use to him and the business. Plus, I type and know shorthand."

"Hmmm," the man said, scratching his beard. "It almost sounds too good to be true, as I was just thinking how desperately I needed help to organize the factory up to the Reich's standards. And here you walk in…"

Aniela pressed her advantage. "I'll happily oblige you, sir."

The man appraised her from head to toe, and then nodded. "Let me introduce myself. My name is Herr Helmut Neumann. Please, show me your identification card and I'll submit your name to the employment office. If the labor office has no problem with you, you're hired."

Aniela's face broke into a winning smile, her blue eyes flashing with relief. "Thank you! Thank you," she enthused, pulling her ID card from her purse and passing it over.

Herr Neumann reviewed her ID and wrote down the information on a pad of paper and handed it back.

"Well, Frau Aniela Bartosz," he said. "Come back in two days. Be here at nine sharp, ready to work."

"Yes, sir," Aniela said, curtsying, before backing out of the office.

Aniela left the office, running down the stairs, emanating relief. She glanced at her watch — she had landed her old job in less than fifteen minutes! She exited onto the street, and paused. It was so early — she decided to swing by Pani Ostrowska's apartment to share the good news and to discuss getting started with the folk dance lessons. If she was going to be working for the Germans, she must give something back to her community.

Aniela made her way to the apartment and rang the bell. Pani Ostrowska was surprised to have a visitor so early, but happily buzzed Aniela up.

"Forgive me for not having my makeup done," Pani Ostrowska said modestly, though she looked the picture of an aging, elegant dancer, with her hair in a chignon and dressed in a silk housecoat with dragonflies. The windows of her apartment were open, and there was a pleasant breeze wafting in.

"Sit down, Aniela," Pani Ostrowska said, placing a pot of tea on the table and offering Aniela some day-old bread with butter. Aniela sat down and shared the good news about getting her job. She also mentioned that she was open to conducting underground dance classes for any students procured.

Pani Ostrowska beamed at the news. "I knew you would, my dear. This makes me so proud!"

For the next hour, it was as if the war, the occupation, the men lost, and the outside world had no meaning as the two caught up on their daily lives, and talked about the books that they were reading. So many people were losing themselves in books these days as a simple form of escapism.

"You've no doubt heard about the demand for English language books on the black market?" Pani Ostrowska asked.

"Well, I know that everyone is keen to study English these days," Aniela answered. "But no, I had not heard."

"Oh, yes," Pani Ostrowska said conspiratorially. "One of my former students said she got twenty zlotys for a beat-up copy of Thomas Hardy's *Far from the Madding Crowd*."

"Twenty zlotys?" Aniela said, jaw agape. "Wow, my father has dozens of books in English." Aniela paused to correct herself. "I mean, he *had*. I wonder if my mother and I should part with a few — we could use the money."

"Good idea," Pani Ostrowska said. "Just be careful about who you sell them to. You can never be too careful these days. Anyway, this reminds me of a joke that has been going around..."

Aniela took a sip of her tea. "I'm overdue for a good joke."

"People are joking that the pessimists — they are studying German. The optimists — they are studying English. But the realists — they are studying Russian."

Aniela laughed, shaking her head ruefully.

"I pray that they are wrong," Aniela grinned. "Let's not forget about our Polish language in there, heh?"

Pani Ostrowska smiled and clinked her teacup against Aniela's. "I'll drink to that!"

Soon after, Aniela left for home. There was a bounce to her step despite the increasing heat and mugginess, and she smiled, thinking about how pleasant it had been to visit with her dance teacher after weeks of melancholia. Aniela turned the corner, and practically ran into the chest of a navy-blue uniform belonging to the Blue Police.

"Pardon me," Aniela said reflexively, raising her eyes to the officer.

It was the face of Leon Szulc, her old dance partner. Leon had always been on the small side, but he seemed bigger than she remembered. He also looked older and quite official, dressed in the former Polish police uniform. At his side stood another officer, a man perhaps a few years younger than her, with very pale blond hair.

"Aniela Majewska!" he said, his eyes widening with surprise. "Or maybe not anymore?"

"I am Aniela Bartosz now," Aniela replied.

Leon crossed his arms across his chest, leaning back on his heels, his voice hardening. "Well, let me see your identification."

"You know who I am, Leon..."

"I'm an officer, an extension of the great and mighty Reich, so I urge you to refer to me with respect," he said gravely, his eyes cold. "I said: your ID, please."

Taken aback by the cold manner, she fumbled in her purse, looking for her ID. She passed it to him, while the other man sidled up to Leon to take a look.

"Pretty in your picture," the other man said. "But even prettier in real life."

Leon grimaced at this, and turned to his partner.

"Don't be fooled by that pretty face. This woman is as deceitful as she is beautiful." He turned cold eyes to Aniela. "So what business brings you to this block?"

Aniela began to sweat more, sensing that this exchange was not going to be a perfunctory one.

"I was visiting Pani Ostrowska," Aniela said, honestly. "Our old dance teacher."

Leon bristled as if she had insulted him to his face. "Yeah, that stupid folk dance; more fit for the peasantry than a superior class of people. So why were you visiting her exactly?"

Aniela hesitated, her words coming out in starts. "It… was… simply a social… call. Between old friends."

"I doubt that," Leon stated. "I bet you two were conspiring to teach dance, which is strictly forbidden."

Aniela hoped her face belied her. "Of course not…"

Leon grabbed Aniela by the elbow and dragged her across the street to a small park that had several benches and trees arranged in a cozy square. His partner tagged along.

"Leon," he said, his voice tremulous, "what are we doing with her?"

Leon turned eyes to his partner. "Grunwald, just follow my lead, will you? I'm well aware of with whom we are dealing. This woman may very well be an enemy of the Reich. What is a more convincing decoy than a beautiful woman? We must be vigilant and suss out dangers in all its forms."

Fear gripped her like a vise. Was Leon going to haul her to the police station in a roundup? Was she to be sent off to some work camp? Would she vanish from the streets like so many others, never to see her family ever again?

"I'm no enemy to the Reich," Aniela said, her voice full of fear. "Please, Leon, believe me."

"You were always a vision of beauty while dancing, flaunting that body of yours," Leon said, coolly. "Well, why not dance for me and Grunwald here? If we are satisfied, we will let you go. If we are not…"

Aniela stared at him with wide eyes, not comprehending. Dance for them?

Growing angry by her hesitation, Leon's fingers dug into her arm painfully. Aniela winced, as beads of sweat began running down her temples.

"You think I'm joking?" he taunted, his mouth an angry line. "You either dance right here, right now, or we'll send you over to the Gestapo and see what they make of you."

He let go of her elbow and roughly pushed her into the center of the square. Aniela stumbled and then stood in front of him, embarrassed and awkward.

"Dance," Leon threatened. "Or else."

Aniela danced. There was no music, no beat, and no magic in her stilted and awkward movements. Her face burned with shame, and she saw several passersby slow down to see what was happening, only to look away as she danced like a marionette, with Leon and Grunwald watching and pulling the strings. Grunwald, for his part, seemed to find the exhibition embarrassing as well, and whispered to Leon, "Isn't this enough already? You made your point."

Leon kept angry eyes on Aniela. "I haven't even gotten started."

Leon began clapping his hands, and said, "Now to this beat, please…"

Aniela tried to dance to his clapping, and he taunted her by speeding up his rhythm, only to slow it down.

"Now twirl," Leon barked. "Curtsy. Go on, faster!"

Aniela started to pant in the heat, her clothes sticking to her body as she continued to dance and dance. Her cheeks grew red, her hair curled around her face in wet tendrils.

Older men sauntered by, and stopped to watch the show. Here she was, a woman of twenty-five, with summer clothes sticking to her body, made to dance like a strumpet in a peep show window. She followed Leon's barking orders, swirling, raising her arms and knees and trying to empty her mind of the humiliation. Her body was in torment, but she tried to ignore the growing fatigue of her muscles.

Eventually, Aniela began slowing down a bit, her muscles crying out in pain. Her mouth was dry, but Leon kept barking, "Keep dancing. That's right, faster. Lift those knees higher…"

Aniela continued dancing this way for fifteen minutes. Then a half hour. Time seemed to stand still and she was soaked to the skin as she tried to endure, to somehow please Leon so she could just walk away and go home.

Then she felt that familiar throbbing in her breasts, as she was due home to breastfeed Wanda. For several excruciating minutes, all Aniela could concentrate on was the tingling and tightening of her breasts and the pain that ensued when she hadn't nursed. She felt a wave of nausea, and swayed on her feet.

"Keep dancing," Leon bellowed. "It's up to you if you want to trade the *krakowiak* for a *łapanka*!" He laughed at his own rhyme.

Aniela felt her breasts beginning to leak milk. Her blouse was already stuck to her, but now milk dripped through her bra, creating rivers of moisture down the front of her shirt.

Aniela groaned in discomfort, panting heavily as she danced and danced.

Would this ever stop? Was Leon waiting for her to faint? Or to give up, so he had an excuse to drag her to prison?

Aniela's vision grew fuzzy, the world began receding around her. The small crowd of people watching the spectacle disappeared in front of her, and then even her tormentors seemed to fade away, though she could hear Leon's clapping and barking like a drum in her ear.

She dimly registered that she was about to faint. And then a shrill, angry voice broke through Aniela's muddled state.

"Leon Szulc!" An old woman burst into the square, wagging her cane. She had gray hair tucked under a colorful kerchief and looked like she could have stepped out of a fairytale with her old-fashioned dress and style of speech. "Why are you making this woman dance in this heat? Can't you see she is a nursing mother? For God's sake, stop this nonsense right now!"

Leon turned to the woman, recognizing her, and his face registered remorse and shame.

"Pani Gawdzik..." he spluttered. "I am simply doing my job..."

"Nonsense!" the old lady exclaimed. "What job allows a grown man to humiliate a young mother? Stop these antics right now. This is not how your mother would want to see her son, bless her departed soul."

It was as if Leon had been punched in the stomach. All the anger went out of him. His shoulders slumped and he hung his head.

"You are free to go."

Aniela stumbled away, her legs feeling like they were made of planks, and cast a thankful backward glance at the lady who had come to her rescue. She tried to say thank you, but she was panting so hard she could not form the words.

The old woman nodded.

Aniela staggered away, every muscle in her body shrieking in anguish, her mind clinging to the simple statement that she must go home. She must return home. Mother would be worried. Wanda would be hungry. She must return home.

At long last, when she finally made it to the threshold of the apartment and fumbled with her keys, she whispered, "As God is my witness, there is nothing braver than an old woman."

Chapter 37

Secretary

Aniela shakily walked to her job. She hid her hair in a kerchief and kept her head down, making no eye contact. In the periphery of her vision, she kept watch for the familiar dark blue uniforms of the *Volksdeutsche* police. She arrived early, breathless, with a rapidly beating heart. Herr Neumann, already there, greeted her.

"Good to see you," he said, warmly. "Your work papers are all in order, so let's see if you're more than a pretty face."

He pointed to a stack of papers, some written in German and others in Polish.

"Please read these," he stated. "I need you to organize them — which ones are of critical importance, which ones require response, which are unimportant. Can you do that?"

"Yes, sir," Aniela said, taking a seat in the corner at her old desk. She lost track of time reviewing the contracts and correspondence. Some were unpaid invoices and requests for payment, others were questions about unfulfilled orders, and there were letters from former employees asking if there was work to be had. Aniela organized them into stacks, separating those in German from those in Polish, and checked in with Herr Neumann two hours later.

"Herr Neumann?" she queried.

"Ah, yes?" he said distractedly, hunched over his desk.

"I reviewed the documents," Aniela said, trying to keep her voice neutral but confident, though she was nervous. "I'm ready to review whenever you have time."

"You're done already?"

"Yes, sir," Aniela said.

"Okay, let's see what you're made of. What do you see as most critical?"

Aniela sat down across from him and started handing him the documents; each had a paperclip attached with hand-written notes denoting the urgency of the letter as well as key pertinent details.

"Well, this one," Aniela started, "is from a supplier in Biała Góra that supplied the firm with the silica sand, limestone and soda ash used in making glassware. They are inquiring if they can expect an order, as was customary under Pan Urban. This firm is very dependable and fairly priced. Their silica sand is of exceptional quality."

Herr Neumann took the letter and glanced over it. "Good, good. That is an important first step in getting this factory operational. What else have you got?"

"Well, in this pile," Aniela said, picking up a stack of papers, "I have inquiries from some of the previous factory workers and artisans that worked here. I also included a list of all our previous employees, in case you need more labor."

Herr Neumann turned his gaze to Aniela, studying her face for an extended moment. "This is good. My superiors have expectations on profits they expect to see, and I was a bit at a loss where to start. I think, Aniela, we are going to make a good team."

He turned his brown eyes toward Aniela and smiled warmly. Instinctively, Aniela smiled back — a warm, relieved smile that lit up her face and caused her eyes to sparkle.

Herr Neumann continued staring at her. "You're sure that you are not German? You look the picture of a perfect *deutsches Mädchen*."

Aniela paused, unsure how to answer. She didn't want to insult him, or insist too strongly on her Polishness; nor did she want to open the door to a discussion where she'd be "encouraged" to join the *Volksdeutsche*. She settled for a demure, feminine shrug of her shoulders.

"Let us review the roll of employees together. I will need help contacting them to see which ones could return to work," Herr Neumann said. "Pull up a chair."

The two worked for several hours, and at some point, Aniela asked if she could take a lunch break. Herr Neumann readily agreed, apologizing for losing track of time. She excused herself and met her mother with Wanda in the pram downstairs. They found a private place for Aniela to nurse Wanda, and Pani Majewska handed Aniela a sandwich wrapped in wax paper.

Aniela said, "Perhaps it's time to start weaning her from the breast."

"I would agree," Pani Majewska said.

With Wanda's mouth latched onto her left nipple, Aniela thought sorrowfully that Henryk will have missed the opportunity to see his daughter nursing, and that this stage of infancy would soon come to close. She was saddened at the thought of all that he had missed, but the thought of her strong, strapping husband brought unbidden thoughts of desire to mind. She recalled how his lips had encircled her nipple, and how he had looked up at her from her swelling breast, with awe and devotion in those blue-green eyes, and said, "What beautiful nipples you have..." She felt a tingle run down her groin at the memory of those private moments of exploration and discovery. She pushed it aside.

After lunch, Aniela bade her mother goodbye and sweetly kissed her daughter's cheek, to return to the office. Herr Neumann was standing at the window, looking down at the courtyard. His eyes followed as Pani Majewska strolled the pram out of sight.

"I saw you chatting with the woman with the baby," he said. "A relative?"

"Yes," Aniela affirmed. "My mother."

"And the baby?" he queried.

Aniela paused. She had not mentioned to him that she was a mother, but she could not lie to his face. "My daughter."

"Oh!" he said. "You look too young to be a mother. Where is the baby's father?"

"He served at the front," she said, vaguely. No use in making it obvious that he fought against everything that Herr Neumann represented. "We believe he may be in a PoW camp."

Herr Neumann's face softened at this. "Oh, that is difficult. My wife and I have two sons on the front, too. One cannot help but carry your heart in your mouth with worry."

Aniela met his gaze, and nodded sympathetically. Understanding passed between them. Her husband and his sons could have been squaring off against one another, on opposite sides of this war, and yet here they were, commiserating about their loved ones, and perversely working together.

They worked on their plan to hire back the former employees, and to ensure that the products and machinery were stocked and ready for production. With hope in her heart, Aniela realized that they made a good pair.

She knew that Herr Neumann had looked at her beauty and discounted her intelligence and abilities, but she felt that today she had won him over.

Herr Neumann looked at his watch, yawned and stretched.

"Seven thirty already," he mused. "I think we ought to call it a day, Aniela."

"Yes, Herr Neumann," Aniela conceded.

Herr Neumann looked at her, scratching the stubble on his chin. "So, Aniela, did you grow up in Kraków?"

Aniela nodded. "My family has lived here for generations."

"And what do you like about the city? What are its charms?" he pressed.

Aniela paused. Kraków was so changed today, with the sandbags lining the sidewalks, military vehicles belching in the avenues, and the military presence on every corner. She collected her thoughts and closed her eyes briefly, in order to conjure up the Kraków from her childhood.

"I love Cloth Hall and the market square," she said. "Especially in the summer, where people come in their Sunday best. The window boxes are filled with gardenias and the sky is a robin's egg blue. You can buy an ice cream or a beer, and just sit and watch the crowds go by."

Herr Neumann listened carefully as she continued.

"In the main square, we have a tradition called the *hejnal*, where a bugler trumpets out a five-note melody from the top of the watch tower in St. Mary's Church. As tradition has it, the bugler stops his tune mid-song *in memoriam* of a trumpeter who sounded the alarm of Mongolian invaders in the 1200s. His alarm allowed the city to seal its gates against the Tatar ambush, but not before an arrow pierced the sentry's throat, killing him instantly. And so Kraków has ever since honored his sacrifice by playing that melody every hour on the hour, but halting the song at the same moment he trumpeted his final notes.

"And there are lovely cafés, many with live music. On a winter day, when the snow covers the church steeples and lines the street like a blanket, you can warm up with hot tea and homemade *szarlotka* cake with fresh whipped cream…"

Aniela ceased her nostalgic musings. "Why do you ask exactly?"

Herr Neumann replied, "I've been trying to convince my wife, Olga, to join me here. I have the responsibility of getting this factory up and running, and I'd so like her here. But she thinks of the East as some foreign, uncivilized place."

Aniela privately laughed at the idea of Kraków as a foreign, uncivilized place. The only thing that made it foreign and uncivilized was the German invaders.

"Is that enough to entice her?" Aniela asked.

"Yes, yes," he said. "I think it's a start. I'll see if I can campaign to have her join me."

Aniela smiled, packing up her things, and said her goodbye.

She stepped onto the streets, and as it was summer, the sun was still casting its glow and it was not yet dark. But still, Aniela wanted to return home quickly, and avoid any unpleasantness with the police. She adjusted her purse tightly over her shoulder and set off at a brisk pace. She walked a block or two, when she sensed someone following her. Fear crept up her back. Oh, no, she thought, not again.

Aniela began walking faster, and she heard the feet behind her keeping pace. Aniela began almost running, holding her purse to her side to keep it from flapping. She began sweating profusely as she felt terror gripping her throat. Was this a dreaded roundup?

Aniela began to panic, breathing in short gasps. In desperation, she looked over her shoulder to gauge the distance between her and her follower, and then bolted through an open door to a nearby apartment building, hiding behind the door.

She panted, waiting there, urging her breath to return to normal. She heard steps slow down by the door, which was old and swollen from the summer heat, and would not close. She held her breath, and the footsteps continued past. She exhaled, mopping her brow. She waited another ten minutes and stepped outside. Within a few steps, however, she felt a hand on her shoulder and she jumped and squealed with surprise.

"Shhhh," came a feminine voice behind her. "I mean no harm. Are you Aniela Bartosz?"

Aniela gasped, "Yes…" Her heart was jackhammering in her chest. She felt a hand slip something in her pocket.

"Burn this after you read it," said the voice, and then vanished.

Aniela stood there, shaking with fear and cold sweat. After a few moments, she collected herself and reached into her pocket. She found a small piece of paper, folded up into a small triangle. She rushed home, and under the yellow light from the ceiling, she unfolded the little note, carefully pulling back each corner until it was unfurled.

On it were these simple words: *Dancing Girl. Come find me. Tomorrow 6.30 p.m. Where we picnicked last.*

Chapter 38

A Walk in the Park

Aniela checked the clock a thousand times, willing its hands to advance. She was in a state of suspended euphoria — at long last, she had confirmation that Henryk was not only alive but here in Poland, not in some foreign gulag or work camp.

It had been more than a year since she had seen his face, heard his deep voice. She fell into a reverie about the million little things she loved and missed about him.

At a quarter to six, she left work and walked directly to the park. She noted with a bit of surprise that the park had changed since she had last been there with Henryk. The idle dog walkers and the old people reading newspapers on park benches were gone. With some astonishment, Aniela noted a herd of goats grazing on the banks of the river, and plots cordoned-off where people were growing vegetables. With the increasing restrictions on food rations, people were turning to ingenious ways to scratch together an existence.

Aniela walked to the riverbank, watching the green current coursing by. So much time had washed by her and Henryk, flowing like this river. Had war altered him? And then, seemingly out of nowhere, she felt a presence to her left and an old familiar voice.

"Walk with me."

She looked up, but his hat was pulled down low over his head and she could just make out his jawline, covered by a beard. Henryk gently took Aniela by her elbow, leading her to a park bench under a large willow tree. A willow tree always brought her back to the day he proposed.

Henryk checked his surroundings and then sat down, facing Aniela, his breath shallow. Aniela stared at her husband, who seemed both familiar and new to her. A thick, dark brown beard covered most of his face, which was thinner and quite weathered by the sun, and his eyes seemed to be blazing out of his head.

"My Henryk," she whispered, and took his face in her hands, feeling the thick hairs of his beard through her fingers. Her eyes filled, and she kissed him passionately.

Henryk was like a man dying of thirst. His arm slipped around her and he held her head in his hand, tangling his fingers into her flaxen hair. His other hand found her cheek, and he cradled her face, his thumb running down the contours of her cheekbone.

At last she came up for air, and words began tumbling out of her. "Are you hurt? Where have you been?"

Henryk prised his lips from hers, talking over her. "Our baby?"

"We have a healthy daughter, Henryk. She was born on November 26th. Her name is Wanda."

Henryk's face broke into a giant grin, and he pulled Aniela to him, hugging her so tightly she squealed.

"Sorry," he apologized, containing his exuberance. "I am so overjoyed to see you, to hear news. I have spent months in torment wondering about you two."

"Henryk," Aniela said, her eyes wide, "where have you been? What took you so long to come home?"

Henryk lowered his eyes, clearly ill at ease. "I've been working with the resistance after barely avoiding capture. I've been living in the forests, on the fringes, and it's not been safe for me in Kraków. The Gestapo is on high alert as we have been conducting increasing levels of sabotage. They are constantly on the lookout for young men, especially soldiers."

Aniela continued to drink in the image of her husband, noting that he had used some coal dust on his sideburns to make his hair appear gray.

Henryk continued, "We had a mission close by, so I had to see you. I had to risk it. And I want to see our child."

"Can you come home with me?" Aniela asked.

Henryk's face clouded over with regret. "I cannot risk that, dancing girl. Even now, I am putting us at risk. Kraków is a small town. Anybody who recognizes me can turn me in."

Aniela took his hand in hers. "You must know, Henryk, that my father died while you were gone. He was rounded up by the Germans, along with hundreds of other professors, and sent to a work camp. He died there."

Henryk's face darkened as he visibly tried to keep his emotions in check. "Oh, my dear wife," he said, pulling Aniela into his arms again. "I'm so sorry."

Feeling him pressed to her, and taking in the musky scent of him, Aniela whimpered — remembering her father, feeling the familiarity of her husband, wanting to say so much to him, but not sure where to start.

"Any news of my mother?" Henryk whispered, stroking her hair and muffling her cries with his chest.

"She is well, Henryk."

Henryk nodded, his eyes studying her. "I have dreamt so often of you. I went over every detail of your beautiful face. But now that I see you in person, I realize that my memories do not come close to doing you justice. You are truly an angel, I can hardly believe my eyes. But you are real, aren't you?"

She kissed him again, feeling the bristles of his beard scratching her face.

"Oh, Henryk," she breathed. "We are real."

"I have to see our daughter," Henryk stated, his mouth against her cheek. "Whatever the risks. I will be in touch through a carrier girl. You will hear from me soon."

"You must go?" Aniela said, her voice high and plaintive.

"I will find a private place for us to meet," he said, taking her head in his hands firmly, memorizing every detail of her face. "Wait for instructions. I will find a way. I promise."

And with that, he kissed her one last time. He groaned against her willing lips, and with obvious effort, stood up, turned up his collar while he buried his chin into his chest, and walked away.

Chapter 39

Waiting for Contact

Months dragged by, Aniela caught between reliving every stolen moment in the park to wishing fervently to be intercepted by a messenger with a tiny folded-up note. But one day bled into the next, and there was no news or contact made.

Aniela grew worried. He had said it was not safe for him. Had he meant that he was as unsafe as any young man or Polish soldier hiding out? Or was he wanted for some act of sabotage and was being pursued by the Gestapo?

She sat with Wanda on the floor in their living room, playing with wooden blocks. Wanda was ten months old, and was babbling as she sounded out new words.

Aniela cooed to her daughter, "Can you say *ta-ta*? Can you say *Daddy*?"

Wanda smiled up at her mother, banging a block against the floor and causing Harmony to jump from the couch in alarm.

"Wanda," she continued, "can you say *ta-ta* for Mommy? Repeat after me. *Ta-ta*."

"*Kotek*!" Wanda shouted, looking at Harmony.

"Yes, a *kotek*. Can you try to say *ta-ta*? Please, for Mommy?"

But Wanda's attention was drawn to her toys, and she tried to stack up the blocks with chubby fingers and gasped in surprise as they came tumbling down.

"A-oh!" she exclaimed, one of her favorite expressions.

"Yes, a-oh," Aniela repeated. She stood up and pulled the framed picture of Henryk and herself off of the mantel.

"Look, Wanda," Aniela said, returning to her knees on the floor and pointing at the man in the photo. "This is your *ta-ta*. Can you say *ta-ta*, please?"

Wanda flexed her fingers and rubbed the photo with the awkwardness of a child still mastering her digits.

"A-oh!" she repeated.

Aniela smiled, shaking her head ruefully, and wiped the glass with the hem of her dress to remove the smudge.

"Yes, darling. A-oh."

But it was during Sunday mass, another week later, when contact was finally made. Aniela sat in a pew in the middle of the church, nestled between Irena and her mother. Irena was bouncing Wanda on her hip, as the priest invited worshippers to take communion.

"You mind holding her a bit longer?" Aniela whispered to her sister.

"Not at all," she replied, smiling at her niece.

Pani Majewska and Aniela sidled out of the pew, into the aisle and slowly made their way to receive communion. Aniela felt a hand touch the small of her back, the way a husband often does to guide his wife through a crowded space, and then she felt a light touch as someone slipped a note into her jacket pocket.

Aniela didn't turn around, and never saw the deliverer of the note, but she could not resist smiling as she made her way to receive the Eucharist.

"It pleases me," the priest whispered, "to see the Lord bringing such joy to you, my child, especially in these sad times."

Aniela nodded, and returned to the pew. She could hardly wait for the service to end so she could read the note in the safety of home. She caught her mother's eye, and then Irena's. Nodding conspiratorially, they instantly understood their shared secret: contact was made.

Chapter 40

Happy Eyes

The instructions were clear — *Come with Wanda. Arrive at ten a.m. Make sure you are not followed. Burn this note.*

Aniela lay in her childhood bedroom, watching the breeze play with the curtains. For a moment, she could envisage herself as a young teenage girl, waking early before the train ride to Wieliczka, to meet Henryk at his family's home. That seemed so very long ago.

But she was no longer that young girl. She had known loss, suffering and humiliation. She had lived for months not knowing if Henryk was alive or dead, and since those stolen moments in the park, lived in constant dread that he could be lost to her and she'd never know his fate. He said he was an enemy to the Reich, a man of hidden identity. He was both her familiar husband and completely foreign at the same time.

Aniela quietly tiptoed over to the crib. Wanda was a beautiful child, slumbering with lashes resting on plump rosy cheeks. She smiled lovingly. How long had she imagined Henryk holding his daughter? Today, they would finally meet. Aniela idly touched her belly, now flat, and remembered how Henryk had cradled her swelling abdomen tenderly before leaving for the front, kissing it and talking to his unborn child.

Aniela padded to the bathroom and ran the bath. She threw in clumps of lavender from Pani Bartosz's garden and exhaled deeply as the aroma permeated the air. She undressed and slipped into the warm tub, cleaning every inch of her skin till it tingled. She carefully washed her long blonde hair, and combed out the tangles.

She stood in front of the mirror and assessed what she saw. Her breasts were fuller, but still high, but perhaps no longer as perky as they had been before pregnancy. Her stomach was flat, but the skin beneath her belly button showed the signs of having been stretched. She turned to the side and sucked her breath in. She could see the outline of her ribs, but they didn't protrude. She hoped Henryk would still see the girl he fell in love with. Would she still be his dancing girl?

She towel-dried her hair and put on a robe.

"Mama," she heard Wanda call, and went to greet her daughter.

"Good morning," Aniela smiled, reaching into the crib.

Wanda grabbed Aniela's wet hair in her hands and gurgled with excitement as she felt the slippery texture in her hand.

"You need changing," Aniela said softly, and laid her on the table. She deftly pulled off the soiled cloth diaper and put it in the laundry basket.

Aniela's mother popped in with a knowing smile. "You're up early."

"Too excited to sleep," Aniela confirmed.

"Here," Pani Majewska offered, "let me take her. You get dressed. What would you like to see her in?"

"How about the yellow and orange sailor dress that Pani Bartosz made?"

"Perfect choice."

Aniela stood in her robe, carefully reviewing her wardrobe options. She wanted to look perfect. It was a warm, summer day, so she chose a light pink dress with a small flamingo motif with a white patent leather belt. Aniela dabbed perfume behind her ears and on her wrists, and started braiding her damp hair into two braids. If she let it dry while braided, she could let it loose upon seeing Henryk and it would fall past her shoulders in soft and controlled waves.

She walked into the kitchen, where Wanda, neatly dressed and wearing a bib, was being fed by Pani Majewska.

Pani Majewska looked over her daughter appreciatively. "You look lovely, Aniela."

"Thank you," Aniela said. "I'm packing the pram with nappies and a couple sets of clothes. I do not know how long we will have with Henryk and I must be prepared."

"Good," her mother smiled. "Make sure you have enough for yourself, too. And give my best to Henryk. I know that there were no instructions for me to visit, but I would dearly like to see him. Please let him know how much he is in my thoughts and in my heart."

Aniela put a hand on her shoulder. "I will."

Aniela gave her mother a long hug and left the apartment with Wanda, her heart racing with anticipation. She had to watch two trams rattle by before boarding this tram with its "*Für Polen*" sign.

Nothing could dampen Aniela's mood, and she clung to the wooden handlebar as the tram lurched forward. Upon arriving, she looked over her shoulder, and noted with satisfaction that nobody was paying them any mind. She was just a young mother pushing a baby carriage on a sunny, summer Saturday.

Aniela entered a quiet, tree-lined street. She found the building, and carefully hit the button marked "3". She was instantly buzzed up. Aniela walked through the entry doors, closing them behind her. She took Wanda from the pram and her daughter opened her eyes sleepily. With another deep breath, Aniela knocked on the door and waited. A woman in her mid-fifties quickly opened the door and invited Aniela in.

"Were you followed?" she asked, as Aniela stepped into the apartment.

She looked at the smartly dressed woman with coiffed dark brown hair flecked with gray, and an angular face featuring large brown eyes.

"No."

"Good," said the woman, and then smiled. "My name is Dorota. This is my apartment. My husband is also in the Home Army, and he helped arrange today's meeting."

Aniela nodded, her eyes scanning the apartment. Was Henryk not here, then? Was this just a rendezvous point? The apartment had slightly worn parquet floors and large stuffed furniture with throw pillows and blankets bringing in a burst of pleasant color. Various tapestries covered the walls, giving the apartment a regal feeling.

The woman turned and opened a closet, taking out a large canvas bag and hoisting it over her shoulder.

"It is all arranged," she said. "There is food in the kitchen, everything is stocked as well as one can, given the times. Help yourselves! I mean it. You have until this time tomorrow, and then I'll be back from my sister's."

Aniela nodded, a bit overwhelmed. Dorota walked to the door and turned back, noting Wanda slumped over sleepily in Aniela's arms.

"And you can lay her down on the divan," she said, pointing to the sofa in the living room. "Enjoy the time with your husband. Good luck, and remember: Keep quiet."

She quickly exited the apartment, leaving Aniela a bit stunned. Immediately, Aniela heard the latch of a door being opened and Henryk strode toward her with such intensity, she reflexively loosened her grip on Wanda.

Henryk was by her in an instant, hugging his wife and daughter to him, as if he couldn't believe they were both real. He gazed down at her, kissed her soft pink lips, and then stared down at the baby nestled on Aniela's hip between them.

"Our daughter?" he whispered, his voice tight with emotion.

"Yes," Aniela said, her voice choked and thin. "This is Wanda Justyna Bartosz."

Wanda opened her eyes, blinked sleepily, but she smiled.

"Her eyes are just like yours," Henryk said softly, his face examining every detail of her face.

"Yes," Aniela agreed, nestling up beside Henryk, resting her head on his shoulder. "Look, she has the same fingers and fingernails as you…"

Henryk took her small hand by his index finger and examined the features. His face broke into a lopsided grin, revealing his long white teeth and incisor that overlapped ever so slightly.

Aniela beamed back at him, suddenly seeing Henryk as the boy she knew from her childhood. Yes, he was thinner, tanner, more lined and older-looking than before. But that grin was *her* Henryk, and she reached up and pulled him toward her, kissing his lips with longing and pent-up passion.

Henryk groaned as she explored his mouth with her tongue and licked his lips as she made herself reacquainted with the contours of his mouth. He had shaved the beard, but was sporting several days of stubble, and she felt it scratch the soft skin by her mouth, and she relished the idea of being marked by him.

Her body responded immediately to the musky scent of Henryk, the taste of him on her lips, the feel of his hard body pressed against hers. She broke off the kiss and looked down at Wanda, who was groggily trying to keep her eyes open.

"Let's put her down," Aniela said. "She was up early, and she's ready for a nap."

Aniela lay Wanda down on the divan and made a wall of pillows to keep her from rolling off. Henryk watched as Aniela smoothed their daughter's hair, and put a light blanket over the slumbering child.

"She's a very good baby," Aniela said.

"She must be," Henryk said, his smile turning mischievous. "Because all I want to do is ravish you, and she has the good sense to fall asleep..."

Aniela's breath caught in her throat as she was drawn into the intensity of his gaze. She stepped away from the divan and Henryk met her with a long stride. He put his arms around her waist and picked her up so that her lips met his. Their mouths locked as the two tasted, and nibbled, and eagerly explored each other's lips. Henryk carried her, his mouth never leaving hers, her body pressed against his, to the bedroom and laid her down on the bed.

Aniela idly observed the large four-poster bed, which took up a room with wallpaper emblazoned with palm fronds set in gold leaf. But the room receded as Henryk gently unbuckled her sandals and tossed them aside.

"Such beautiful feet," he mused, kissing the top of her foot. "So refined, ever the dancer. I have missed these feet."

His hands gently touched her ankles and began straying up, past her calves, her knees, to her thighs. He kissed her soft skin every few inches, speaking in a low, tender voice.

"And this skin, covering supple muscles." He kissed her kneecap. "So springy and soft. I have missed these calves. And this knee, and this birthmark..." He kissed the spot on her inner thigh.

Aniela gasped as she felt his hot lips, and her hips naturally rose to meet his mouth. She was so excited; she was practically panting with anticipation and desire.

Henryk's hand pulled up her dress's skirt and he stared at her mound, hidden under a pair of lacy underwear. His mouth descended on her pubis, and she could feel the heat of his kisses through the lace. She threw her head back, her eyes rolling behind closed lids, as she felt his fingers slowly move the fabric away and touch her hot, pulsating skin.

"And I've missed this beautiful sight," he said, his voice thick. "I love how you smell, how you taste. Everything about you makes me feel so primal; every fiber of me just has to have you."

Henryk pulled the panties off of her in a single motion and buried his face in her wetness. Aniela arched up to meet his tongue and her legs fell to the side as he sucked her swollen lips and gently stroked her with his tongue.

Aniela thrust her hips up as his face went deeper into her, exploring her with deep groans of intense pleasure. She felt his stubble against the softness of her inner thighs, but ignored the incongruous sensation, and swiveled her hips in a pattern to meet his dancing tongue. He had found her core, the key to her desire. She gripped his head as she thrust herself into his mouth, into his face, and he toyed with her feminine core until, at last, she could resist no more, and she stifled a cry. His hands snaked around and cupped her buttocks, as he lifted her up and buried himself even more deeply into her gyrating, climaxing body. She tried to keep quiet, but was breathing and panting heavily.

Henryk pulled away, wiping away her wetness with his forearm. He hesitated and savored the moment.

"God, Aniela," he whispered. "I have missed this... so much."

He crawled up to her on his forearms and unbuckled her white patent leather belt and pulled her dress over her arms. He quickly unhooked her bra and hovered over her, his face dark and forceful.

Very tenderly, he leaned down and kissed her as she struggled to catch her breath. He gulped in her breath as he kissed her.

"We share the same breath," he murmured against her cheek, as Aniela's breathing slowly began to recover. She tasted her own musky saltiness on his face.

Henryk pulled away and quickly stripped down, and then positioned himself on top of her.

"Are you ready, my love?" he whispered, his member grazing the wetness of her swollen femininity. "Can I at last have you?"

"Yes," Aniela whispered, as his mouth came crashing down on her lips and she felt the full size and girth of him fill her up. She gasped against his mouth, and he pulled away enough to gauge her expression.

"Okay?" he whispered, his hips still.

"Yes," she breathed, as her body slowly acclimatized to the size and feel of him. It had been so long since she had felt him inside of her, and she reveled at the feeling of fullness, of completeness. "Don't stop..." she pleaded.

And he did not. Their hips found a familiar rhythm, a cadence of their primal passion. Aniela's mouth never left Henryk's as their bodies fused into one, and he held her to him, his hands lifting her buttocks to drive deeply into her, her fingers digging into his shoulders and gripping his hair as they were overcome by their passion.

And Aniela orgasmed again, her body convulsing, and Henryk could no longer hold back his pleasure. He gritted his teeth and groaned deeply as he let go, as he, too, was unable to hold back his desire for her. And then he collapsed over her, still inside of her. Aniela felt a wave of fatigue and of complete tranquility wash over her with such intensity, she could not keep her eyes open. And they slept.

***

Aniela opened her eyes to find Wanda lying in between them, with Henryk cooing over his daughter. He examined his child with a fierce focus. Aniela gulped with the realization that he didn't know when he would see Wanda again and he was memorizing every feature, burning it into his mind to carry him through the months ahead.

"Hi, you," she said softly, and reached over to touch Henryk's hand. He turned his gaze to Aniela, and she could see the love shining through his eyes.

"I thank you for bringing our child into the world," he said, his voice hoarse. "For carrying the burden without me. If I live a thousand years, I do not know if I would have enough time to express my immense gratitude." His eyes filled with tears, and he threaded Aniela's fingers through his and kissed the back of her hand.

"I have missed so much," he said sadly. "I have missed... this... you... everything... so much."

Aniela's eyes watered in response to his. "I have, too, my love."

Time slipped by as they enveloped themselves in their private world. But after a while, Wanda woke up and began to fuss. Aniela looked at the clock, and sat up. "It's about time to feed her," she said, rubbing her eyes.

She rolled back to the other side of the bed and got up. She felt Henryk's eyes glued to her silhouette as she retrieved the clothes strewn about. Aniela pulled the dress over her head and walked over to where Henryk lay, and leaned over him to meet his mouth with hers.

Henryk's hand snaked around her, and she felt him grip her buttocks with his bare hand, squeezing appreciatively.

"Hmmm," he groaned. "I want to stay all day in bed with you..."

Aniela smiled, and reached over him to pick up Wanda. "We can do that, Henryk. Let me feed her and change her first..."

"Let me." Henryk got out of bed, pulling on his pants. Together, they made their way to the unfamiliar kitchen and set the table for lunch. Aniela pulled out a bowl of puréed vegetables from her bag, and offered it to Henryk. She put Wanda on her lap and tied a bib around her neck.

Henryk fed Wanda tiny spoonsful of the puréed vegetables, coaxing Wanda to eat with funny faces and noises, and Wanda ate each spoonful, eager to please him. Aniela watched the interplay with a smile. This was heaven, just being here with her husband and baby, acting like today was a normal occurrence.

"*Ta-ta*!" Wanda said, as she gulped down a spoonful of carrots.

Henryk stopped, spoon in mid-air, and turned surprised eyes to Aniela. "Did she just say *ta-ta*?" he said, incredulously.

Aniela glowed with pride and joy. "She did! You smart girl..." she said, kissing Wanda on her pink cheek. "You brilliant girl, you did say *ta-ta*!"

"*Ta-ta*!" Wanda said again, enjoying the attention.

Henryk whooped with joy, and kissed Aniela and then Wanda in excitement.

"We have been practicing all week," Aniela admitted. "In all honesty, I never actually got her to say it. She has a flair for timing, doesn't she?"

Henryk laughed, and Aniela joined in. Wanda started laughing, too, the way children do when they want to be included but don't understand. Nothing was more beautiful than the sound of the three voices laughing together.

Henryk just stared at Aniela's laughing face, her eyes sparkling with vibrancy and joy. He sighed, almost to himself. "How I have missed your happy eyes."

After lunch, they moved to the living room, where Henryk played with Wanda on the floor and the couple caught up on the many things they had each missed in one another's life.

Henryk spoke vaguely about his life. "I have a pseudonym. I won't reveal it to you, Aniela, for your protection. I cannot give away any information that could lead them to you or us. All you need to know is that my code name is Ox. We conduct attacks on Nazi targets, and it is dangerous."

Henryk's face clouded over. "And I must tell you, there is a chance that I may not come home. The Nazis are feeling the brunt of our efforts. We blow up rail lines, transformers, electrical stations, depots and warehouses regularly. We are disrupting their war machine, but the Germans become more and more ruthless in trying to hunt us down. We were each given a pill in case we are captured. By oath, we must be prepared to take our own life rather than reveal secrets under torture."

Aniela stared at her husband with wide, frightened eyes. "I understand. Is there any way for me to get in contact with you?"

Henryk lay on his back and picked up Wanda over his head, who squealed with delight.

After a few minutes, he put her down and turned his gaze to Aniela. "If you really needed to be in touch, you can come back here and ask Dorota to pass me information. It may take a while, and it would put others at risk, so don't do that unless you direly need me."

"And Dorota?" Aniela pressed. "Would she come find me if something happened to you? If you were hurt, or…" She couldn't bring herself to say "dead".

"Someone from the Home Army would find you and let you know… if that comes to pass," Henryk said, his jaw firm and his face grim. He stole a look at Aniela, who sat on the couch, head lowered, looking at folded hands in her lap. He could see the tension and worry emanating from her every pore.

"Why don't you do something safer, Henryk?" Aniela asked, her voice thin. "Couldn't you write for the underground newspaper?"

"Of course I could," Henryk said with exasperation, running his hand through his hair. "Now is the time for action. I can no longer sit on the sidelines and *report*. I'm fighting for everything I love here."

Aniela swallowed, at a loss for words. Henryk glanced at her, noting her face entombed in deep sadness.

"But we do have our fun at the Krauts' expense," he said, trying to lighten the mood.

Aniela looked up to meet his gaze, seeing a coaxing smile in those eyes. She smiled tremulously, allowing herself to be drawn in. "Do tell."

Henryk smiled widely. "OK, dancing girl. This story has been passed around throughout the Home Army and we all love sharing it.

"As you well know, nothing pleases the Germans more than lording themselves over those that they perceive as weak or subhuman. Nothing infuriates them or undermines their act of terror as completely as a joke at their expense.

"My buddy from Toruń spoke of an incident involving the statue of Copernicus in the main square. There was an inscription on the base of the monument that read: *To Copernicus. From His Countrymen*. Well, the Germans removed the inscription and had it replaced with a new one: *To the great German Astronomer*. The statue was right across from the Gestapo headquarters. One day, a crew of workmen in overalls strolled up to the statue and unscrewed the new plaque and took it away.

"The German sentry on duty had no suspicions, and assumed the removal to be sanctioned by the authorities, as no one would dare such a brazen act, in broad daylight, no less. Three weeks passed before anyone in authority even noticed that their plaque had been removed.

"A proclamation was posted all over the town, signed by the Governor himself, that said, *Recently, criminal elements removed the tablet from the Copernicus monument for political purposes. In reprisal, I order the removal of the Janko the Musician monument for political reasons. At the same time, I give full warning that, should similar acts be perpetrated, I shall order suspension of all food rations for the Polish population of Toruń for the term of one week.*"

"Janko the Musician?" Aniela interrupted, leaning forward. "The protagonist of the Henryk Sienkiewicz story about the peasant child with great musical talent?"

"The very one."

"They removed a statue of a *fictional* character for political reasons?" she pressed, a look of surprise on her face.

"Yes, exactly," Henryk continued with a grin. "And sure enough, the Germans dragged the statue of Janko the Musician from his pedestal and into the museum vault. But the very next morning, no one could miss the large inscription painted in tar on the walls of the museum that read: *People of Toruń: I am here. Signed, Janko the Musician.*"

Aniela laughed, holding her hands over her mouth.

"But here is the best part," Henryk continued, delighted to see his wife's laughing face. "A week or so later, a new poster appeared all over town, in the same exact font, format and typeset as the Governor's. Very official-looking. It read: *Recently, criminal elements removed the Janko the Musician monument for political reasons. As a reprisal, I order the prolongation of winter on the eastern front for the term of two months. Signed, Nicolaus Copernicus.*"

Aniela guffawed. Henryk laughed along with her, as Wanda watched her laughing parents with observant eyes.

At about five, the buzzer rang and Henryk sprang to attention. Startled, Aniela gave Henryk a worried look. "Are we expecting anyone?"

Henryk looked at the clock on the wall and laughed quietly. "I can't believe it slipped my mind. My mother has instructions to meet us here. That must be her. Can you check and let her in?"

"Of course," Aniela said. "What a lovely reunion."

Henryk caught his breath and whispered, "Yes, I have all my girls close to me."

Aniela checked the peephole, and seeing her mother-in-law, quickly ushered Pani Bartosz in.

Upon seeing Aniela, Pani Bartosz's face lost its tension and a look of pure relief settled over her features. "So it's true then if you are here. Henryk is here!"

"Mamo!" Henryk said, pulling her in from the hallway and wrapping his mother in a bear hug. Stunned, she tried to hug back and sniffled with emotion.

"My boy!" She took his face in her hands. "My beautiful boy. It is so good to see you, my son."

Henryk sat his mother on the couch and told her as much about his life with the Home Army as he could share. The whole time, he had Wanda on his lap, and bounced her up and down until she grew bored. Then they were on the floor, and he played horsy with her until Wanda was exhausted and wanted to return to Aniela. Aniela laid Wanda down between herself and Pani Bartosz, who was watching everything with misty eyes.

"It is so nice to see you as a family," she stated. "To see us as a family again. This war has split so many families up; one has to wonder if we'll ever see another day like today again."

Aniela quickly responded, "Of course we will. The work that Henryk and the Home Army is doing will bring the Germans to their knees. And before long, Britain and France will unite to defeat the Nazis. We will have our country back."

Henryk looked at Aniela with surprise. "You speak with such confidence…"

Aniela smiled, a bit sadly. "When I think of all that I've lost during this war, all that we've lost, I must believe that we will persevere and that our lives will be worth living after this is all over. I must believe that the risks you take are not in vain. If not, what is all this loss and suffering for?"

"You are right." Henryk gazed at her with fresh eyes. The naive, somewhat apolitical girl had left him, and now sat a self-possessed woman, his wife, ready to fight for what was hers.

An unbidden thought came to mind, when they had argued about his favorite book, *With Fire and Sword*. He had argued that war was noble, and that the death and destruction that encircled war was part of a valiant and necessary struggle. Henryk had to admit, he had doubts. He was fighting for what was right, but facing defeat after defeat. Seeing friends and comrades blown up senselessly and babies growing up never knowing their fathers, it was hard to justify the valor of war.

"Let's not talk of war today," Henryk said. "Tomorrow, I'll leave and go underground. We are safe for this one night. Let us just be a family."

Pani Bartosz volunteered to prepare dinner, and was pleased to find the kitchen stocked with flour and potatoes. She prepared dumplings while her family mooned over one another in the next room. She hummed as she worked, pleased to know that her one surviving child was safe and under the same roof as she, even if for just one night.

The apartment was soon filled with delicious aromas, and Aniela set the table and helped Pani Bartosz with the final touches of the meal. They sat down, just looking at one another, as if they each couldn't believe that this was all real.

"Gratitude," Aniela said, after the prolonged silence. "How can I express my gratitude for such a day as today?"

Pani Bartosz nodded. "I feel God's presence protecting the Bartosz family. I often wondered about God's existence, especially in war, but today, I feel his presence."

Henryk gave his mother an indulgent look. "From what I have seen in battle, I do not feel that God cares one whit about the arguments and squabbles of man. But I do feel that the love of family... the feeling I have today is... transcendent. It's as close to God as I have ever felt."

"Hear, hear," Aniela said, clinking glasses.

And as the sun set, they lingered over their meal, hanging on to each other's words.

Aniela visited her mother-in-law in Wieliczka at least once a month. In turn, Pani Bartosz plied her with staples from the farm, which helped the family avoid some of the food shortages. Aniela somewhat envied the choice her mother-in-law had made, to turn away German customers and hide herself on the family farm. But Aniela had a daughter and a mother to take care of, and she could not be so choosy. It didn't always go down easy, working for the oppressors knowing that Henryk was fighting the very system that employed her.

"I have given up tailoring," Pani Bartosz said. "Poles have no money for such things. And I am not eager to land German customers."

"We all have to give up things we love," Aniela said softly.

Pani Bartosz nodded. "If you ever tire of living with your mother, consider moving to the countryside. It may be safer there for a girl with your looks."

Henryk turned surprised eyes to Aniela. "You no longer live at our apartment?"

Pani Bartosz shot Aniela a look of contrition, realizing that this news would likely upset Henryk.

"No, I don't, Henryk," Aniela said softly. "I gave it up right before Wanda was born."

A muscle danced in his jaw as he took this in. "I understand, of course." But he looked upset, and Aniela and Pani Bartosz shared a look of concern as they both read his discomfort.

"Lots of apartments are being seized by the Nazis," Aniela continued. "There is no telling how long anyone can keep an apartment these days. The best places are now all inhabited by Germans, and more and more keep flooding in."

"Yes, yes," Pani Bartosz said in quick agreement. "That's why it is good to share and economize. Who knows how long this will last before things get better?"

Henryk stood up and gathered up the dishes, placing them in the sink. With his back to them, he said in a quiet voice, "It is hard on a man to not be able to provide, and protect, the people he loves. I know you have had to make some hard choices, to sacrifice. I do not judge that. I just wish…" He sighed deeply. "Never mind."

Aniela stood up and hugged him from behind, resting her head on his strong back.

"We're all trying our best, Henryk," she whispered. "Let us just enjoy this night together… Let's not let reality creep into our cocoon."

Henryk turned around and looked down at his wife, whose eyes sparkled with devotion, and he sighed deeply, pushing his negative feelings aside. Just Aniela's touch made desire jolt through his body as he felt her pressed to him and he breathed in her lavender scent. He looked over Aniela's crown of hair to where his mother sat at the table, spooning food to Wanda.

"Mother," he said, his voice firm, "I hope you will understand, but I need to be alone with my wife now. Will you keep Wanda occupied for us?"

Pani Bartosz, shocked by the brazen request, recovered and stuttered, "Of course!"

"Good," Henryk said, taking Aniela by the hand and leading her back to the bedroom. "I have just one night and I'll be damned if I'm going to waste it."

Chapter 41

Different Preparations

Aniela was back at work, reviewing an order for supplies for Herr Neumann's approval. She had a hard time concentrating on the figures in front of her, and forced herself to start again for the third time.

Aniela's brain kept drifting back to those magical hours with Henryk. She recalled waking up to see Henryk's loving face as he studied his daughter. She smiled to herself as she envisioned him still playing on the floor with Wanda, or holding Wanda up over his head, with Wanda giggling infectiously.

It was difficult to concentrate on factory work, to the humdrum of paperwork and invoicing and payroll after the stolen moments they had spent together.

Aniela and Henryk had hardly slept at all Saturday night. Henryk had drunk from her lips like a man who had been lost in the desert.

"My dancing girl," he whispered, deep inside of her. "My dancing girl."

"Aniela," Herr Neumann's voice interrupted her reverie.

"Yes, sir," Aniela said automatically, blinking her eyes.

"I would like to dictate a letter to you," he said.

"Of course!" Aniela said, grabbing her notepad and walking toward his desk. She took a seat in front of him, awaiting his dictation.

"Dear Olga," Herr Neumann said, "I trust that this letter finds you well. I've been giving much thought about your concerns. I want to assure you that you will find Krakau very much to your liking. I have secured us a lovely home, close to the city center, which is within the very exclusive, Germans-only district and close to the General Government's seat. Many of the highest-ranking officers live in this area, and most have come with their wives and children. You will not be at a loss for fine company or social events. The ladies are active in organizing teas, socials and various activities, and there is no shortage of posh cafés and lovely restaurants. You will delight in the medieval architecture, the well-laid-out parks, and overall picturesqueness of this city. Unlike other parts of the territory, there are little signs of war here as it is a functioning capital city. I urge you to organize the packing up of our household in Essen, and to join me soon. Perhaps we can celebrate Christmas together here? I hope so. Yours truly, Helmut."

Herr Neumann concluded, brow arched, "So, what do you think? Will that convince her?"

Aniela looked over her notes. "I think so."

Herr Neumann paused. "Would you be willing to show her around a bit, if she does come? You know, give her a glimpse of the parts of Krakau you like?"

"Of course."

"So perhaps we should add something to that effect," he continued. "Please add something that my secretary, a fine Polish woman with perfect manners and perfect German, can be her personal tour guide. She won't be without female companionship. That is important to her."

"I will type this up for you for your approval."

"Excellent," Herr Neumann said, relieved. "I hope this will do the trick. Thank you."

Aniela returned to her desk. As she started converting her shorthand stenography into German, she paused at one of Herr Neumann's sentences: "there are little signs of war here". She stared at that sentence for quite a while. For her, war and occupation were as present and real as the empty space greeting her every morning in bed. Herr Neumann's reality was so different from her own. How could they really be living in the same place and time? How could two realities be so different?

Chapter 42

A Little Teatime

January, 1941

To her husband's delight, Olga Neumann arrived by Christmas. She was in her fifties, with the thickening waist and ankles of middle age. She had a round face that featured dark blue eyes, a snub nose, a small mouth and wide forehead under mousy brown hair. She was not a pretty woman, but nevertheless there was a pleasantness to her face that reminded Aniela of a doll. It was almost as if a child's facial proportions were shifted onto the face of an adult, middle-aged woman.

Olga entered the factory dressed in a twill coat, woolen scarf and fine hat with a feather. She looked around the office with critical eyes, laying a gloved finger on the top of a filing cabinet to check for dust. The office was on the second floor, and looked over the manufacturing floor, where workers and artisans worked the large ovens and blew glass.

She stood in front of the window, appraising the hubbub.

"This is quite an operation, Helmut," she said, a note of appreciation in her voice.

"It wasn't easy setting up a factory, but we managed to do it. And the Reich is very pleased with the quality of our wares and the pace of production. Many of the finer families know of our work and products."

"Is that so?" Olga asked, adjusting her hat. "I do hope I will be able to meet with some of these finer families. It is very important for the wife of a leading manufacturer to be in the right circles. It is only befitting your station, and mine."

"Of course! I'm sure we'll meet all the best families," he assured her. "I have not had much time for socializing due to my workload, but now that you are here, my dear, we will make that our priority."

Olga Neumann nodded in satisfaction and turned to Aniela. "And you, young lady," she said, noting Aniela's trim form and pretty face. "You are the woman Helmut suggested could get me accustomed to Krakau, are you not?"

"I am."

"Good, then. Well, Helmut dear, I hope you don't mind, but I'll have your secretary take me around presently. I want to see where the society ladies convene. Aniela, will you take me to the cafés Helmut mentioned?"

Aniela paused. Working for the enemy was a necessary evil, one that she did to provide for herself, for Wanda and for her mother. Playing a tour guide for her boss' wife was not something Aniela wanted to do. It felt a bit like inviting someone into your home and having them walk off with the family china.

Helmut sensed Aniela's reluctance and gave her a reassuring smile. "It's fine, Aniela. I can manage on my own here and any service you perform for Frau Neumann is a service to me."

"Excellent," Frau Neumann said. "Grab your coat. Let's be off." She turned to her husband and gave him a kiss on the cheek, and left with Aniela.

"What's the best way to go?" Olga said, her eyes twinkling with excitement.

It was a cold but dry day, but Aniela doubted that Olga would be up for walking — it was about forty minutes by foot to reach the fine cafés on Floriańska Street from the factory.

"Do you mind going by tram?" Aniela offered, smiling tightly.

"Not at all," Olga said, and they made their way to the stop. As the tram pulled up, Aniela automatically entered by the rear doors, where the back benches were reserved for Poles and were separated by a rope from the Germans at the front.

"No, no," Olga said, taking Aniela gently by the arm. "Please sit with me up front."

"If they ask for IDs, they could arrest me for being in the wrong section, Ma'am. I would rather not take the risk."

Olga's mouth opened in surprise, but she nodded in understanding.

"I'll sit at the front of the Polish section so I'll be close to you," Aniela offered. "And I'll signal when we're at our stop."

"Of course," Olga agreed.

Aniela signaled to Olga to exit the tram and they rejoined each other on the curb.

"My word," Olga mused. "I keep forgetting that you are not a real German. With your perfect German, and your pretty blonde looks, I'm sure nobody would question you. You look like you belong in our advertisements for the Vaterland."

Aniela smiled at the attempt at a compliment. "Thank you, Frau Neumann. But there are a lot of guards and checkpoints all over the city, so I must take care."

"Yes," Olga quickly agreed. "I must talk to Helmut about this. Surely, with his influence, he may be able to get you exactly the paperwork needed. That way we can travel together and not have these little inconveniences."

Aniela nodded, but kept quiet. She was well aware that the path toward access to German zones was through the *Volksdeutsches*, and she prayed neither Helmut nor Olga would pressure her to renounce her Polishness. How such an act would have tormented her late father and eviscerate Henryk, who was now God knows where, hiding out and risking his life in the effort for them to remain truly and utterly Polish.

Aniela escorted Olga to Café Merkury, where the sign on the door clearly read "For Germans Only".

Olga hesitated, a bit nervous to be entering by herself. Through the windows, they could see finely dressed women, laughing and enjoying coffee and desserts, as if they had not a care in the world. Many had lovely mink stoles around their necks, and tailored gloves on their hands.

"I'll wait outside here for you, Ma'am," Aniela said.

Olga's face registered trepidation. "It is frightfully cold for you to wait out here. I'll just pop in to take a look. I shan't be long."

Aniela nodded, and Olga entered the café. She could see Olga smiling conspicuously at the ladies dining there, hoping to be drawn into their circle and trying to look nonchalant as she appraised the venue. She sat down by herself at a table in the corner and ordered herself a tea, her eyes never leaving the other customers. Whenever someone's glance happened to land on Olga, she smiled brightly and congenially, reminding Aniela of a dog that was desperate for a pat.

To her word, Olga finished her tea quickly and paid the bill. She rejoined Aniela on the street within twenty minutes.

She was breathless with excitement. "Yes, yes. Such a fine place. Thank you for taking me here. I believe I overheard two women talking about a great society ball that is to take place at the governor's quarters at the end of the month. The ladies mentioned what an elegant and fine affair it is to be. I must ask Helmut about an invitation. Such an event will surely put me, uh, put us on the map in Krakau!"

Chapter 43

Henryk's Mission

January, 1941

S hots whizzed by his head. Henryk ducked, and sprinted away from the railway tunnel. They had chosen this night to lay the bomb because it was dark and moonless. The bullets ricocheted off the stone tunnel walls, missing him, as he made it to the tree-line and stumbled into the forest.

The forest had become a haven for him, as well as the many men and soldiers that now made up the partisan Home Army. Henryk didn't pause to catch his breath, and continued deeper into the forest until he heard a familiar call, like an owl, that signaled that Marek was close by.

Henryk cupped his hands around his mouth, replying with the same call. Moments later, the two men found each other and hugged warmly. They were both thin, wearing increasingly threadbare clothes, with four days of beard growing on their rugged faces.

Henryk's face split into a relieved smile. "I set up the charge. When the weight of the train hits it early this morning, both the train and the tunnel will be dust."

"Well done," Marek said. "Any trouble?"

"There was a guard in the watch tower," Henryk admitted. "He spotted me just as I was finishing up."

Henryk patted himself down, to make sure. "He fired. And missed."

"Well, let's keep moving, then," Marek said. "He'll likely send out the dogs."

Henryk nodded, and the two continued trekking through the barren forest. Moving helped them feel warmer, though in reality they were cold, hungry and tired. They kept a brisk pace. They began to relax after an hour, when they stopped to listen for pursuers, and heard just the sounds of birds waking.

They made it to a small stream and navigated alongside of it, hugging it until they came upon a small cabin, hidden deep in the forest. Relief flooded through Henryk at the sight of smoke escaping the chimney. With hands and fingers stiff with cold, Marek knocked on the door using the secret cadence of a friendly caller.

Moments later, the door was unbolted and they were ushered inside a rustic, one-room cabin. They both moved straightaway to the tiny coal-burning stove and started rubbing their hands, not bothering to remove their coats or hats.

They were greeted by Kuba, Piotr and Bendyk, the other members of their group. Each of the men used a pseudonym, and nobody knew one another's true identity.

"Everything went all right?" Bendyk inquired, handing a cup of ersatz tea to them.

"Yes," Henryk said, too tired to elaborate. After months of living the life of an underground soldier and freedom fighter, it no longer seemed relevant to cite all the close calls and near-death experiences. It was all in a day's work. As a partisan soldier, his journey to the warm cabin had been one of living on the edge, of lucky breaks, split decisions and extreme caution.

Two years earlier, after he had pushed the dead body of his compatriot, Arek Bukowski, off of him in the large expanse of a battlefield in Tomaszów-Lubelski, Henryk had stumbled into a forest much like the one he had run to tonight. But that night, he had no plan — just the simple primal desire to live, to survive and to escape the Germans.

That forest was dense and large, and after a night of wandering aimlessly, he came upon a ragtag group of Polish soldiers who had also escaped and were trying to figure out what to do.

One of the soldiers knew of Henryk's platoon and gave him unwelcome news. "General Dąb-Biernacki ordered the platoon to surrender, and fled to save his own skin, abandoning his men. So much for Polish fortitude and leadership, huh?"

Henryk shook his head. "We're losing this war: our leadership is in disarray, communications are totally cut off, our weapons are inferior."

"So what are we to do?" an infantryman said. "We surrender, they'll take us as Prisoners of War."

Henryk's jaw was firm. "I can't speak for you, but I'm not going to stop fighting. Even if our leaders surrender and abandon us, I will not abandon my country."

The men put their fists to their hearts and erupted, "Hear, hear!" in solidarity.

They lived in the forests for an erratic week. They traveled by night, avoiding main roads. They had no leader, no ammunition, no rations and no plan. Some of the men argued they should try Kraków, and seek to make contact with other resistance fighters and regroup there. Others wanted to make it to Warsaw, but the villagers that sheltered them warned that Warsaw was still under siege.

And then they heard from a priest that on September 28th, 1939, General Czuma had finally capitulated after twenty-eight days of heavy fighting, artillery bombings and mass destruction. About ten percent of Warsaw's buildings were demolished and another forty percent were heavily damaged. The water works were destroyed by bombers and Warsaw neighborhoods had no potable water, nor water with which to extinguish the fires caused by the constant bombardment. No Allied support came, food and ammunition were scarce or non-existent, and it became pointless to continue fighting two enemies with no chance of winning. The city, once the jewel of the East, was in ruins. Dead bodies, those of citizens, soldiers, horses and house pets, littered the streets amongst piles of rubble and chaos.

On those final days of September, 1939, the President of the Polish Republic, Ignacy Mościcki, resigned. Power was transferred to Władysław Raczkiewicz, who was in Paris setting up Poland's government in exile. Raczkiewicz immediately took his constitutional oath at the Polish Embassy and became President of the Republic of Poland. Raczkiewicz then appointed General Władysław Sikorski to be Prime Minister, and following Edward Rydz-Śmigły's stepping down, made Sikorski Commander-in-Chief of the Polish Armed Forces.

By October 1st, 1939, the Polish government and military leadership were either safely in exile, or making their way to the border in attempts to leave the country. Those who were not abroad or trying to escape fell into two camps: those who surrendered and became PoWs; and those, like

Henryk and his band of men, who stayed in Poland and vowed to continue the fight as part of the remaining Home Army.

General Sikorski, the new Commander in Chief of the Polish Armed Forces, made contact with the generals still left in Poland and instructed them to set up a Home Army, a resistance organization, that would aid the Allies in all matters needed: espionage, intelligence, sabotage, field reports, propaganda, etc.

For the months of October and November, the numbers of soldiers were thinned out by raids and ambushes by Germans and Russians alike. Eventually, those who had managed to elude such a fate were told of the Home Army and the mission to protect Poland from within.

Henryk immediately joined, taking the vow:

Before God the Almighty, Before the Holy Virgin Mary, Queen of the Crown of Poland, I put my hand on this Holy Cross, the symbol of martyrdom and salvation, and I swear that I will defend the honor of Poland with all my might, that I will fight with arms in hand to liberate her from slavery, notwithstanding the sacrifice of my own life, that I will be absolutely obedient to my superiors, that I will keep the secret whatever the cost will be.

Henryk was assigned to the Kraków district, given the pseudonym Damian Fatela, and eventually false documents. He was assigned to an outpost commander, "Felicjan Zaleski", who headed a platoon of fifty men. Each platoon operated as a basic organizational and tactical unit. The men were divided into groups of five, and nobody knew true names or identities. Each member of the group was allowed to know only his four fellow members, each one of them in his turn creating a new group of five. Their main aims were to disrupt the German war operation by putting on pressure through resistance: diversion, sabotage, and of course, propaganda.

This had been Henryk's existence. Exhausted, Henryk lay down. He fell asleep almost immediately, but one particular face appeared before him, golden hair loose over her shoulders, smiling at Wanda.

Chapter 44

Digging Up the Past

March, 1941

There was a welcome break in the bitter winter temperatures. The mission was to retrieve weapons buried when the Polish troops surrendered in Tomaszów-Lubelski. The defeated soldiers knew that weapons would be confiscated by German or Russian armies, and they wisely hid them away. Henryk's squad was given a general map of the area with information on where each platoon had buried their weapons back in October, 1939.

It had not been safe or feasible to retrieve the weapons before, as the area had been teeming with enemy soldiers, and then the freezing temperatures entombed the weapons in the hard earth. The task was a daunting one. First, they had to locate the sites, then they had to clandestinely dig up the weapons — which should number in the thousands and would likely include tommy guns, machine guns, grenades, and flame-throwers.

"We'll not likely find any ammunition," Henryk muttered, as he and Marek descended on the first site. Kuba, Piotr and Bendyk were fanned out, keeping watch.

Marek grunted in agreement. It was late afternoon and the sun would set in an hour or so. They hoped the ground would be warm enough for their shovels to move the earth.

They had no idea what condition the weapons would be in. The soldiers had been trained to oil and seal the guns to prevent rust, but such methodical tasks are hard to ensure on the best days, never mind in the heat of battle.

They started digging, strenuous work as the earth was thawed but still heavy and unwieldy. After about half an hour, they came across the first cache. Sweat poured down their backs and dripped off their noses, despite the cool air.

They pulled out waxed canvas bags, covered in dirt, and peered inside. The bag was full of *karabinek* rifles, a bolt-action short rifle. There was some evidence of rust on the blades, but in general, they were in good condition.

"Felicjan will be pleased with these," Marek said.

They dug up several more bags full of similar weapons, each bag containing about twenty-five rifles. They arranged them onto their backs and began trekking through the woods. Marek and Henryk hunched under the taxing weight. They were in for several trips.

They met up with Kuba. Piotr and Bendyk were standing sentry and would take the next shift of digging up and carrying the weapons to their depot.

Seeing Marek and Henryk laboring under the heavy loads, Kuba jumped up and helped them shake the packs off their backs. They fell to the ground in a heavy clatter.

"Well done," Kuba said, admiring the load.

Marek arched, stretching his aching back. "We're in for a long night," he groaned.

"We procured a horse and wagon," Kuba said. "That will help us transport these to the checkpoint."

"What I wouldn't do for a truck," Henryk said, ruefully.

The Nazis outlawed the use of cars and trucks by ordinary Poles, and only those with proper identification and work permits could get access. Life seemed to be evolving backwards, as almost everything was now transported by horse and wagon. Nevertheless, a horse and wagon would attract a lot less attention as they moved the weapons south.

They worked all night, digging and moving the guns, amassing a huge arsenal. Though exhausted, they could not rest, and around six in the morning, Piotr directed them to a path in the forest where a large draft horse and wagon waited. They loaded up the bags onto the wagon and covered the bags with bales of hay. Two men would drive together in the front, one would be hidden with the guns under the hay, and the two final men would hug the road, watching from the front and back for danger and to employ the signal.

They set out at seven in the morning, well within curfew hours, and when most farmers were up and hauling their goods alongside country roads. They kept off of lanes that were flagged as busy or potentially dangerous, and they made their way slowly to their destination.

Henryk sat in the front with Kuba. Henryk had the most experience with horses, and he held the reins confidently as the kilometers slowly ticked by. Watching the swaying back of the brown gelding in front of him, his mind wandered to Willow, the farm on Wieliczka, of proposing to Aniela under the willow tree by the stream. That life seemed so far away now, one could almost imagine it was all a dream, if they allowed themselves to believe the Nazi propaganda that this life was the new Polish reality.

Chapter 45

In Search of Cheddite

After the squad's success in digging up and transporting the guns to a safe house, the men were briefed about their next mission.

One of the main challenges facing the underground army was armaments. While retrieving the buried arms was an important first step, many of the guns rusted or were older models that were not suitable for modern warfare. The Home Army needed more than their old weapons to be an effective force against their occupiers.

The Home Army Commander-in-Chief, "*Grot*" or spearhead, stated a main directive was to secure materials to make explosives. The materials were desperately needed for the making of hand grenades, bombs, and other explosives.

Outpost commander Felicjan met with Henryk's squad at an abandoned shed at the edge of an industrial area outside of Kielce. The shed was damp and smelled of mold, and there was dim light emanating from a single light bulb hanging from a wire.

Felicjan explained that the greatest difficulty was procuring basic materials for explosives, such as saltpeter. All such materials were heavily guarded and controlled by the Nazis. Partisan technicians brainstormed on how to recreate or procure these essential materials, and they soon settled on cheddite as the best option for the army's needs.

Originally manufactured in the town of Chedde, France, cheddite consisted of a high proportion of inorganic chlorates mixed with nitroaromatics as well as paraffin or castor oil as a moderate for the chlorate. Cheddite made the ideal explosive material, as the main ingredients were likely to be available or produced locally for quarrying or farming.

For cheddite, the army needed potassium chlorate, which was not easily had. Felicjan said Polish Intelligence had zeroed in on the one German-controlled plant that produced the chemical, in a town called Radocha, a few hours west of Kraków.

Felicjan, a hearty man in his late forties, was a commanding figure, with salt and pepper hair, a gray beard of at least five days' growth and dark, intense eyes.

He addressed the squad in a deep, confident voice. "We had other squads try procuring potassium chlorate, but each ended in failure. The Germans are on high alert. The first attempts were to steal the material directly from the factory. But the factory is too highly fortified. We now believe the only option for us is to stage a raid on railway wagons loaded with the chemical and leaving the plant."

Felicjan rolled out a map of the factory, which included the outgoing train lines. The men bent over to take a closer look in the dim light.

"We've information from our friends at the railway that they are to ship the material next Thursday between two and four a.m. That will be our chance," Felicjan said.

The friends he was referring to were Polish workers employed in rail transportation in various capacities. While many Germans were moving into the area, displacing Poles from their homes, towns, and provinces, there simply were not enough Germans to do all the necessary work. The Germans had to rely on Poles to operate the train lines, to work in factories, and to transport materials. Of course, the Poles held no positions of management or power, but these friendly allies were the Home Army's moles implanted right in the heart of the Nazi system and eager to help. Many men and women risked their lives by aiding the partisans in simple and dramatic ways, and the Home Army could not function without their support.

It was a worker at the train depot that fed the information to Felicjan about the upcoming transport, and Henryk and his team got down to business organizing the raid. They settled on creating a diversion and using their meager firearms to overpower the guards on watch, unloading the potassium chlorate into awaiting trucks and hiding it in a designated safe house.

They decided to block the train tracks with large logs a few kilometers after a rail switch junction. The obstacle would slow the train to a stop, and the guards would likely deboard to investigate. From there, Henryk and Bendyk would crawl under the train and detach the last two cars. The railway worker had advised them that, if after disengaging the cars, the two could make it into the caboose and get the train moving, he'd switch the tracks to allow the train to progress in the opposite direction, away from the diversion and factory.

With luck, they'd drive a few kilometers, where another set of squads would be waiting in the shadows. There, they would quickly unload the train of its contents into awaiting trucks.

They went through the plan over and over. Henryk and Bendyk practiced disengaging a train car in pitch darkness, using a stopwatch to mark the decrease in time. For days they practiced, with help from their railway friend, and were able to execute the task in mere minutes.

Each man knew his role and was aware of the danger involved. Drivers were ready, porters were primed. Procuring the getaway trucks was no easy feat, but Felicjan said cryptically, "We have our ways," and nobody pressed the point.

They counted down the hours to the raid, positioning the logs in place at one thirty a.m., then hid in the shadows as they awaited the transport. Henryk could feel the blood pulsing in his temples as time slowly ticked by.

At 2.23 a.m., the train appeared in the distance. Kuba used a flashlight to signal its approach, and then the plan was put into action.

The conductor pulled the emergency brake and halted the train. Seconds later, Bendyk and Henryk skulked unseen under the carriage of the train, wiggling the connector, and using tools strapped to their bellies, quickly disengaging the cars.

Now came the really dangerous part — moving into the caboose to take control. They scaled the outside of the car until they made it to the end of the train, and on the count of three, burst into the caboose in unison. There were two men on guard, but they had the element of surprise, and Henryk threw himself at the first man, knocking the breath out of him, and he thrust him roughly against the wall. He pummeled his fists into the man, who crumpled with a groan. Henryk pulled twine from his pockets and quickly tied the man's hands together, relieved him of his guns, and threw him out of the train. Bendyk had also been successful in subduing the other guard, though he did take a couple of blows to his face, but was able to eject him from the caboose as well.

Henryk flashed the signal that they were in, and began moving the train in the opposite direction. The rail switches shifted their tracks, and they were on their way. They drove the train for what seemed like an exorbitantly long time, but was, in fact, only ten minutes, until flashing lights revealed the waiting crews and trucks in hiding.

Bendyk hit the brakes and they jumped out of the train and rushed to unload the cars with the containers of potassium chlorate. They worked like machines. Not a word was said while the cars were emptied, the train was abandoned, and the trucks driven away into the night. Lights turned off, they slowly made their escape.

Hours later, the men regrouped at the safe house, where Felicjan was waiting. He slapped each man on the back.

"You men did an amazing thing today," he said, pulling out a bottle of vodka from his duffel bag. "We secured two whole railway wagons. That's one and a half tons! Well done, my brave compatriots!"

The men passed the vodka around, each taking a celebratory swig.

"We really got them this time," Piotr bragged. "Not a shot was fired, no one was injured. Triumph!"

"Hear, hear!" the men exclaimed, drunk on their success. They were the first squad to procure potassium chlorate, and had succeeded where others had failed.

Henryk felt overwhelmed with pride, camaraderie, and of purpose that was so intense, he vowed to do anything for his squad and the call of the Home Army. He thought about his time writing about political events for the newspaper, and as he sat down on an old chair and stretched his legs out in front of him, he had to admit to himself that, despite the risks, he much preferred to be a man of action in the midst of events than to be reporting on them from some smoky newsroom.

He had never felt more important or needed in his life.

Chapter 46

Podgórze

Spring, 1941

The latest proclamations had residents on edge. The news was everywhere: posters, in the German-produced Polish language newspaper, on State-run radio, blaring from loudspeakers across every corner of town: the Jews of Kraków were to be resettled to Podgórze.

Podgórze was a rather shabby neighborhood on the other side of the Vistula River, and many of the fine Jewish families didn't understand how they could be forcibly removed from their own homes and relocated to such a slum.

Irena burst in, upset by the news, and found her mother.

"All of my in-laws are being told they must relocate," she said with a grimace. "Why are they putting all these Jews in one neighborhood? How will they all fit? There are sixty-eight thousand Jews in Kraków — have you seen Podgórze? It's a dump."

Aniela entered, leaning over to hold her daughter by the hands as Wanda was taking steps. Wanda was now walking by herself and a bit unsteadily, and had to be watched like a hawk as she streamed around the apartment in a blur of uncoordinated movements.

"And what of you, Irena?" Aniela asked. "And Adam's family?"

Irena paused, a pained expression on her face. "As I am not Jewish, I am not compelled to relocate, as long as I can show my birth certificate. I feel awful for my in-laws and Adam's siblings. As you know, many of them are not even practicing Jews, so they feel like they are being swept up in some religious dragnet!"

"So that means Pan Rozenberg, too?" Aniela said, realizing the scope of the edict.

"Yes, everyone," Irena said. "Can you imagine? They are relocating every Jew to one neighborhood. The deadline is March 3rd. If any Jew refuses to comply, they risk being hunted down by the police and shot. And if anyone tries to help or hide a Jew, their whole family will be shot."

Aniela sat down on the couch next to Irena and reached for her hand. She squeezed it, offering what little comfort she could tender. But what was there to say? Their world was descending into madness. Nothing made sense.

By the March 3rd deadline, vast neighborhoods and streets throughout Kraków were emptied of Jewish residents. Podgórze, which previously had three thousand residents, now absorbed huge numbers. The people who lived in Podgórze were kicked out; some were actually able to move into apartments and homes vacated by the Jews.

Krakovians watched in grim silence as the streets were filled with Jews rolling their possessions in carts and wheelbarrows. German police lined the streets, separating the Polish Jews from their non-Jewish population. If someone broke from the sidelines to help or embrace a Jewish neighbor, they were severely beaten by bully club or shot on the spot. The Jewish population, many of whom had lived in Kraków peacefully since the thirteenth century, vanished virtually overnight.

Hans Frank had vowed to make Kraków a "racially pure" city, and residents soon understood the full import of his plan. Not only were the Jews crammed into Podgórze, as many as four families to one apartment, but forced labor crews constructed walls around the area, and it became apparent that the Jews were being penned in. Even the buildings facing non-Jewish areas had their windows bricked, as Jews were forbidden to see "normal" life. Jews and non-Jews noted with alarm that the walls that enclosed Podgórze had rounded arches, resembling tombstones. Rumors spread that it was Hans Frank's wife, Brigitte, who had insisted on this morbid touch.

The entrance to the ghetto was guarded and no one could come in or go out. The food rations allotted to working Jews in Podgórze resulted in a mere three hundred and fifty calories a day, and people began starving, then dying in the street. It soon became commonplace for a crew of men to roll a cart around collecting corpses at the end of each day.

Many residents were stupefied by this brutal change of circumstances, and struggled to comprehend how to help. Smuggling food or medicine into the ghetto meant a death sentence. Smuggling someone out of the ghetto was also a difficult task, yet enterprising underground groups started using the sewer tunnels to bring in help or bring out people, often children. Still, most non-Jewish Poles stood by in shocked silence, afraid to risk their families, paralyzed by fear.

A couple of months later, Olga stopped by the factory in a chipper mood. She was elegantly dressed as usual, and strode in and headed towards Aniela.

"Aniela, my girl," she said warmly. "I desperately need to go shopping. I've managed to secure several invitations to society events and I must have the right thing to wear."

Aniela nodded politely. Olga turned to her husband. "Helmut, can you spare Aniela this afternoon? I could use her language skills."

Helmut, glancing at the pile of invoices, acquiesced. "Of course, dear. There is nothing that could not wait till tomorrow."

"*Wunderbar!*" Olga clapped her hands. "Oh, what fun we shall have, Aniela. I have a car waiting downstairs."

Aniela looked at her half-finished ledger with a pang of regret, and then grabbed her spring jacket and purse from behind her chair. She smiled at Herr Neumann and waved goodbye, knowing that he'd much rather have her stay and finish her work. But instead, she followed Frau Neumann down to the street, where an elegant Mercedes ran idling, complete with a driver.

"I didn't want to bother with that tram business," Olga said, conspiratorially. "Plus, a woman of my station should have a car and driver. Helmut agreed; he knows how important it is to keep up appearances."

Aniela paused, then opened the door and slid into the plush leather seats next to Olga. As Polish automobiles had been confiscated, it felt quite foreign to be sitting in a car.

They began weaving their way through the streets. It all seemed so different from inside; it felt safer being whisked away behind metal and glass, away from the random terrors of the Blue Police, chance roundups, or even just the ugliness of daily occupied life.

But with a sinking feeling, Aniela realized where they were going. They crossed the bridge over the Vistula and pulled up to the guarded entrance along the bricked-up walls to Podgórze. Frau Neumann unrolled the window to address the German guards manning the entrance to the ghetto.

"We are here to do some shopping, young man," Olga said.

"Let me see your papers, Ma'am," the guard said, noting the fine car and elegantly dressed woman.

Frau Neumann pulled out her Reich identity card and said, as if revealing a secret, "You may recognize the name. My husband, Helmut Neumann, is a great friend to the Reich. He runs the crystal and glass factory on Fatimska Street."

"Your ID card," the guard said to Aniela.

"She is my translator," Frau Neumann interrupted, "as well as my husband's secretary. She is harmless."

"ID, please," the guard repeated, and Aniela reached into her purse to present him her ID card and working papers. He examined her documentation carefully.

He turned to Frau Neumann. "We don't like to admit Poles into the ghetto for security reasons."

"Oh, nonsense!" Frau Neumann continued. "How am I to haggle without someone who can translate? This Pole is absolutely necessary for me to conduct my business here today."

The guard hesitated, clearly afraid to cross such a well-connected and influential lady, and nodded. "You may pass."

The driver slowly pulled the car into the ghetto, and Olga leaned over with a self-satisfied smile. "That's how it's done. Just a little confidence can go a long way in life. I heard that Brigitte Frank herself comes to the ghetto to shop for the best deals. I had to do the same."

Olga stepped out of the car, and a crowd of desperate Jews quickly encircled her, each begging her to buy some item or another. Aniela joined her, a bit overwhelmed by the melee. She could smell the stale scent of bodies living in too close quarters with too little soap or water. Several men competed for Olga's attention, wearing finely tailored clothes that looked like they had slept in them, offering fine, leather-bound books, a beautiful detailed globe, and an empty birdcage.

"I'm not interested in books or this... junk," Olga said haughtily, wrinkling her nose in distaste. "I heard there are fine deals to be found — furs, frocks, shoes, jewelry..."

She shot a look to Aniela, clearly needing a rescue.

Aniela stepped up and said in Polish, "I'm sorry, gentlemen. This German lady is only interested in ladies' clothes and jewelry."

One man's face broke open in naked hope. "Please ask your German to wait a moment. My wife has such items to sell..."

The man dashed away, and within five minutes, word had rippled throughout the ghetto that a German lady was shopping for women's clothes and accessories. Olga and Aniela were soon surrounded by women and men, each dangling items for sale. The noise of their offerings was deafening in Polish, German and Yiddish.

Olga examined every offering. There were designer dresses from Paris and Vienna. Mink and fox-fur stoles and muffs. She tried on several pairs of leather and satin gloves, splaying her fingers to examine the fit. Many of the Jews knew enough German to bargain directly with Olga, and her eyes narrowed as she haggled over price.

From time to time, Olga turned to Aniela and asked for her opinion. "What do you think? Does the blue fit me, or how about this garnet color?"

Aniela stiltedly replied, "I think the blue goes well with your eyes, but the garnet is very regal."

"True, true," Olga replied. "I'll take both."

She began negotiating the price down further. Olga spent two hours carefully inspecting the items, checking labels and seams for flaws, and coming back to the ones that she liked with an even lower price. Trapped in the ghetto, with no chance to earn unless employed in one of the local factories or working for the Jewish police, they were desperate for any chance of getting their hands on currency to buy food or medicine. What good was a mink stole or satin gloves? Those were sad vestments of a life no longer lived, and practicality and survival was the only currency that mattered now.

As Olga bartered, Aniela surveyed the dismal conditions. Down the street, she glimpsed several bodies lying on the sidewalk, frail and thin. She didn't know if they were alive, but from the awkward angle of twisted limbs, she didn't think so. Children, disheveled and dirty, wandered around her with glassy eyes, begging for food, whining in hunger. She felt sick to her stomach; it was hard to stand there knowing she was working for the very people who had created such an existence, such a perversion of capitalism, with no regard for the human misery.

The people trying to lure Olga to buy their items emanated desperation. Many had been well off before being forced into the ghetto, and they were slowly fraying in the cramped and undignified surroundings. There were Jews from all social strata, some Orthodox and wearing traditional garb, others in fine three-piece suits, looking like they needed a laundress. An old woman with a parasol, her hair in an old-fashioned bun and wearing a lace shawl, walked by the crowd and paid them no mind, as if she was out for a stroll.

Aniela had an apple in her purse, and she gave it to a pregnant woman. She asked about the Perelmuters and Pan Rozenberg, but to no avail. Aniela's heart broke when approached by begging children, and she couldn't help but see Wanda in their needy eyes. Where were their parents? Were they orphans? She reached into her purse and pulled out all her money, handing it to begging children and wailing old people.

Aniela's face was tense and drawn, as she tried to keep her emotions in check. She wanted to leave this hellish place, but was assailed by guilt because she, as a non-Jew, could leave, while they, for no fault of their own, could not. She wanted to go home, hug Wanda, and cry on her pillow.

At last, Olga was satisfied with her "shopping", and asked the driver to pop the trunk. She beamed with pride, having picked up four evening dresses, a fox stole, a mink coat, a tiara, two pairs of gloves, and various jewelry.

She motioned to Aniela to get into the car. The driver reversed, as hordes of people jumped out of the way, begging for one last look and a chance of a purchase. Aniela's head ached with suppressed emotion.

Olga turned a satisfied grin to Aniela. "Oh, boo-hoo! I didn't get a single thing for Helmut. Next time, we'll make sure to pick up something for him!"

Chapter 47

Barbarossa

May, 1941

L ife was a daily exercise in degradation. New proclamations were constantly posted — reminding the occupied of everything that was forbidden. It was forbidden to aid or hide Jews, forbidden to own a radio, forbidden to enter entire neighborhoods, or hide or assist a partisan. The German word *Verboten* was branded into their minds.

Many residents found the lack of news on the war's progress as well as the difficult conditions too harsh to surmount, and suicides were reported with alarming regularity. It was hard to remain hopeful as Germany's war machine rolled over and through Europe and as Poles wearily approached two years of occupation.

Irena, too, gave up her apartment. She had found work playing the violin in an exclusive, for Germans-only restaurant, but could not stay in her apartment, which bordered Kazimierz, the Jewish neighborhood. With most of its residents relocated to Podgórze, Kazimierz had become a ghost town, and few residents wanted to move into the desolate, dark and unsafe neighborhood.

Irena's mood was dark and gloomy. She fretted about the lack of news from the ghetto and from Adam. She was unsure of how to help her in-laws and felt the same bitter conflict as her sister did — while working for the enemy was required, it still left a poisonous taste in one's mouth. The household grew a bit again, as both daughters — both husbandless — lived with their widowed mother and Wanda and Harmony.

Germany was preparing for something big. Huge convoys of military vehicles, hundreds of thousands of horses, marching troops and heavy machinery were crossing the countryside and clogging up the city streets, all heading east.

On June 22nd, 1941, Germany attacked their ally, the Soviet Union. With tremendous force, the Germans crossed over their agreed-to border, the Molotov-Ribbentrop line, which divided Poland. The skies filled with war planes heading east, and Poles hunkered down, privately expressing some glee that the Soviets were betrayed by the Germans, just as the Poles were betrayed by the Soviets.

The Germans pushed the Russians back, and while no Pole was happy to see the advancing German troops, there was some solace in the artificial border dividing Poland being gone. Families separated could finally reunite, and there was a feeling that Poland was once again, not restored exactly, still occupied, but stitched together. News from the other side began trickling in. Ewa wrote a letter that she was safe in Białowieża and considering returning to Kraków if it were ever safe enough.

Irena received a letter from Adam, smuggled in from the underground. To her delight, she learned that Adam had been released from a work camp in Russia. He wrote that he would follow General Władisław Anders, who was en route to Persia, where the Polish army would meet with British Allies. After two years of living as a Russian prisoner, neither Adam nor other Polish PoWs could stomach the thought of fighting alongside their captors, who were now "on the same side" since the Russians had joined the Allies. Instead, the soldiers preferred to follow their charismatic General to Persia to recover, regain strength, and rejoin the fight for Poland's freedom.

As summer bled into fall and the earth froze, news trickled in that Japan had attacked a port in Hawaii called Pearl Harbor, and the Americans had finally joined the fight on the side of the Allies, on the same side that Poland was fighting for.

This information brought a renewed sense of hope in occupied lands, and belief began to grow that the Nazis' days were numbered, that they all just needed to hold on a bit more. But freedom was a long time in coming. 1942 began with no joy among Poles, and muted celebrations from Germans who were unhappy about the entrance of America into the war, and despite victories in the east, tensions were running high.

Even more proclamations, edicts and warnings plastered the city. One stated to turn in foreign currency, another to turn in gold and precious stones. The penalty for failure to comply was death or a one-way trip to a work camp. Corpses were strung from nooses in the town square, with signs which read "traitor" and "partisan" pinned to their chests. The Germans, perhaps fearing a turning tide in the war, doubled down on their efforts to control every facet of the lives they oppressed.

Germans seized local farms outside of Kraków, forcing people from their homes. The farmers were given just hours to pack, and within an instant, their hard-earned harvests were sent to enemy soldiers in the east. For the residents of Kraków, food supplies became immediately scarce. The markets displayed less and less, and ration cards couldn't buy food that wasn't there.

The pressure of the Yanks joining the war seemed to push the Nazi agenda into overdrive. Starting in June, 1942, the Germans began removing Jewish citizens from Podgórze. At first, those inside and outside the ghetto speculated that those selected were going to work details on German farms or factories. But the selections kept up at a brisk pace, and often included the young, the sick, even the pregnant. It became apparent that those selected were not going to work at all.

By June, 1943, all Jews had been liquidated from Podgórze. The loss of more than sixty-eight thousand Jews from Kraków was felt like a phantom limb — the remaining Poles felt the presence of long-time neighbors, friends, doctors, shop owners as if they were still there. But they were all gone, most never to be seen again.

Chapter 48

Lebensborn

April, 1944

It was a lovely spring day, and Pani Majewska brought Wanda to the factory in order to escape the apartment and to walk home together.

Aniela came down the steps and picked up Wanda, kissing her cheek warmly. Wanda was now four years old, and was a lovely girl with golden hair that grew in darling ringlets that framed big, light blue eyes.

A Mercedes pulled up and Olga Neumann stepped out, looking more elegant than ever. She wore a silk navy blue dress with butterfly sleeves, stockings with a smart, crisp seam up the back of her legs, and carried a Chanel purse.

She seemed surprised to see Aniela, and approached warmly.

"And who do we have here?" Olga said, crouching to be eye level with Wanda.

"This is my daughter, Wanda, and my mother, Kinga Majewska. Wanda, darling, can you say '*Guten Tag*'?"

Momentarily shy, Wanda looked up to her mother for encouragement. Aniela nodded patiently and mouthed the words "*Guten Tag*".

"*Gu-ten Tag*," Wanda said softly, momentarily bashful.

"Oh! Such a delightful child," Frau Neumann extolled. "Lovely eyes, and look at those long lashes! Such a beautiful child!"

Aniela smiled with pride, gazing down at her daughter. "Can you say '*Vielen Dank*? Thank you very much'?"

A little more confident now, Wanda responded quicker, "*Vielen Dank!*"

"She really is the picture of a perfect *Mädchen!*" Frau Olga said enthusiastically. "Well done, you clever girl! Well done."

Olga turned to Pani Majewska and Aniela. "I'm sorry to dash off so quickly, but I simply had to drop by to pick up Helmut for a reception at the Palace Hotel tonight. It's going to be a dashing event, and I won't allow him to make us even a second late."

"Well then, we shan't keep you," Aniela said politely. "Do have a good time."

"Thank you," Frau Olga said, rushing to fetch her husband.

Aniela turned back to her mother and daughter with an indulgent smile, and they started for home. They ambled with Wanda in the middle, the little girl holding tightly to her mother and grandmother's hands.

From that moment, Olga Neumann could not stop talking about what an impression Wanda had made on her. As a mother of two sons, both away at the front, she seemed to be entranced by the beautiful child. Aniela imagined that Olga, now past childbearing, and with no grandchildren in her near future, was drawn to Wanda like the daughter she longed for. She started to bring gifts for Wanda to the factory. Many of the gifts were items that no Pole could dream of attaining under occupation, including chocolate candies laid out in decorative tins, and a sunhat with silk bow with beautiful eyelet detail.

"You are too generous," Aniela protested, as Frau Neumann came by with a porcelain doll from famous German doll-maker, Käthe Kruse.

"I'd love to give her this gift personally," Olga Neumann said. "To see her face. As a girl, I always dreamed of having such a doll. It would mean the world to me to give it to her."

Aniela nodded her head. "I'll ask my mother to bring Wanda after my shift tomorrow, if you can stop by the factory after five p.m.?"

"*Wunderbar*," Olga said, packing up the doll. "I will take it home tonight. I'm not sure it will be safe here, even locked in the office, with all the Polish workers. Better safe than sorry, you know."

Aniela smiled tightly, letting the dig wash over her.

The following afternoon, Olga Neumann arrived at the factory with a large wrapped package. She smiled widely upon seeing Aniela, and placed the package on her husband's desk.

Herr Neumann smiled at his wife indulgently. "Did you have a nice day, dear?"

"Oh, very much," Olga replied, smiling widely. "I met some very important people this morning at the club, a Herr Grossman and Herr Schreiber, husbands of Gerti and Hedwig. They are eager to meet you, and tour the factory. I told them about what a fantastic job you have done turning this place around."

"Oh, that's nice, dear," Helmut said, rubbing the bridge between his eyes.

"I hope you don't mind," Olga said, lowering her voice, "but they may even stop over this very evening."

"So soon?"

"When it comes to making social connections," Olga said firmly, "one should never dally."

Moments later, Pani Majewska arrived with Wanda. They ascended the steps to the factory office, and Aniela immediately hugged her daughter in a warm embrace.

"Hello, Mama," Wanda said, putting her hand in her mouth. Pani Majewska gently pushed it away, with a slow negative nod.

"Can you say hello to Herr and Frau Neumann, Wanda?" Pani Majewska urged.

Wanda wiped her hand on her skirt and said, "Hello, Herr and Frau Neumann!" in perfect imitation of her grandmother's order.

Herr Neumann laughed. "Such a clever girl!"

Olga took the large wrapped package and presented it to Wanda, crouching down. "Do you know who this is for? It's for you, Wanda. Do you want to open it?"

Wanda nodded, a bit shyly, then sat down on the floor with the large package in her lap and tried to rip the paper away. She struggled a bit, as her fingers were still growing and were uncoordinated, and Aniela cooed, "Do you need help, Wanda?"

"No!" Wanda said firmly. "I can do it!" She stuck her tongue out in concentration as she fought with the paper and managed to pull it off the box.

After much concentration, she opened the box to find the beautiful porcelain doll with golden ringlets and painted glass eyes.

"Isn't she wonderful?" oozed Frau Neumann. "She looks like you, Wanda. That is why I had to get you this doll."

Wanda stared at the doll with wide eyes and reached out to touch the doll's stiff face with her little fingers.

"Pretty," Wanda said in Polish.

"Yes, *hübsch*," Aniela translated. "*Sehr hübsch*."

There was a knock on the door and Aniela rose to let in two men. She noted with surprise that they were dressed in the dark green wool uniforms of the SS. She had never seen such uniforms within the walls of the factory.

Olga jumped to attention. "Oh, please, do come in, Herr Grossman and Herr Schreiber," she said warmly. "This is the factory of my husband, Herr Helmut Neumann. Let me introduce you properly."

Herr Neumann stepped forward and offered his hand, greeting each man warmly.

"Herr Neumann," he said formally, saluting. "Heil Hitler."

"Heil Hitler. I'm *Gauleiter* Schreiber," one man corrected, and offered his hand to Herr Neumann.

"Nice to meet you," Herr Neumann replied. "Won't you take a seat? Aniela, can you offer these fine gentlemen coffee or tea?"

Aniela nodded. "Of course. What would you prefer, gentlemen?"

Herr Grossman took a seat and said, "Coffee, if you don't mind."

Aniela turned to the other man. "And you?" she asked politely.

Gauleiter Schreiber stared at Wanda, who sat on the floor with the large doll in her arms.

"Is this the little girl you told us about?" he asked Olga.

"Yes," Olga said quickly. "Isn't she just the picture of perfect Germanity?"

"She is," Gauleiter Schreiber said, patting Wanda on the head. "She looks like my Liesel did at that age. Amazing!"

Aniela hesitated, but seeing Gauleiter Schreiber's distraction, left to prepare coffee.

When she came back, she found Wanda clutching the doll, being held by Gauleiter Schreiber on his hip. Aniela put the coffee down and looked at her mother, for she felt something was amiss.

"She is perfect for the *Lebensborn* dictate to find suitable Aryan candidates," Gauleiter Schreiber said, brushing Wanda's soft cheek with the back of his fingers.

"I thought so," Olga said eagerly. "She is a clever girl, and already speaks quite a few German phrases. She'll adapt beautifully."

Aniela's skin prickled as she faced the man holding her daughter. "I'm sorry, sir. What are you referring to?"

"Our Aryanization policy," Herr Schreiber said. "Herr Heinrich Himmler has asked us to locate suitable children of Nordic traits to be sent to childless homes in Germany. I believe Wanda will do perfectly."

Aniela, at first speechless, eventually sputtered, "I'm not sure I understand. Are you suggesting that my daughter is to be sent away and Germanized?"

"Yes," Gauleiter Schreiber said firmly. "I'm sorry if this causes you pain, but this is the order from above and cannot be questioned."

He looked at his colleague. "I suggest we leave presently. Forget the coffee. I have found this part can be filled with all kinds of hysterical unpleasantness, and I'd rather not draw it out."

Gauleiter Schreiber, still holding Wanda and her doll, began exiting the room.

Aniela looked at her mother in panic, and then flew after him. "No! No! Wait, you cannot do that. She is my daughter. You cannot just take her from me!"

Gauleiter Schreiber, holding Wanda in one arm, pushed Aniela away roughly with a strong arm. Aniela stumbled into her mother, who was pleading between sobs, "Please, sir, you cannot do this. You cannot do this…"

Wanda burst into tears and began wailing, trying to escape from the arms of the large man holding her.

"Enough," Gauleiter Schreiber said with distaste. "Olga spoke of what an elegant family this girl comes from, and I'd rather not have to deport you to a camp like the last mother who gave me trouble. Please calm yourselves! I cannot abide hysterical women."

Herr Neumann, who stood pale and shocked behind his desk, whispered in a thin voice, "Please, sir. Have pity on these women. Surely you can find another candidate and leave Wanda be."

Gauleiter Schreiber ignored him and nodded to Olga. "I thank you for your service, Frau Neumann."

He exited, with Wanda screaming in his arms, and descended the stairs. Aniela and Pani Majewska fled after him, crying and begging, but he quickly disappeared into the back seat of a car with Wanda. Aniela threw herself against the window, tears streaming down her face, trying to get a glimpse of Wanda.

"I am here, Wanda," she cried. "Your mother, Aniela Bartosz. I'll come for you. Remember who you are. You are Wanda Bartosz. I'm your mother, Aniela Bartosz. I will come for you…"

Herr Grossman entered the car from the other side, and they pulled away. Aniela and her mother ran after them, eyes crazed, tears running down their cheeks. When Aniela could run no further, she collapsed in the middle of the street in a crumpled pile of devastation, muttering, "I will come for you, baby. I will find you. I will come for you…"

Eventually, Pani Majewska caught up to Aniela and gently enveloped her daughter in her arms.

"Get up," Pani Majewska said, hoarsely. "Get up, my darling. Off the street, before they arrest us, too. You must get up."

Aniela looked at her mother with a bleak and dazed stare, but shakily stood up, leaning against her mother. They slowly made their way home, as Nazi banners billowed above in the breeze.

Chapter 49

Wilderness

Aniela was in a state of panic and despair.

She could not believe that Wanda had been kidnapped, and that there was nothing she or anybody could do. The authorities — they were part of the same fabric that was smothering the country with harassment, thievery, bullying, kidnapping, forced labor, and murder.

She didn't know what to do. She could not sleep; she could not eat. Nor could she go to work and face Herr Neumann or the despicable Olga. Her brain registered that Herr Neumann had been just as shocked by the turn of events as she and her mother had been, but how could she go back in and pretend that her life hadn't been totally and utterly destroyed? How could she continue to support the very regime which stole her child?

Her mother also was in a state of shock, at a loss on how to support her daughter amidst her own desolation. Irena, who quietly intimated that she knew people in the underground and that she "overheard things" at her place of work, tried to get information.

Three days later, Irena brought news. "The Germans are kidnapping Polish children with blonde hair and blue eyes that have so-called Nordic traits. Many of the children being kidnapped were taken from orphanages. But any child that fits the criteria can be seized."

Aniela stared at her sister, hanging onto every word.

"They apparently send the children to a secret location, where they are examined for their suitability, given new identities, and indoctrinated in German culture and language. If the child qualifies, he or she is sent west to a German family."

"And what if the child doesn't qualify?" Aniela asked, her heart in her mouth.

Irena said very quietly, "My source said that they're sent to a camp."

"A camp?" Aniela asked, her brain seizing on the idea of a children's summer camp.

"A work camp," Irena clarified. "Or a concentration camp. Like the one in Oświęcim."

Aniela stopped breathing as she took in this information. Since 1941, everyone had whispered about the camp in Oświęcim, which Germans called Auschwitz. It was a former Polish military barracks that since occupation had been used to house the German army, then used to imprison Polish political prisoners. It now had a sinister reputation as a place where enemies of the Reich were sent to work and were hardly ever seen again.

"This is tragic," Aniela said, her voice breaking. "I must get a message to Henryk. Maybe he will know what to do."

****

Henryk and his three compatriots slept on thin mattresses in a safe house, with Bendyk on sentry duty.

The men were exhausted, having just completed a routine mission outside of the match factory in the town of Błonie. The crew had infiltrated the German-run factory by forging alliances with key Polish workers. The need to find factory workers who were willing to put themselves at risk was rooted in a very elemental need: phosphate.

As the Home Army needed cheddite, an explosive material used in bombs and grenades, they also desperately needed phosphate, which was closely regulated and controlled. The raid on the train supply that Henryk and his team had done had solved a short-term problem for the Home Army, but the partisans were in desperate need of a steady source.

The difficulty was that there was only one match factory left in all of German-occupied Poland, and the Germans were well aware of the need for phosphate for bomb-making and sabotage. The factory was heavily guarded, the employees were under close watch, and it took months of careful surveillance to determine which employees were worth getting close enough to.

From there, they hatched a plan to create a steady source of phosphate. The team came up with a simple solution. They created a dummy account, complete with a German company name, the name of a procurement individual making the order, an address in Berlin, and an account number. The Polish workers slipped the fake customer profile into the accounting system, and made sure to separate the phosphate order from the rest of the inventory every week, and hid the materials behind a false wall near the back exit.

Once a week, Henryk and his team snuck onto the factory grounds and clandestinely removed the phosphate under the dark of night. They now had a steady supply of phosphate, and because the Home Army was forging invoices and receipts under the fake customer name, there was no reason for the management to question the veracity of the arrangement.

Henryk and his team were pleased with their efforts. For six months now, they had secured the precious phosphate and the Polish workers had proven to be honest and trustworthy. Felicjan was thrilled that the group of five had already managed to smuggle over ten tons of the material.

Henryk felt a hand on his shoulder, gently shaking him awake. He opened his eyes to see the stubbled face of Bendyk leaning over him.

Henryk snapped to attention, reaching for his gun.

"It's okay, Damian," Bendyk whispered, using Henryk's alias. "I have received word from a courier that Felicjan has news for you."

Henryk cocked his brow. "Just for me?"

"Yes," Bendyk said. "It appears that there has been a communiqué delivered from Kraków. Felicjan wants to deliver it to you personally."

Henryk felt a chill go down his spine, and quickly got himself ready. He couldn't imagine Aniela would risk getting information to him unless it was urgent. Bendyk passed Henryk a sealed note from the courier. Henryk carefully unfolded it, read it, committed an address to memory, and burned the note in a small basin by the window.

"I'll meet Felicjan. I'm not sure when I'll be back."

Henryk looked at the slumbering forms of Marek, Kuba, and Piotr, regret etched on his face.

"I will let them know what is going on," Bendyk promised. "And extend your *pozdrowenia*."

Henryk nodded, shaking Bendyk's hand, then roughly hugged him. "I thank you, my good man. Goodbye, may we see one another again."

***

Henryk sat in Dorota's living room, nervously tapping his fingers against his thighs. It had taken six days of traveling at night to get back to Kraków, and now that he was here, he was impatient to see Aniela.

Dorota was making tea. He glanced over at the bedroom, the room in which he had spent one magical, much remembered evening with his beautiful wife more than four years ago. Even now, he could feel Aniela's skin pressed to his, the faint smell of lavender clinging to her hair.

With a constricted throat, he thought of Wanda. He had but one day in his whole, on-the-run existence with his cherished daughter. He remembered carrying her around on his back, spinning her until she was in a fit of giggles, and the sweet abandon of her laid-out form as she was slumbering in bed between him and Aniela. She had been but ten months old then, he reminded himself, and now she was almost five years old.

He jumped to attention when he heard a light knock on the door, and Dorota quickly checked the peephole and let Aniela in.

Aniela was, of course, as beautiful as ever. She swept in, with a courteous nod to Dorota, and ran directly to Henryk. Her eyes were large in her face, and there were purple shadows beneath them. Her skin was very pale, and he could see the vein under her right eye pulsing. With concern, he noted that she was thinner than the last time he'd seen her. She threw her arms around his neck and buried her head in his chest, and began to sob.

Henryk had been around men for so long that he was a bit startled by the feel of her slight frame next to his. He belatedly wrapped his arms around her, lifting her off the floor, and held her close as his chest muffled her sobs.

"My darling girl," he whispered. "I'm sorry. I'm so sorry."

He saw Dorota signal to him that she was leaving, and she quietly left the apartment, mouthing, "One hour."

"Henryk," Aniela finally managed to say, her voice strangled. "Were you able to find out any news? Do you know where Wanda is?"

Henryk lowered Aniela to the floor and took her hand in his and led her to the sofa. He sat down next to her, hands entwined. Her hands were cold, as if there was no blood flowing through her frame.

"My contacts said that thousands of Polish children have been kidnapped by the Germans," Henryk said, his voice tight. His eyes were glued to Aniela's shimmering eyes.

Aniela nodded, fighting back a sob.

"They send the children to holding centers, where they are examined, brainwashed, and there their suitability for the Reich is determined."

Aniela nodded impatiently. "Yes, yes, Henryk. But where is she? Do you know where this center is?"

Henryk took Aniela's face in his hands, surprised how smooth her skin felt against his weather-beaten and calloused fingers. "No, my love. My sources have not been able to get us this information."

Aniela stared at him for a beat, disappointment all over her face. "So you don't know anything more?"

"No," Henryk said. "We have our networks of spies, so there is no telling when we will get useful information. But for now, that's all we know."

"So you gathered as much as Irena?" Aniela removed her hand from his. "You, who has dedicated more than four years to the underground, have no more than that? How can it be that I know as much as you do?"

Henryk was at a loss for words. He had come here to comfort his wife, and it was clear that she had expected him to come with a solution. He exhaled, feeling powerless.

"I'm sorry, Aniela. This is a recent development, and the Home Army's network is struggling to get information. There is no chance of organizing a rescue when we don't even know where the children are being kept."

A chill went through Aniela as she stared at her husband. He seemed a stranger to her, stiff and informational, as if he was delivering a message to a spy and not to his wife. It was as if he was talking about someone else's child, someone else's loss. Her mouth fell open as she looked at Henryk, trying to see if anything was left of the man she had fallen in love with, the man that had made love to her to the wee hours of the morning on their last meeting. But he felt remote and alien to her.

"You don't seem upset that your daughter's been kidnapped by Nazis," Aniela accused, face hard.

"How can you say that?" Henryk choked.

"But how could you be?" Aniela continued, her eyes blazing with recrimination. "You hardly know Wanda. You have chosen to live on the lam, forsaking responsibilities to wife and child, in order to pursue your own selfish desire to be a 'man of action'. And now, when I need you to take action the most, you have nothing to offer."

Henryk's voice grew very quiet, as if it hurt him to speak. "Aniela, that's not true. I love Wanda very much. It's been a sacrifice, the biggest sacrifice a man can make, to be separated from you and her."

But Aniela was inconsolable. She had pinned all her hopes on Henryk, expecting that his position in the Home Army would somehow return Wanda to her, to make this nightmare end. With a sinking feeling in her heart, she saw that he could do nothing.

"Nobody asked you to join the partisans, implementing sabotage and going on dangerous missions. There are spies that live and work right next to Germans, right here in Kraków. There are those who write for the underground newspaper. You could've chosen a different calling, one that didn't keep you cut off from Wanda and me. You could've chosen to stay in Kraków and protect us!" she lashed out in fury and hopelessness.

"My work with the partisans is done precisely to protect you and Wanda," Henryk cried, his face filled with anguish.

Aniela turned cold eyes, filled with tears, toward her husband, and she said softly, "Well, Henryk. You have failed. You have failed us completely."

Part Three
May-December, 1944

Chapter 50

Raw Recriminations

Their parting was rancorous and strained. Henryk, so used to keeping his emotions in check, knew he seemed distant and uncaring. Aniela, bereft and emotional, blamed the man in front of her because she had no other place to put her swirling emotions.

The couple had just an hour together and parted with a stiff embrace, each not knowing when they'd again see one another. Aniela placed the leather case of Henryk's cherished watch into his hand before parting, saying, "Do everything in your power to find our daughter and bring her back." He took the case with stiff, cold fingers, her intention clear.

Henryk left Kraków and knew he should return to Felicjan in the north, to beg him to find the resources within the Home Army to locate Wanda. But due to the cold parting with Aniela, her words carving lashes deep on his heart, he felt the need to be comforted by the only person in the world who could. He longed to see his mother. His younger self would have guffawed at this childish yearning — to have mamo hold her little boy once more and tell him everything would be okay. But war had changed him in so many ways, and he was drawn to his mother as if she could provide a miracle.

He traveled by night and safely arrived in Wieliczka. He hid behind dumpsters at Wiktor's bar, hoping for a chance to intercept him. At around eleven, Wiktor stepped outside, pulling a package of cigarettes out of his pocket and striking a match.

"Wiktor?" Henryk said quietly, emerging from the shadows.

Wiktor jumped and recovered. "My God, Henryk! You almost gave me a heart attack!"

"I'm sorry, my friend. I have been waiting here for hours, hoping you'd appear."

Wiktor hugged Henryk to him. "Look, we must be quiet. There are Germans swarming in my bar; no place is safe here."

Wiktor offered Henryk a cigarette. Henryk paused, and shrugged off a demon. "Yes, thank you." He took the cigarette and inhaled deeply, like a man who hadn't had a drink for a long time.

"What are you doing here?" Wiktor said.

"I need to see my mother," Henryk said. "Do you know if it's safe for me to organize a meeting with her?"

"It's bad, Henryk," Wiktor said. "The Germans have taken over the salt mine. They've rounded up the Jews and are now taking over farms."

Henryk shook his head. "Do you know of our farm?"

Wiktor paused. "I think it's safe, but Marian would know better. I'll contact my brother and have him arrange a meeting with your mother. Come back tomorrow at this time and I'll try to have some information. But Henryk, be careful. There are young men and partisans hiding out in the woods, so the Krauts are constantly raiding homes, looking for men to conscript or partisans to hang..."

The next night, Wiktor said, "Marian passed on information that you are to meet up with your mother at our old chicken coop. Meet her there at five a.m. It's before curfew, but should be dark enough to go undetected."

Henryk met his mother in a dilapidated chicken coop that sheltered a few pigeons and a family of field mice. Pani Bartosz threw herself into her son's arms upon entering the old coop, barely registering the sight of her ragged son under his shaggy beard of more than a week's growth. The feel of his mother's arms unlocked something in Henryk, and he sobbed, "Mamo!" as he hugged her tightly to him.

After their embrace, she pulled back and took a better look at him. The light came dimly through the broken slats, yet she could see the deep crevices along his set mouth and purple shadows under his eyes.

"What is it, my son?" Pani Bartosz said.

"The Germans, they have taken Wanda."

"Taken Wanda?"

"Kidnapped her," Henryk said. "I got word from Aniela. We believe she was taken for their Aryanization program. I have tried to get information from our spies, but there is... nothing. No information on where Wanda may be."

The tears that did not fall in front of his wife sprung to his eyes. "Mamo," he said, his voice mournful, "I have failed my daughter and my wife. Aniela is beyond distraught. I just returned from Kraków and I fear she'll never forgive me."

Pani Bartosz, shocked by the thought of her precious and only granddaughter being ripped from Aniela's arms, could think of nothing to say to comfort her frantic son.

"That is terrible news," Pani Bartosz said, her tears joining his. "Poor Wanda. How scared she must be…"

"I know," Henryk said, mother and son openly weeping. "I have never felt so powerless in my entire life."

Pani Bartosz brushed tears from her face and turned to study her son. Her heart was aching for Aniela and Wanda, but here in front of her stood her child in need of comfort. She took his face in her hands. "It is not your fault, my son. You have always tried to protect Aniela, from the moment you met her. You are just one man against an army of barbarians. Not you, nor any man, can protect us from this hell we are living in."

"But as a husband and father," Henryk lamented, "is it not my duty to protect my family?"

"Duty," Pani Bartosz said, grimacing. "Who knows what that word means anymore? We must all do what we believe is right. You're a soldier in the Home Army. Surely that is good and right. Young men are targets; there is no guarantee that you'd be better at protecting your family coming out from the shadows."

"But what can I do?" Henryk pleaded. "Aniela called for me, expecting me to save her. I have no idea where to even start. Perhaps Wanda is lost to us forever?"

"Have faith," Pani Bartosz said, clinging to her beliefs. "God is testing us again. We are being tried as a nation. As a community. As a family. But we must come together, as one, in faith, and believe in our hearts that our heavenly father will deliver Wanda and deliver us from war."

Henryk looked at his mother sadly, knowing that in his heart he did not share a belief in a benevolent God or a higher power. He had seen too much. He had done too much. He could not believe that this senseless suffering offered deliverance and redemption. But her words comforted him when nothing in the world could. And so, for a moment, he let himself believe.

Chapter 51

Synagogue

Henryk crouched in the corner of an abandoned synagogue, anxiously awaiting the arrival of an unknown man. His senses were on high alert, and he felt acutely how exposed he was. For he was alone here: no Kuba or partisan compatriots to watch the door or sound an alarm.

The mission he was on was a private one, and the risk was borne by him alone. A mystery contact had the power to provide the information that could lead him to find Wanda or the power to betray him. Through inquiries by way of his network, Henryk had been lured to the town of Nidek. It was in this nondescript village in Silesia where many stolen Polish children had been sent for "evaluation and re-education". Given German names and identities, the children were relentlessly drilled in German language, songs, and pledges to ensure they were worthy of the great honor of joining a German household. Only those who "passed" would be adopted into the households of party loyalists.

Henryk had been tipped off from an old lady picking blackberries that the person he was to meet had been a caretaker at the school where the children were taken. Henryk hid in the corner, watching his breath condense before him in the dim light. All the windows of the synagogue were broken, and the wooden pews torn out, likely used for firewood or a Nazi bonfire. It was early in the morning hours, and he was cold and stiff, yet his ears were trained to the sounds around him. Dogs barked in the distance, menacing German shepherds that the Nazis seemed particularly fond of.

A pigeon flew into the building, splattering excrement onto the marble floor, before nestling in a rafter. Henryk fidgeted, his body craving a cigarette. These days, one had to take comfort wherever one could.

The truth was that the Germans were becoming less predictable.

Henryk could not reliably count on information on the progress of the war — what battles were being fought and how the Allies were progressing. From the shadows, he saw the mobilization of German vehicles, troops, and resources heading east to west and west to east. More and more Polish families were being expelled from their farms, making it harder for Henryk to find a safe place to spend the night, and forcing farmers to raid their own larders in an effort to survive.

Henryk's stomach growled, but he ignored it. Everyone who was not a Nazi or a conspirator was hungry. He wondered if his mother, aunt and uncle were managing on their farm and if they had enough to eat. Their farm was modest in size. Perhaps it was too small to be noticed by the Germans, who were desperate to feed their troops.

Henryk heard the sound of footsteps approaching and held his breath. Was this his contact? He waited, every nerve on edge. A second set of footsteps entered the synagogue, the sound reverberating through the empty building. Henryk's hair stood on end. He was supposed to meet the caretaker. One man. The sound of a second set of footsteps was neither anticipated nor welcome.

Henryk listened as one set of footsteps drifted away from him. He heard the sound of a man unzipping his pants and the stream of urine hitting stone. A man laughed, speaking in the flat sounds of Plattdeutsch, "I'll just use it as a commode…"

This was definitely not his contact, but rather two drunken German sentries using the abandoned synagogue as a latrine.

"Good idea, Günther," the other voice chimed in. This set of footsteps came closer and closer to where Henryk was hiding, tucked in the corner. He tried to slow his breathing to keep the condensation in front of his nose from giving him away. Seconds seemed to last an eternity as he tried to control his breath, fear turning his blood cold.

His stomach growled again. The second German drew a breath, pulling out his flashlight. "Who's there?" He turned his flashlight into the corner, illuminating Henryk.

The German's eyes widened in surprise. "Hands up, you dirty Jew!"

The other soldier quickly abandoned his urination and rushed to his comrade's side, gun drawn.

"*Ich bin kein Jude!*" Henryk said, hands in the air.

Günther grabbed Henryk by the arm and forced him into the glare of the flashlight.

"On your knees," he yelled, forcing Henryk onto the floor. The second soldier trained a rifle on Henryk's head. "What are you doing here?"

"Looking for firewood," Henryk improvised, keeping his hands in the air and his eyes down. The men were young, slightly drunk, and clearly surprised to have found him lurking here. They looked at one another with uncertainty, each waiting for the other to take the lead.

"Prove that you are not a Jew," said Günther, kicking Henryk with a shoe splattered with urine. He hoisted Henryk to his feet, and poked him with the butt of his rifle.

"Okay," Henryk said, pausing as he unbuttoned his pants. He choked back his shame as the other soldier shone his flashlight on his uncircumcised penis.

"*Kein Jude*," Günther agreed, looking at his mate with an expression that read, *now what?*

"We can't just leave him here," the other man said. "He could be a partisan or a danger to the Reich."

Henryk offered, in his broken German, "Not a partisan. Farmer. Kicked off land, looking for wood to warm family make."

Günther's flashlight traveled from Henryk's head to his toes. "He does *look* like a farmer. The commander will know what we should do if we bring him in."

The other man paused. "Or we could just kill him."

Henryk reached into his pocket and pulled out his beloved watch. "A gift. In return for freedom."

He put forth the Audemar, Piguet & Co. watch, its gold face gleaming in the brightness of the flashlight. Günther plucked the watch out of Henryk's palm and stashed it in his pocket. "We will take your watch, filthy Pole, but not your life. We'll let our commander decide your fate."

The other man laughed, forcing Henryk out of the synagogue with a rifle pressed between his shoulder blades.

"How do we split a watch?"

"Who knows?" the Northern German said, a satisfied smile on his face. "The grimy Pole probably stole it anyway. No farmer could afford something so fancy…"

***

For days, Aniela buried herself under blankets in a desperate attempt to cocoon herself from her spiraling world. She emerged from bed as a phantom, slowly examining every object in the apartment with sad eyes. She saw the fingerprints that Wanda had left on the glass of their curio cabinet. How many times had she scolded Wanda to keep her fingers off the glass? But Wanda had loved to peer inside, looking at the delicate porcelain figurines and painted bowls her grandmother collected. Aniela's throat tightened at seeing those tiny marks, regretting that she had ever let something as petty as dirty glass stop her from adoring her daughter.

Because now, with her daughter's lively presence in the home absent, time had ground to a crawl. The clock ticked loudly in the living room — a bleak reminder that minutes faded away and turned into hours and then days, and that there was nothing that anyone could do that would bring Wanda back. The sounds of Wanda babbling to herself while playing with her dolls and in a world of her own — the squeals, complaints and giggles that had become the metronome of their life — were gone.

Aniela spent hours gently touching everything that was connected to Wanda. She held her toys in her hands, and looked at her favorite objects with tormented eyes.

She and her mother had taken turns reading Wanda's favorite book before bedtime, and sometimes Aniela groaned internally at the monotony of Wanda wanting the same story read to her. Now, Aniela took the book, chokingly saying the words out loud as if Wanda could somehow hear them across the great expanse. Was someone reading to Wanda? Was she being taken care of and tucked in? Was she scared and frightened? Where was she?

These thoughts gripped Aniela with dread. She opened a drawer, removing the sweater that Pani Bartosz had knitted for Wanda last Christmas. Aniela breathed in Wanda's smell deeply. She had done the same when Henryk had left — and now she inhaled the sweet smell of her daughter, desperate to remain connected.

She spent hours just sitting in Wanda's room. She had nowhere else to go. Aniela carefully put the sweater back in the drawer. Harmony, perhaps also missing the precious girl, was curled up on Wanda's pillow.

"Get off!" she shrieked, pushing the cat roughly off the pillow. Harmony yelped and skittered away. Aniela picked up the pillow and inhaled, and realized that the scent of her daughter was lessening — replaced by the faint smell of cat.

Aniela collapsed on the floor, hugging the pillow to herself, and quietly wept. She felt her mother's arms encircle her, and that only made Aniela cry more.

"That stupid cat!" Aniela said unfairly. "I can't smell Wanda on this pillow. It smells like the cat!"

"I'll try to keep her out of Wanda's room," her mother said softly.

After a few minutes, Pani Majewska cooed, "We are all missing her, Aniela."

Days turned into weeks, then weeks into months, and Aniela heard no news of Wanda or from Henryk. Aniela knew that she should find a new job, as all Poles needed a work permit, but she could neither bring herself to return to the factory nor look for work. After a week of mourning, closeted in Wanda's room, she got up and spent her days instead wandering the streets looking for signs, trying to convince herself that she'd overhear a conversation that could lead her to her daughter. She could not sit idly at home. She had to do something. Anything.

She strolled past Wawel Castle, the fine cafés and social halls, seeking any information that may lead to a break. But as the months slipped by with no news, the cold hard reality began eating away at the corners of Aniela's mind: she may never see her daughter again.

Aniela was filled with impotent rage. She did not recognize the world she lived in. While she had spent her whole life in Kraków, the city was no longer hers. The posted proclamations, the pro-Nazi propaganda blaring from the loudspeakers, the sound of the German language spoken everywhere, and the daily subjugation of her brethren settled over her like a shroud.

After her initial shock and debilitating grief, her mental state shifted. She was furious, her anger focused on Olga, who had befriended her only to betray her. Yet she had always seen Olga for the opportunist she was — so eager to make connections with senior Nazis and their wives, Olga would have sold out her own child for social advancement. Instead, Aniela thought bitterly, Olga had sold out Wanda.

Then her anger was placed on Henryk's shoulders. She cursed him for not being there to protect them. She blamed him for his ineffectiveness, as he had no information that got them closer to having Wanda returned.

After months of focusing her anger, she sadly realized that her fury was displaced. While Olga was without a doubt the conduit that allowed Wanda to be kidnapped, it was the occupying forces of Nazi Germany that had set the stage for her loss. With forlorn clarity, she realized that the Reich had first taken her husband from her — turning him from newspaperman to soldier to partisan saboteur. The Reich had seized and murdered her father. And now, the Reich had stolen her daughter. Little by little, this regime was destroying her family and everything she held dear.

She felt a pang of regret, recalling her cruel words to Henryk. She had ridiculed him for being a "man of action"; but now, with no recourse ahead for her, she understood why he had risked everything in order to achieve *something*. She could see no action that would bring Wanda back, no action that could undermine the Reich, no action that could turn back time, and the feebleness was both devastating and humbling.

After the harassment from Leon, Aniela had not gone back to Pani Ostrowska, nor had she taught folk dance lessons. She had lacked the courage. With shame, Aniela realized that Henryk's path took a tremendous amount of courage and sacrifice, and that she was just trying to get by, risking less but somehow losing everything.

And with woeful clarity, she recognized that Henryk had lost so much, too. He had lost precious time with her, he had missed the birth of his child, he had missed all the marvelous milestones of watching an infant turn into a toddler, and into a talking, opinionated child.

Rambling through the streets of Kraków aimlessly, Aniela began to cry as she imagined Henryk's pain, his plight. How she regretted blaming him for Wanda's kidnapping! How she regretted spoiling their one hour together with anger and harsh words. They should have held one another, grieved with one another, affirmed their bond to one another; but Aniela's anger and anguish had prevented that.

"Your ID," a uniformed man said, breaking Aniela from her reverie.

Aniela blinked her eyes of tears and focused her attention on the green uniform of the man in front of her. He was German police, a man in his late thirties, and he was looking down at her with cold eyes.

Aniela reached into her purse. She took out her ID and passed it to him. With alarm, she realized her work permit was stamped for a six-month duration. As Aniela had not stepped foot in Herr Neumann's factory since that awful day in early April, she had no idea if her work permit was still valid.

The policeman looked over her ID. "What are you doing here? This area is for Germans only."

Aniela's mouth went dry.

"Your work permit," he demanded crisply.

Aniela reached into her purse and pulled it out. She quickly looked over the expiration date — it had expired two months ago.

Trying to use her looks as a way of distracting the policeman, she smiled brightly, batting her eyelashes at him. "Oh, I'm such a scatterbrain. Here it is. Or maybe this is my old one."

The policeman took it, and quickly grimaced at seeing the expired date.

"This is expired," he said flatly. "You clearly do not belong here. Come with me."

The man took Aniela by the elbow and roughly escorted her to a cargo truck idling on the corner. He pushed Aniela up into it, and she practically fell in the lap of three men and two women who were already on board.

"What's going on?" Aniela spluttered, trying to get up.

One of the women was crying, and she looked at Aniela with devastated eyes. She whispered like a cancer diagnosis: "*łapanka*."

Aniela's face drained of color. She had just been caught in a roundup.

The policemen had combed the city, selecting young men and women, some of whom had problems with their IDs, work papers or possessed suspected forgeries. Others had simply been in the wrong place at the wrong time. In the end, Aniela was driven to Kraków prison, along with twenty-three other unlucky souls.

They were taken to prison, the men separated from the women, and put into holding cells. Aniela entered a large, drafty room with a shared toilet and wooden bunk beds. The women were all frightened, and eager to share their shocked story of how they wound up there.

One by one, each prisoner was interrogated. There were two Germans in the room during her interrogation, one that did all the questioning, and a lanky guard who stood by the door, staring at Aniela's face with a queer look.

"What were you doing in an area clearly marked for Germans?" the man asked.

"I was looking for someone," Aniela stated.

"Who were you looking for? And why is your work order expired?" the man asked, his face impassive. Aniela decided to tell the truth.

"My daughter was seized almost three months ago," Aniela said, a slight edge to her voice. "By the Nazi authorities. This happened at my place of work. I could not bring myself to return there."

The interrogator seemed surprised by her response. "Hmmm," he said. "I see. Regardless, all Poles are required to work. We cannot make exceptions due to personal circumstances. Do you have any connections to the partisans?"

"I do not," Aniela said firmly.

"Where is the husband, the father of your child?" he asked.

"I have not heard from him since August, 1939. I assume he is dead or in a camp in Russia."

The man looked at her with narrowed eyes. "Well, if he was in a PoW camp in Russia, the Soviets emptied those out when Russia joined the Allies. But chances are, he is dead. He likely got a bullet to the back of the head like the rest in Katyń. Who are your parents?"

Again, Aniela chose the truth. She hoped that she would not endanger her mother or Irena, but she could see no other way. "My father, Bogdan Majewski, is dead. My mother is Kinga Majewska."

He nodded, checking some papers in his folder. "Yes, yes, we see that your father was arrested in November, 1939, with the other agitators at Jagiellonian University."

Aniela said nothing, though she felt sweat break out on her upper lip at this man labeling her kind, intellectual father as an "agitator".

"So why is your German so flawless?" he asked, eyes on her face.

"I studied German philology at university," Aniela said simply. "And I used this knowledge at Herr Neumann's glass and crystal factory."

"You studied German yet never joined the *Volksdeutsche*?" the man pressed. "Why not? The only reason I could see for not joining is if, like your father, you are an enemy to the Reich. Are you a spy?"

"I'm no spy," Aniela said. "I'm simply looking for my lost child."

The interrogator marked down several notes on her file. He then nodded to the guard, dismissing her. "You may go for now."

The guard took Aniela by the arm and walked her back to the cell. He kept his eyes trained forward, as if he was afraid to look at her, after having stared at her with unblinking eyes during her entire interview.

Once back in the cell, Aniela lost control of her limbs. She sagged limply against the cold, stone walls of the prison cell, her face ashen. Could she get a note to her mother and to Irena? Did they know she had been ensnared in a roundup? She had no idea if anyone witnessed her fateful moments with the *Ordnungspolizei* and whether they would get information back to her mother and sister.

She cursed her stupidity. How could she have been foolish enough to wander the streets near the seat of Nazi power, ears trained for news about Wanda, with an invalid work card? Had she not been harassed enough times by the police to know better? Had she not seen the bodies hanging by the neck in the town square?

Had she allowed her grief of losing Wanda to cloud the one thing that could give her a chance to find her? Her reason? She castigated herself for her idiocy, her stomach in hard knots, thinking about the worry her mother and sister surely were feeling. Her mother, who had lost a husband and a granddaughter, would be devastated at losing Aniela.

And Henryk? Aniela's mind strayed to her husband and recalled his haunted eyes from their last encounter. She squeezed her eyes shut as she breathed shallowly. Would her mother be able to locate Dorota on her behalf and get news to Henryk? Aniela had worried about how information would flow her way if Henryk was hurt, caught, or worse; but she hadn't thought to have a contingency plan if she was the one who was captured.

In her whole life, she had never miscalculated so badly. She had been foolish and selfish, and everyone around her would pay the price. With eyes pressed closed, she wept in the corner of the prison cell.

Chapter 52

Selection

Aniela was hustled to the train platform, where a cattle car awaited them. The German guard, who always stared at Aniela with slightly bugged-out glassy eyes, pulled Aniela away from the throng of people that were being jammed into the car. He grabbed her by her upper arm and said quietly, "Just wait."

Aniela was surprised by the soft statement, mainly because she had never heard the guard address her. She had found his eyes resting on her hundreds of times during her three-day stay at Kraków prison, and she was always disconcerted by the gaze. Sometimes he appeared embarrassed and looked away; other times he just continued to stare at her with a look that gave her a chill down her spine.

But the soft tone, spoken like a lover's secret, stopped her in her tracks. Was she not to board this train after all? Her illusions were shattered no more than ten minutes later, when all the prisoners were crammed onto the car. Cries of discomfort and indignation came swiftly from within, as the prisoners were so tightly packed and there was little room to stand, and everyone grew hot despite the late Spring weather.

"You last," the guard said. He escorted Aniela onto the train, as if she was traveling first class to Paris, not being herded onto a cattle car as a prisoner.

There was hardly any room for her, and she stepped in, landing on the feet of the others packed inside. The door to the car quickly shut them in and the sound of locks being bolted silenced the internal protests momentarily. Aniela realized how lucky she was to have gotten onto the car last, as she was now standing, crushed against the wooden slats, but she could gasp the air through the vents and see glimpses of the platform as well.

The wood was rough and unhewn, but at least she could rest against it, keeping her body weight from resting completely on the sweating strangers to each side of her. She quietly reflected on the role her beauty played in her life. Had her beauty, with the coveted fair hair and blue eyes, been the attraction that led to her losing Wanda? Would she have been perhaps a luckier and happier woman if she blended into crowds and didn't excite the passions of men? People were swept up every day, whether they were young or old, homely or beautiful, so beauty was surely no safeguard here. But for the guard, the young German who never said a word to her, but stared at her with unsettling eyes, it was her beauty that had singled her out in his eyes, and that special treatment meant a slightly more bearable trip to the dreaded work camp.

But what would await her there? She had heard the stories; some so fantastical it was hard to believe they were true. Then, Aniela thought of her father's ashes, sent home with a note from Sachsenhausen. Who would imagine an old professor was a threat to the Nazis? And she would never forget the petrified face of her daughter as she was ripped from her own arms — the brutality of these Germans knew no bounds.

Aniela felt beads of sweat dripping down her spine, and carefully tried to regulate her breathing as a way to calm herself. The car was filled with panicked and uncomfortable people, and the smell of that fear was taking over the dank air. The train lurched forward, and Aniela peered out the gap in the slats as best she could, seeing the platform disappear.

The train ride to Oświęcim, as the Poles had long called the small farming town that was renamed Auschwitz, would have taken a couple of hours before the war. But this train moved slowly, and made random stops in the middle of fields, for no apparent reason. The wails of the people who were trapped in the center of the car grew louder at first, and eventually quieted down as thirst, fatigue and lassitude seemed to take over.

Aniela smelled the camp before it came into view. Her nose was assaulted by a sickly-sweet burning smell, of unwashed bodies, and an odd chemical smell that she couldn't place. The last observation gave her a bit of hope: maybe there would be work in a chemical plant nearby.

Aniela focused on the big, wide-open fields that met her eyes, and then witnessed barbed-wire fences, watch-towers, sentry posts. The train slowed down to a crawl and passed through a bricked archway and crawled to a stop.

The door opened, and Aniela was pushed forward by the desperate people who wanted out. She tripped down the wooden plank, holding her arms out like a dancer to gain her balance, and stepped out onto the platform.

The noise was deafening, tall Nazis in green uniforms barking orders to the passengers.

"*Raus*," they yelled in shrill voices. "Out, quickly — quickly, you pigs!"

Aniela glanced around in confusion. Many of the people that were packed into the car with her were neighbors and families. She was alone, and watched from a strange distance as families reunited on the platform in desperation and were hustled along by strange, gaunt men in striped — pajamas? — who were doing the bidding of the screaming Nazis.

One of the men in stripes took a look at the people spilling onto the platform, and said grimly, "Poles."

He had spoken in Polish, and Aniela stepped in front of him and asked, "Please, sir. What is this place?"

He gaped at her.

A fellow striped prisoner called over, "Jacek, keep moving, man."

Aniela looked over to the man who had called out, and stopped short. There was something familiar about him. She searched his face, the dark eyes and thick brows. His hair had been shaved to the skull and he wore an odd striped cap. He was of average height and had an odd, gray color around his eyes and mouth. Yet, Aniela felt she knew him but could not place how.

"Aniela Majewska?" he asked hoarsely.

"Yes."

He looked her up and down, crumpled from the train ride and three days in prison, but still comparatively elegant, wearing a dark blue dress with a white leather belt and matching eyelet collar. Her blue eyes were wide, her well-formed mouth slightly agape as she took in the mayhem around her. Her cheeks were flushed pink, and he could see the braided girl he had desperately wanted to impress so many years ago.

"Julian," he said, taking her by the arm and walking her to the far edge of the platform. "Julian Piotrowski. We went to elementary school together."

Julian — the boy who knocked her language books to the floor in the library all those years ago. The boy whose behavior had elicited a tender response from Henryk, who helped pick up the books and walked her home from school from that day forward.

Aniela swallowed as the thought of the young Henryk stole her breath. Would he ever know what happened to her?

"This is a horrific place," Julian said, bringing her back to the present. "We Poles have some of the choice assignments here. We practically run the camp for these Nazi bastards."

Julian approached another striped man, a burly man with muscles like a street fighter who had a big K on his shirt.

"Kapo," Julian said quietly, "this is an old friend. Can you see about getting her on a good detail?"

He scrutinized Aniela with shrewd eyes.

"You're very beautiful," the man said. "Only the most beautiful girls become camp secretaries. Can you type? Have you skills?"

Julian gave her arm a squeeze, encouraging her.

"Ah, yes," Aniela said. "I was more than a secretary for a company that exported crystal abroad. I know shorthand, how to type…"

"And you speak German, right?" Julian said. "You were always studying."

"Yes," Aniela said. "I majored in German. I'm fluent."

The Kapo nodded briefly, and walked off to talk to one of the Nazis that was flanking the platform.

Julian looked back at Aniela, his eyes penetrating. "With luck, he'll get you in with the secretaries. Whatever you do, try to get a work detail inside. And don't trust anything that the Krauts say; always watch your back."

Aniela nodded. "Julian, how did you get here? What is this place?"

Julian looked around furtively. Conversations with other prisoners were forbidden, and he was growing nervous.

"A group of us partisans were caught in a raid about a year ago. We are slaves here, Aniela. This is a work camp, but also a death camp."

A guard yelled at Julian to keep working, and he scurried away, pushing other passengers toward the end of the platform. Aniela tried to keep track of him, but she soon lost him in the bustle of the platform, all the striped men looking alike.

The Nazi and brawny Kapo walked over and stood over her.

The Nazi rubbed his jawline. "She is very pretty, as you said," he said in German. "Herr Beckmann may be pleased. He recently lost his secretary and may appreciate one that looks… like this."

The Nazi looked directly into Aniela's stunned eyes.

"You speak German?"

"Yes, sir, I do," Aniela responded fluently.

"And can type? File?"

"Yes," Aniela said, her voice shaking a bit.

"Good, then," the Nazi said in a clipped tone. "Good work, Kapo, bringing this one to me. Have her taken in with the rest, but make sure to keep her hair."

***

Aniela was pushed to the front of a line, where crying and screaming women were separated from husbands and male family members. Dogs snarled at them, uniformed men prodded them like cattle, and yet somehow she could hear an orchestra playing Strauss in the distance.

The line of women was culled again as the young, the fit, and the beautiful were told to go to the right, and the old, pregnant, handicapped and middle-aged were sent to the left.

Aniela was led, along with the others from the right line, into a long room with pegs on the wall with marked numbers.

"Remove all your clothes and put them on the hook. Remember your number so you can retrieve your items after a health inspection and de-lousing," said a German woman with a bully club.

Aniela placed her purse over the peg, knowing her coveted work card and ID cards were more valuable than any other contents.

"Leave *everything* on the peg," a guard repeated. "Remember your number."

With alarm, Aniela and the women voiced a unified protest: there was a group of German soldiers lined up to watch the spectacle, enjoying the free show of naked women.

"Do it," the female guard barked. "Underwear, too."

Women stiltedly undressed, removing each item with embarrassment. Many had never been naked in front of any man, others only in front of their husbands; many were simply shocked to be leered at by the sneering German soldiers.

Aniela held her head up, removing her clothes with her back to the line of Nazi men. She had experienced this before. With or without clothes, she knew what it felt like to be stripped naked in front of a stranger. She held her head high, eyes forward, and allowed herself to be pushed through the throng of women without clutching her breasts in modesty or bending over to shield her body.

After the audience of leering men were cleared out, she was pushed into a large room labeled "Shower". The floor was wet and cold. She stood near the edge of the shower wall, having been hustled to the front by one of the attending guards. She stood quietly, absorbing the din of wailing and frightened women with dull awareness. During the entire journey to the camp, Aniela castigated herself for failing Wanda and allowing herself to be caught. She was so distraught and disgusted with herself that, as she waited for the shower to begin, her mind wandered once again to all the things she should have done and said when she had been rounded up and later interrogated. The women stood, shifting weight on stiff and cold legs, for quite a while before they heard a clank of the pipes engaging and cold water scented with a noxious chemical engulfed them.

"I'm glad that this is a shower," one woman said, her voice emanating relief. "I was afraid they'd kill us all in here."

Without towels and never returning to the numbered peg with their clothes and purses, the women were then given stiff and obviously worn, striped pajamas that emanated a strange chemical odor. They were hustled forward to a room where a Nazi camp doctor examined the women with cold hands without gloves. His fingers violated Aniela's vagina and spread open her buttocks, searching for smuggled items, before she was seated in front of another shorn prisoner who held the camp registration papers.

In shock, Aniela was asked to reveal her name, her nationality and next of kin.

She paused at this, knowing that she'd never reveal Henryk as her next of kin, as he was a wanted partisan and enemy to the Reich. With an internal blanch, she again wondered if she would die here and if he'd ever know her fate.

"Kinga Majewska," she said, citing her mother.

Aniela then had her photo taken at three angles, before moving on to get a number tattooed onto her left wrist. The pain brought tears to her eyes as she watched with a disbelieving gaze as her wrist was marred by the digits 81455. She was now nothing more than property.

Chapter 53

Assignment

Aniela was assigned to SS Economics Main Office Director, Herr Joachim Beckmann. Beckmann was a senior SS official working in the Economics office's accounting division, whose sole responsibility was to calculate the value of the goods being pilfered from the incoming transports. The items were amassed in huge warehouses, where prisoners sorted through every compartment of every suitcase and piece of clothing, extracting valuables for further sorting. All the money, jewels, precious metals, watches and fine clothes that came in suitcases or as dental fillings had to be weighed and their value calculated, and Herr Beckmann was part of the enormous team dedicated to this task. Each month the department calculated the value of their plunder and sent the valuables back to Berlin, where the Reich was dependent on these spoils to finance their war. Lately, the pace of transport had picked up significantly, as the Reich rushed to liquidate Jewish ghettos all over Europe.

The sorting room had been long ago dubbed "Canada" by prisoners who saw the *lager* as a place of tremendous riches. Nobody had ever seen a place with such bounty: jewels, embossed leather belts, wallets and briefcases, furs, piles of foreign currency. Canada, they imagined, was the most prosperous place in the world. But the Canada in Auschwitz was simply a warehouse of stolen riches.

Aniela was escorted to the office by a female guard, who kept a bully club in a holster on her hip. They stopped at the threshold of his office, where a large, imposing wooden desk sat in the middle of the room and in front of double windows. This was a private office, and featured a map of the camp on the right wall over a chaise lounge, and a framed portrait of Adolf Hitler on the left wall over a large bookcase. A man sat at the desk, poring over figures. Near the front of the room and to the right of the chaise lounge, a Continental Silenta black typewriter was placed on a small desk facing the wall.

"Your new secretary, Herr Beckmann," the guard stated.

Herr Beckmann was a lanky, angular man. He was a good foot taller than Aniela, with wide shoulders, gangly limbs and a protruding Adam's apple. He had a strong jawline, that was perhaps too sharp to be handsome, and a beakish nose set between small eyes. His eyes were the most eerie of his features, as his right eye was slightly off center, a so-called wandering eye, which made it difficult to ascertain his focus or intent.

He took a step forward. She was dressed in oversized striped pajamas and clogs, her hair tucked under a kerchief. She felt ridiculous as she stood across from this man in his fine dark green uniform.

"You type?" he asked, his voice flat and low.

"Yes," Aniela said, her speech raspy.

"How fast?" he pressed.

"Eighty words a minute," she said.

"Any other skills?" he asked, his eyes never leaving her face.

"I know shorthand," Aniela offered. "And I did some bookkeeping and contract negotiations for a crystal and glassware factory in Kraków."

Herr Beckmann examined her, his eyes traveling up and down and noting her stiff stance. Moments passed as his gaze continued to bore into her. Aniela wanted to shift her weight in anxiety, but forced herself to stand still, her arms pinned to her side, not moving a muscle.

"You're not German?" he asked, noting the P patch on her striped shirt.

"No."

"Hmmmn," he grunted. "All the other secretaries are German."

Aniela said nothing as he continued to examine her.

"It may be good to have a native Polish speaker, though," he said, scratching his jawline. "Thank you, guard," he said. "You may leave. We'll see how she works out."

He directed Aniela to the small desk with the typewriter.

"Sit," he ordered, and Aniela sat in front of the machine. He pulled a typed letter from his desk and laid it down next to her.

"Type this," he said, and checked his watch.

Aniela placed her fingers on the keys and typed, knowing her life depended on the outcome. She concentrated on every word, making sure her fingers struck the exact right key, and that her cadence was quick. She tried to block out the large man looming over her, but her breath came shallowly as she focused on the task at hand.

After a few minutes, she concluded and removed her hands from the keys, placing them on her lap and staring at the paper in front of her. If he asked her what the letter was about, she could not have said. She looked over her work, and noted two typos with a sinking feeling.

Herr Beckmann reached over to pull out the sheet of paper. Aniela sat ramrod still, facing the typewriter, afraid to see his reaction. She could hear his deep breathing as he read over her work. He put the letter down on the desk and folded his arms in front of him.

"What do *you* think?" he said, eyes narrowed, using the informal you — a sign of disrespect and often reserved for children.

Aniela shakily took the letter, her hands trembling.

"I can do better, sir," she said. "I see that I made two typos."

He paused as he decided on his response. At long last, he said, "Yes, I saw that, but you perform under pressure better than most."

Aniela looked at him, noting his narrowed eyes, an indication that he was still deliberating her fate. She smiled sadly.

Finally, he said, "I need someone who is honest. We'll see how you do. What is your name?"

"Aniela Bartosz."

"Aniela," he said, trying out the sound of it. "Pretty. How old are you?"

"I'm twenty-nine."

"OK," he said. "You'll report to this office at eight a.m. every morning, along with the rest of the secretarial pool. You will sit at this desk. You are to keep everything that transpires in this office completely confidential. I won't have you gossiping with the other girls about the business conducted here. If I don't like your work, if I don't like your attitude, if I don't like your tone, you are back to the main barracks. You understand me?"

"Yes," Aniela breathed.

"Good," Herr Beckmann said in a clipped tone. "So let's get to work."

Chapter 54

A Proper Secretary

Aniela was housed in the women's barracks in Birkenau, the neighboring camp, with the other secretaries. As Herr Beckmann had pointed out, the women were almost all German, mostly German Jews. They welcomed Aniela with reserve, and she soon realized that compared to the rest of the prisoners, the secretaries had a charmed life. First of all, they were not required to stand roll call every morning (called *Appell*), which was a brutal affair that often entailed standing in either freezing or sweltering conditions for hours on end, fighting hunger, fatigue and the random beating of the guards on duty.

The secretaries, instead, reported to the Secretarial Kapo, an older German woman who was a political prisoner named Sabine Richter. Sabine was tough but fair, and made sure that the secretaries were up, washed and fed in order to march over to the Auschwitz administrative offices by eight a.m.

Aniela noted that the secretaries were all uncommonly beautiful. There was Rachel, with her striking red hair and dark brown eyes fringed with curled lashes. There was Ulricke, with dark hair and eyes, her face reminiscent of Lulu from the silent film era. Aniela was the new fish in the pond, and the women sized her up accordingly, a bit surprised to have a Pole in the secretarial pool, assigned to a top SS man.

"Well," Ulricke said, as they sat down at a rough-hewn dining table, "your German is perfect. I wouldn't have known if not for the P."

Aniela nodded, sensing a lowering of her status defining her existence in the camp. Their breakfast was a tasteless porridge, but seeing Aniela playing with her food, Rachel whispered that she should eat it. The other prisoners often got one meal a day, usually soup made with rotten vegetables, and if they were lucky, a rock-hard piece of bread. While their own meal was not good, there was enough and it was nourishing. The women ate with concentration, making sure to lap up every last bite, and kept conversation to a minimum.

Aniela reported to Herr Beckmann daily, afraid to displease him, afraid to be sent to the barracks. Just a little over four months ago, she was at home in her childhood apartment, her daughter sleeping by her side. Now she was a lowly prisoner, and so she ate her breakfast mechanically, her stomach in knots.

"Be very careful of Herr Beckmann," Ulricke said, as they readied themselves for their morning march. "He had his last secretary, Gertrude, for years and then she displeased him. We never saw her again."

Aniela swallowed, stomach gurgling in fear. She knew that she was luckier than most people who had passed through the gates of Auschwitz, but each person here had a life and identity before, had lost loved ones, and were living shadow lives as prisoners and slaves. It was hard to quantify in one's mind the existence of *before* with the existence of the present.

With heavy clogs, Aniela marched alongside the other secretaries to the administration offices, lined up in rows of five. It was summer and the day was already hot, despite the early hour. No breeze could be felt, and the 3.2-kilometer walk was in the blazing sun, along a dusty, well-worn gravel road.

Aniela sat down in front of her typewriter, sweat forming on her brow. She was on edge all the time, hardly able to eat, and when she did, her food went through her. She was consumed by worry and a sense of constant fear. Her eyes were drawn to the tattoo on her wrist. Her mind was stuck in a loop, wondering if Wanda was fed and safe. How was her mother managing, a widow with a kidnapped grandchild and a daughter who left one day and never came back? And Henryk? Had he gotten any news of their daughter? Perhaps he was trying to get in touch with her, and not a soul in Kraków knew where she was.

Herr Beckmann entered the office shortly after eight, and sat behind his desk within two strides of his long legs. He picked up correspondence arranged for him in piles, and began reading, drumming his left hand on the desk. Although he was mostly cold and distant, Aniela became keenly attuned to the subtle changes in his mood.

He often seemed incredibly wired, and had energy like a pouncing cat, even at this early hour. She had seen him reach into his breast pocket and pull out a vial of pills and pop them into his mouth, while drinking cup after cup of coffee. She wondered if those pills were what had him always on edge.

He appeared to be under great stress, always moving even when he was seated at his desk. For hours, he would ignore Aniela — she sometimes wondered if he knew she was there — only to raise his head and dictate an order. She would take down a letter, or locate files that he needed; sometimes he would ask her to go to the canteen and get him a drink. She did as she was told, never speaking unless spoken to, keeping her eyes trained ahead — which meant that she was constantly staring at the silver buttons of his uniform when they addressed each other standing.

One day, after lunch, Herr Beckmann came in and stopped short upon seeing Aniela, as if he was surprised to find her there. His eyes raked over her, in the same fashion of their first meeting, and Aniela started to become nervous, not knowing where to look.

"I can't have you wearing those pajamas, Aniela," he said flatly. "Given my position here, you need to dress like a proper secretary. No more clogs and bare legs."

Aniela nodded, not knowing how she would manage finding more suitable clothing.

"I'll bring some items up for you to try tomorrow. From now on, that is how you will dress here."

The next morning, Aniela entered his office and found several outfits folded over her chair. She closed the door and tried them on. They were each tailored suits, of good quality, with fashionable pleated skirts and matching jackets. There were also silk blouses with ties around the neck. There were several pairs of hose, with a seam up the back; and most miraculous of all, a pair of brown leather pumps with embossed detailing. Aniela chose the light blue suit with white blouse, as it was the lightest, airiest material. There was no mirror in his office, but she used the glass from Hitler's portrait to adjust her hem and smooth her hair. She looked quite professional, much better than the woman swimming in pajamas, which she folded and put under her desk.

Herr Beckmann strode in and stopped when he saw Aniela at her desk in her new outfit.

"Good," he said. "Stand up. Let me take a proper look."

Aniela stood up, smoothing her hands on the skirt.

"Turn around," Herr Beckmann ordered. He grunted in satisfaction. "That is more like it. You can leave the clothes here each night, and I'll make some room for them in the *garderobe*. Get here early and be suitably attired. Tell Kapo when laundering is required."

"Yes, sir," Aniela said.

And the peculiar thing was, the clothes did make her feel like a proper secretary, though she lived in fear of doing the wrong thing and ruining her privileged position. Taking off the stiff pajamas and donning tailored suits gave Aniela the feeling that she was a person, not a prisoner, certainly not a despised Pole, but a working woman.

She needed to be smart and play it safe if she were ever to get out of the camp and find Wanda. If she were to find herself in her husband's arms again. Those simple thoughts kept Aniela alert and focused, forcing herself to eat the tasteless food that never agreed with her, to smile at the man that growled over his coffee each morning, to get along with the other women in her block, a friend to all, enemy to none.

Often, Herr Beckmann tuned into a radio station from Katowice. Aniela listened intently as she heard the latest news about the victories the German soldiers were having in the East, as well as in Africa. She sadly continued typing, wondering if she would live the rest of her life as a slave secretary, estranged from her husband, her daughter lost to her. The thought of Henryk and Wanda brought tears to her eyes, and she quickly blinked them away lest Herr Beckmann see.

But Herr Beckmann was engrossed in calculations, and seemed to be in another world. Aniela checked her calendar with his appointments, and noted that he had a meeting with a colleague in ten minutes.

"I'm sorry to interrupt," Aniela said, speaking over the wireless, "but I wanted to remind you that you have an appointment with Herr Schwarzkopf in ten minutes."

Herr Beckmann looked up, focusing his eyes on Aniela. "Yes, yes. Thank you for the reminder. I'll be gone for at least an hour."

He grabbed his jacket and hat and left the office with a sense of purpose. Aniela paused, and then got up to see if Herr Beckmann was down the corridor. He was moving at such a brisk pace; he was almost out of sight. She smiled and quietly walked to his radio.

A radio! When was the last time she listened to one? She surreptitiously turned the dial, looking over her shoulder, knowing that touching a radio was strictly forbidden. There were the classic propaganda stations, but she stopped turning the dial when she heard the haunting classical strains of a violin concerto. It was so beautiful to hear the music that she gasped, transfixed by the melody.

The next song reminded Aniela of a mazurka, and she swayed to the music, looking out over the treetops from the office window, and closed her eyes. Could she imagine herself listening to her mother and Irena playing beautiful music, skipping on parquet floors, practicing her dance moves? Music seemed to transport her back to a happier time, to a distant place, and she extended her arms and pointed her toes, and swirled in abandonment to the joy of the chords that were wafting beautifully through the room. She pirouetted and curtsied, and opened her eyes to find Herr Beckmann standing in the doorway, watching her with mouth agape.

"I'm so sorry," Aniela spluttered. "Forgive me."

"What were you doing?" he said, his eyes narrowing in that eerie way.

"I was dancing," Aniela said sheepishly.

"I saw that," he said. "But why?"

Aniela paused, and turned her blue eyes to look at him directly. "I don't know why. I just had to. Before the war, I taught folk dance and performed all over Kraków. The music just... moved me."

He scratched his chin, appraising her. "Interesting," he said, and grabbed a document from his desk.

"Carry on," he said, and departed a second time.

Chapter 55

The Performance

The next day, Herr Beckmann was in the office when Aniela arrived. Still dressed in her prison clothes, Aniela said with regret, "I apologize, Herr Beckmann, to have you see me dressed like this." As usual, she kept her eyes trained on his silver coat button at eye level.

Herr Beckmann waved his hand. "No matter. I had an excellent idea that will help the morale of our department, and you, Aniela, can help."

Aniela cocked her head, a question on her face.

"You said that you were a dancer, correct?"

Aniela nodded.

"Well, we Germans are very fond of the quaintness and charm of Slavic music and dance. Lately, we have been buried under Berlin's quotas. I suggested to the men to have you perform for us this evening after dinner in the social club. We even have musicians lined up."

Aniela stared at Herr Beckmann.

"Don't worry, Aniela," he said, pleased with himself. "I saw that you had that air of a dancer when I walked in on you yesterday. Just bring that to the stage and everything will be fine."

That very night, Aniela found herself dressed in a commandeered peasant top, lace-up boots and a long striped skirt. With shaking hands and butterflies in her stomach, she took to the stage with a violinist and accordionist. The stage overlooked a smoky room, filled with uniformed SS men enjoying a drink and a smoke after dinner. Immediately, the SS men hooted, seeing Aniela's form in the traditional garb, and the musicians launched into a lively polka.

At first, she felt strange dancing by herself — as most of the traditional dances required a partner or an ensemble. But after a few moments of awkwardness, Aniela felt the singing strains of the violin and familiar chords of the accordion reawaken muscle memory and a sense of time and place.

The lights kept her from truly seeing the audience, and Aniela imagined herself at her first recital. Could that be her father and mother, sitting in the front row? Was that her mother beaming with pride? She could practically see their blurred faces while she swirled. Aniela could see Henryk and his mother not far behind them, feet tapping in rhythm. The music was like a seduction — how long since she had heard notes of her beloved traditional music? When had she last danced, her heart light and mind clear? Aniela felt entranced by the intoxicating live music, the once-common leather boots, and she was swept away. She was a girl again — dancing in front of the boy she loved and her dear parents — and she felt, for that moment, free.

After several dances, the musicians played their final notes and Aniela took a bow, breathing heavily.

Joachim Beckmann sat unmovable, drinking in this dancing vision with fierce eyes. He was drawn in by her light, expert motions, the way her blonde hair floated around her like a cloud of gold. Her full lips, tilted at the corners, offering up a seductive smile as she moved across the stage. The music dimmed in his ears; it was as if she were dancing privately for him and him alone.

As Aniela curtsied, smiling demurely to the audience, Herr Beckmann became aware of the howls and the whistles. Behind him, he heard a man say lewdly, "Did you see the legs on that girl? I'd like to have them wrapped around my neck..."

Laughter erupted all around him, as the men ogled Aniela, making jokes about what each of them would do to her.

He noticed that her peasant blouse, a thin borrowed garment in white, was clinging dangerously to her breasts. None of the prisoner women had brassieres, and the lights blazing down on her revealed the dark outline of her areolae. And all the men were eyeing her like a wolf eyes a lamb. Aniela took her final curtsy, men yelling and whistling. She retreated behind the curtain with the two musicians.

Joachim stood up, pushing his chair back. What the hell was he thinking? Exposing her like that in front of all these drunken and lewd men? What a stupid peacock of a man he was, parading her out there like a tail feather. It was one thing to have the prettiest secretary working for him, but now she was lit up for all to see and desire.

Hans Strohmayer slapped him on his back, a knowing smile on his face. "Well done, Beckmann, you devil. I hope she moves that well flat on her back. What a specimen she is!"

Pushing past him, Herr Beckmann found Aniela behind the stage curtain. She stood, dressed in her ersatz folk costume, chatting happily in her native tongue with the violinist and the accordionist. She had her right foot out in front of her and pointed outward, her hips slightly thrust forward in the common stance of a dancer at rest. Her head was held high and her slender arms danced through the air as she chatted with the musicians, and they smiled at one another warmly.

She saw him approach, and took a few steps toward him with a dazzling unguarded smile and shining eyes. Her skin was dewy with perspiration and her breasts were clearly outlined through the sheer blouse.

"How did we do?" she asked, blue eyes fixed on him, the look of a woman seeking approval.

For the first time, he saw her not as a subhuman, not as a Pole, not as a slave, but as she was: a beautiful young woman of slight stature in a world designed and plundered by men. A woman without protection, a woman who could easily be plucked, manhandled, and cashed in as easily and carelessly as a diamond found sewn into a Jew's hemline at the *Effektenlager*.

Suddenly, Herr Beckmann felt a profound wave of protectiveness wash over him. It was at once an unfamiliar yet familiar feeling — bringing him back to the days before the war. The days in which he would have offered his jacket to cover her, and insisted on walking her home. He had not felt any pathos for anyone at Auschwitz; this was a grim job filled with the unpleasant business of exploiting, organizing, extracting value from lesser races of humanity.

Yet here he stood, looking down at that heartbreakingly beautiful girl with the open smile and beseeching eyes, and he felt impotent. He could not pick her up and spin her around, telling her he was proud of her performance. Nor could he offer her a jacket to cover her exposed body, a body that had excited all the men in the audience, thanks to him.

He stood erect and cold, furious with himself and his shallow blunder, a muscle throbbing in his jawline, face firm. And before his eyes, he saw her rare unguarded smile disappear. He saw the warm and open body language dissolve into her usual, straight posture, toes in line, arms by her side. She lowered her eyes and fixed them on a button on his jacket. She transformed back into his *untermenschen*, and the moment was lost.

Herr Beckmann gruffly called over to one of the female guards. He ordered her to escort the prisoner back to the barracks.

"Stop for no one," he said privately to the guard. "Our men are worked up by her performance and I won't have my... secretary... molested."

The guard nodded and ordered Aniela to march back to the barracks, poking her softly in the back with her club. Beckmann scowled at the musicians as she was led away, adjusted his hat, and returned to the club and to the oblivion of a stiff drink.

Chapter 56

Canada

Something had changed between them. Aniela sat at her desk typing, and looked over to find Herr Beckmann staring at her bleakly.

"Is everything okay, Herr Beckmann?" she ventured.

"Yes, yes," he said, returning to his work.

One day in early September, he brought in a set of leather gloves with fox-fur trim and a matching stole. They were beautiful. Aniela had no doubt that the items were pilfered from Canada, and belonged to some poor transport who was likely dead. During her first day walking back to the secretarial barracks, Aniela had remarked to Ulricke about the awful plume of smoke that furled into the sky without pause. Was it a chemical plant of some kind?

Ulricke's response was chilling. "That smoke and fire you see all night? There goes our people."

"Our people?"

"Yes," Ulricke said grimly. "Mostly Jews. My own parents were gassed and put in the crematorium within an hour of arriving. I remember crying to the Nazi I work for, how dreadful it was to go up in smoke… and he tried comforting me by saying, 'Don't worry, little Ulricke, you'll be the very last Jew we burn!'"

Aniela's attention was brought back to the present.

"I'd like to see how this looks on you," Herr Beckmann said, offering the gloves and stole to her.

She hesitated, afraid to touch the soft, silky items, as if they'd come to life and might bite her.

"Please, Aniela," he said impatiently. "You have such a refined beauty, I thought these would suit you."

She took the items and wrapped the stole around her neck and pulled up the gloves over her slender fingers. She turned her eyes to his. A foot taller than her, he loomed over her, examining her for a long time, until he finally said, after clearing his throat, "As I suspected. You look ravishing."

Aniela smiled tremulously. "Thank you." She began taking off the gloves.

"No, no," Herr Beckmann said. "They're a gift for you."

Aniela looked at him like he was mad. She could not wear such items around the camp. Every guard and Kapo would target her, assume she'd stolen them, and she'd be beaten or killed without a second thought.

Herr Beckmann seemed to understand her expression. "What I meant is, they are yours while you're in this office with me. I'll make a special place in the *garderobe*. While you are here, if you want to listen to the wireless, if you want to dance, or wear a fur stole, all you have to do is ask, Aniela. You have nothing to fear from me."

Aniela nodded, unsure where this kindness was emanating from. She remembered Julian's warning to never trust the Germans, and she wondered if he was setting a trap for her. Looking pleased with himself, Herr Beckmann returned to his desk and sat down. "Now, then," he said amiably, "let us get down to business. Come sit in front of me and let me dictate a letter to you."

Aniela went to her desk and grabbed her steno pad and a pen, then sat expectantly in front of him. He looked up from his dossier and leaned back in his chair as if a thought had come to him.

"You know," he mused, "I like your hair down. While here, can you wear it that way?"

Surprised, Aniela nodded and undid the pins of her hair. Unlike the other female prisoners, she and the other secretaries actually had hair — though they had hair cut to a sensible shoulder length and always kept it up, pinned and tidy, as the Kapo insisted.

"Better," Herr Beckmann said, and returned to his dictation.

Aniela continued with her shorthand, though the skin along her neck was tingling.

Chapter 57

Mein Kampf

Auschwitz
September 27th, 1944

Aniela arrived at Herr Beckmann's office at eight a.m. She sat stiffly, awaiting his arrival. It was now almost noon. He had not appeared, so she busied herself with some filing, opening and sorting letters, and tidying his office.

Once again, she thanked the heavens for the graces bestowed on her. It was a dreary, cold, rainy day, and the march over to the administration offices had chilled her to the bone. But unlike so many others, she was now warm in an indoor detail, and seeing the windowpanes blurred with rivulets of rain instead of having them soak her clothing. She imagined herself as a proper secretary, thinking of Antoni. With Herr Beckmann absent, she was not as keyed up anticipating his mercurial moods. She could pretend that she was merely doing her work, and that the boss was on a business trip, and it was her job to keep things going. That her daughter was waiting for her at home, tended by her mother. How normal it all seemed to be. Her musings were interrupted when Herr Beckmann stalked into the office, throwing his briefcase down on a chair with a thump. Aniela, startled, tried to collect herself.

"Good day, Herr Beckmann," she said tightly.

Beckmann took off his hat and hung it on a peg on the wall, and shrugged off his outer coat, water droplets spraying everywhere. He turned quickly and stared at Aniela, his eyes emanating an eerie glow.

"Quotas, quotas," he muttered, stalking around the office. With his long legs, he reduced the office to a few strides, and the entire room seemed to shrink around him.

"Never enough, always more," he grumbled. "How the hell does Berlin think we can manage?"

He picked up a paper from his desk, glanced over it briefly, then threw it down in disgust.

Unsure of how to respond, Aniela tentatively offered, "May I get you something? Perhaps some tea or coffee? It is quite chilly out."

Beckmann stopped short at her voice, his eyes boring into her. Aniela swallowed hard, unnerved by his penetrating gaze. Eventually, she looked down and folded and refolded her hands, trying to hide her nervousness. She realized what was so disconcerting about his gaze. His pupils were dilated, making his green eyes appear almost black.

"Yes," he said, very softly. "Please get some coffee."

Beckmann stood a few feet in front of the doorway, blocking her, and she gingerly tried to step around him to pass. His hand shot out and grabbed her by her arm, stopping her exit.

He looked down, his face bent over her, eyes foreboding. "You really are so beautiful," he whispered. "You must have a fair amount of German blood in you to be so fine. Why were you not classified as *Volksdeutsch*?"

Aniela swallowed, trying to pry her arm out of his grasp. She could think of no response.

Eventually she managed, "So kind of you to say…"

Herr Beckmann snaked his other hand around Aniela's back and took her hair and skull in his large hand, forcing her head back. He loomed over her, head and shoulders bent, his mouth mere inches from hers. Her lips parted in surprise and fear, seeing those frightening eyes so close to hers. With one of his hands on her arm and the other holding her skull, she could hardly move.

"So pretty," he murmured to himself. "I have been fighting my desire for you since the day I first saw you."

He lowered his mouth and kissed her passionately, grinding his mouth down on hers with such force, she tasted metal. She could also taste alcohol on his breath, and tried to push him away, but was trapped in his grip.

"Let me," he groaned, and spun her around and forced her against his large wooden desk. His hands were running up and down her body, squeezing her breasts, and she felt him take her earlobe into his mouth. She was being pushed, face first, into the desk, and she felt his leg split her thighs open as he pushed her down.

She whimpered, "No, please stop…"; but he ignored her, pulling up her skirt as it bunched awkwardly around her waist. He then took her hands, and placed them in front of her and over her head, and with one hand, kept them there — immobile. She was flattened onto the hard contours of the desk, her arms pinned, her face pressed into the wood.

She realized with grim certainty that he was going to rape her, and that there was nothing she could do about it. She could not call for help — nobody would care nor dare rescue her, nor could she overpower him.

The dilated eyes and tainted breath suggested he was overtaken by some stimulant, and his frenzied movements spoke of some inner demon. Her underwear was torn off, and she heard him spit on his hand as he lubricated himself, and she closed her eyes tightly as if not seeing could somehow stop what she knew was about to happen.

He thrust himself into her with a groan of desire, and she gasped from the pain and the shock of it. His hand left hers and found her neck, and he encircled it and pressed her down against the desk as he thrust into her again and again. She coughed and gagged, fighting for air, as her fingers dug into the corners of the desk. Tears streamed down her face and tortured whimpers came from deep inside her.

How long she was violated in this manner, she did not know. He kept up his violent assault on her until, finally, he cried out as he climaxed, pulling out. She could feel his hot semen on her thighs as Herr Beckmann leaned over her, bracing himself with his arms, his fiery breath on the back of her neck.

Aniela stared ahead, eyes on his bookshelf. She could read the title *Mein Kampf* from this awkward angle, and she emitted a cry like a wounded animal. Herr Beckmann stood up, noting his pants around his ankles, and awkwardly pulled them up. Aniela rolled off the desk and tried to stand up straight. Her head was swimming and her vision blurry.

She thought of Henryk, and a pang of longing and despondency overtook her with incredible force. Her face drained of all color; a trickle of blood sprang from the corner of her lip. She looked at Herr Beckmann, her guardian, her tormentor and violator, and she crumbled to the floor, head bent over and breath ragged. Her vision was closing in on her, and her field of view narrowed at the edges.

Herr Beckmann strode over to her and picked her up by her armpits. Aniela tried to get her limbs to work, but they would not cooperate. She was dragged to the chaise lounge and he laid her on it. She closed her eyes, trying to stop the room from spinning, amidst her shallow gasps for air.

Herr Beckmann sat down next to her, noting her pale cheeks and rasping breath. Overtaken as he was by drugs and alcohol, his brain was struggling to register what his eyes were taking in. Eventually, he collected himself, and felt a cold sense of shame wash over him. He had taken his prisoner, his secretary, roughly and from behind. She was clearly going into shock. He took her hand; it was ice cold and trembling.

What kind of man was he? Had he just raped her, or was this his right as her racial superior and as a man? He pushed these thoughts aside and slowly unbuttoned her shirt to lay his hand on her heart.

It was beating incredibly fast, and he noted that his hand more than enveloped her breast. He blinked, trying to clear his mind, and noted the body panting in front of him.

He'd seen Aniela naked that first day when the women were stripped and paraded naked in front of the soldiers after selection and on their way to the showers. He recalled the women hunching over, trying to cover themselves with their hands, in shame and humiliation. And then there was Aniela, who walked through the melee, standing straight — the body of a dancer, with soft rounded hips, golden skin, a narrow waist, and full breasts tightened in the cool air. Her hair, in a thick braid, hung down to her mid-back then. Her eyes were trained forward, ignoring the leering men.

Now he could see how clearly she had changed. Her breasts, once so full, were less so, and her rib cage, expanding up and down with her breathing, was clearly exposed. He could see the gaps under her ribs, and the hollow that led to her belly. He looked again at her neck, noting the protruding clavicles and tight skin around her jawbone. The full-figured woman that had caught his eye was slowly wasting away. Dressed in the layers of tailored clothing, how had he not seen it? A curl of dread spread out in his stomach, as he leaned over to lift up her head and to sit her up.

"Just breathe," he whispered, his voice rough. "You're going to be okay. Breathe." Herr Beckmann put a hand tenderly on her breast, willing the heart to regain its normal beat. Aniela opened her eyes, seeing his concerned face, his hand on her heart. Her eyes widened in panic, fear in her eyes.

"Please don't be alarmed," he said gently. "You are okay. I think you haven't been taking care of yourself enough, Aniela." He brushed away any thoughts of how he had seized her, violated her and reduced her to this panicked form. "You need to eat more; you're getting too thin."

He got up and made a quick call, then unbuttoned his suit jacket and took it off, laying it over Aniela for warmth. Aniela lay there, confused and in shock. This man, just moments before, had thrown her on the desk and raped her without compunction. And now, he was stroking her with warm, concerned hands as if she was the most precious thing in the world to him. Tears formed at the corner of her eyes. His ability to shift from angry aggressor to concerned — what was he? *A lover?* — was stupefying. She had no idea how to behave with this dangerous man.

There was a knock on the door and Herr Beckmann went to it, took something and then closed it quickly. He came back and knelt in front of Aniela, Thermos in hand. A mélange of fragrant aromas sprang forth from the Thermos, and Aniela heard her stomach grumble as she registered the smell of warm chicken soup.

"Take a sip," he ordered, his voice soft.

Aniela took the Thermos and felt the warmth emanating through the canister to her chilled bones. She took a sip, and the warm, comforting taste of consommé slid down into her belly, and for a brief moment, this nostalgic reminder of home and normal life settled her.

She looked up, where Herr Beckmann sat with concerned and dilated eyes.

"Herr Beck…" she said.

"Better?" he interrupted, placing his warm hands over hers, encircling the Thermos. "And in here you can call me Joachim."

She took another sip.

Chapter 58

Sehnsucht

S he could not sleep. Her mind kept drifting back to her honeymoon with her Henryk.

On their final evening in Zakopane, Henryk and Aniela went to the large ballroom, where a famous orchestra from Warsaw was playing with a big band. They drank champagne freely, and danced to the band with abandonment.

The ballroom held hundreds of people and the hall grew warmer, the only fresh air coming from the oversized windows on one side of the room. Cigarette and cigar smoke clouded the air, and after hours of dancing, Henryk pulled Aniela off the dance floor.

"Let's get something to drink," he offered.

"Just water, please," Aniela said, wiping her brow.

"Stay here. I'll see if I can fight the crowds and make it to the bartender."

Aniela nodded, and found a sliver of wall next to the large open window and wearily leaned against it, closing her eyes.

A deep male voice, with a hint of an Austrian accent, broke Aniela's reverie.

"Are you okay, young lady?"

Aniela opened her eyes to find a very tall, lanky man in his forties studying her with a worried expression on his face.

"Oh, yes," Aniela said, smiling. "I was trying to catch my breath."

The man smiled. "I'm sorry for interrupting you, then. But allow me to introduce myself. I'm Wilfred Mayer."

"I'm Aniela... Bartosz," she offered, extending her hand, her heart clenching over her name being joined with Henryk's. Wilfred took it and kissed the back of her hand with a gentlemanly flourish.

"Do I detect a bit of an accent?" she queried.

"Yes, afraid so," Wilfred said. "I'm Austrian, but my mother is Polish. I'm afraid I never got my tongue around those blasted Polish consonants."

Aniela laughed, switching languages. "Well, then, we can converse in German if you prefer."

Wilfred's eyes widened. "If you don't mind! What a delight to hear my native tongue, and so perfectly delivered, here in the mountains of Poland!"

Aniela took a closer look at this friendly man. He was dressed in a smart tuxedo, and had black hair slicked back. His face was friendly, with warm brown eyes, and skin lined in an attractive and friendly way. There was a warmth about the man that immediately put her at ease. After a moment, he offered, "Do you think you have your breath back sufficiently to favor me with a dance?"

He gestured to the floor.

"Oh, I'm sure my husband will be back any minute with drinks…"

Nonplussed, Wilfred continued, "Of course. I promise to hand you back to him the moment he arrives…"

Aniela hesitated, and then smiled back at his warm face. "Sure, why not?"

Wilfred found some space on the corner of the crowded floor. He expertly took Aniela's hand and immediately began leading her, using arm tension to cue her as he moved her from spins, to turns, to behind the back releases. Aniela instinctively fell into line, and laughed gleefully as Wilfred moved her around the floor. Other couples made room, clearly impressed by this pair.

"You are quite an accomplished dancer," Aniela exclaimed breathlessly in German.

"Why, thank you," Wilfred said. "I used to live in Berlin, and loved to go dancing at the various cabarets and clubs…"

"Is your dance partner here tonight?" Aniela asked, glimpsing a wedding ring on Wilfred's hand.

Wilfred paused. "Miriam, my late wife, was an avid dancer…"

"I'm sorry," Aniela offered.

Wilfred smiled as he led her through various moves. After a few moments, Henryk appeared — drinks in hand — and a false smile on his face as he interrupted, "Do you mind if I cut in… with my wife?"

Wilfred quickly released Aniela, and bowed to her formally and shook Henryk's hand.

"Of course," Wilfred said, speaking in his accented Polish. "I thank you for the pleasure of dancing with such a lovely woman. It was the highlight of my evening..."

Henryk glowered at the lanky, older man and passed a cool glass of water to Aniela. "Here is your water," he muttered grumpily.

Aniela gratefully took the glass, and Wilfred faded into the crowd. Henryk and Aniela moved away from the dance floor to sip their drinks.

Aniela looked up at her husband, and placed a hand on his arm. "Are you mad at me for dancing with Wilfred?" she asked gently, sensing a dark mood.

"So it's Wilfred now? Hmm." He pulled out a cigarette from his breast pocket and angrily lit a match, drawing on the cigarette like it was a lifeline. He muttered something under his breath: "Doesn't take but a minute and the bees come swarming around your hive..."

Aniela couldn't catch exactly what he said, but could read him. He obviously was jealous, and knowing that he had no real qualm, he was being petulant. She reached up to her glowering husband and whispered in his ear, "Why don't you put that cigarette down and take me up to our hotel room?"

Henryk looked down at Aniela smiling sweetly at him, and dropped the cigarette and stamped it out under foot. He let her take his hand and lead him out of the crowded ballroom, into the hallway, and up the winding staircase to their room. He was miffed, and she encouraged him on demurely, looking over her shoulder and batting her eyes.

But he was not quick to let go of his annoyance.

Fine, Aniela thought. It's time to tame this tiger.

She unlocked their door and pushed him into the room and onto the bed.

"You stay there," she ordered firmly. She stood in front of him as he lay haphazardly across the bed, still in his evening clothes.

"So... my dear Henryk didn't like to see me dancing with another man, hmmn?" she teased softly, and started to slip off her dress, one shoulder bared and revealing the top of her lace slip. "You'll need to get over that, my love, as that old widower was harmless... a fine dancer... but harmless."

Henryk's eyes latched on to her as she started to sway, seductively dancing to the music that was wafting up from the ballroom below.

"But you..." she continued, in her soft lilting voice. "You are dangerous. Like a caged animal, ready to pounce..."

She swirled around, facing away from him, and let the dress fall to her hips. She wiggled suggestively while bending over, and slipped out of the dress. She turned back to him, still swaying to the music, her hands traveling up and down her own body in her pink slip, teasing Henryk as her nipples hardened under her own hand as she danced in front of him.

Henryk groaned, his eyes on fire. He stood up to reach for her.

"No," she ordered, pushing him back down on the bed. "I'm not done dancing yet, my love," she cooed, as she let her slip fall off her shoulder, revealing a breast with an erect nipple. "Hmmm," she murmured, emboldened by his intense stare, enjoying this new sense of power as he stood enraptured by her every movement. "Do you like what you see?"

Henryk swallowed hard, finding his voice. "I love what I see. I want to touch you so badly..."

"Oh, you will," she promised, letting the other side of her slip fall, revealing her naked breasts, her silk slip resting on her hips. "But tonight, I'm in charge. You don't touch me until I ask you to. Can you do that?"

"Yes," he answered huskily. "I will do whatever you say."

"Good boy," Aniela praised, and walked over to Henryk as he perched on the bed.

She placed her nipple in front of his waiting mouth, and gasped as his tongue snaked out to flick it.

"Just a little taste," she teased, and pulled away from him, dancing and swaying provocatively to the music, swiveling her hips and pressing her breasts together like an exotic dancer.

"Now," she said softly, returning to the bed, "do not touch me yet, not until I give you permission. I am going to touch you."

"Please," Henryk offered, his eyes locked on her half-nakedness.

Aniela bent forward, giving him an eyeful of her dangling full breasts, and slowly removed his bowtie. She heard his ragged breathing as she unbuttoned his dress shirt, pulling it off his tense shoulders, admiring the veins that were protruding on those strong arms.

"What a tense, coiled cat you are..." she whispered, and made her way to his pants. He lifted his hips eagerly as she unzipped his pants and pulled them off, along with his underpants.

She giggled a little, unused to being the wanton boss she had turned into, and finding it oddly humorous to see this powerful man naked on the bed, his erection hard and throbbing and practically begging for her, and yet still wearing his dress socks and shoes.

"This will not do," she said sternly, leaning over with a smile and pulling off the shoes and socks. "Much better…"

He was completely naked, sprung and at attention, and she lifted her slip up to reveal herself to him as she shimmied out of her delicate panties, her slip still bunched around her waist and her breasts free.

"Lie down," she ordered, and Henryk quickly lay down in the middle of the bed, his face locked on hers, his eyes like nothing she had ever seen before.

A sense of power, of dominance, of feminine force swept over her, and she understood that with Henryk's all-consuming desire for her, she had him in the palm of her hand. It was a heady realization.

"Tell me that you love me," she said softly, getting on the bed and straddling him, her hips hovering over his hard torso.

"I love you," he groaned, reaching up to drag her on top of his waiting member.

"Not yet," she breathed, gently biting his earlobe. "I say when."

"Yes," he gasped, his eyes wide and unblinking.

"Tell me that you were being very silly for being jealous, when it's you I have between my legs."

"I was very silly…" Henryk whispered, his hands running up and down her toned back, cupping her buttocks.

"Now that's a good boy," Aniela teased, and slowly slid down, dripping on his lower torso until she felt the tip of him against her wetness.

Aniela's eyes blazed with passion as she looked down at her husband beneath her, who had an almost heartbreakingly desperate look on his face. She relented, and slowly lowered herself on top of him, taking the full size of him into her, and arched her back by the surprise of the rigid feel of him. She had never ridden him before, and this position accentuated their intimacy; he seemed bigger and fuller, and she felt an almost painful sensation of completeness.

She arched some more, bending backward in a seductive pose, and began gyrating rhythmically. She closed her eyes and swiveled her hips, and heard a deep, abiding groan of desire erupt from him. She opened her eyes to look down at him, and his face displayed ecstasy mixed with a desire for mercy. He was totally in her power.

Aniela continued her motions, letting him delve into her, arching back and forward to force him deeper, and she felt an animalistic drive take over her body as she rode him harder and harder, pushing him even deeper into her.

Henryk's face was fixed on hers, so enraptured was he by the view of her over him. He was almost silent as his senses locked onto every sound and motion that she made; every gasp, every moan, every squeal took his excitement up to a new plateau.

He murmured as if in a daze, "Always my dancing girl…"; and his hands circled gyrating hips, his body moving to the motion and the rhythm her movements dictated.

And at last, she arched her back one last time and came on top of him. And then he let go, emptying everything he had into her. She lay over him like that for a long time, until his spent penis retracted and quietly slipped out of her, their wetness mingling with each other as they fought to catch their breaths.

Finally, Aniela pulled herself up to her arms to look at her husband. His face was filled with such awe, such love, and a great tenderness as he kissed her deeply.

"My God," he said to her, "I can't imagine loving you any more than I do today. You surprise me, you delight me, you are my everything, dancing girl. My everything."

Aniela kissed him gently, and whispered, "I love you, husband," before she lay her weary head on the pillow. She fell asleep almost immediately, the thought dancing in her head that she had found a sure-fire method to tame her Henryk, her tiger.

Each day presented a question for Aniela: which Joachim would show up for work? Some days, he was consumed by business, poring over figures, barking orders over the phone, rushing to and from appointments. On those days, though the stress of being around him was great, she could be just a secretary and maybe even fade in the background for a little while.

But the other days, when his eyes were strangely dilated, or he had the smell of liquor wafting off of him, was when he was most dangerous. He would enter the office and talk to Aniela like a lover, or as a man does to a wife, often bringing a gift for her stolen from Canada.

Today was one of those days. Joachim burst into the office with his usual energy, and urged Aniela to stand up and go to the window with him. The sun was shining brightly through the panes, though it was a cold day.

"Look what I brought for you," he boasted, his voice like a purr. He pulled a red leather box from his jacket and flipped it open, revealing a stunning necklace and earring set sparkling with diamonds and rubies. He gently pulled the necklace from the box and placed it around Aniela's slender neck, admiring how the light bouncing off the windows reflected the brilliance of the precious stones.

"*Wunderbar*," he said, taking the back of his hand and rubbing it against Aniela's cheek. "You look like a queen, my little angel."

"Herr Beckmann…" Aniela protested.

"Joachim," he corrected. "When it's just you and me, call me Joachim."

Aniela started, "Joachim, why are you bringing me these gifts? You know I can't keep them."

"I know," he said, looking deeply into Aniela's eyes. "I want to pamper you. You know that you… are special to me, right?"

Aniela nodded and took a gamble, seeing his desire to please her reflected in his dark green eyes.

"I do, Joachim, of course I do," Aniela said softly, forcing herself to turn her face sweetly up to him. "But there are things about my life that I want you to know. So you understand me better."

Joachim smiled, and led her to the chaise lounge. "Tell me, then," he urged. "What do you want me to know?"

"I am married," Aniela said, then amended, "Or *was* married. I have not heard from my husband since 1939, so I don't know if he is alive or dead."

"I understand," Joachim said, stroking her hand.

"And we had a daughter, Wanda. She was taken from me on April 5th,

1944, by the Nazi authorities in Kraków. The man who took her was Gauleiter Schreiber."

"Taken from you?"

"For the Germanization program," Aniela said, her voice a whisper and eyes brimming as she formed the hated words. "She looks a lot like me, blonde hair, blue eyes. So-called Nordic traits. She's only five."

Joachim stopped, surprised by the news. "So your daughter was taken away from you and sent to Germany for Aryanization?"

"I believe so," Aniela said, a tear running down her face. "I never saw her again. I don't know where she is, if she is safe with a German couple, if they treat her well and love her. Or if she didn't qualify… They say that children who don't qualify are sent to camps like this one."

Joachim put his arm around Aniela, and the feeling of a comforting shoulder seemed to cleave her. For so many months, she had repressed her pain. But as she sat there, speaking of her daughter and seeing the gold ringlets and sparkling eyes in her mind, Aniela forgot for a moment that she was crying out her woes to a Nazi, and just succumbed to her grief.

Joachim held her tenderly as she cried, murmuring to her, "I'm sure she is safe somewhere. She is likely being loved by a nice couple somewhere safe in the German countryside…"

But this just seemed to make Aniela more despondent.

"Easy, my angel," Joachim said, kissing the tears from her cheeks. And then his mouth was on her salty lips, his hands tangled in her hair. Aniela registered that he wanted her, and unlike the time on his desk, he was tenderly asking her if she'd give herself to him. If she would allow him in.

It felt so good to be comforted, after so many years of torment borne alone, and Aniela leaned into him, opening her mouth to take his exploring tongue. Joachim groaned deeply, and began unbuttoning her blouse, his hands seeking her breasts. She clung to his wide shoulders, as she felt his ardor increase as she returned his kisses.

"I want you, Aniela," he whispered, pulling her blouse over her head and lowering his large head to her erect nipples. She was momentarily surprised how large he looked compared to her own compact frame, but closed her eyes as he took one nipple, then the other, in his mouth, his tongue flicking them in turn. The thought of Henryk flitted through her mind, but she pushed it aside, and let her desire unfurl in her belly.

Instead, she thought of Wanda and what this man could do for her if he would only try. If this was the way to get a man to do what she wanted, well, she was going to give him all that she had.

And so she made love to him; she clung to him and gasped in his ear as he entered her. He looked down at her, concern in his eyes. "Am I hurting you?"

She shook her head and hugged herself to his large frame, driving him deeper into her. She heard his breath grow ragged in her ear, and she quietly urged him on.

Her endearments seemed to be his undoing, and with a blazing intensity in those eyes that seemed black with passion, he convulsed with frenetic energy. He collapsed over her, and she breathed shallowly under his crushing frame, but made no effort to move.

When he came to his senses, he rolled off of her, facing her on the couch, their bodies touching. He fingered the necklace, admiring how it rested against her flushed skin.

"You are so beautiful. The sounds that you make. The way your face changes when I'm in you. It's just so... beautiful." He reached over to touch her face, gently stroking her full lower lip with his thumb.

"That was wonderful," she said, complimenting him shyly. "So wonderful."

He stared at her, memorizing every angle of her delicate face, a look of pure awe etched on his angular face with the pronounced jawline.

"I will try," he whispered, and Aniela's heart skipped a beat, for she understood what he meant. But she needed to hear more.

"What will you try, Joachim?" she said softly, her eyes like velvet.

"I will try to locate your daughter," he said. "I will make inquiries. Write down every detail — her birth date, birth name, what she was wearing..."

"Oh, Joachim! Thank you," Aniela said, her eyes glistening, and she kissed him with such feeling and such passion, he would have sworn she was madly in love with him.

Chapter 59

Presents

She was sweet as cream to him, smiling when he entered the office, no matter what his mood, no matter if there was that dreaded eerie dilated look in his eyes. She ignored that far-off look or the smell of alcohol on his breath, and welcomed him with such pleasure that at times, it undid him. Her face beaming up at him, with turquoise eyes sparkling, often had a calming effect on him, bringing him back to the man that he wanted to be and not the man drowning under the pressure of financing what looked to be a losing war.

Aniela vowed she would be nothing but lovely to him every second in his presence so that he wouldn't question her devotion or delay in helping locate Wanda. And in this way, she learned more about this enigmatic man. He told her that he had been born in Augsburg, and had been swept up by the National Socialist movement as a way to get ahead in his career. Joachim's father had been a mechanic for the Mengele company, who manufactured farm equipment locally, and he had urged Joachim to get involved as a way to get beyond their modest social standing.

Joachim Beckmann was seduced by the mantra of the elite Nazi party. He had been a meager accountant at the local granary, a man with no particular distinction or prospects. By joining the party, a new path appeared before him — brightly lit and full of opportunity. To get to the highest ranks, he had to forego fealty to religion, to conventional institutions such as monogamy or to childish notions of fairness. His new philosophy was heroic realism, the idea that men were the natural leaders in the world order, and that fighting and subjugating the weak was the natural state of the manliest of men.

Women were to be revered for their fecundity and ability to produce more perfect German citizens, and through those numbers, Germany would take its natural place as the leader of all humankind, ensuring a thousand years of prosperity through the Third Reich. The best specimen of man had a duty to spread his seed and populate the world with his superior offspring.

Heroic realism favored men that fit a certain build, height and temperament. In this world, there was no pity for the weak. Pity, they argued, was an inherently feminine and Semitic notion, not fitting for warring, thinking and dominant men. There was no honor in pity, no benefit in protecting the weak, the ill or old. When confronted with thoughts of empathy, compassion or tolerance, the men reminded themselves that those ideas were the result of a Jewish propaganda machine eroding the progress of all mankind with outdated and sentimental ideals.

And so Joachim found heroic realism flattered his sense of importance in the world, and reminded him every day that he was better than the next man, and certainly more valuable than any woman. His wife, a devout Catholic, was horrified to learn that Joachim would abandon his faith and profess loyalty to Adolf Hitler and the National Socialism party. Joachim shrugged off her concerns as evidence of the childlike intellect of women and the old-fashioned brainwashing of antiquated religions; silly ideas that had no place in the world they were striving to build. The only honor was in fighting for one's own people, for one's own success and prosperity. Anything else was puerile.

Joachim admitted that he was married, but that his wife, a very religious woman, had not agreed with his decision to join the party and that their marriage had been over for ages, but as a Catholic, she would never divorce. They had lived separately for years and had no children to bind them.

"You were raised Catholic?" Aniela asked in surprise.

"Yes," Joachim said. "I was an altar boy, too."

Aniela stared at the large, lanky man in front of her, confusion in her eyes. What decisions, what concessions, what bargains had led a former altar boy to be counting gold and jewels amassed by murdering Jews, Poles, and the elite of Europe in this corner of her native Poland, now woefully occupied?

"I was raised Catholic, too," Aniela said, pushing away her thoughts. "Though that was more my mother's influence than my Dad's. He was a humanist, a scholar…"

"Is your father alive?" Joachim asked softly, noting wistfulness in her voice.

"No, Joachim," she said, looking down at her hands. "He was a professor at Jagiellonian University and was sent to Sachsenhausen in November of 1939. He died there in the Spring of 1940."

Joachim swallowed hard as he took in this news. "You have lost a lot, haven't you, little angel?"

She looked at him with sincerity, and nodded. "Yes. But still, there are those who have lost more."

She thought about all the skeletal prisoners that she saw every day on her way to and from her secretarial detail. Those souls had lost their families, too, as well as creature comforts, dignity, and hope. Once again, she was thankful that her youth and beauty had granted her special privileges — whether it was fair or not didn't register in this corrupt world. The concept of fairness was something for children or the demented.

"Oh!" Joachim jumped up from his chair and reached into his jacket hanging on a peg by the door. "I've something for you…"

With a big grin, he pulled out another fine leather box. She opened it, and found a simple gold necklace with a pendant of a little angel, with two small diamonds encrusted in the wings.

"For my little angel," he said softly. "You might be able to wear this under your prison clothes…"

Aniela shook her head no. "Don't ask me to take that risk, Joachim. This is very beautiful and thoughtful. But let it remain here with the other gifts. I'll put it on every morning when I change for work. If this is found on me, I don't have to tell you what will happen…"

"Yes, you are right, of course. I just like the idea of a part of me touching you at all times, my angel," Joachim said, kissing her on the forehead.

Chapter 60

Blok 42

It was early October, and a light snow was already drifting by the windowpanes, obscuring the tree limbs from view. The earth was beginning to freeze, and winter winds howled outside. Aniela sat at her desk, typing up correspondence.

Yesterday afternoon, Joachim had brought a bunch of flowers into the office, setting them on her desk. The sight of the colorful blooms — they were white peonies with a hint of pink — was like a window into a foreign world. Somewhere outside the bleak walls of the camp was a greenhouse where out-of-season flowers were cultivated to adorn fancy homes and tablecloths in the finest of restaurants.

Her mind had strayed to the wildflower wreath that Henryk had woven in Wieliczka, plucked by his own hand and placed on her head like a crown on a golden summer day so long ago. She stared at the flowers, her face expressionless.

She realized that Herr Beckmann was awaiting her reaction, and recovered. She turned a beaming smile to him, her face emanating joy, her turbulent memories hidden.

"Do you like them?" he pressed, eager to please.

"They are extraordinary," she said honestly.

"And the chocolates?" he pressed. She had shared the chocolate with the girls in the barracks, making sure to give Kapo Sabine the biggest piece. She had not touched it herself, finding that little offers such as these went a long way in improving her station among the secretaries as a non-German.

"It was heavenly," Aniela lied, noting Herr Beckmann's satisfied smile.

Aniela looked up from her correspondence, noticing that one of the peony petals was yellowing already. She grimly noted that beauty did not last, especially in Auschwitz.

The door swung open, and two senior, important-looking SS officers dressed in immaculate crisp black uniforms strode in.

"Heil Hitler," the men said in formal greeting, extending their right arms. Herr Beckmann stood to attention and saluted in kind.

"We are investigating the loss of great amounts of money," said a man in his late fifties with wireless spectacles. His tone was hard and flat, his demeanor haughty. "These sums are expected by Berlin to help continue to finance our fight. And as you are high-ranking in this department, we will start with you and all the senior officers. I am Herr Krabbenschmidt, and along with Herr Stengel, we are part of a team sent to conduct a raid of all offices and personal lodgings at exactly the same time, so we can root out who is stealing."

Joachim's mouth opened in surprise. "I can assure you, *mein kommandant*, that we run a tight ship here. Everything is in order."

Krabbenschmidt gave Joachim a withering look. "We shall see about that…" He turned and saw Aniela standing by her desk, her face pale.

"Ah, yes," the senior Nazi continued. "We had made our inquiries about all our senior officers. You are Herr Joachim Beckmann. There has been some discussion about your fondness for pretty secretaries."

The man looked Aniela up and down, making her feel as if she had been publicly undressed, and she lowered her eyes in shame.

Stengel began opening up every drawer in Joachim's desk, searching for hidden compartments and false bottoms. Satisfied, he moved to the bookcase and began examining the books, and making sure nothing was stashed in their bindings. He then moved to the *garderobe*, and Aniela and Joachim exchanged a look of panic. They both knew what he kept there — behind his row of uniforms and suits were Aniela's secretarial clothes. But in the back at the bottom, there was a shoebox where the jewels he had bestowed upon her were kept, as well as a large leather hat box with the fur stole and lined gloves.

It didn't take long for the man to pull out the box, and he laid it on the desk for his superior to see. The older man slowly opened up the box, seeing the ruby and diamond necklace, earrings, the gold necklace with diamond-encrusted angel, and he turned accusatory eyes to Herr Beckmann.

"So," Krabbenschmidt said in a clipped tone, "we have found one of our thieves."

Herr Beckmann spluttered, "I'm sorry, sir. I've never seen these items before."

The senior Nazi turned a skeptical eye to Herr Beckmann, fingering the fine jewels with a gloved hand. "Really? You, who has direct access to the *Effektenlager*, have never seen these items before?"

"I have not," Herr Beckmann said firmly, his voice growing in confidence. "What use would I have for such feminine items, anyway? These clearly were stashed there by my Polish secretary."

Aniela gasped, as the two Nazis turned their gazes onto her.

Krabbenschmidt turned an incredulous eye to Herr Beckmann, then continued staring at Aniela as he said, "So, we are to believe that your secretary waltzed into the *lager*, and managed to smuggle these items right under your nose..."

"All the secretaries accompany us to the *lager* from time to time," Herr Beckmann improvised, pressing his point. "Many of the women working at the *lager* are Poles, and you know how they stick together, always looking for a way to cheat us... they could've colluded."

"Is that right?" the senior Nazi said, his eyes never leaving Aniela.

"I swear, I had no idea about those items being hidden in my office," Beckmann said, sweat popping out on his forehead.

Krabbenschmidt looked at Joachim Beckmann with penetrating eyes, sizing him up carefully. Beckmann stood there, trying to hide his nervousness; he knew his life hung in the balance.

After a long while, the senior Nazi said, "As you wish. We will note that your secretary is the thief. We will add this to your file, Herr Beckmann, that you lacked the judgement and acumen to be aware there was a thief working for you, in your very office. You have dishonored us all."

"Clearly, you were bamboozled by a pretty face." Krabbenschmidt turned to his compatriot. "Please bring her outside and have her executed, Herr Stengel."

Aniela blanched and her face drained of color as Herr Stengel grabbed her arm and started dragging her to the door.

"Wait," Herr Beckmann exclaimed, his face taut and strained. "You are right that she is an uncommonly pretty woman. And yes, I'm sure that I was foolish not to see beyond her charms. But don't you see, *mein kommandant*, what a waste it would be to destroy such a beauty by a bullet?"

The commander looked at Herr Beckmann with disbelief. "What are you suggesting, sir?"

"Send her to Blok 42," Beckmann said. "Such a woman will do more good there than executed against the black wall."

Krabbenschmidt turned pale eyes to Aniela as Herr Stengel gripped her tightly around her bicep.

"An interesting thought," the commander said, stroking his chin. "You may be right, Herr Beckmann, that she may be of better use to us all there."

He turned to Stengel and said in a clipped tone, "Take her to the brothel."

Chapter 61

Haraeth

Since America had joined the fight, the Germans were aware that the tide of war was turning against them. There were doubts whether Germany could continue to press onwards, with America and Russia joining the Allies. But a cynical desire was not to be subverted, even as the war raged on. They may lose Russia, they may lose some battles, but they would not abandon their Final Solution. Himmler proudly discussed the Final Solution in 1942, a radical idea that every last Jew was to be purged from the earth's surface. Previous discussions about shipping the Jews of Europe to Madagascar were replaced with a much bolder idea: total and utter annihilation.

But two years later, the Germans concluded that at the current pace of rounding up Jews into ghettos and sending them to work or concentration camps, they'd never reach their goal of ridding Europe of its Jews. Orders were issued to accelerate the pace. Ghettos were to be liquidated immediately, from the smallest hamlets of northern Poland to the busiest cities. The Nazis turned their attention to the Jews of Hungary, many of whom had been protected by a government that had tried to assuage the Germans while still avoiding their cruel demands.

Mass deportations clogged the rail lines, and the concentration camps were inundated with transports from all over Europe. More and more prisoners were needed to unload the wagons and force the scared and shell-shocked passengers to separate from their loved ones, line up, disrobe and walk into the fake showers that were truly gas chambers. The Nazis in charge of the camps needed more hands to sort through suitcases, purses, wallets and clothing. The pace of the demands was crushing, and many a prisoner preferred to "take a stroll to the electric fence" rather than to continue gruesome tasks such as shoveling cadavers into chimneys.

The Germans realized that incentives, even for the most powerless prisoners, were needed. And women, as was always the case in times of love and war, provided the motivation.

***

She had discovered the odd skill of disassociation. It was as if her entire self was cleaved in two. There was the mind, a mind that lived in a loop of memories of the past — Henryk carrying books after school, Ewa and Aniela dancing in a recital as Pani Ostrowska beamed with pride, evenings sitting in a warm, cozy living room with a book in her lap, her father chewing on his pipe as he worried over some prose, Irena and her mother playing music together.

She kept away from thoughts of Wanda as if it were a sentence to recall the first moments when she felt her daughter move inside of her, or when she first held her, or the swell of her heart when Henryk picked up his baby for the first time. Those bittersweet memories had the power to sever the soul and crack the mind. Nor did she think about the intimacy that lay in the past between Henryk and herself. Her mind never strayed to their honeymoon in Zakopane, where they first learned each other's sighs, gasps and groans, exploring every inch of each other with the force of a dam bursting. She could not bring herself to think about the look on his face when he was over her, inside of her, and about to climax — the grimace of pleasure mixed with a twinge of awe that signaled ultimate release, pleasure and love.

In her life as a sex slave, Aniela could not bring herself to think about sex at all. The body became some distant extension — a tool, as functional as a hammer or a rolling pin. Her body was now an object to be used to get a job done, but nothing more intimate or personal, and certainly not a part of her.

Breasts, waist, hips, legs, vagina — they were just outside expressions of someone else's desire, fantasy and biological need. As man after man entered her room, she could see from their reactions that they saw her as something designed and created expressly for their pleasure. The men assigned to Aniela were all Polish — in keeping with the German system of things — and she grew numb and indifferent to their eyes that widened

288

upon seeing her. There was a blok where Jewish sex slaves serviced the Jewish men who manned the crematoria, and the Kapo said that there were even *"FeldHuren"* on the front, servicing German infantry. Those whores were, of course, German, as no mixing of the races was permitted.

The unwashed men would come in, smelling of sweat, dust, and ash, their penises dripping with the acrid smell of spermicide. Hair cut short but still oily, with gaunt faces that had an eerie gray twinge, each man would set his gaze upon her and reacted as if she was a vision from another world.

Sitting in a robe, with hair washed and brushed, with neither sunken cheeks nor concave bellies, she was certain that the "brothel" women looked like pinups compared to the cadaverous, shrunken women that the prisoners glimpsed across the yard or from their work details. Out there, only one out of ten women made it through selection, and those who did were stripped of their femininity and humanity instantly. Aniela was thinner than she had been in the pre-war days, but still had breasts, her hips flared narrowly, and she didn't have the knock-kneed look of a starving prisoner.

"My God, you're lovely..." Each number would utter a similar platitude, eyes raking her over, imagining possessing her body. "I had heard that there was a certain Polish angel in the brothel; I never dared hope I'd get the chance to be with her."

The men even addressed her in the third person, as if her body was a stranger to them both, so it became almost natural to let the brain drift to some other faraway place as the clumsy and vulgar reality of her existence played itself out.

"No talking!" barked the Nazi guard on duty, who watched the proceedings from a small sliding window in the door. His job was to ensure that no talking transpired between Aniela and the male prisoner, and that coitus would ensue perfunctorily and in missionary position, keeping to the schedule of fifteen minutes per man.

From there, the man would discard his prison clothes. She made no effort to welcome or seduce the "number", but sat on the bed — naked under her robe, eyes and face blank of emotion or feeling.

Most of the men would become erect immediately, and stroke themselves as they came over to the bed, eyes huge in their heads, resembling something akin to an insect, with their wiry limbs and bulging eyes and penises. These creatures bore no resemblance to any men she had ever known.

She lay down on the bed and allowed the robe to open. Quickly, the man would crawl on top of her, and she turned her head to the side to avoid breathing him in. She forced her brain to go somewhere else as his weight shifted over her — she sought and found the loop in her head of pleasant memories and allowed herself to linger there like a broken record, disconnecting brain from body as she felt rough fingers grab breasts, hands pull apart thighs and an unfamiliar penis slide up between them into her.

There were the men who called out the names of a lover. Aneta. Maria. Danuta. A wife, a girlfriend, the one who got away, or a woman killed? She knew not, nor did she care. These were the ones who, like her, were somewhere else in their heads, and she recognized and even understood their impulse to escape into their own fantasy, even if it was for just fifteen minutes. Her body was the vessel to enable their escape.

Others came with the primacy of an animal. Those were the men who seemed to have nothing more than a pent-up biological need. She lay under them as they grunted and groaned in her ear, their hips gyrating over her in a mad rhythm that would have reminded one of a humping dog or jackrabbit, if one chose to think of those things. But her mind was somewhere else, and while she registered the actions on her body as she was shaken and thrust upon, it seemed as if she was witnessing the whole affair from some distant vantage point, like watching two animals copulate in a zoo.

Such a man tended not to linger, and would be done quickly and loudly. Only then would he look into her face. There was one man who had shaken her roughly under his driving hips and finished within less than a minute, who looked into her eyes and asked, "How was it for you?"

She looked at him in astonishment, at a loss for words. *It was rape*, came to mind, but she said nothing, not only because of the non-talking rule, but because of the absurdity of even formulating a response.

"That was my first time with a woman," he whispered. With gray taut skin, shaved head, and the skin around his eyes dark and bruised, she would have taken him to be in his forties. It occurred to her absently that he was likely younger than she.

"Thank you," he said. "I hope to see you again."

And then there were those who would weep during or after sex. Those numbers were often older — although nobody could guess anyone's age in the camp. These men sometimes managed to creep into her disconnected mind, even when she had so trained and fixed it on a distant place. These sad men experienced sex as if transported to an age where a man could lay with a woman and be as one. A time when sex was consensual and not a transaction. A time when a man had dignity and was not vanquished by enemies who had stolen his country, a time when a man could own his life, have a sense of agency, and not live life like a beast under a whip.

Those moments of touching soft, feminine skin brought on a rush of memories of a life that was lost, and the floodgates of emotion followed the release of their loins. The Polish men at the camp who visited her room were political enemies or suspected partisans — men who had risked and lost everything. Simply lying with a beautiful woman unhinged and gutted them more completely and quickly than the months of unrelenting roll call, work details and degradation.

Aniela could almost pity such a fellow creature if she had any feeling left at all. Then the inevitable comment, "You have it so good here" would snap any feeling of humanity that existed between sex slave and prisoner rapist, and they were all reduced to the white heat of shame and indignation and hopelessness that had taken over their existence. Compassion for someone else had little perch in the camp — better to think of oneself, to be convinced that your life was worth more than the one next to you. That was the way to survive this horror of a place — only the strong were rewarded here; weakness was exploited and trampled on by others.

It was why the conditions for women were so much worse than the men's. She had seen other women on her return to the women's barracks in Birkenau. The sad, gaunt creatures — who resembled malnourished children more than women — so many didn't even have enough clothes to protect their shrunken bodies. These women worked like mules in fields and subsisted on potato skins and gruel. They eyed Aniela and the other brothel workers from a distance with dead eyes. Did they resent them for better food and clothes? The more tolerable living conditions? But like them, all the women owned nothing and counted for nothing. Even their bodies had become the property of not only their captors, but of other prisoners, underscoring how little value was placed on the "weaker" sex.

This travesty was truly a man's world — where men exploited and dominated other men, and together they colluded to exploit women, whose children were rounded up to die in chambers or left to scrounge for themselves. This world was a nightmare of the most perverted and distorted kind, and it would drive one mad quickly and to utter despair.

And so she disconnected brain from body — and lived in memories of the past, or fantasies of an imagined future. She lived in a world of characters from books read, and cast herself as part of their story, not living in the filth and shame of her own.

Another man entered her room. Fifteen minutes had come and gone, and it was time for the next prisoner.

Chapter 62

The Visit

Three weeks passed, and Aniela was still breathing. The fact that the men referred to building 42 as a brothel made her blood turn to ice. A brothel? There was a woman ceremoniously put in charge — resembling a madam, but truly a Kapo — but she still reported to one master officer, Oswald "Papa" Kaduk. And just because women had sex here with strange men, didn't make this place a brothel. What a euphemism it was to normalize the reality of it!

Because, of course, there was no payment. And no consent either, though she had heard enough stories from the other women to learn the sad ways many had found themselves forced into the paid sex trade before the war. These women, marked as anti-socials by a black, upside-down triangle patch sewn onto their shirts, had known a life of selling their bodies for money. Some were working off a debt, others were trying to feed children, others were tricked into it and lacked the intelligence and resources to escape. But the removal of the red upside-down triangle patch (denoting Polish political prisoner) that was replaced with a black patch (antisocial) showed that the system for classifying prisoners was a fluid one in this regime.

No, this was no brothel. It was a place for sex slaves, of systematic rape — all designed so that the male prisoners would work a little harder, or resist a little less. Female bodies were nothing but bait to motivate male behaviors, and the only payment received for this work was better meals, better hygiene, and except for those fifteen minutes, separation from all other prisoners. And yet these "perks" didn't exist because of any concern for the women, but rather because the men who visited would complain if the girls were too sickly, skinny and not womanly looking.

The men thought the women of Blok 42 had it so good because the women were not skeletal and smelled clean to them. They had no inkling of the horror of the daily lives, forced to be invaded by stranger after stranger, locked in a room with nothing but a robe and a lumpy bed. The women were not their sisters, daughters, mothers, neighbors. Even the fact that they were all Poles seemed to be lost, as Blok 42 women were simply objects — a means to an end. The men referred to the Blok as the "puff", which sounded light and airy. Really, what a romp, what a good time a visit to the puff must be for them!

It was on a Thursday evening, after Aniela's last "number" had left, when Joachim purposefully strode in, dressed immaculately in his uniform. He filled up the small room with his presence, stopping short when he saw her sitting slumped on the bed, robe open and revealing breasts that had been touched and tortured by countless hands.

She looked up at him and resisted the urge to cover herself. Her eyes bore into him, anger bringing color to pale cheeks.

"I…" he started awkwardly, looking down at Aniela with a tense face. "I wanted to see how you were doing."

She opened her mouth to speak, and closed it.

He glanced at the window in which the guard watched over her visits. "I sent the guard away. We're alone."

Perhaps he was here for the exact same reason as all the other men? The thought must have shown on her face and he came toward her, kneeling in front of her and gently pulling her robe closed. "I am here to see how you are, Aniela."

He was almost even with her, so she could stare directly into his face. She noted that he looked more haggard since she last saw him; there were shadows under his eyes, and his wandering eye gave him that slightly demented look. A muscle twitched alarmingly in his temple. His body was stiff and tense in front of her.

"Talk to me, goddammit," he exploded. "How are you?"

She looked into that face — the beakish nose, the overly defined jaw, and blazing eyes, and saw only the face of the man who betrayed her.

"How am I?" she whispered hoarsely.

"Yes, please tell me." He took her hands in his; he was almost begging.

"I am a sex slave," she said flatly, looking over his shoulder and not meeting his eyes. "I have sex with strange men in fifteen-minute intervals.

In return, I'm told how good I have it to have better food."

Joachim's Adam's apple noticeably bobbed as he searched her emotionless face.

"This is not what I wanted for you," he said raggedly. "You must see, this was my only choice. The only way to protect you."

Her eyes snapped to his, full of fury. "Protect *me*? You were protecting *yourself*!"

She noticed beads of sweat appearing on his brow, as he took her by the shoulders and shook her.

"No! No!" he said forcefully. "You must see, if I had not blamed you for the theft, I would've been shot as a traitor. And with me dead, you'd be sent right back to the barracks in Birkenau. My reputation at the camp is compromised and I have been severely disciplined, but they can't afford to lose men. Can't you see? I have managed to protect you here."

She looked around the stark room, the sheets soiled and reeking of sperm, spermicide, sweat and soiled bodies. Her nose flared in disgust for this atrocious place and for him.

"You were the one that assuaged your guilt by pampering me with pilfered jewelry and furs. You thought you could bite the hand that fed you and you drew them to us," Aniela spat. "Why couldn't you be satisfied with just doing your evil job? No! Instead, you had to believe in your own heroism and chivalry, to disguise the facts that were in plain sight: you are a criminal, a thief, and a rapist. Your actions have led me to this horrid place."

A chill went down her spine as she faced Joachim, drained of any fear of him. Drained of the protocol to stay silent. She had lost her husband, her baby, her dignity and her freedom. There was nothing left to lose.

"Only you sick, delusional Nazis would envision a brothel as a place to protect women," she seethed. "Look at this horrible world you created. You corrupted the world with your greed masked as ideology. The horrors you have foisted on me and my people — it's all just an elaborate way for weak men to feel strong by nothing more than thuggery. You bully, beat and intimidate the old, the weak, the frail. You delight in stealing possessions from Jews and the rich. You murder old professors and steal babies from mother's arms. You set up barracks for women to be systematically raped. You fill up buildings with the spoils gained by robbery, as people who have worked hard and honestly their whole lives are reduced to ash."

Hatred for him and his entire people pulsed out of her like a fever.

"It's not like that," he said feebly, shocked by her diatribe.

She shook her head, gazing over his shoulder and not meeting his pleading eyes. "It is exactly like that. You and your compatriots are criminals who justify your behavior behind Nazi bullshit."

Her eyes met his. "And you, Joachim, who were raised Catholic — like me. You should know better. You know the difference between right and wrong."

Joachim reached out and took her face in his hands, his eyes moist, his face full of regret.

"You have it all wrong," he said, voice breaking. "I'm a good man. If you had met me in my previous life, you would've seen that. You and me, we would have been..."

She looked at him, eyes cold, daring him to continue. "We would have been what?"

"You would have loved me," he said quietly.

She could have laughed, if she still knew how to. Love him? The man who she had feared as both protector and captor? She thought of Henryk, his strong wide shoulders, green blue eyes, and thick dark hair. Her heart constricted tightly in her chest. Henryk's was the face of love. Joachim's was the face of a monster.

"Never," she said, knowing that he was not used to being defied. She was daring him to strike her, to drag her out of Blok 42 and to throw her against the electrified fence. She was so sick of his deceit; she was reckless in her candor.

"No," he said, standing up and backing away. "You are wrong, Aniela. I have protected you here. I have done the honorable thing — it was the only way."

He made his way to the door, and stopped to take a final look at her. She sat on the bed, the robe covering her nakedness, as still as a statue and just as cold.

He turned and left, the door to her prison locking behind him as he strode away.

Chapter 63

Lost Girls

Aniela returned to the shared rooms where she lived with the other women forced to work at the brothel. She was greeted by the Kapo "Madam" in charge, Karolina. Karolina had been a madam on the outside, and had a grim, no-nonsense view of the world. She had always known men as exploiters of women, and profited quite handsomely for over twenty years. Now somewhere in her mid-forties, Karolina expressed mild resentment that there was no money as a Kapo keeping women primed and ready for Polish prisoners. But when she was ensnared in a roundup, she was happy to ply her lifetime's trade in the prison — for better food, softer beds free of lice, the occasional chocolate or bottle of nail polish, and she had stopped giving a damn what anybody thought long ago.

"Working for the enemy?" Karolina scoffed, when one of the girls asked if she minded having the Krauts as her pimp. "Inside or outside these walls, they are all men: led by their simple desire for sex. I don't concern myself which uniform they wear. Using our bodies for profit or favors is of value, and I'll be damned if I wind up being slowly killed carrying rocks from one pile to another all day."

Liliana sat on the edge of her bed, painting her nails. Karolina encouraged the women to take care of nails, hair and skin the best they could.

"*Being a woman is a terribly difficult task, since it consists principally in dealing with men*," said Liliana, with a dramatic pause. "Joseph Conrad."

Aniela leaned against the bunk's bedframe shakily. Liliana looked up, seeing Aniela's wan face.

"Are you all right?" she said worriedly, patting the bunk. Here in the brothel, the women happily shared manicures and brushed out each other's hair — as a way to take pride in routines that could be shared only with fellow women, and not as a siren call for the men who took up their days.

"I don't know," Aniela said, her throat still tight. She sat down, and told her friend about the unexpected visit from Joachim Beckmann.

Liliana listened intently, nodding sympathetically, and patted Aniela's frigid hand. Liliana was only twenty-three, and had black hair that had grown back around her well-shaped head like a dark helmet. She had been working in the brothel for six months before Aniela arrived. It was Liliana who made the evenings worthwhile, because she intentionally kept her conversation away from the horror of their present reality. She called it "meditation" — the act of talking about anything other than the men that they were forced to service. She said the highest form of meditation was one of "supreme vegetation" — where one thought of nothing at all. That, she said, was the key to sheer contentment.

"The only thing that I think of," Aniela continued, "is the need for me to keep my wits about me in order to survive and find my daughter."

"It is hard to keep one's brain from returning to the only person that gives one the will to survive," Liliana said in commiseration. Aniela knew she was thinking of her younger sister, Anna.

They had bonded over their grief about losing a loved one. In Liliana's case, she was swept up in a roundup along with her mother and little sister. Liliana relayed the horrifying first moments on the grounds of Auschwitz, where the women were separated from the men. She recounted the shock of seeing tall, blond men wearing high black boots, armed with bully clubs and whips. They were petrified by their snarling, barking German Shepherds.

"The meanest ones got those jobs," Liliana recalled.

Liliana and her mother had held the hand of her sister, Anna, who was just thirteen years old. From their porch, the Nazis bayed at the women — directing them to form a line to the right or to the left. Liliana and her sister were separated from their mother, who was ordered to join the line on the left. Liliana and Anna went to the right.

Liliana had hesitated, wanting to keep the family together — she tried to join the line on the left. The left line was filled with women holding babies, cripples and old women.

But her mother said, "No! You must go with Anna to the right."

Liliana did what her mother told her to do. Along with the other young women, they were hustled into a building, where they were stripped of their clothes and told to put their items on a numbered hook. Naked and confused, they huddled with strangers in the showers, as they were doused with cold water and chemicals.

Despite the indignity of it all, Liliana tried to calm her sister with reassuring smiles. They never returned to the hooks with their clothes, but instead were given a hodgepodge of clothes and a permanent tattoo on the wrist. Liliana was scandalized to be given a black, sheer evening gown. Anna received a short red dress with ruffles.

"Add a few years to your age," she advised her sister, as if an angel was whispering in her ear.

Anna nodded, her face red with mortification.

"They were absolutely ridiculous outfits," Liliana recalled. "Nothing fit. I had two left shoes and an evening gown. Despite our fear and confusion, I tell you, everyone laughed."

They were marched, in groups of five, to Birkenau. They entered a crowded barrack built for fifty-two horses that now housed eight hundred women. The smell of the unwashed bodies in the tight quarters was another shock. But it was later, when the kapos turned off the lights and the women were crammed into wooden bunks lined with straw, that many of the women realized that their children and family members were not to be seen again. A wail of anguish erupted and spread through the barrack like a virus, and there was nothing the kapo could do to keep the lamentations at bay.

Liliana held her sister close by and the two clung to one another like barnacles. During that first week, when, like everyone else, Anna remarked on the smoke billowing from the stacks, they were shocked to hear a prisoner say, "That is the left line."

After three miserable months, Liliana had been singled out by the kapo for a new detail. She found herself in Blok 42, a sex slave like Aniela, and she grieved over her sister's fate. How was the young Anna managing without her? Did she have a tolerable work detail, protected from the elements? Was she able to hide her real age? It was these worries that struck a chord with Aniela.

In their misery, they found comfort and became fast friends. After sharing their grief about their losses, they found they needed something different to talk about in order to not sink into an abyss of pity and hopelessness. Most days, they fantasized about food. About the best ice cream cone they ever had, about how butter used to be slathered on a fresh roll without a second thought. They talked about meals they would one day eat and vacations they would one day take. Those elaborate dreams helped keep reality at bay, giving it a fuzzy dimension, as if the lives they envisaged were more real than the ones they actually lived.

***

Aniela lived another month in misery, ticking the numbers off in her head, lost in the reverie she created each day. Today, she was trying to remember in exacting detail how to make *szarlotka*. It was a specialty of her mother-in-law, and Aniela transported herself back to Wieliczka and slowly imagined every detail on how to make that delicious cake. She imagined walking beside the carefully trimmed apple trees outside of the house, filling a basket with the plump fruit. She examined each apple carefully, noting bruises and spots where the worms had been there first. She felt the cool water on her hands as she washed the apples and sorted them. She took a sharp knife and began peeling the skins away. (The skins! Those would have been thrown to the pigs. Here at the camp, people would kill for the taste of an apple peel.)

Aniela chastised herself for that unbidden thought. No, let us return to the careful peeling of the apples. How many would she need for the cake? How thinly must she slice them?

The groan of a man who had finished climaxing over her reminded her that number 11 was done, and Aniela pressed her eyes tightly closed — trying to breathe in the smell of the orchard on a fall day and not to the sweating stranger on top of her.

She felt his weight shift off of her as he got out of bed and made his way to the door. She sat up, straightening her robe, face blank. Just three more numbers and she could return to the barracks, to the oddly comforting camaraderie of Liliana and the other "antisocials", and perhaps tonight a piece of bread with real jam. Maybe even apple butter.

The guard barked, "Next, number 12", and Aniela lowered her eyes to folded hands in her lap. She imagined those hands covered in flour and butter as she sat bent and waiting for the next prisoner.

He stepped in. She heard a sharp intake of breath, as if someone had been punched in the stomach, and looked up in alarm.

Eyes and brain were on separate tracks, and she gaped at the man before her. Dressed in ragged prison clothes, this man had wide shoulders stripped of all but the very last of its muscles. His bony frame hinted of heartiness that once was, but now stood gaunt. His hair was shorn, his brow pronounced, cheeks hollow, and he had a gray cast to his skin. Only the blazing blue green eyes were the same. On wobbly legs, Aniela stood up and strode to him, thinking perhaps this was one of her daydreams come to life, but daring herself to believe her senses.

"Henryk?" she whispered, standing in front of him with beseeching eyes.

With a jerky motion, he reached out to her and violently hugged Aniela to his thin body. She felt his hip bone, his ribs pressing into her flesh, and she embraced him with mad fervor.

Henryk was alive, he was here, he was with her. But… how?

"No hugging!" the guard yelled through his window, breaking their rough embrace.

Henryk released her and took a step back, appraising Aniela.

"You look well," he said flatly, his stare scorching her like a flame.

She was tongue-tied by the comment and searched his face, but could find no emotion there. Was he angry that she was forced to prostitute herself? Or that the act of prostitution ensured her a better meal?

Aniela took a step back, torn between joy at seeing her Henryk alive, but shocked by the man who stood in front of her. She was at a loss at what to say to him. There was no etiquette on what to say when one meets their husband in a brothel, she thought madly.

Finally, Henryk recovered. "What are you doing here?"

Aniela swallowed, not sure where to begin. "I was caught in a *łapanka*," she said, staring intently at the angular face, trying to reconnect with the boyish Henryk of her memory. "And… I was sent to… work here." There was no point in mentioning Joachim or her secretarial work, at least not now.

"But but," he said in confusion. "Here are prostitutes and whores. Antisocials. How can you be among them?"

"No talking!" shouted the guard in German.

A flash of anger quickened her heart even further. "It would be convenient for you men to presume all the women in Blok 42 are antisocials, prostitutes and criminals. But yet I am here... and you are here, too. What crime brought you here?" she asked bitterly.

"No communication between prisoners!" the guard bellowed again.

They stood staring at each other, torn between the desire to hold one another and the shock of the circumstances. But it was Aniela who took her husband's hand and led him to the bed. Henryk's face drained of all color, as he smelled the sweat and sperm on soiled sheets and came face to face with her reality.

She could not talk to him, she could not explain herself to him; the only option she had in front of her was to comfort him in the way that her entire existence was designed.

She reached for him, eyes pleading with him to see her as his dancing girl with the happy eyes he once loved and cherished. She kissed him gently on his hard mouth, suddenly desperate to connect with him, and there in the prison of a room, she knew this was the only option in front of her. She so bitterly regretted their last cold meeting, and she wanted him to find her again.

He was as still and cold as a stone at first, but her familiar soft lips knew the contours of his mouth and it was the memory of that taste and smell that jolted him out of his dazed state. She heard a deep groan in the back of his throat, and he started to kiss her back. They had not seen or touched one another for such a long time, neither knowing if the other was alive.

"No kissing!" screamed the guard.

Aniela ignored the orders from the window in the door, and pushed Henryk, her beloved husband, back on the bed, her mouth never leaving his lips.

Henryk was a shadow of the man she once knew. She could see, from his physical condition to the lackluster sheen of his eyes, that he was surviving on willpower alone. This place had taken his amazing strength and reduced it to a whimper. She felt the need to fortify him, to bolster him, to fill him up with her love and a will to live to make sure that they would meet again outside the walls of this camp.

Aniela climbed on top of him, letting her robe fall open so her breasts dangled freely over his open mouth, and she started to ride him in the rhythmic dance of days past. She felt him grow hard against the fabric of his pants, and she reached down and shimmied them down off his hips. His eyes were large and fixed on her, giant in his head, and with a look that was a combination of entreaty and desire.

"Only missionary position," the guard said weakly, and Aniela knew he was enjoying this show much too much to enforce rules. She was learning her way around men and their rules.

She turned back to Henryk and kissed his mouth, his jaw, his neck, his chest. He grabbed her breasts as she slowly found his member and pressed herself down on him, bringing his full girth easily into her body. She arched back and gasped at the welcome feeling — an odd sensation of novelty and familiarity and so utterly divorced from the "intervals" that had been her daily existence.

"Oh," he cried. "My beautiful dancing girl…"

She leaned down and kissed the tear from the corner of his eye, bringing hips grinding down on his.

"That's right," Aniela whispered in his ear. "It's just you and me, husband and wife, making love. I am sanctifying my love for you right here and now. Nobody can take this away from us. It's ours and ours alone."

Henryk grabbed her around her waist tightly, pressing her down to him. Her breasts flattened against his bony chest, with her breath in his ear as they found a familiar and ancient groove. They danced together, clinging to one another, and brought one another to a place so powerful, she lost all sense of time and place.

She collapsed on top of him, trying to catch her breath. Henryk's breath was ragged, and when she lifted her head to see his face, she realized with a squeeze to her heart that he was weeping.

"Henryk?" she whispered, taking his face in her hands.

"How am I to go back?" he cried softly, his chest shaking. "How am I to go back to the ashes, knowing that you are here? How can I abandon you to… this?"

She started kissing the tears, stroking his face, eyes locked onto his. "You will go back, Henryk. You must survive. I will survive this for you and for Wanda. You go back and survive your daily hell for us. We will be together again. This is not the end."

"What kind of man…?" he whispered, his voice breaking.

"We will be together again, my darling," she said, weeping over him. "Find the strength in us and believe it."

"*Genug*! Enough!" the guard shouted. "*Raus, numer 12!*"

Henryk wiped his face and stood up, looking at her with a desperately bleak expression.

"Hear what I have said, Henryk," Aniela said urgently, grabbing his hand. "Survive."

Henryk stumbled out of the room, as the guard took him by the collar and hurried him along. He did not have a chance to take one final look back.

The door clicked behind him, and Aniela numbly grabbed her robe and tightened it around her, imagining the robe to be Henryk's arms still warm on her body. She sat on the edge of the bed and let out a wail of such desperate and complete sadness that her cries ricocheted around the small chamber, filling up the prison with the sounds of despair.

She had not asked him how he was, or how he had found himself in this godforsaken place. All they had was stolen conversation and fifteen minutes on a mattress, and she suddenly felt the shock of seeing him. On one hand, she felt a blazing joy so intense that it made her feel a bit lightheaded. He was alive. On the other hand, she could not get the haunted memory of his ragged and reduced state out of her brain. He looked as if he was being worked to death, and that he was holding on by pure determination and that amazing brute strength. But how much longer could that strength persist?

But it was seeing her strong husband weeping in front of her, stripped of any power, any ability to protect, shield or save his wife, that reminded her that they had both lost more than their dignity in this brutal camp.

The next number came in and dropped his pants to his knees, and the smell of spermicide reached Aniela's nose.

Her shoulders were convulsing, her face red and swollen. She could not control the tears spilling out of her, as she sat on the edge of the bed, wailing and weeping like some wounded animal.

Number 13 stopped short, and said, "Why are you crying, *pani*?"

Aniela struggled to respond, and after a few moments of desperate gasps, she managed hoarsely, "I'm crying because I just met my husband here in this room."

The man looked a bit surprised, and said absently, "I didn't know any of the whores were married."

And he strode toward her and roughly grabbed a breast through her robe and pushed her down on the bed.

"Sorry to hear about your troubles," he said. "But I have waited a long time to be here, and I'm not going to waste my chance."

He crawled on top of her and jammed himself into her, as she buried her head in the pillow and cried, her body convulsing with sobs, and the man over her grunted in approval.

Chapter 64

News

After that, it was harder for Aniela to cling to her fantasies. She awaited each number with dread and anticipation; maybe this time it would be Henryk again. Living in the moment dragged her back to reality, made her ability to cling to happy memories, fold herself into plot lines of favorite novels, or transport to her domestic past all the harder.

Days ticked by, and Aniela struggled anew with intervals of continuous violation. She longed for the once-strong arms of Henryk nestled around her as they burrowed together like spoons. Fifteen men came and went, and she whispered to each of them, "Have you any news of Henryk Bartosz?"

A grunt, or a sad, "I'm sorry, pani, never heard of him" met her inquiries, and the weeks dragged by with no sighting or news of Henryk. Aniela grew tense and nervous, replaying their last meeting over and over in her head like a broken record. She imagined a thousand conversations not had. Why had she not asked what detail he worked? Why had she not asked the name of his kapo? These were the important questions to ask, and she castigated herself for her stupidity.

Aniela went over the experience with Liliana night after night, her face contorted. For whom was the shock worse? Was it worse for her, to discover her once-robust husband turned into a drained shell of a man, being worked to death by their enemies? Physically, he was more altered than she. Or was it worse for him, to see his wife — also a prisoner — forced into sexual slavery, also by the designs of a mutual foe?

Could he find strength in the fact that she was alive and that someday this hell would end and they could join hands and find their daughter together? Aniela imagined the gates to Auschwitz opening. She would pass under the damnable "*ARBEIT MACHT FREI*" sign and into the grassy fields of her homeland, to find Henryk, to take his hand, to find Wanda, and to begin living again.

But as weeks ticked by and she heard no news of Henryk, Aniela started imagining the worst. People died every day in Auschwitz. Not just those who were condemned to die immediately, but also the young, like Anna, the fit, the strong. They also died every day. Some wasted away from the work and the meager rations; they lost the will to live, and stumbled through their days as *Muselmänner*, a creature that fell easily to one's knees and lacked the strength or the will to get up, and would die alone and stepped over on the ground or beaten to death by a camp guard who demanded the prisoner stand.

Others had accidents. Carrying logs and heavy stones was hard work, and one slip of the foot or loose grasp, and a man could be killed easily on any of those tasks. Or maybe during daily *Appell*, a prisoner unwittingly wore his hat askew and garnered the cruel gaze of the Nazi in charge, and for that crime the prisoner was singled out and forced to stand outside in one position all day and all night until he collapsed from fatigue, went to the hospital and died by an injection of phenol barbital. Aniela had heard those stories and more, and chewed her lip wondering if Henryk could escape the myriad ways death found you at Auschwitz.

She forced herself to eat, though she had no appetite. She could not afford to get too thin and lose her appeal to the men, the men she despised. She needed to remain attractive — her own survival depended on it.

Another week dragged by, terror lacing its grim fingers around her icy heart. Number 9 was pulling on his pants, and she whispered, as always, "Have you any news of Henryk Bartosz?"

The man stopped, looking at her with penetrating eyes.

"Do you know him?" Aniela pressed.

"I think I know of him. I believe he worked a logging detail with a guy from my village."

"Really?" she said quietly, not wanting to draw the guard's attention. "How is he?"

Number 9 looked at her intently, and she felt a shiver of dread crawl down her spine.

"How do you know him, pani?" he said softly.

"He's my husband."

He took a deep long breath, and ran his hands along his skull, a habit that Henryk had, as if he still had hair. "I'm sorry, but I heard that a man named Henryk... I thought it was Bartosz... threw himself against the electrified fence a week or so ago."

She gulped, not grasping what he was telling her.

He saw her confusion, and said gently, "If it is the same man, he is dead, pani."

"What did the man look like?" she pressed, desperately.

"What do we all look like here?"

The guard burst in and pushed the man out of the door. "No talking. You... *raus!*"

Aniela stood dumbstruck, reeling from the information. Her mind could not wrap itself around the news. Thrown himself against the electrified fence? Took his own life? Henryk? Could he have been driven to that, knowing that she was here? Or did he do it precisely because she was here? Could it be true? Could Henryk have decided it was better to die than to continue living this life?

Could he have really given up on her, on Wanda, on *them*? Or had he given up on himself, eviscerated by his powerlessness? Could his indomitable strength have finally been vanquished?

Chapter 65

A Mother's Advice is Heard

*I*t was the long-awaited day of Henryk and Aniela's wedding. On that morning of June 26th, 1937, she woke early, lying in the single bed in her childhood bedroom, relishing the moment. From now on she would be sharing her bed with Henryk. It was a thrilling thought, and she also felt a pang of nervousness at their pending honeymoon. Her life was about to change.

The morning still carried a hint of coolness as she slid her feet into her slippers and padded to the window. A few early risers were strolling the streets, bringing home fresh bread or the morning paper. The cobblestones were slick with morning dew and the evening cloud cover had yet to clear.

She entered the kitchen. Her mother was already up, sitting in a dressing gown and sipping tea. She smiled warmly, the wrinkles bunching up around those warm turquoise eyes that were so like Aniela's.

"Good morning, daughter," she said. "Our beautiful bride."

Aniela leaned over and hugged her, too moved to speak. Pani Majewska cleared her throat and urged Aniela to sit. Daughter complied as mother brought over a teacup and saucer and poured Aniela some tea.

"Today," Pani Majewska said, concentrating on the task, "is your day. Try to just enjoy yourself. Don't worry about the little details..." Her eyes welled up and she gathered herself together.

"A woman's life changes when she is married," she continued. "In many ways, your life becomes an extension of someone else's. Your husband's, and God willing, your children's."

She reached over to take Aniela's hand in hers. "That is the natural way. To give up little pieces of yourself to mold and meld yourself into this new existence with another. But remember, there should always be a part of you that is for you alone. Protect that part fiercely; keep it safe in a *hidden place. It is where you will return when you hit hard times. You need to have that place, the place that is the essence, the core of you, to return to for strength, courage and fortitude."*

Aniela listened intently, trying to understand the wisdom her mother was desperately trying to impart. She nodded, eyes locked on her mother's intense gaze. "I will, mama," she said. "I promise."

The memory was so vivid, Aniela could see the dust specks in the air as a morning sunbeam illuminated their kitchen table and turned her mother's dark blonde hair, with its streaks of white, to a cloud of gold. She could see the swirl of steam curling up from her teacup. Aniela missed her mother with such an intensity in that moment, she felt she could crawl into the fetal position and wail like a baby.

But there she was, lying on a stiff cot in a drafty barrack with Liliana and six other women, all sex slaves. She thought about her mother's words on her wedding day so long ago. She tried to imagine where that place resided in her. Was it locked somewhere deep in her heart? Or was it hidden in her brain, like a gateway to enlightenment?

Did she have the strength to carry on, not knowing whether Henryk was alive or dead? Was there another level of strength in her that she could tap into? That part that her mother mentioned that was for Aniela only — for her dreams, for her desires, for her existence? The part of her that didn't live for someone else — for a husband, or parents, or a job, or even one's children — but for love of oneself? A fundamental belief in oneself and what that life was worth, irrespective of all the emotions, entanglements, guilt, hope and obligations that went with loving someone else?

Aniela closed her eyes, trying to imagine that place within herself. She lay like that for an eternity, willing herself to find the will to live, to carry on, to persevere. Yes, for Wanda, and for her mother, and for Henryk. But mostly, and urgently, for herself. For Aniela.

Somehow, in those dark moments, with the din of suffering around her, Aniela drew herself inside and found some peace. And in that quiet place, she found what her mother had told her about, a place she didn't truly know she had until this moment when she realized that she had no power or freedom, she was not in charge of anything in her life — not even her own body. Her daughter was stolen, her husband caged like an animal and likely dead, her father turned to ashes. Aniela had nothing — yet there was still *something* there, something that had not been sullied, stolen or destroyed. It was her will to live, and it had not been defeated. She would not let her story end here.

Chapter 66

Camp Unraveling

Aniela sat on her cot, staring blankly ahead, willing her imagination to kick in, to take her away from yet another day of misery. It was a gloomy, overcast December morning and her feet and hands were cold.

"Could that really be? That's so close to Poland!" Liliana murmured, breaking Aniela's reverie.

The ladies in the barracks had been very excited last night about the news (or were they merely rumor?) that was trickling into the camp. From scraps of newspaper smuggled in from the Nazi houses, the women had learned that the Allies were advancing. Major cities in France had been liberated; in Belgium and Holland, too. The Brits were being sieged daily by V-1 bombs, but were still progressing elsewhere in Europe, freeing Brussels and Lyon. The Allies were experiencing victory after victory, as the detested Nazis were being pushed back and out. The Soviet troops were also advancing — they heard that they had already taken Hungary and were pressing on in Czechoslovakia.

"They'll be liberating us by Christmas," said Halina.

She was a striking woman in her twenties, with the body of a lithe dancer. She also wore the badge of an "antisocial", but from her mannered speech and elegant manners, Aniela suspected that she had not been doing this kind of work before the war. More than likely, her beauty was what had her reclassified as an antisocial. By affixing an antisocial label on Halina's lapel, the men could kid themselves that she was a career prostitute and old hand at this dirty business, and not some woman caught up in a roundup, betrayed by a jealous neighbor, or a Polish patriot arrested for her political acts against the Nazis.

"You can tell things are getting worse for them," Halina continued, eyes flashing. "One of my numbers told me that Hitler is calling up children and old men now. He called men from age sixteen to sixty to serve."

"That surely means that they are on the ropes," Aniela mused, an ember of hope catching flame in her belly.

The women whispered on, voices low but trembling with excitement, noting the other changes apparent in the camp. The kapos — some of whom were notoriously harsh and cruel — were beginning to look the other way, as the SS guards seemed to be distracted by the news trickling in and feeling the cold hand of dread on their hearts as they doubted their own Nazi propaganda.

Some of the older, stalwart Nazis had packed up and gone, and were replaced by teenagers in ill-fitting uniforms. Their youthful skin was pale and pink, blemished with acne. They stood white-knuckled at their post, with a look of fear, and the prisoners began testing the resolve of these green guards. These young men were a bit more dangerous and unpredictable than the previously stationed men, but everyone felt that the system was breaking down. The great powerful Reich was beginning to crumble.

The sense of order — viciously and incessantly pressed upon the prisoners — was also fraying. They could see it by the work details that passed by their barracks. Hair was growing back in, prisoners were no longer only wearing the striped cotton prison pajamas, but now street clothes were mixed in, providing warmth and perhaps a sense of resistance and a shred of individual identity? Prisoners were trading goods from Canada — as food parcels and luxury items were still amassing in the warehouses — flooding the camp with much-needed sustenance and ample opportunities for theft and bribery. The guards themselves were trading with kapos and highly-respected prisoners, enriching themselves with one eye to their own future, should the Reich truly fall.

And to the delight of them all, they learned that there was an uprising in Warsaw. It had begun in August — already four months ago! No, Poland was not yet dead — the capital city still had the grit and the determination to fight, despite six years of brutal occupation. Upon hearing about the uprising, the women spontaneously started humming the national anthem quietly and with deep feeling. They did not dare sing the words out loud, but Aniela could hear the lyrics in her mind, as clear as a bell, and felt in her heart the beat of an army drum:

313

Poland has not yet perished,
So long as we still live.
What the alien force has taken from us,
We shall retrieve with a saber.

March, March, Dąbrowski!
From the Italian land to Poland.
Under your command,
We shall rejoin the nation.
We'll cross the Vistula and the Warta
We shall be Polish!

Aniela was jolted out of her reverie when the door swung open, and there stood Joachim. He drew a startled breath as he saw her sitting on the bed, eyes closed, her face towards the window, where weak beams of sun tried to break through the gray. He collected himself and grabbed her roughly by the arm, pulling Aniela to her feet.

"Come with me," he ordered, his voice like gravel.

Chapter 67

An Unlikely Gift

"Keep quiet," Joachim growled, as he dragged Aniela out of the room. He stared down the guard as they pushed past and out of Blok 42. Aniela was dressed in lingerie and a robe, and Joachim pulled out a jacket from under his coat and roughly put it on her, providing both warmth and modesty as they stepped outside.

He was holding her roughly by the arm, and she had to run alongside him at an awkward angle, trying to keep up with his long legs and brisk gait. He led her through the corridors of the camp, past the execution wall and the so-called hospital, and pushed her down an alleyway to the back of an old brick administration building.

Her breath was coming in shallow gasps, as fear chilled her limbs so that she could hardly move. Her brain had frozen on the single idea that he had come to finish her off. Was he there to pull a revolver from his pocket and coldly execute her here by the trash cans? Or would that be too messy? Would he simply take those giant hands and place them around her neck and snap it?

He let go of her arm to quietly test the back door, which was indeed unlocked, and he turned to drag her inside. Aniela broke out of her frozen state and tried to fight against him as he reached to draw her into the building. She panted as she futilely tried to struggle against his grip.

"Stop it, Aniela!" he said through gritted teeth. "I'm not going to hurt you. Just come with me and keep fucking quiet!"

He picked her up under the armpits, his arms folded over her bosom as he dragged her backwards up the few steps into the building. They fell through the door awkwardly, and he immediately shoved her into a room marked "broom closet".

Aniela stumbled into the room, blinking as her eyes grew accustomed to the dim light. The room was small and cramped, smelling of old mops and mildew. She looked up at Joachim's tense and glowering face, shirking back due to his great size advantage. He seemed even bigger than she remembered.

"Aniela," he said, a little more gently. "Listen to me. I'm trying to help you. I have very warm, quality clothes in that bag to your left. Go and put them on. Every layer."

With stiff and numb fingers, she reached down to the canvas bag and pulled it open. Sure enough, there were warm woolen women's pants in a deep navy color, high-waisted with pleats, and a matching blazer. There was a cream sweater with navy polka dots, a brand-new pair of underwear and matching bra in ivory silk, as well as thick, knee-high woolen socks and leather boots.

She looked up at him, eyes registering her confusion.

"Just put them on," he ordered.

She turned her back to him as she did as he instructed. It was a ridiculous act of modesty given their history, but she did so anyway, as she briskly got out of her nightgown and robe and put on the offered clothes. The room was cold and unheated, and her body tingled with goose flesh; she was glad he could not see her stiff nipples and cold breasts as she put on the undergarments.

The clothes fit perfectly, as if they were made for her.

"Yes," he breathed. "Perfect. That will do."

He turned and pulled out a large paper package that was hidden on a shelf behind cleaning supplies, and pulled out a fine mink fur coat, wool gloves, scarf and hat.

"This, too."

She hesitated, afraid that this was a set-up, that this act of "theft" would end with her head splattered against the execution wall that had turned black with dried blood and gore. He registered her fear and hesitation, and brusquely started putting the coat on her himself.

"Don't argue with me," he said, his voice tense. "You are walking out of here on my arm. If anyone asks, you are my wife. Got it? Don't say a word, let me do the talking."

Once the fur coat was on, he adjusted her hat and reached into his pocket and pulled out a lipstick.

"Purse your lips," he ordered, and inexpertly painted her lips crimson.

She dimly registered that the lipstick that was being applied likely came from a woman who's entire being had been reduced to ashes. She swallowed hard.

"Now come," he said, as they exited the closet and out the back door. He took her by the arm, this time with her arm cradled into his side, the way a lover holds his woman close. His pace was leisurely, as if they were strolling through the camp on some sort of tour, if the thought were not too preposterous.

They ambled through the brick administration buildings, and eventually came to a black Mercedes that was parked alongside.

"Here, my treasure," he said smoothly, opening the passenger door for her. "Please get in."

She stepped into the car, noting the cool, clean leather seats and luxuriousness of the car. The last time she had been in a car was with Olga.

The feeling was surreal — her dressed as an elegant German Frau, wrapped in a mink coat that emanated warmth; and him, playing a solicitous husband with fine manners. She felt as if they were actors in some film, but the billowing chimneys of death still pumped away in the distance, and the never-ending clamor of barking dogs and the groaning of suffering humanity kept any such illusion at bay.

Joachim got in, his hands trembling a bit as he fit the key into the ignition. Aniela looked over at him, eyes like saucers.

"No worries, my darling," he said smoothly. "We are simply a couple taking a ride to Kraków. Enough of this country living, let's enjoy what the city has to offer."

She said nothing, as he started the car and slowly drove through the camp streets to the exit checkpoint. He looked smart and important in his black uniform, his medals polished and gleaming. He pulled the car to a halt as two young guards approached the car, peering inside. One of the men approached the driver side.

"Papers?" he asked.

Joachim reached into his pocket and pulled out a few documents, handing them to the guard.

The guard looked them over, his eyes moving from Joachim to Aniela. His eyes noted the large turquoise blue eyes, sparkling perhaps too much against the fine wool hat she wore, and the bright red lips.

No one looking at her now could imagine her as a Polish prisoner, a sex slave and enemy to the Reich. She was a genteel married *Deutsche* woman, taking a drive with her husband. The guard nodded briskly, said "Heil Hitler" and opened the gate. And with that, they drove away.

Aniela dared not look back, and she swallowed nervously, her mouth completely dry. She blinked furiously, trying not to let her emotions overtake her. Was she leaving her husband behind? Or was he already reduced to embers? And what about Liliana? Would she ever see her again?

Joachim drove on, his hands stiffly on the wheel as they left the camp behind and passed through the rolling countryside and farmland that opened up before them. This was still Poland — she had never left it — but Aniela stared numbly at the relatively normal and pedestrian lives that surrounded them. Lives that seemed so alien to the existence eked out behind the barbed wire and electrified fences.

Though it was December and many trees had lost their leaves, the countryside dazzled her with color. The fields still displayed the hues of fall — amber wheat and hay fields, the boldness of maple leaves turning a vivid red, and the golden hues of silver birch trees about to drop their leaves. Everything in the camp was monochromatic — even its inhabitants were gray and ashen.

After some time, Joachim pulled off the main road onto a dirt one and drove deep into a pine forest. Huge trees towered on either side, and he slowed the car down and came to a stop.

He got out and opened the door for Aniela. The air was clean and fresh, she could smell the pine resin and the needles as she stepped outside, and she gasped from the purity of it.

Joachim took her gloved hands in his. He struggled to find the words, but eventually managed, "The war is all but lost for Germany. It is just a matter of time."

She nodded, still not able to find her voice, as the fear and shock of her escape from Auschwitz rendered her mute.

"You must understand, Aniela," he said, "that had I met you before the war, as the man I once was, you would have loved me with the intensity that... I love you now. You would not see me as this twisted monster, but as a man of great integrity, loyalty, and action. I was that man."

He said that last sentence bleakly, like a plea. "I know you would have loved me. I would have swept you off your feet and married you near the Chiemsee, and we would have been happy. We would've had four beautiful children, and our house would have been filled with laughter. You would be the envy of all the other wives, with a husband who adored and exulted you.

"But alas, I am now on the losing side. And I must run, and attempt to escape from the wrath that is surely coming. The Russians are advancing; they are just a month or so away. And so, my darling, my one true love, I am setting you free to find your own way. I can dream that your path may find its way back to me, but who knows what fate has in store?"

She finally found her voice. "And what of Warsaw? I heard there was an uprising."

Joachim shook his head. "It is gone, Aniela. The partisans fought through October, but the rebellion was vanquished."

"What do you mean, vanquished?" she asked, heart in her throat.

"The Allies didn't send provisions, armaments or support. The Russians never joined the fight, so we... so, in retaliation, Germany bombed the city to the ground. I'm sorry, Aniela, but Warsaw is in ruins."

She stood dumbly, absorbing the news. The capital gone? How could that be true?

"Aniela, you must listen to me closely," Joachim said, squeezing her shoulders. "The reports I'm hearing about the invading Russian soldiers... they take everything that is in their path. They have no code of ethics. You must hide yourself when they are close. Women, especially women like you, are not safe."

She looked into his green eyes, absorbing his message, while still registering the absurdity of his warning. He was worried she would be raped by Russian soldiers? The man who placed her in a brothel? Was he mad?

"I must go," Joachim said, his voice cracking. "If you continue on this road a bit, you'll find a cluster of houses, and I pray that someone there will take you in and help you. You can speak to them. You Poles seem to stick together. I trust you will be safe there. Check the linings of your coat; you can also bribe them if you need to."

"Where are you going?" she asked, still reeling.

"South," he said. "God willing."

319

He took her in his arms and hugged her roughly to him. Aniela's face was pressed into the wool fibers of his coat as he held onto her as if for dear life. The embrace was so tight, she struggled to take in air.

At last, he loosened his grip and took her by her upper arms, gazing down into her face with a pleading look. "Tell me, Aniela, that you would have loved me, too. If you had met me under different circumstances. Leave me with that knowledge. With that gift."

She looked up at that face, with its beakish nose and square jaw. His green eyes were blazing with an intensity that was frightening, and his fingers dug into her arms. It would have been easy to concede, to tell him what he wanted to hear, as payment for breaking her out of Auschwitz. She could have easily said, "Yes, I could have loved you." But she hesitated, as she found deep in herself the place of courage, of self-respect, that her mother told her to protect like a lioness.

She thought of Henryk, of the teenage boy who protected her from library bullies, transformed into the broken prisoner she last saw. The man who had cried out his anguish when she made love to him on a bed in which she had sex with hundreds of strangers, and yet with him she was still able to feel something tender, unspoken and all-knowing in those final moments.

Unconditional love. The kind of love that doesn't end even in death.

"No, Joachim," Aniela said, eyes glistening with tears for Henryk. "I cannot offer you that promise. I made a promise to another, and that will go with me to my death."

A strangled cry escaped Joachim's lips, and he pulled away, his movements mechanical. He stepped into the Mercedes, and without a final look, drove away.

How long did she stand there by the side of the road? Time, once measured by prisoners on a mattress, had no meaning here. She remained standing, bundled up and warm, in a pine forest — with the cool December breeze tickling her cheeks and reminding her to come back to the present. A crow called in the distance and finally she blinked and returned to reality and to herself.

After a few dazed moments, she removed a glove and wiped her mouth, the red lipstick staining the back of her hand like blood. She reached into the fur coat and ran her hand along the lining and felt a hand-sewn seam that popped away to reveal a deep pocket.

She pulled out the contents of the pocket. There was a small velvet bag, wrapped with a satin bow. She emptied the bag into her hand. Six brilliant stones shone in the palm of her hand — two diamonds, two rubies, a sapphire and an emerald.

Her breath caught in her throat. Joachim had given her the currency she needed. These stones represented a future, and maybe in some dark way, he had offered her what he considered payment in full. Aniela stared at the stones for quite a long time, marveling at their beauty and purity. She had no illusions from whom these stones came. They were the spoils of war, stolen by the Nazis. It was hard to believe that something so beautiful was so sullied.

Eventually, she decided to put the stones back in their velvet bag and hide them in the seam of her fur. But as she opened up the little bag to drop the stones carefully inside, she saw a scrap of paper folded up neatly at the bottom.

She carefully extracted and unfolded it. The note was written in Joachim's hand, in flowery German script. It read:

She lives.
Family Rudolf Hausmann.
Dresden.

Stay tuned for the sequel to Blok 42!

For more information, visit www.debriannaobara.com